FINDING KENNA

SEAL Team Hawaii, Book 3

SUSAN STOKER

CHAPTER ONE

"Let me get this straight," Carly said with a huge shit-eating grin on her face. "You jumped *on* the poor man? You couldn't figure out anything else to do to try to save him than literally jumping on top of him?"

"Shut up," Kenna grumbled with a small grin. "I mean, it wasn't like I *meant* to land on him. I misjudged."

"Apparently," Paulo said wryly as he leaned on the edge of the bar.

"And they were SEALs?" asked Kaleen, on duty behind the bar with Paulo.

"Yup," Kenna confirmed. "I was running along the Ala Moana Park out by the Magic Island Lagoon, minding my own business, when I looked over and saw him floating face-down in the ocean. I didn't think. I took off my shoes and shirt and jumped in to save him. But, as you all know, he didn't need saving. He was watching his friends under the water, who were doing some sort of military training. I was embarrassed as hell and couldn't believe I'd actually done that."

"I swear that's like the best meet-cute ever," Kaleen said.

"What's a meet-cute?" Paulo asked.

"Seriously?" Kaleen asked.

"I wouldn't have asked if I wasn't serious," Paulo returned.

Kenna smiled at her coworkers' ribbing. She loved working at Duke's. The other waiters and waitresses were all pretty cool and it felt like working with a large family rather than coworkers. The restaurant was located in the heart of Waikiki on Oahu and was pretty much always crowded. It was at the back of the Outrigger Waikiki Beach Resort, situated right on the beach.

The restaurant was named after Duke Kahanamoku, who was a native Hawaiian, six-time Olympic swimmer and water polo medalist, as well as the father of modern-day surfing. There were three of the restaurants in Hawaii and three in California, all well known for their cocktails and decadent hula pie dessert.

It was Friday night, which was always busy at the restaurant, and that meant great tips.

"A meet-cute," Kaleen explained patiently, "is when a guy and a girl meet in a super cute and unique way."

"So only a guy and girl?" Paulo asked.

"Well, no, I guess not."

"I mean, is it a meet-macho if it's two guys who are into each other? Or a feminine-frolic if it's two women?"

"Shut up," Kaleen said, rolling her eyes at her coworker.

Kenna had always enjoyed the banter between the two bartenders. They were reason one thousand and twenty-two why she loved working here.

It was also well-known around Duke's that Paulo really wanted to find a serious boyfriend, so they all tried to set him up at least once a night. So far, everyone—including Paulo—had struck out. A shame, because he was one of the best guys Kenna knew. Always volunteering to walk someone to their car and insisting all the waitresses text when they got home.

"What'd I miss?" Charlotte, another waitress, asked as she rushed up to the bar with her tray and drink order from one of her tables.

"Kenna was about to explain why she thought inviting the Navy SEAL she jumped on top of to hang out here tonight was a good idea," Carly helpfully offered with a grin.

"It wasn't that I thought it was a good idea, but he asked if he could see me and my brain kind of short-circuited," Kenna defended.

"He said seven, right?" Kaleen asked.

"Yes."

"Well, it's seven-fifteen. He's late," Paulo said with a frown.

"The traffic down here sucks," Kenna said, defending Marshall despite not even knowing the man.

"You gonna ask Vera to put him in your section?" Charlotte asked.

"Not sure Alani would like that," Paulo said.

Alani was the manager on duty tonight. And while she was pretty cool, she had a thing about the servers chatting up friends and family who came into the restaurant. Kenna couldn't blame her. They were usually always busy and work was work. Which was why it had been the worst idea ever to invite Marshall to come to Duke's tonight. It wasn't as if she could hang out and get to know him.

"Tell Vera to put him here at the bar," Paulo said with a gleam in his eye.

"Yeah, we'll vet him for you," Kaleen agreed.

"No way," Kenna said with a laugh. "You guys'll scare him away for sure."

Everyone chuckled.

"Fine. But maybe if I'm lucky, he'll bring his SEAL buddies with him," Paulo said. "We could use some eye candy around here." He placed a mai tai and a lava flow cocktail on Carly's tray.

"I hope he does bring his friends. And that they're single," Charlotte replied with a wink.

"Not me," Carly said as she balanced her tray. "I'm done with men."

"Just because Shawn didn't turn out to be the one doesn't mean you should give up dating altogether," Kaleen told her.

"Men are dogs," Carly retorted before turning and heading for the table with the couple who'd ordered the drinks.

Kenna watched her friend walk away with a frown on her face.

"What did her ex do to her, anyway?" Paulo asked.

"Treated her like shit. Made her feel guilty for coming to work or hanging out with her friends. Talked down to her. And when Carly had enough and told Shawn she was done with the relationship, he pouted, begged, cried, and did everything he could think of to get her to stay. Then, when she didn't fall for it...he got mean," Kenna explained.

She and Carly were pretty close, even though the other woman was five years younger than her thirty years. They'd talked a lot about Shawn, and Kenna had never been so happy as when Carly had finally broken up with him. Or tried to.

"That sucks," Paulo muttered as he wiped down the bar.

"Definitely," Kenna agreed.

"Holy mother of God. Please tell me one of those perfect specimens is your Marshall," Charlotte muttered under her breath.

Turning, Kenna saw a group of men, and a couple of women, being led into the restaurant by Vera. It seemed as if everyone they walked past did a double take. It wasn't just that they were good-looking, it was more the air of confidence that seemed to ooze out of their every pore as they followed the hostess to their table. It might be fanciful, but they even *looked* like men who could absolutely be counted on if shit hit the fan.

"Woo-wee," Paulo said, fanning himself with his hand.

"So? Is one of those guys him?" Kaleen asked.

"Yup. And I'm gonna go tell Alani that I quit," Kenna quipped. "I'm too embarrassed to talk to him. I'm moving to a deserted island."

Charlotte laughed. "You are not. You love this place too much."

She was right...but damn.

Kenna normally had pretty high self-esteem. She wasn't a beach bunny, but she worked out and did her best to keep snacks to a minimum. She loved her long hair, which was light brown, but she frequently experimented with fun colors. Sometimes a streak, sometimes just the tips. She was five-eight, so fairly tall, had toned arms and legs, and people always told her that her smile lit up her face.

All in all, Kenna was satisfied with her looks...but at the moment, she couldn't help the pang of insecurity that hit upon seeing Marshall again.

He wasn't wearing a scuba suit this time, and it was more than obvious the man was in shape. His age was hard to guess, but she supposed he was probably around the same age as her. He was taller by a few inches, and the five o'clock shadow on his face was sexy rather than scruffy. He had on a black T-shirt that showed off his huge biceps and wide shoulders.

Yup, it was official. Kenna was intimidated.

"I'm guessing your Marshall isn't either of the men holding those women's hands," Kaleen observed wryly.

"No. He's the last guy," Kenna said. He was looking around the restaurant as if taking in the ambiance...or perhaps looking for someone.

Her.

"Well? Go say hello!" Charlotte said as she nudged Kenna.

"Nope. I think I'm gonna pretend I have no idea who he is."

"Um...but he knows who *you* are," Paulo said in confusion.

"Shit," Kenna mumbled.

Kaleen laughed. "The unflappable Kenna Madigan is flapped."

"What does that even mean?" Paulo asked. "That makes no sense."

"Yes, it does," Kaleen insisted.

"It looks like Vera put them in Carly's section," Charlotte said, interrupting the bartenders' banter. "You need to go say hello."

Taking a deep breath, Kenna nodded. She'd been the one to invite Marshall to come here tonight after almost landing on his head in the water during her morning run. It would be rude to ignore him. And Kaleen was right, even if she wanted to pretend she didn't know him, he knew *her*.

"I'm going," she told her friends.

"If he orders any of our frou-frou drinks, he's a big fat no," Paulo said under his breath. "Although...he might be worth it anyway."

Paulo had a bad habit of judging people based on the kind of alcohol they ordered. Kenna supposed it was a job hazard —and she didn't think it would help the poor man find a boyfriend.

Taking a deep breath, Kenna headed toward the table of six men and two women. Vera had sat them in the huge circular booth the servers called "the stage." It was on a slightly raised platform at the back of the room, facing the beach. It gave the people sitting there a good view of both the entire dining area and the sunset. Normally, ten or so people could easily fit around the expansive table, but with

Marshall and his friends' sizes, there wasn't much free space.

"Come on, you can help me with the table," Carly said, materializing out of nowhere.

Kenna chuckled. "The day you need help with a table of eight is the day I quit to become a hula dancer."

Carly winked. "You can't dance worth shit, so that wouldn't work. But don't worry, I'll report on anything I overhear that would indicate your Marshall's a douche."

"He's not *my* anything. And he's not a douche."

Carly merely smiled.

Kenna shook her head in exasperation.

"Come on," Carly said. "He's totally looking for you and you need to explain what's going on."

She did. Kenna knew it. But she dreaded seeing the irritation that he'd likely feel when he realized she couldn't hang out with him. That she was working.

But then again, *he'd* shown up with seven other people. He couldn't really have been expecting any kind of intimate date, could he?

Marshall continued to surprise her. In a good way. He hadn't gotten pissed when she'd interrupted his training that morning. Or bitched that she could've really hurt him if she'd landed on his back or something. He'd brought his friends along tonight, which was...unusual. Kenna didn't know what his reasoning was, but she was relieved he hadn't arrived with flowers and dressed to impress.

Oh, she was impressed with his jeans and black T-shirt all right, but it didn't look like he was trying too hard, which was a relief. While she wasn't opposed to dating, she was happy with her life the way it was. She didn't *need* a boyfriend to be happy or content. She loved her job, her apartment was cozy, and she had some great friends.

But something about Marshall had her doing things she

wouldn't normally do. Like inviting him to come to Duke's while she was working.

Please don't be a douche, she thought as she approached the table.

* * *

Marshall "Aleck" Smart saw Kenna from across the restaurant as he walked toward their table. She was near the bar, laughing at something one of the bartenders said. He was struck immediately by her smile. He wanted to find out what was so funny. What had her looking so happy.

"That her?" Jag asked as they arrived at a large circular booth. As Elodie and Lexie scooted around the table to sit in the middle, Aleck nodded.

"She's cute."

Aleck whipped his head around to glare at his teammate.

Jag simply laughed. "Easy, tiger. I just didn't get a good look at her this morning. Besides, she looked different with wet hair."

"Your waitress will be with you soon. There's a cocktail menu on the table, and we have wine, as well as beer on tap. I highly recommend Duke's blonde ale, if that's your thing, or a traditional mai tai, or perhaps a coconut mojito for an island flair. Aloha!"

Aleck didn't even look twice at the blonde woman as she walked away from their table. He only had eyes for one person.

"Here she comes," Pid said from next to him.

Aleck had already noticed Kenna walking toward the table with another woman. It didn't take a rocket scientist to see from their uniforms that both of them worked at the restaurant. Aleck was confused for a split second, and he couldn't help but feel a small pang of disappointment that he obviously wasn't going to dine with her and get to know her as he'd planned.

"Hi! I'm Carly. I'll be your waitress tonight," the smaller woman said.

"And I'm Kenna. I was the woman who jumped on your friend this morning. Well, not jumped on him, but almost."

It was clear Kenna was nervous, but Elodie beat him to reassuring her.

She stood up as best she could in the booth and reached her hand across the circular table. "It's so good to meet you!" she gushed. "When Scott came home this morning and told me what happened, I could seriously picture it in my head."

"And I swear that's something I would've done," Lexie said with a wide grin. She shook Kenna's hand as well.

Kenna smiled at them both. "Thanks. But it was so embarrassing. I'm sure poor Marshall was wondering what the hell was going on. One second he was supervising all you guys, and the next there was a huge splash and I was there."

Aleck slowly stood and held out his hand. Kenna smiled shyly up at him, and he couldn't help but notice how smooth and soft her hand was when he shook it. His own was covered in calluses from his job and working out. "I was surprised for sure," he told her. "But once I realized what had happened, I was impressed. Not many people would do what you did. Get involved. In fact, no one has ever done what you did before today."

She blushed, and it made her even prettier. Her high ponytail had a cute flip at the end and her dark brown eyes were so expressive. He loved that she was only a few inches shorter than he was, so he could see her gaze clearly. Right now, he could tell she felt awkward and maybe a little embarrassed about how they'd met.

"Which just means everyone else is smart enough to

realize you were in the ocean for a reason and that you weren't actually drowning," Kenna said.

Everyone chuckled, and he could see Kenna visibly relax.

"I'm Jag," his teammate said, making Aleck realize that he needed to introduce Kenna to the rest of his friends. But when he turned, he saw that Jag wasn't looking at Kenna.

He was staring at the other waitress.

"I'm Carly," she replied, staring back at Jag as if they were the only two people in the restaurant.

Knowing he'd give Jag shit later, Aleck quickly introduced his other friends to Kenna. "This is Mustang and his wife Elodie. That's Midas and his girlfriend Lexie. Jag already introduced himself, and that's Slate and Pid," Aleck told her.

"Hi," Kenna said, waving a little self-consciously before turning back to Aleck. "Can I talk to you for a second?"

"Of course," he said without hesitation. As if it was the most natural thing in the world, he reached for her elbow. There wasn't much privacy in the busy restaurant, and Aleck heard Carly asking the others what they wanted to drink as he led Kenna into a small hallway that connected the dining area to the reception podium.

"I'm sorry I didn't tell you I worked here," Kenna said without hesitation. "I wasn't trying to mislead you or anything. Honestly, you threw me off guard by asking me out, and when you asked when and where, Duke's just kind of popped out. Probably because I'm here a lot."

"It's okay," Aleck told her. "I'm sure you didn't expect me to show up with all my friends either. But when I told Midas that I was meeting you here tonight, he invited himself and Lexie along. Lex told Elodie, and the next thing I knew, *everyone* had invited themselves to our date."

She blushed again, and Aleck had to force himself not to reach up to cup her cheek.

"I wish I could hang out and get to know everyone, but I really am working tonight," she apologized.

"It's okay. We'll just have to plan something for another night," Aleck said, the words coming easily and naturally. He wasn't just saying them to be polite; he really did want to see her again.

"I think I'd like that."

"Good. Me too."

"Kenna! Table thirty-five wants their check," a man said from the end of the small walkway they were standing in.

"I'll be right there, Justin. Thanks," Kenna told him.

The man waved and disappeared into the dining area once more.

"I guess I need to go take care of that," she said, looking up at him.

"Okay."

"If it's all right...I'll stop by to talk as much as I can."

"It's more than all right," Aleck said.

"And...at eight-thirty, I get a fifteen-minute break," she added. "If you'd be interested in hanging out with me?"

"Definitely."

"Okay."

"Okay," Aleck echoed.

They stared at each other for a long moment before Kenna chuckled and scrunched her nose. "This is weird. I'm sorry."

"It's not. It's fine," Aleck reassured her. "Elodie and Lexie were thrilled to have a girls' night out. I'm guessing they'll bail on us guys at some point and go hang out at the bar."

"Paulo will love that. He'll probably grill them about all of you. I don't suppose any of your friends are gay?"

Aleck laughed. "Sorry, no."

Kenna shrugged. "It's probably better. Paulo is kind of a man-whore. In a good way, of course."

"Of course," Aleck agreed, even though he had no idea what that meant.

"And now I'm babbling. Anyway, thanks for coming tonight. It's nice to see you."

Aleck knew his gaze was raking her from head to toe, but he couldn't stop himself. He'd gotten an up-close look at her ass that morning as she'd climbed up the rocks to get out of the ocean, and he'd be lying if he said he hadn't admired the view. But somehow, seeing her in a pair of khaki shorts, a Duke's T-shirt tied in a knot at her waist, and a sensible pair of tennis shoes was even more of a turn-on than her running shorts and sports bra had been.

Shaking his head slightly, he realized that he'd been staring at her without saying a word. "You intrigued me this morning," he said. "I wanted to see you again."

"And now you know I'm a simple waitress who sometimes doesn't think before she acts," Kenna quipped.

"And I'm even *more* intrigued," Aleck admitted. "Go on," he urged, knowing he could stand in the hallway and talk to her all night, which would surely get her in trouble. "You've got people waiting on you."

Kenna took a step backward. "Thanks for being cool about tonight," she told him.

Aleck nodded and watched as she turned and walked away from him.

He stood there for a moment longer, then headed back to the table. Things weren't turning out as he'd expected tonight, that was for sure. He'd planned on asking if Kenna wanted to sit at a table away from his friends, so they could get to know each other before joining the group again. He hoped she would get along with Elodie and Lexie, as well as his team.

While he was disappointed he wouldn't get to talk with

her like he'd hoped, he couldn't be upset about spending the evening with his friends.

"So?" Pid asked when he returned to the booth.

"So, what?" Aleck asked.

"What's her deal? She's obviously working tonight. Did you know she's a waitress? Are you gonna get to talk to her at all?"

"Jeez. I had no idea you were that interested in my love life," Aleck quipped.

"I'm not," Pid protested. "It's just weird that you asked her out and she suggested you come here, and now she can't spend time with you."

"It's not weird," Elodie said, breaking into the conversation. "It's smart. I mean, think about it."

"Yeah," Lexie agreed. "I think it's hilarious how you guys met, but you're still a stranger. And having you come here, where she knows everyone and you don't, is much safer than meeting you at a random restaurant."

Elodie nodded in agreement.

"It's fine," Aleck said. "She said she'd pop by as much as she could. Besides, now I get to hang out with you guys."

Jag rolled his eyes. "Right, because we haven't gotten to see each other in soooo long. It was, what, an hour between when we last saw you on base and when we met up to come here?"

"I wonder how long it's gonna take for food to come out. It looks pretty crowded," Slate muttered.

Everyone laughed at his mild grumpiness. It was hilarious how their friend was so impatient about everything. Even his food.

"I'm sure you won't waste away," Elodie told him with a smile. "Carly will be back with our drinks soon. We'll order some appetizers to tide you over."

Aleck tuned his friends out as he watched Kenna, who

smiled at a couple as she passed their table on the other side of the restaurant. She moved quickly and gracefully and seemed to be in her element. Her body language definitely showed that she enjoyed her work.

As he was watching, she glanced in his direction. Aleck gave her a small chin lift, and she smiled at him in return, before turning her attention to the patrons at another table.

Damn. He may not be sitting next to her, but seeing her in action and observing from afar was kind of fun. And Aleck couldn't help but love that her gaze kept straying to him. There was something to be said for flirting like this. It was... interesting. And different. Kind of like Kenna herself. He definitely liked it.

CHAPTER TWO

"Oh my God, you guys are giving off enough sexual tension to make me all hot and bothered," Carly teased Kenna a while later.

Kenna did her best to hide her grin, but failed when Carly rolled her eyes. "He doesn't seem too upset that I didn't tell him I wouldn't be able to hang out with him much tonight," she said, fishing for more information.

"I don't think he is," Carly said, assuaging her fears immediately. "I mean, every time I go over to the table he's super friendly."

Kenna was relieved. And happy that he was nice to her friend. Carly was amazing and awesome, but she was still dealing with her asshole ex, so her thoughts about men in general were pretty low right about now.

Without thinking about it, her gaze flicked over to the table where Marshall and his friends were sitting. And like the other five hundred times she'd done it, she found him looking at her already.

"See? That's what I'm talking about," Carly said with a sigh. "But I wouldn't be a good friend if I didn't warn you..."

Kenna tensed a little and looked back at her friend. "About what?"

"That's how Shawn started out too, and I thought it was about him being protective. Watching me all the time. Wanting to keep me in his line of sight. Remember that first night he came here and sat at the bar all night? We all thought it was swoon-worthy that he got all pissed when that tourist guy hit on me?"

Kenna did remember that. But if she recalled the situation right, *Carly* had been the one who was all swoony. Paulo and Kaleen had told her later that they thought Shawn was creepy. And it wasn't cool of Shawn to practically start a fight in the middle of the restaurant. It was obvious Carly hadn't been interested in the tourist she was serving, and Shawn should've realized it.

But she knew Carly's heart was in the right place, and she'd much rather have a friend who was honest with her than one who got all googly-eyed over a guy. "I know, thanks," Kenna told her.

Carly nodded.

"What about the rest of his friends? Do they seem cool?" Kenna asked.

"Oh yeah. The two girls are hilarious. Lexie spilled her entire drink on her boyfriend, but he didn't get pissed at all. He just laughed and ordered her a new one."

Kenna would've pointed out that someone accidentally tipping over a glass wasn't cause for *anyone* to get pissed, but didn't want to bring down her friend's mood. Shawn had done a number on her, and tonight seemed to be the first time in a long while that she was mostly back to her old self.

"What about Jag...that's his name, right?"

"The guy who looks like he could kill someone with just the intensity in his eyes?" Carly asked.

Kenna smirked.

"What?" Carly asked.

"Nothing. He's nice too?"

"Yeah. They all are," Carly said. "Your break is coming up, right?"

"Yeah."

"Cool. I'll watch your tables for you so you can take a bit longer if you want."

"That wouldn't be fair," Kenna said.

"Screw fair," Carly said. "Look, I might be done with guys for a very long time, but that doesn't mean you are. And Marshall seems nice. Not impatient that he hasn't been able to talk to you much tonight. He just watches you with those smoldering brown eyes of his and a half smile on his face. Kenna, you're one of the nicest people I've met here. You've been really supportive and you always help me out with my tables. So helping *you* for an extra fifteen minutes isn't that big of a deal."

"Thank you so much," Kenna said, reaching out and pulling the younger woman into a hug. "Seriously."

"Whatever," Carly said. "When you guys get married and have a dozen babies, you can thank me."

Kenna laughed. "Now if I could just get the assholes at table twenty-seven to eat faster, my night would be perfect."

"What's up with them? The women are being total bitches, and the guys they're with aren't saying anything."

"I know. I swear they're making stuff up to make my life harder. The last time I went by to see if they needed anything, the blonde asked for a new fork since she dropped hers—*again*—and the brunette wants more napkins. She said it's ridiculous to assume she could eat her wings with what I'd already brought her."

"Which would be a valid argument if *she* was actually eating them, not the guy with her, and if you hadn't already given her like twenty napkins," Carly commiserated.

SUSAN STOKER

"I better get going and take care of the princesses, I wouldn't want them to make a scene. Thanks again for giving me the extra time with Marshall."

"Anytime," Carly said.

Kenna headed for the kitchen to grab another fork and more napkins before heading back to table twenty-seven. She passed the booth where Marshall and his friends were sitting on her way to deal with the difficult guests, and stopped for just a moment. She'd been doing that all night, finding excuses to walk by their table and stopping to say hello. She wished she could sit and really get to know everyone, because honestly, they seemed like a fun group of people.

"Hey. Everything okay?" she asked.

"It's great!" Elodie told her. Her cheeks were flushed and it was obvious she was more than enjoying the mai tais she'd ordered. "After we have dessert—that hula pie thing—Lexie and I are gonna head to the bar and pretend our guys aren't here."

Kenna eyed the woman's husband and Lexie's boyfriend, and saw nothing but amusement on their faces.

Lexie leaned over the table, and Midas quickly moved her plate so she didn't get food all over her chest. It was a little thing, but Kenna had observed countless couples over the years, and this guy's attention to his girlfriend was to be commended. "I would never be able to do what you do. Those women over there are such bitches!" she whispered loudly.

Kenna blinked in surprise. She knew the women weren't nice, of course, but she hadn't really let it get to her much. She dealt with all sorts of assholes in her job, but preferred to concentrate on the nicer patrons. She shrugged. "They're not so bad."

"Not so bad?" Elodie exclaimed. "You've been running

18

back and forth to their table the entire time they've been here. But don't worry...Lexie and I have a plan."

Kenna frowned. "A plan?"

"Don't ask," Marshall said quietly.

Kenna glanced at him. The moment their gazes met, a jolt of electricity seemed to go through her once more. It had been like that all night. Every time she looked at him, goose bumps broke out on her arms. The chemistry they seemed to have was surprising.

"Nothing bad, promise," Lexie said, getting Kenna's attention.

"I need to get back to work, but..." She looked at Marshall again. "I have a break in ten minutes, and Carly said she'd cover for me so I could take a bit more time."

"Great news," Marshall said with a wide smile.

Kenna felt as if she was in junior high school all over again. She was giddy with excitement and definitely looking forward to getting to know this man.

"If we're not here when you get back, we'll be at the bar," Elodie's husband said. "Watching over Elodie and Lexie."

"I think I'm gonna get going," Pid said.

"Same," Slate agreed.

"You can stay as long as you want," Kenna told them. "It's not a problem. We don't usually get large groups this late, so we won't need the table." She didn't want the guys leaving if they truly didn't want to go.

"We're good," Midas said.

"I think I'll stick around. Someone has to make sure these guys don't get into trouble," Jag said with a chuckle. He was referring to his friends, but his eyes were focused on something behind her.

Kenna turned to see who he was looking at and saw Carly coming toward the table. She inwardly smiled. It was more than obvious Marshall's friend was interested in Carly. She didn't have the heart to tell him she'd sworn off men for the foreseeable future.

She looked back at Marshall. "Meet me in ten minutes by the podium at the front of the restaurant?"

"I'll be there," he told her.

Kenna gave him a shy smile, then turned to deliver the fork and napkins to table twenty-seven. She'd missed the two women getting up and heading her way, so when she turned, she ran right into the blonde, dropping both the fork and the napkins she'd been about to deliver.

"Watch it!" the brunette exclaimed, then she and the blonde giggled as they walked toward the restrooms.

Sighing, Kenna knelt to pick up the mess she'd made—and realized Marshall was right there next to her, reaching for the napkins.

"I've got it," she told him.

"I know," he said, not standing up or returning to his seat.

It was a little thing, but she appreciated his help even though it wasn't a big deal to pick up the items. Ten seconds later, they'd collected all the napkins before they could blow away from the slight breeze coming off the ocean.

"Bitches," Marshall muttered as they stood, and he handed her the napkins he'd picked up.

"It's fine. Trust me, they don't even rate on my asshole-patron scale."

"I'd say I'd love to hear stories, but I have a feeling hearing how you're treated would just piss me off," Marshall said.

"Ten minutes?" she asked again, holding the napkins to her chest.

"Excuse me, gotta use the restroom," Elodie said with an edge to her voice.

"Oh shit," Pid muttered as he moved out of the way so Lexie and Elodie could scoot out of the booth.

The women headed in the same direction the blonde and brunette had gone. Kenna glanced at their men. "Should I be worried?"

"No," Midas said.

At the same time Mustang said, "Maybe."

"Ten minutes," Marshall said, lightly touching her arm.

Kenna nodded, then turned to head back to the kitchen. She dumped the dirty napkins in a bin inside the door. Making a split-second decision, she headed for the bathroom. She didn't really know Elodie or Lexie, but she didn't want them to get in trouble because of her. She'd been dealing with people like the blonde and brunette for years, so nothing anyone said or did ruffled her feathers anymore.

She pushed open the bathroom door and saw Elodie and Lexie standing at the sinks. There was no sign of the other two women, but since both doors to the stalls were closed and she could see feet on the other side, Kenna assumed that was them.

Elodie winked at her before turning back to Lexie. "I'm told one of the waitresses here is related to one of the producers of the latest *Jurassic Park* movie."

"Really?" Lexie exclaimed in the fakest voice Kenna had ever heard.

"Yeah. You know they film on the northeast side of the island at that ranch...what's it called again?"

"Kualoa Ranch?" Lexie asked.

"That's it!" Elodie said with an overabundance of drama. "Anyway, so I heard Chris Pratt is on the island filming and they need extras for some of the scenes."

"Ooooh, cool," Lexie gushed.

"Right? And rumor has it the waitress helps her dad, or uncle, or whoever he is, find extras. Since she meets so many people, she asks random guests if they might be interested in working out at the ranch for a day," Elodie said.

Kenna put her hand over her mouth to try to keep her laughter in.

"Who is she?" Lexie asked. "I want to kiss her ass so maybe she'll ask me!"

"I don't know," Elodie said in a dejected tone. "But I plan to be as nice as possible to the waitress. I mean, can you imagine being a bitch to the staff, then finding out later you could've been hired for a *Jurassic Park* movie if you'd just been nicer?"

"That would suck so bad," Lexie agreed with a huge smile.

"I think my hair is as good as it's gonna get," Elodie said. "You ready to go back? I need another drink."

"Ready," Lexie agreed.

The two women in the stalls hadn't said a word, but Kenna figured Elodie and Lexie had gotten their point across more than adequately. She backed out of the restroom, with both the other women following and grinning like lunatics.

The second the door shut behind them, Lexie burst out laughing.

"Shhhh," Elodie scolded in a whisper. "They might still be able to hear us!" They walked down the hall toward the dining area, and only then did Elodie join Lexie in laughing.

"That was awesome!" Lexie exclaimed.

"They're gonna be kissing all the waitresses asses now for sure!" Elodie agreed.

Kenna couldn't remember if someone had ever gone out of their way to do something like that for her. It was harmless and funny, but would likely be effective. Of course, there would always be patrons who felt it was perfectly all right to treat the waitstaff like shit, but for tonight, those two women would almost certainly do an about-face and change their attitude.

"Thank you so much," Kenna told them. "They honestly weren't all that bad, but I appreciate it all the same."

Elodie got serious as she met Kenna's gaze. "I've had more to drink tonight than usual, and I'd probably never say something like this otherwise..."

Kenna braced.

"I like you. I mean, I don't really *know* you, but I like how Aleck can't take his eyes off you. I like your smile and how you're always looking over at him. And I freaking *love* that you didn't hesitate to try to rescue him when you thought he was drowning. Aleck is a good guy. He's funny—and yes, he's the smart aleck that he's named for. But when we all invited ourselves tonight, he didn't say no. He didn't pitch a fit. I think he was kind of glad because he was nervous. And he'd only be nervous if you mattered. So...all that to say...I hope things work out between you guys."

Kenna was surprised. She kind of thought Elodie would tell her not to fuck with her friend or something. She definitely liked this woman. "Me too," she admitted.

Lexie nudged Elodie and gestured not so subtly with her head toward the table they'd been sitting at. Their men were headed their way.

"Wow, they gave us a whole five minutes," Elodie joked with a laugh.

Not able to stop herself, Kenna looked back at the table, and her gaze met Marshall's.

"You okay?" he mouthed.

Kenna nodded at him.

Marshall made a big deal out of lifting his arm and looking at the watch on his wrist. Kenna smiled and held up five fingers. He nodded.

"See? You guys can have an entire conversation from across the room," Elodie said. "That's awesome."

It *was* awesome.

Kenna nodded at Midas and Mustang as they arrived to collect their women.

"You good?" Mustang asked her.

Kenna couldn't help but smile. "I'm good," she told him. "Your wife and Lexie were awesome."

"They can be a little...enthusiastic," Midas said, wrapping an arm around Lexie's shoulders.

"We *are* awesome," Lexie agreed, snuggling into her man.

"Dessert arrived while you two were delivering your smackdown," Mustang told them.

"We didn't do any such thing," Elodie protested. "We just had a conversation. That may or may not have been overheard."

"We'll see if it was when the bitches go back to their table," Lexie said.

"Speaking of which, I'd better get more napkins for them," Kenna said. "Thanks again."

"Anytime," Elodie said. "That's what friends are for."

Kenna smiled at both women and headed back toward the kitchen. She heard Mustang ask, "So you're best friends with Aleck's woman already?"

"Yup," Kenna heard Elodie say, right before she entered the kitchen area. Smiling, she gathered up the napkins and fork, grabbed the appetizer for another table that was ready, and headed back into the dining area. She had time to do one more check on each of her tables before her much-needed and anticipated break.

After dropping off the poke tacos and crab wontons to table forty-three, she headed back toward table twenty-seven.

This time, the blonde and brunette couldn't have been nicer. They apologized for being a pain and the blonde even complimented Kenna's hair. It was such a crock of shit, because the ponytail Kenna wore wasn't anything to gush about. But she merely smiled and asked the group if they needed anything else.

Kenna had to admit that Elodie and Lexie's ploy was crazy

effective. They hadn't started a knock-down drag-out fight. Hadn't shamed the two women. Had just lied their asses off with their elaborate tale, which had worked like a charm.

Making a mental note to never underestimate either woman—that was, if she had the chance to spend time with them in the future—Kenna headed for her next table to make sure all was well.

Five minutes later, she took off her apron, hung it on a hook near the kitchen door, waved to Carly, and headed for the front of the restaurant. She still had a couple hours of work in front of her, but she'd never been as excited for her break as she was tonight.

CHAPTER THREE

Aleck stood apart from the patrons waiting to be seated at Duke's and realized he was fidgeting. He never fidgeted. But anticipation over spending time with Kenna, even if it was only thirty minutes, had him shifting back and forth on his feet like he was a ten-year-old kid in the principal's office.

He had no idea what it was about her that had him so off-kilter. All he knew was that he was excited to get to know her better.

When Aleck saw Kenna headed toward him, he couldn't help but smile. She was laughing as she stopped by the hostess stand to speak to the woman working there. Then she was headed toward him.

"Hey," she said as she approached.

"Hi," he returned.

They stared at each other silently before she asked, "You want to take a walk or something?"

Aleck shook his head. "No. You've been on your feet all night. I'd prefer to find a place to sit where you can actually relax for a while."

She didn't say anything for a long moment.

"But if you're set on a walk, that's okay too," Aleck added awkwardly.

Kenna shook her head. "No, sitting sounds heavenly. I just wasn't sure you'd want to do something so...lame."

"Kenna, you've been working your ass off tonight. I'd be a dick if I insisted on adding to your fatigue." He looked around the bright lights of the shopping area and inwardly groaned at the lack of privacy and the fact that all the benches were occupied.

But Kenna came to his rescue. "We could sit outside by the beach...if you wanted," she suggested.

"Yes," Aleck said immediately. The sun had set not too long ago and the temperature was absolutely perfect.

"We have to go back through the restaurant," Kenna said. "I mean, we don't have to, but it'll be the fastest way to get to the beach."

"Lead on," Aleck said, gesturing toward Duke's with his arm.

He followed close behind her, selfishly hoping like hell no one would need her as they walked past the tables toward the beach. Luckily, no one stopped her and soon they were walking on the sand, headed for a lounge chair.

"Is this okay?" Kenna asked.

"It's perfect," Aleck assured her, and it was. The hustle and bustle of Duke's was behind them and the sound of the calm ocean lapping at the beach was relaxing. He waited until she sat on the chair, then took a seat next to her.

"I know I already apologized, but I kind of feel I need to again—" Kenna started.

But Aleck cut her off. "No, you don't."

She looked over at him. "You don't even know what I was going to apologize for," she protested.

"It doesn't matter. You have nothing to be sorry about. If you thought you might apologize for jumping into the water this morning, I'm *definitely* not sorry you did that. The training we were doing was boring. Yes, it was important, but being safety monitor isn't my favorite thing in the world, so you did me a favor. And why would I be upset about a beautiful woman jumping on top of me?"

"I didn't jump on you," she protested with a small smile. He saw her glance down at her hands in her lap. It was endearing. Aleck had been observing her all night, and it was obvious she was outgoing and an extrovert, so seeing her shy whenever she was around him was kind of cute.

"And if you were thinking about apologizing for asking me to come tonight when you had to work, don't. I've actually enjoyed watching you interact with others, and it's been fun to see Elodie and Lexie let down their hair and truly relax."

"You really like them, don't you?" she asked, then scrunched her nose adorably. "I mean, of course you do, because they're your friends, but sometimes guys don't like their friends' girlfriends and merely tolerate them."

"I know what you mean. And if you mean 'like' in the sense that they're my best friends' women and they amuse me? Yes. They're good people who have been through hell, and came out stronger on the other side."

Kenna tilted her head at that. "But they're okay?" she asked.

Aleck liked the genuine concern he heard in her voice. "Yeah. I'm sure they'll tell you all about their experiences if you ask. They aren't shy about it, and honestly, they're some of the strongest women I've met. In a nutshell, Elodie was a chef for a mobster who took exception to the fact she wouldn't poison a guest for him. She ended up cooking on a cargo ship, which was hijacked by pirates in the Middle East. She came to Hawaii but the mob guy wasn't willing to let her go, so he tried to kill her."

Kenna's eyes were huge in her face. "Holy shit!"

"Yup. But she's okay now, and the mob guy is out of the picture, and she and Mustang got married and they're madly in love."

"It's obvious," Kenna said, nodding. "I'm glad she's okay."

"Me too."

"And Lexie?" Kenna asked.

"She was working in Africa and got kidnapped, along with a coworker. We rescued her, but unfortunately the man she was with didn't survive the rescue. He had a heart attack. She came to Hawaii to work, but the twin of her coworker wasn't happy that she survived and his brother didn't, and tried to take out his frustration and anger on her."

"Wow, you weren't kidding about them having gone through hell!"

"Nope. But anyway, seeing them happy and relaxed is always nice. Lexie's thing wasn't too long ago, so seeing her so carefree is refreshing. So you have nothing to apologize for," Aleck said. "Besides, I was pleasantly surprised by the food here."

"What, you thought it would suck?" Kenna teased.

"No. But Waikiki isn't my go-to spot to hang out or for food."

"I know, but I think the area has gotten a bad rap for whatever reason. There are some amazing places to eat down here. And the business owners are super nice too."

"I guess I need to get out of my comfort zone a little more," Aleck said.

"I'd be happy to show you my favorites," Kenna told him.

"Yes," Aleck answered immediately.

They smiled at each other.

"So...what brought you to Hawaii?" Aleck asked, wanting to know everything about the woman at his side. He was aware that the clock was ticking and he didn't have nearly the time he would've liked to get to know her better.

"I came here in college with some friends and fell in love with everything about it. The weather, the sunsets, the people, the culture. After I graduated, I got a job in Pittsburgh that I hated. The winters sucked, and I spent most of my days in a cubicle. I made an impulsive decision to quit and move out here. I arrived with three suitcases and huge expectations." She shrugged. "My life hasn't turned out how I thought it would. You know, making big bucks at some huge corporation, changing the world in the process...but I'm happy."

"That's good," Aleck told her. "You been working at Duke's long?"

"I tried to find an accounting job, which was what my major was, and even though I was offered one or two, something kept me from accepting. I couldn't imagine living here and being stuck in another cubicle, staring at numbers all day. It was one thing to do that in Pennsylvania, where it's grossly hot in the summer and freezing and gray in the winters, but to do it here in Hawaii, where the weather is literally perfect all the time, just seemed wrong.

"So, while I was trying to figure out what I wanted to do, I took a waitressing job. It was awful, and the pay sucked... but I realized I loved meeting all sorts of different people every day. That job led to another, and after a while, I met someone who put in a good word for me here. It's been a few years now, and I can't imagine working anywhere else."

The enthusiasm and honest enjoyment of her job was clear in her tone. She wasn't blowing smoke up his ass. She honestly seemed to love what she did. It was somewhat of a revelation for Aleck. He just assumed she was waitressing temporarily while she looked for a "real" job. But it was obvious this *was* a real job for her.

"What about you?" Kenna asked.

"What about me?" he asked.

"You're a SEAL. How'd that happen? Were you one of those kids who always dreamed about joining the Navy and becoming a superhero? Or were you forced to join up because you were a troublemaker?"

Aleck chuckled. "Neither, actually. I was an okay student, didn't get into trouble, and was voted class clown," he told her. "After high school, I was kind of lost. Didn't know what I wanted to do with my life. Wasn't really ready for college. I went down to the recruiting office in San Francisco and talked to all the recruiters. The Navy offered me the most money and benefits. So I joined up."

Kenna smiled. "You totally played them off each other, didn't you?"

"Yup," Aleck said without remorse. "I got through boot camp and sat through a recruiting session about the SEALs. I thought it sounded like a challenge, so I signed up."

"And here you are," Kenna said.

"Well, it wasn't quite that easy," Aleck said with a snort.

"I know. I'm not an expert, but I know about BUD/S."

"Yeah, Hell Week and BUD/S sucked, but there's so much more to becoming a SEAL than just that."

"I figured. So...you're from San Francisco?" she asked.

"Yup. My parents still have a home there too. They travel a lot, but that's home base." He wasn't about to get into the fact that they were multi-millionaires right now. Or that he had quite the healthy trust fund. He wanted Kenna to like him for who he was, not for how much money he had.

Silence fell between them for a long moment. But it wasn't awkward. Not really.

"How old are you?" Kenna asked.

"Twenty-nine," Aleck said without hesitation. "You? Or... am I not supposed to ask that?"

"I'm thirty. I just wanted to make sure you weren't like twenty-one or forty. I mean, there's nothing wrong with either, but after Carly's recent terrible experience with an older man, I'm not sure I want to go there. And twenty-one just seems super young to me."

"It is," Aleck agreed. He was curious about her friend's situation, but Aleck knew he only had a little bit of time to talk to her tonight. He wanted to know more about *her*, not her friends. "You grew up on the East Coast?"

"Yeah. Richmond, Virginia, actually. I went to Virginia Tech, then got that job in Pittsburgh."

"Any siblings?"

"Nope. I'm an only child. My parents are divorced but still friends, weirdly. They were one of those couples that had a whole parenting plan. I spent weekends with my dad and was with Mom during the week."

"That had to suck," Aleck said.

Kenna shrugged. "Not really. As I said, my parents were friends. They didn't fight, and I didn't think much about my situation until I was in middle school and realized it wasn't really normal. My dad got remarried, and I really like my stepmother. She's very different from my mom, which is probably why she and my dad's relationship works so well."

"Did your mom ever get remarried?" Aleck asked.

"Nope. But that doesn't mean she doesn't date. She always made sure I was well taken care of, but she loved having her weekends free so she could hang out with her friends and boyfriends."

"She sounds...interesting," Aleck said.

Kenna smiled. "She is."

"And your folks are all right with you being out here?" he asked.

Kenna's brow furrowed. "What do you mean?"

"Well, it sounds like you had a stable job, then you left to come out here to Hawaii without a plan and are now only a waitress."

"They want me to be happy," Kenna said, the friendliness in her tone gone. "And being here makes me happy, so yeah, they're all right with it. My mom visits every few months and my dad's been here a few times too. But it doesn't sound as if *you're* all that impressed with me or my job."

Aleck blinked and realized she was offended by his questions. And no wonder. "Shit, it's my turn to apologize now. I didn't mean to disparage what you do."

Kenna glanced at the water without responding, and he knew he needed to dig himself out of the hole he was in. "Honestly. That was a shitty thing to say. I just know my parents at first weren't all that thrilled about me being stationed out here in Hawaii. They complained that it was too far away. They've come to appreciate me being out here, though. They come visit all the time, but I'm just a convenient excuse. They see me for like three hours, then spend the rest of the week on the beach and being tourists."

Aleck was relieved to see Kenna's lips twitch.

Taking a chance, and hoping like hell it wouldn't backfire, Aleck reached over and took her hand in his. He ran his thumb over her knuckles, once again noticing how silky smooth her skin was. "I'm sorry for being insensitive," he said softly. "Most people I've met are always trying to work their way up the corporate ladder. Even in the Navy. It's all about rank and moving upward."

Kenna didn't yank her hand out of his grip, which Aleck appreciated. She stared at him for a long moment before saying, "You're a snob."

Aleck blinked. Was he?

Yeah…he probably was.

"I mean, you're cute, so you have that going for you though." Kenna smiled. "I know being a waitress isn't what most people aspire to do with their lives. But I had that cushy accounting job, and I hated it. I felt hemmed in. If I had continued to work there, it would've smothered me. I might not be making a million dollars a year, but I'm happy. I meet all sorts of interesting people. I get to spend time at the beach during the day and I'm not trapped in a cubicle, staring at a computer."

Aleck felt horrible. He *was* a snob. He'd never considered that someone who worked as a waitress might *want* to do so. Might actually like it.

"Do you like your job?" she asked.

"Yes." He didn't even hesitate.

"Even though you could die? That you could be shot and no one would ever know the circumstances behind it? Even though you can't really talk about what you do? I'm just assuming that's the case, by the way. I don't know for sure. Some people would look at you and think you're crazy. Why would you want to put yourself in danger for people you don't even know? And while the world isn't like it used to be—most people appreciate our soldiers and what you do—there are those who still think you're the devil incarnate, that you enjoy killing people. And yet...you still do what you do."

"Point made," he said quietly.

"I just...it frustrates me that people look down on me because of my job," Kenna said. "There are some shitty parts of being a waitress, for sure. My feet always hurt at the end of the night, I have to deal with entitled people who can't understand why they have to wait longer than two-point-three minutes for their food. They treat me like a servant, give me shitty tips or no tips at all. I've been yelled at for refusing to serve alcohol to someone who's obviously already had enough, screamed at because their food wasn't to their liking, and even spit on.

"But you know what? The good outweighs the bad. Just as I'm assuming it does for you. I don't save lives—well, I take that back. I *have* saved two lives...one was a kid who was choking and the other was a man who'd had a heart attack, and I did CPR until the paramedics got there. But anyway, my job might not be at the top of the importance scale, but I work damn hard, and like I said...the good outweighs the bad."

Kenna paused for a deep breath. "And now you're probably regretting coming tonight."

"No," Aleck told her. "Actually, I'm even more impressed. You're pretty damn amazing."

"Yeah," she said with a short laugh. "I've chastised you for feeling the way I'm sure most people do, have ignored you because I've been working, and kinda insulted your own job— which, by the way, is cool, and I want to know everything about it."

"You're real," Aleck told her. "You have no idea how refreshing that is. You rightfully called me on my bullshit, you're obviously smart, you're independent, and it's more than obvious how much the people you work with like you. All that adds up to someone I really want to get to know better. If you can forgive me for being an ass."

Kenna smiled. "You're a guy," she said with a shrug.

Aleck laughed. "I am," he agreed. "But we're not all assholes. At least not all the time."

"I'm thirty years old, Marshall," Kenna said. "I probably say what I'm thinking more than I should. I don't have the patience to deal with angst in a relationship...friendship or otherwise. I am who I am, and I want to be around other people who are just as honest. I can't stand secrets and subterfuge. I'm probably screwing everything up here and jumping the gun, but...I like you."

"I like you too," Aleck said immediately. "And I want to see you again."

"Me too," Kenna agreed.

They smiled at each other.

"I do work the dinner shift a lot though," she warned him.

"But not every night."

"No, not every night."

"I can work with that," Aleck told her. "I work during the day. Meetings, training, and there will be times I'll be deployed for indeterminate periods. But I think you're worth any effort it takes to work around both our schedules, Kenna."

She smiled at him. "I've got enough seniority here that I can pretty much pick which shifts I want...although I do have to plan ahead."

"Great," Aleck said. He was more than aware he was still holding her hand. He hadn't really been a hand-holder in the past. But with Kenna, the connection felt...good. Especially because he was more than aware he'd almost fucked up.

"Can you see the fireworks the Hilton Hawaiian Village sets off on Friday nights from here?" he asked, steering their conversation back toward a more neutral topic.

"Well, not from the restaurant, no. But if you walk a bit down the beach and sit on the breakwater wall down that way," she said, pointing down the beach toward the Hilton's large hotel complex, "you can," Kenna said. "Is it bad for me to admit that the fireworks don't do anything for me anymore?"

Aleck chuckled. "Nope. Fireworks aren't my thing either."

"Oh, because of PTSD?" Kenna asked in concern.

"No. I mean, that doesn't help, but we had a dog back home who hated thunder and fireworks. Like, they'd both totally traumatize him. So around the Fourth of July, we had to sedate him in order to help him get through the night, as well as the week before *and* after. Unfortunately, we had neighbors who bought a shitload of fireworks and would set them off every night. It was awful."

"Aw, what kind of dog?"

"Doberman."

Kenna tried not to laugh.

"Yeah, Maximus wasn't exactly the best guard dog," Aleck said with a grin. "He would lick someone to death rather than bite them if they broke in."

"I miss having a pet," Kenna said. "My dad and stepmom had cats."

"You could get one," Aleck suggested.

"My apartment complex doesn't allow them," Kenna said simply.

Immediately, Aleck thought about his own place. He had no idea if pets were allowed or not, but he had a feeling if he wanted to get a dog or a cat, he'd be allowed. Living in the penthouse had its perks.

And that thought was how he knew for sure that Kenna was different.

He'd never, ever contemplated getting a pet because of a woman before. His schedule was definitely not conducive to having a dog. A cat...maybe. If he could find someone to check on it while he was deployed.

"Am I allowed to ask how you and your friends got your... unusual names?" Kenna asked.

Aleck chuckled. "Of course. You can ask me anything. I might not always be able to answer your questions...operational security and all. But if I can't, I'll tell you why. Anyway, yeah, so my nickname is Aleck. My last name is Smart."

Kenna laughed. "Smart Aleck, huh?"

"Yup. And I'll warn you, it fits me pretty well."

"Noted," Kenna told him.

"Mustang's name is kind of complicated, but it involves a prank when he first joined the Navy. Midas was an amazing swimmer in high school and won a bunch of gold medals. Pid's first name is Stuart—or Stu, for short."

"Oh, man, that's harsh," Kenna said.

"Yeah, nicknames often are. The more someone protests about it, the more it'll stick," Aleck told her. "Jag's first name is Jagger, and Slate's last name is Stone."

"So most of your nicknames are because of your real names," Kenna noted.

"Yeah. They usually come about because of our name or something stupid we did," Aleck said.

"It's a good thing I don't have a nickname based on that," Kenna quipped. "I've done a lot of stupid things."

"Nope, I don't believe it," Aleck said.

Kenna laughed, and once again Aleck was struck by her beautiful smile. It lit up her face. And he loved that she didn't seem self-conscious about laughing either. Some women he'd known had covered their mouths with their hands while laughing. Or they'd just giggle. Or they'd complain about getting laugh lines on their face. But Kenna's laugh was genuine.

They sat on the lounge chair for a while longer, talking about nothing important. The amazing Hawaii weather, how impressive surfers were, the necessary evil of tourists in Hawaii, and Kenna told him that it was a personal mission of hers to find the best beaches on the island, even if they weren't open to the public.

"The best beaches?" Aleck echoed.

"Yup. Some of the best places to body surf, or lie on the sand without having to deal with hundreds of tourists, or to snorkel, are privately owned. I've been able to find a lot of them, have been kicked off a few, but for the most part, as long as you aren't being a jerk, no one cares if you're there." She gave him a side-eye. "I bet the Navy base has some good beaches."

Aleck chuckled. "Probably not as many as you'd think. Unfortunately, the top officers don't really look kindly on sailors lounging around on a beach while at work."

"Darn," Kenna said.

"But I'm happy to get you on base and drive you around if you want to look for yourself."

"Yes!" Kenna said enthusiastically. "And in return, I'll be happy to show you some of my favorite private beaches. But you have to promise not to do anything to get us kicked out."

"Promise," Aleck said.

The beeping of an alarm sounded from inside Kenna's pocket, and Aleck reluctantly let go of her hand so she could shift on a hip and pull out her phone.

"Shoot. My break is over," Kenna said as she turned off the alarm.

Aleck was surprised at how fast the time had gone. But then again, he had a feeling he could've talked to Kenna all night and not gotten bored.

"I really would like to see you again. Maybe on one of your nights off," Aleck said.

"I'd like that," Kenna said.

Aleck let out the breath he'd been holding since his screwup. He was happy she was giving him a second chance after putting his foot in his mouth. "Can I get your number? Or I can give you mine," he said, not wanting to be too pushy or get a set of fake digits.

"Give me yours," Kenna told him.

Aleck rattled them off and she programmed them into her phone. He felt his cell vibrate in his pocket after a moment.

"I sent you a text so you'd have mine too," Kenna told him.

Aleck beamed. "Awesome." He stood and held out his hand. "Come on. Let's get you back. I don't want your boss to be pissed."

"Alani's cool. She'd understand."

"Still."

Kenna put her hand in his and let him help her up. And

instead of letting go immediately, she held on as they walked back toward Duke's. The lights of the restaurant seemed extra bright after their time on the beach.

A loud burst of laughter came from the bar area, and Aleck couldn't help but smile.

"Sounds like Elodie and Lexie are having fun," Kenna noted.

"Yup." Looking over at the bar, he saw the women were laughing it up with the two bartenders. Mustang, Midas, and Jag were sitting at a table near the bar.

"Should I be worried about how much they're drinking?" Kenna asked tentatively as she looked over at Elodie and Lexie.

"No," Aleck said. "Mustang said he was going to have a word with the bartender and ask that they go easy on the liquor in their drinks."

Kenna stared at him. "That's...kind of presumptuous, isn't it?" she asked.

"Not really," Aleck said easily. "Both Elodie and Lexie already knew, since Mustang and Midas discussed doing it in front of them."

"Oh."

"We're a protective bunch," Aleck told her. He was somewhat warning her as well as trying to explain. "It's not like they mind their women getting drunk, but they don't want them getting sick. And both Elodie and Lexie are all right with it, since they're not big drinkers. They know they're being looked after, even as they let loose a little." He shrugged. "It works for all of them."

"And your other friend? Why's he still here?"

"Carly," Aleck said with a smile.

"Ah, of course," Kenna said.

"He likes her, even though he's not ready to admit it."

"I think I told you earlier that Carly dated an older man?

Well, it didn't go well. Not at all. She's definitely not ready for another boyfriend right now."

"I can understand that. But that doesn't mean Jag is gonna give up."

"He's got his work cut out for him," Kenna warned.

"If a thing is worth doing, it's worth doing well. If it's worth having, it's worth waiting for. It it's worth attaining, it's worth fighting for. And if it's worth experiencing, it's worth putting aside time for," Aleck said.

Kenna stopped in the middle of the dining room and looked up at him. "Oscar Wilde said that."

"Yup. I've always loved that quote. I'm paraphrasing a bit, but I memorized it in high school, and it's amazing how many things it applies to. My job. Friendships. Relationships. Spending time with someone you want to get to know better."

"Shit," Kenna muttered. Then she straightened her shoulders and looked him in the eye. "Just for the record, you've more than made up for being snobby earlier."

Aleck grinned. "Good."

"Kenna!" Charlotte called when she saw her. "Good timing. Vera just sat someone in your section. You want me to grab their drink order for you?"

"I've got it!" Kenna told her. She looked back at Aleck. "Time to get back to work."

Aleck dropped her hand and nodded.

They smiled at each other for a moment, before Kenna spun around and headed for the kitchen.

Aleck watched her go, feeling a pang of disappointment. He supposed he would've felt it no matter when they parted ways. Kenna was pretty different from the women he'd dated in the past...in a very good way.

He strolled toward the bar and overheard Elodie telling

the bartenders the story about what they'd done in the restroom. They all burst out laughing again.

"I'm totally gonna keep that ruse up," the female said. "Shouldn't be hard. And if it makes people be nicer to the waitstaff, all the better."

Aleck couldn't agree more. He headed for the table where his friends were sitting. He saw that Mustang had a glass of water in front of him, and assumed Midas was drinking iced tea. Jag was nursing a beer.

He pulled out a chair and sat.

"You good?" Mustang asked.

"Yup," Aleck told him.

"How good?" Midas pressed.

"We exchanged numbers, and even though I said some stupid shit, she still wants to see me again," Aleck said with a smile.

"Awesome. Even though I don't believe you said anything stupid," Jag said.

Aleck grinned ruefully. "Kenna called me a snob. And she wasn't wrong."

"You aren't a snob," Midas said in surprise.

Aleck shrugged. "I try not to be, but obviously not having to worry about money has affected me in ways I hadn't realized."

"But you two are cool?" Jag asked.

"Yeah."

"Good." Jag paused, then asked, "She talk about her friend at all?"

He smirked. "You mean the cute waitress you haven't been able to take your eyes off of all night?"

Jag shrugged.

Aleck sobered. "Just that she's not all that keen on dating right now. I guess she's got an asshole ex."

"Shit," Jag swore softly, then straightened in his chair. "Well, the only easy day was yesterday."

Aleck rolled his eyes at the same time as Midas and Mustang. The phrase was a fairly popular SEAL saying, but he wasn't sure it really applied to dating a gun-shy woman. Though it wasn't as if he was an expert in relationships.

Just then, the woman in question headed for their table, and Aleck smiled when Jag sat even straighter.

"Can I get you something to drink?" Carly asked Aleck.

"Iced tea, please," he said.

Carly smiled. "Of course."

They all watched as she glanced briefly at Jag, blushed, then hurried away after making sure everyone else was still good with their drinks.

"She might be gun-shy," Mustang said softly. "But she isn't un-interested."

"I can be patient," Jag said, sipping his beer.

His friend's interest in the waitress was intriguing, but Aleck's attention was already caught by Kenna. She was welcoming a couple sitting on the other side of the bar, and he couldn't take his eyes off her. He hadn't been this into a woman in a long while.

When she'd taken their order and headed back toward the kitchen, her gaze met his, and she smiled.

It felt good to know the attraction wasn't one-sided.

Aleck sat back, happy to chill for as long as Elodie and Lexie wanted to stay. Even if he couldn't talk to Kenna, it was nice to simply be in the same place as she was.

CHAPTER FOUR

Kenna felt almost giddy. She hadn't been this excited about a guy in...

She wasn't sure *how* long it had been, just that it had definitely been a while. Marshall was funny, and clearly not afraid to admit when he'd made a mistake. She'd been disappointed at the way he'd looked down on the fact that she was a professional waitress, but he'd seemed genuine with his apology.

And she couldn't help but remember how good it felt to hold his hand. It was silly, but his thumb brushing back and forth over her knuckles had sent goose bumps racing down her arm.

She liked how close he seemed with his friends too. She wanted any man she dated to have his own interests. She'd seen how clingy Shawn was with Carly. At first it had seemed romantic that he wanted to know where she was all the time and when she'd get home. But then it had started to get...overbearing.

"So, that went well, yeah?" Carly asked when they had two minutes between orders to talk.

Kenna couldn't keep the huge smile off her face. "Yeah, it did."

"Good. I like seeing you happy."

"Now, don't go getting all crazy. We just talked for half an hour. We weren't planning our wedding or anything," Kenna warned her friend.

"I know, but seriously, you're glowing," Carly said.

"He's a good guy. I mean, I know I don't know him all that well yet, but he didn't hesitate to apologize when he said something insensitive, and I honestly think he meant it."

Carly wrinkled her nose. "Not sure it's a good sign he's already put his foot in his mouth," she said.

"I know. But I'd much rather him be honest than blow smoke up my ass. He's real, Carly, which I like."

"True," her friend mused. "Shawn did everything he could to be perfect when we first started dating, and it wasn't until a couple months had gone by that he started slipping and being an ass."

"Exactly," Kenna said with a nod. "I mean, I don't want to be with a guy who's constantly a jerk and apologizing for it, but I also don't want to be snowed by someone who's going out of his way to say what he *thinks* I want to hear."

"So...what'd he say?" Carly asked.

Kenna sighed. "He just made me feel as if he thought waitressing wasn't a 'real' job. That it should be something I'm doing while I'm looking for some corporate career."

Carly shrugged. "Lots of people feel that way."

"I know. It just caught me off guard."

"You made sure he knew the error in his thinking, right?" Carly asked.

"Yeah. We talked a little about his job as a SEAL, and I think he realized pretty fast that he'd been rude. I called him a snob," Kenna admitted.

"You didn't!"

Kenna shrugged. "I did. But in my defense, he kinda was acting like one."

Carly studied Kenna for a long moment.

"What?" Kenna asked.

"You came back in here all smiles and glowy, like I said. So you obviously worked it out."

"We did," Kenna confirmed.

"I'm happy for you," Carly said. "I mean, the fact that you guys could have a serious conversation like that and still like each other afterward...it's...good, Kenna. Seriously."

"I think so too," Kenna admitted softly.

The two friends smiled at each other but were interrupted by Justin sticking his head into the kitchen and saying, "Carly, there's someone here to see you."

"Me?" she asked in confusion. "What do they want?"

"Don't know," Justin said. "Vera just told me to tell you that someone was here for you. That's all I know. He's up front."

"Okay, thanks," Carly said.

Justin disappeared and Carly turned to Kenna. "Seriously, girl. I like him. He was polite and courteous the whole time I was serving their table. They all were. I admit that I don't have any desire to date right now, but if I did...I might give you a run for your money."

"You aren't interested in Marshall," Kenna said with a smirk. "But Jag, on the other hand..." Her voice trailed off.

Carly held up a hand. "Nope. No way. Not going there."

Kenna laughed. "Okay, okay. I'll shut up about it. I'll take the order to your table so you can go and see who wants to talk to you. I hope it's an old guy with a million-dollar tip he wants to give to you for being such an awesome waitress."

"From your lips to God's ears," Carly said with a smile. "And thanks for taking my order."

"Anytime." Kenna headed to where the orders were sitting

under heating lamps, staying warm, and made sure she grabbed the right meals, loaded up a tray, and headed out into the restaurant.

After she'd dropped off the food to a very appreciative couple, Kenna heard a commotion from the bar area. Turning, she saw Carly talking with a man.

Her ex. Shawn Keyes.

Kenna had heard more than enough stories about how horrible he was to Carly. When they'd first started dating, Carly had been flattered that an older man was interested in her. Everything had been all sunshine and roses for a couple months, until Shawn's crazy started coming out. Carly had tried to explain away his abusive and aggressive behavior, but eventually it became too much. And when she'd come to work with a huge bruise on her upper arm, Kenna and the other waitstaff had convinced her to leave the asshole.

That should've been the end of it. But Shawn decided he didn't want to break up with Carly, and he'd been emailing, calling, and texting her nonstop, apologizing and trying to get her to come back.

Carly had held strong, doing everything in her power to try to make him understand that they were over...but for some reason, Shawn wasn't getting the hint.

And now it seemed as if he was escalating his campaign to get Carly back. Kenna couldn't hear what he was saying, but he stood too close to her friend. At six feet tall, he was looming over Carly's five and a half feet, obviously trying to intimidate her.

Kenna didn't even hesitate. She was pissed on her friend's behalf and determined to make Shawn understand once and for all that his relationship with Carly was over and done with. She headed straight for the pair.

When she neared them, she overheard Shawn say, "You're acting like a spoiled brat."

Kenna saw red. "No, she's acting like a grown-ass woman who doesn't want to be talked down to as if she's a little kid," she bit out.

Shawn turned to glare at her, and Kenna refused to back away, even if the hate in his hazel eyes made her want to. He'd cut his dark hair short since the last time she'd seen him, almost a buzz cut. He had on a pair of jeans and a polo shirt, making him blend in with the crowd of locals and tourists without any problem. Kenna had to admit at first glance, the man seemed harmless. Even though he was in his forties, he'd kept himself in shape, didn't drink or smoke—according to Carly—and had a steady, well-paying job doing something with the local government.

But the crazy in his eyes, the way his hands clenched into fists, and the snarl on his face all showed his true colors.

"No one's talking to you," Shawn sneered. "Butt out."

"I'm sorry, but no," Kenna said, trying to sound braver than she felt. They were in a public restaurant with people all around them. Shawn wouldn't do anything to her, she was almost certain of it. "Carly's told you she doesn't want to see you anymore. You need to move on."

"Our relationship is none of your business," Shawn retorted, then turned his back to her and reached out, grabbing Carly's bicep. "I just want to talk," he said. "You owe me that."

Kenna ground her teeth together in frustration. She was taller than Carly, but not strong enough to take this guy on. She was also well aware that she was at work. Alani was a great boss, but Kenna didn't think she'd approve of her hauling off and hitting this asshole. Not to mention, she was one hundred percent certain Shawn would call the cops and get her arrested for assault or something.

"There's nothing to talk about," Carly said. "We're through."

"We *aren't*," Shawn insisted. "After all I've done for you, I can't believe you won't just talk to me. When we started dating, you were a naïve little girl. I turned you into a *woman*. You can't just throw me away."

Kenna wanted to scream. Shawn had always belittled her friend. Tried to come off so worldly because of his age. He'd mocked Carly's much younger age since almost the beginning. Yes, she was twenty years his junior, but in Kenna's eyes, Carly was the mature one. His behavior tonight proved it.

"Give me a break. We didn't date that long, and you didn't turn me into *anything*. So I can and I *am* throwing you away," Carly retorted bravely, lifting her chin. She tried to jerk her arm out of his grasp, but Shawn tightened his grip, pulling her closer so he could grab her other arm as well.

He physically shook her as he said, "You stupid bitch! No one breaks up with me!"

Kenna was done. She reached for Shawn and tried to push him away from Carly, but his grip on her friend was too tight. He stumbled and ran into a chair, making it tip over with a loud crash. "Let go of her," Kenna ordered.

"Fuck you," Shawn hissed, turning to Carly once more. He shook her again, harder this time. Kenna watched as her friend's head bounced back and forth, even as she struggled in his grasp.

Desperate to help, she took a step toward them, but suddenly an arm wrapped around her waist, pulling her backward, away from Shawn and Carly.

She fought for a second, then heard a low voice at her ear. "Aleck and Jag have this."

Turning her head, she saw it was Mustang who'd pulled her away from what was going on. Midas was standing on her other side, posture tense, as if ready to make sure Shawn didn't turn on her.

Glancing back, she saw that in the few seconds she'd

taken her attention off her friend, Marshall and Jag had gotten Shawn to let go. Jag's arm was around Carly's shoulders and he was escorting her away from the bar area.

"We aren't done!" Shawn yelled at Carly as she hurried away.

"You're done all right," Marshall told him. He spun Shawn around, twisting his arm behind his back, wrenching it upward in what looked like a very uncomfortable position.

"Let go of me, asshole!" Shawn yelled.

"No," Marshall said calmly. "Not until the cops get here."

"Cops? That's bullshit!" Shawn said, trying to get out of Marshall's hold, but he held him secure. "I didn't do nothin'. I was just having a talk with my girlfriend."

"She's not your girlfriend," Kenna couldn't help but growl.

"Yes, she is," Shawn insisted.

"It's a moot point," Marshall interjected. "You don't put your hands on a woman. *Ever.*"

"I wasn't hurting her," Shawn said.

"Oh, so those bruises on her arms that were already forming weren't from you?" Mustang asked. "And you were shaking her—hard."

"Fuck you!" Shawn retorted.

"That's mature," Kenna muttered.

"The cops are on the way," Paulo said from behind the bar.

Kenna nodded. She knew there was an emergency button behind the bar for situations like this, when people got out of control. She was so glad there was a Honolulu Police Depot not far from Duke's. In the past when the police had been contacted, they'd been there within minutes.

"Let go of me, you asshole!" Shawn shouted, managing to wrench his arm out of Marshall's hold.

Mustang grabbed Kenna's elbow and pulled her farther out of the way.

Midas joined Marshall in subduing the pissed-off man and within seconds, they had him on the floor. Marshall had a knee on his back and held both of his arms, while Midas secured his legs. It didn't look like they were exerting much energy to control Shawn either. Kenna couldn't help but be impressed.

"Relax, man," Midas told him.

"Get off me!" Shawn yelled.

"How's it feel to have someone bigger and stronger manhandle you?" Marshall asked. "Sucks, doesn't it? How do you think Carly felt?"

"Fuck you!"

"Seems to me things between you and her are done. Move on, man. Doing shit like this just makes you look pathetic, not macho or manly."

"I said, *fuck you!*" Shawn repeated as he continued to struggle under the two SEALs.

Kenna wanted to roll her eyes.

By this time, she noticed several patrons had their cell phones out and were filming the altercation. She winced. Alani probably wouldn't care too much, since there hadn't been any damage to the restaurant. Midas and Marshall had easily taken control of Shawn and prevented him from hurting Carly any further, but it still wasn't exactly great publicity to have something like this happen on the premises.

Shawn continued to fight their hold, to no avail, and within five minutes, three police officers were there. They nodded at Marshall and Midas and took control of the swearing and out-of-control Shawn.

They tried to talk to him, but he just continued raging at everyone around him.

"Fuck all of you! I didn't do nothin' wrong! I was talking to my girlfriend and these two assholes jumped me for no reason. You should be arresting *them*, not me! Do you know who I am? I know the governor! If you don't let me go, I'll have your fucking badges!"

Two of the cops led Shawn out of the bar and through the restaurant. Then, and only then, did Kenna let out a sigh of relief.

The second Shawn was out of sight, Marshall was there. He put his hands on her shoulders and moved close. "Are you all right?"

"Of course. Are you?"

His lips twitched. "Yeah."

"There's nothing funny," Kenna scolded.

He immediately sobered. "You're right. Sorry. But for the record...subduing that shithead wasn't exactly hard."

Kenna shook her head. Of course it wasn't. Not for the big bad SEAL. She was suddenly very glad he and his friends had been there. "I need to go check on Carly," she said.

"Jag's got her. But if she's not all that keen on pressing charges, I hope you can convince her otherwise."

"Oh, she'll press charges," Kenna said with confidence.

"If she doesn't, I will," Alani said, coming up next to them. "I saw him shaking her. It's unacceptable. Thank you for your assistance," she told Marshall.

"You're welcome."

"Sir? We're going to need your info and your statement," the police officer said. "If you can please stick around for a while."

Marshall nodded.

The officer turned to Kenna. "You too, ma'am."

"I'll be here. I need to get back to work though, will that be a problem?"

"Not at all. We'll let you know when we're ready for you."

"Thanks."

The officer turned to talk to Midas, and Kenna looked at Marshall. "So much for a relaxing night," she joked.

"Are you really all right? That was pretty intense," he said in response.

"I'm fine. Shawn didn't touch me."

"Even so," Marshall insisted.

Kenna couldn't help but melt a little inside at his concern. "I'm really okay," she told him. "I'm *very* glad you and your friends were here though. I wasn't sure what else I could do to get him to let go of Carly."

"Me too," Marshall said. "The thought of that asshole turning on you is gonna give me nightmares. Can I...Never mind."

"What?" Kenna asked.

"I was just going to ask if I could give you a hug," Marshall said a little self-consciously.

Without thought, Kenna moved forward. She stepped into his personal space and within seconds, his arms were around her, and she had her nose buried in the crook of his neck. She sighed, realizing for the first time how tense she'd become during the altercation.

She heard Marshall inhale deeply as he nuzzled her hair.

Smiling, she pulled back, but didn't step out of his arms. "Did you just smell me?" she asked.

"Yup," he said without embarrassment. "You smell like coconut and fried food."

Kenna burst out laughing. She never would've thought she could be laughing so soon, after something so intense, but she was beginning to think that with this man, anything was possible. "That's what happens when you work at a restaurant," she told him. "Although the coconut is my shampoo."

"I like it," Marshall said simply.

They stared at each other for a long moment before Kenna heard Elodie talking to her husband.

"What an asshole. Too bad you didn't get any licks in."

Kenna chuckled. She wholeheartedly approved of how

bloodthirsty the other woman was. She kinda wished Shawn had struggled *more*, just so the guys would've had to use more force to subdue him.

"I really do need to go check on Carly," Kenna said. "And take care of my tables."

Marshall nodded, but didn't immediately let go of her.

"Marshall?" she asked.

"Sorry. I just...I know things between us are new, if there's even an 'us.' But when I saw him grab hold of Carly and glare at you, I couldn't get to you fast enough. And when you shoved him, I swear I aged ten years."

"Because I shoved him?" Kenna asked in confusion.

"No. Because I was afraid of what he'd do in retaliation," Marshall told her.

Kenna licked her lips. "I'd like there to be an us," she blurted.

"Good." Then Marshall slowly dropped his arms from around her and took a step backward. "Go do your thing."

"You aren't leaving yet, are you?" Kenna couldn't help but ask.

"No. We'll stick around. Need to give the cops my statement, as do the other guys, and I'm sure Elodie and Lexie will want to throw in their two cents as well. I'll be here for a while."

"Okay. I'll talk to you in a bit."

Marshall nodded.

It was harder than it should've been for Kenna to head for the kitchen, where she'd seen Jag leading Carly. It was safe to say that she was definitely "into" Marshall. Time would tell where things between them might go, but for the first time in a long time, she was definitely looking forward to getting to know a man.

CHAPTER FIVE

Aleck glanced at his watch. Ten forty-seven. In some ways, the night seemed to have gone by extremely slowly, but in actuality, he'd been there less than four hours. His emotions had definitely been on a roller coaster during that time. Anticipation, excitement, contentment, confusion, horror, relief...he'd felt all of those and more in the span of four hours.

He had to hand it to Kenna. She seemed to bounce back from what had happened fairly quickly. But he supposed she had to. She smiled and laughed with the people at her tables and acted like the professional she was.

Watching her, Aleck realized once more how unfair he'd been. He really *had* wondered if her parents were all right with her being "only" a waitress. It wasn't until she'd pointed out how rude his question was, without actually coming out and saying those exact words, that he'd realized he'd fucked up.

Luckily, Kenna seemed to have forgiven him. It was crazy how relieved he was. He'd only met her...today? Had it truly only been this morning that she'd jumped on top of him in the water? She had such an engaging personality, and the chemistry they shared made it seem like he'd known her for much longer.

He'd been impressed how well she'd dealt with that asshole Shawn. He hadn't realized what was happening until Jag said something and stood up. When he saw Kenna trying to pry Shawn's hands off of her friend—and then push him—he'd almost had a heart attack.

It was obvious Shawn hadn't taken Kenna's actions well, and by the look on his face, Aleck thought he was getting ready to shove her back. All sorts of awful scenarios had run through his head as he rushed across the bar.

"Hey."

One word, that was all it took for Aleck to snap out of his own head and focus on her.

He and Jag had been waiting by the front of the restaurant for Carly and Kenna. Midas and Mustang had taken their women home a few minutes earlier.

"Hi," Aleck returned, eyeing Kenna carefully. She looked okay. Tired, but not freaked out. Which was a relief.

"Thank you both for walking us to my car," Kenna told them.

"No way in hell we were going to let you head off into a dark parking garage after what happened," Aleck told her honestly.

She narrowed her eyes. "Let?" Kenna asked.

Aleck sighed.

"You guys have your conversation, we'll head to the car," Carly said with a tired smile.

It was a testament to her resiliency that Carly also seemed to be all right. She headed toward the street with Jag at her side. His friend had been fairly quiet after he'd made sure Carly was okay. Jag wasn't the most talkative man, but he'd been even less chatty for the last hour or so.

"I suppose I should say that came out wrong..." Aleck started.

"But it didn't, did it?" Kenna said.

"No," he said. "Look. I'm not saying you aren't perfectly capable of taking care of yourself. But the fact remains that I'm stronger than you. As is that Shawn asshole. He's a typical bully. Backs off when confronted by someone his own size, someone stronger, but has no problem manhandling you or Carly. I'm well aware we just met, and that you've been taking care of yourself for years. But when I saw that asshole glaring at you, all I could think of was making sure he didn't get the chance to do anything.

"I'm not the kind of person who can simply turn my back on someone who needs help. So yeah, I wasn't going to *let* you and Carly walk through a dark parking garage to your car when we don't know where that asshole is."

"He's probably still at the police station," Kenna said.

"Maybe. Maybe not." Aleck's voice lowered. "I'm not trying to be controlling here. I swear."

Kenna eyed him for a moment, then nodded. "I know. I'm sorry. I'm being unreasonable. I'm actually grateful you and your friend are here. Paulo or Justin usually walk me to my car after work, but having you here is..."

Aleck raised an eyebrow when she didn't finish her thought. "Is?" he asked.

"Nice."

"Come on," he said, gesturing ahead of him. "I'm sure you're exhausted."

Kenna smiled slightly at him and nodded. "Yeah."

They walked side-by-side until they got to the street and took a right. They could see Carly and Jag ahead of them, and there were quite a few people milling around the sidewalks, even at the late hour.

The silence between them was comfortable rather than

awkward, but eventually Kenna broke it. "Tonight's been...interesting."

Aleck smirked. "That's one word for it."

Kenna returned his smile. "I..." She paused, then muttered, "Shoot."

"What?"

"I hope after everything that's happened, you might still want to chat?"

Aleck looked down at her. "Chat? Oh yeah," he assured. "You're the most interesting person I've met in a very long time, Kenna. I definitely want to 'chat' with you some more."

"Good. Me too."

Without thought, Aleck reached for her hand. She didn't pull away when his fingers curled around hers. And long before he was ready, they reached the parking garage, where they got in the elevator with Carly and Jag and headed up to the floor where Kenna had left her car.

She led them toward a brown Chevy Malibu that had seen better days. Figuring he didn't want to push his luck, Aleck refused to comment on the beat-up looking vehicle.

As if she could read his mind, Kenna said, "It looks much worse than it is. I've got a great mechanic and he keeps her running. Besides, no one's gonna want to steal it."

"That's for sure," Jag muttered.

Kenna simply chuckled.

"Thanks for the assist tonight," Carly said, speaking for the first time since they'd all gotten in the elevator together.

"You're welcome," Jag said.

"Of course," Aleck told her.

"First thing tomorrow, go and apply for that protective order," Jag ordered.

"I will."

"I wouldn't mind if you kept me updated," Jag told her.

Carly looked uncertain. Then, even though Aleck and

Kenna were standing there, she blurted, "I'm not looking for another boyfriend."

To Jag's credit, he didn't even flinch. "What about a friend?"

The look on Carly's face screamed "skeptical." She turned and looked at Aleck. "Has he ever had a friend who was a woman before?"

Aleck was immediately uncomfortable. He didn't want to throw his buddy under the bus, but no, Jag hadn't ever had a female friend as far as he knew. Hell, he didn't have any friends period, other than the guys on the team.

On the outside, Jag looked friendly and easygoing, but he was definitely the most intense—and deadly—of everyone on the team.

"Right, that's what I thought," Carly said, when Aleck took too long to respond.

"If Jag says he's okay with being your friend, you can absolutely trust that," he said quickly.

"And I think he's proven tonight that you can count on him," Kenna threw in.

"Fine," Carly sighed. "But at the slightest sign you want to cross that line, we're done," she warned.

"Thank you. You won't regret it," Jag told her.

Kenna let out a small chuckle.

"What?" Carly asked.

"I never thought I'd see the day when you had to warn someone not to get too attached to you," Kenna told her.

Carly blushed furiously. "I didn't mean it that way."

"I know," Jag said. "Come on, let's get you settled." He threw a look at Aleck, then returned his attention to Carly. "You need to get home. You've had a hard night."

Aleck nodded at his friend and pulled Kenna around to the driver's side of her car. He turned his back on Carly and Jag and squeezed her hand. "You sure you're okay?" he asked.

"I'm fine," she reassured him. "I wasn't the one Shawn was pissed at tonight."

"Well, you weren't at first," Aleck said dryly.

"Yeah, he wasn't real thrilled with me, was he?"

"Nope. But then again, he doesn't seem to be the kind of guy who's very impressed with any woman who has the smallest speck of independence in her veins."

They heard the car door shut on the other side of the vehicle, and Aleck turned to see Jag give him a chin lift and head back toward the elevators. They were carpooling back to the base, and Aleck figured Jag would wait for him down on the sidewalk.

Not able to stop himself, he lifted his free hand and ran the back of his fingers over Kenna's cheek. His heart rate increased when she tilted her head into his touch.

"When can I see you again?" he asked.

"I'm not sure. I'm going with Carly to apply for the protection order tomorrow, then I work tomorrow night. I've got some errands I need to do this weekend as well. What's your schedule?"

"Pretty much eight to five," Aleck admitted. "I work out with the team in the mornings and sometimes we have training, like we did this morning. If something comes up, we might have the occasional late meeting."

Kenna frowned. "When I work the dinner shift—which is really the only shift I work anymore—I have to be there around four."

"We'll figure it out," Aleck told her. "If you think I'm gonna let something like our work schedules keep me from getting to know you better...you're wrong."

She smiled up at him. "I have Sundays free. Because I've worked at Duke's so long, I'm able to request not to work them."

"Me too," Aleck said, returning her smile. "Except if I'm on a mission."

"Does that happen a lot?" Kenna asked.

Aleck shrugged. "Enough."

"Right. So, um, you want to do something Sunday?" she asked. "Not this one, because I have errands, and I want to hang out with Carly and make sure she's okay, but the next one?"

"Yes," Aleck said without having to think about it.

"Cool."

"Yeah. Cool. In the meantime, do you mind if I call? I know you work evenings, but I could call on my lunch break...if that works for you."

"That sounds great. And are you a text kind of guy? I admit that I am," she told him.

"I have a feeling I am now," he said with another smile.

"Just ignore me if I get too annoying," she said.

"Never."

"Famous last words," she said with a chuckle.

"Nope. If you text me, that means you're thinking about me and wanted to reach out to share something. How could I ever get annoyed knowing you contacted me because I was on your mind?"

She blushed. "Well, when you put it that way..."

"I've dated my share of women," Aleck said, hurrying to continue when she frowned. "Some have only been with me because I'm a SEAL. Others were hoping we'd get married and they'd be set for life...because let's face it, the military has some pretty good benefits. A few were just out for a good time. And a couple were with me for another reason...which we can talk about later. But none of them have made me feel like you have after just one day."

Aleck knew he was being sappy, which totally wasn't like

him. He was the smart aleck, the joker. But around her, he couldn't seem to play that role.

"I like you, Kenna Madigan. And while I might not be able to text you back right away if I'm in meetings or something, know that seeing a message from you pop up on my screen will make me smile, and that I'll *always* like hearing from you."

She stared up at him for a moment. "Another reason?" she asked. "Should I be worried?"

"That's what you got out of all that?" he asked with a small chuckle.

"Hey, I've learned to listen to the little things. They're usually the most important."

"No, you shouldn't be worried. Not at all." Aleck looked at his watch, then said, "We've known each other for three-point-two seconds and we've already had a good amount of drama. We can save any more revelations for another time."

"Fair enough," Kenna said. "I've dated my fair share of men too, and plenty were just looking for regular sex. Or they thought they liked me until they got to know me. Or they wanted me to be more...reliant on them. I'm independent and I like it that way. I'm an extrovert who loves meeting new people. I like my job, as you know, and I have no intentions of quitting and becoming a stay-at-home mother. Not that there's anything wrong with that, but it's not for me. The stay-at-home part, not motherhood."

"You want kids?" Aleck blurted.

Kenna shrugged. "Sure. Someday."

For a split second, he couldn't get the image of her pregnant out of his head. Which was even crazier than all the *other* crazy tonight. But still...

"Marshall?" she asked.

"Yeah?"

"Please don't be a psycho."

He burst out laughing. "I'm not."

"Promise?"

"Promise."

"Even if things don't work out between us, you aren't going to be all...weird...right?"

"If you mean weird like Shawn was tonight, no. I have no desire to chase after a woman if things between us aren't working out, especially one who doesn't want me. And even if I fall madly in love with you, but you don't reciprocate my feelings, I swear I won't be...weird...if you break up with me."

Kenna nodded. "Okay." She looked behind him at the car, then met his gaze once more. "I should go. Get Carly home."

"Yeah."

Neither of them moved.

Aleck wanted to lean down and kiss the intriguing woman in front of him, but knew it was too soon. He settled for squeezing her hand. "Drive safe. Would it be presumptuous of me to ask you to let me know when you get home?"

"Only if you'll do the same," Kenna said.

"Deal." Weirdly enough, no one had ever asked him to let them know when he arrived back at his place safely. Maybe it was because he was a guy. Maybe it was because he was a SEAL. But he couldn't deny her concern felt good.

He forced himself to let go of her hand and reached for the door handle of her car. He opened it and, once she was seated, leaned over. "Be safe, ladies. Carly, I'm glad you're okay tonight. And for the record...you will *always* be one hundred percent safe with Jag. He's one of the good guys."

"I just don't want him to get the wrong idea," she replied quietly.

"He'll follow your lead," Aleck assured her. And he would. That didn't mean he wouldn't do whatever he could to change her mind about being just friends. His teammate definitely couldn't take his eyes off Carly tonight, making his interest loud and clear to his friends.

It was a good thing he'd taken Carly away and kept her safe, because if Jag had stayed to deal with Shawn, things would've gotten ugly. Aleck had no doubt about that.

"Thanks for walking us to the car," Kenna said.

"My pleasure. I'll talk to you later."

Kenna nodded, and once more Aleck had to force himself not to lean over and take her lips with his own. He shut the door and stuffed his hands in his pockets. He gave the women a small chin lift and headed for the elevators.

Shit. He was a goner.

He'd seen it happen with Mustang. Then Midas. And now he was acting the same way his friends had after they'd met Elodie and Lexie, respectively. But instead of being freaked out about it, contentment filled him.

It was hard to believe twenty-four hours ago, he didn't know Kenna existed. It felt as if the entire trajectory of his life had changed since meeting her. That sounded nuts, and he knew it, but he also didn't care.

Maybe he and Kenna wouldn't work out. There was a lot they needed to learn about each other. But Aleck had a feeling he could be in it for the long haul...and he was one hundred percent all right with that.

Smiling, he greeted Jag with a grin and they headed down the sidewalk toward another parking garage, where Aleck had left his Jeep. Neither spoke, both lost in their heads. Things had changed for both of them that night, and it was a lot to process.

CHAPTER SIX

One week.

That's how long it had been since Kenna last saw Marshall, and she was almost giddy with the thought of getting together with him later that morning.

While she may not have seen him, they'd talked every day. She'd texted him when she'd gotten home from the work shift from hell and ten minutes later had received a note back. He'd let her know he was also home. Even though it was late, they'd talked back and forth via text for another thirty minutes before she called it a night.

When she'd woken up the next morning, Marshall had already left her a good morning message.

She hadn't lied, she liked texting. Liked using emojis. And so far, he hadn't seemed annoyed with how often she shot him messages. Kenna thought back to the parking garage, where he'd admitted that he liked the thought of getting texts from her because it meant she was thinking about him.

He wasn't wrong.

But then again, Kenna found herself thinking about Marshall all the time. He intrigued her. She'd met her fair share of military men and women at Duke's, but something about Marshall, and his friends for that matter, seemed different. More intense. It was probably because they were Navy SEALs, but she didn't think that was the only reason.

They were definitely protective—look at how fast Mustang had gotten to her and pulled her away from Shawn, how quickly Jag had gotten Carly out of Shawn's grasp, and how easily Marshall and Midas had subdued him. But it was more than that.

They were good men. Kenna would bet her life on it. She was a fairly good judge of character. She'd learned from years of waitressing to sum up patrons at a glance. She could tell who were tourists, who would probably be stingy with tips, and which customers were going to be a pain in her butt. And she was rarely wrong.

Marshall could've been an ass about her interrupting his training session. He could've yelled at her, told her to get the hell away from him. He could've been pissed that he'd gone all the way down to Duke's with the expectation of a date, and instead she was working. He could've wanted nothing to do with her and Carly after what happened, deciding the entire situation was simply too much drama. But that didn't seem the case.

Carly knew men in general were good at hiding their crazy from others. Heck, serial killers didn't exactly wear a sign warning people away from them. She'd seen enough murder shows to know most people acquainted with a killer said something to the effect that they "seemed so normal."

While Marshall might not be perfect, he was certainly the most interesting man she'd met in a very long time. And for some crazy reason, he seemed to like her. Not that Kenna thought she wasn't likable. She was. But her dating life had been pretty pathetic recently, so it was nice—really nice—to find Marshall so into her.

She was excited about meeting him near the Naval base today, where he'd give her a tour. They didn't have long, since it was Friday and she had to work later, but he'd gotten permission from his commander to take a few hours off.

Marshall had offered to come into the city to pick her up and bring her back to the base, but she'd declined. Kenna liked him, but she wasn't ready for him to see where she lived. It wasn't smart, even though he seemed amazing and she felt safe with him.

Her phone vibrated with a text and she looked down and smiled at seeing the note from Marshall.

Marshall: Looking forward to today. It feels like it's been a month since I've seen you.

Kenna: Me too (and please tell me you're wearing your uniform! Hubba hubba!). And I feel the same way.

Marshall: I've got on my BDUs. Nothing special.

Kenna rolled her eyes. Guys had no clue how much women liked a man in uniform. There was no explaining why, at least for her. It just was. And she couldn't freaking wait to see Marshall in his. He was hot in jeans and a black T-shirt. But camouflage? Be still her heart.

Marshall: Cat got your tongue?

Kenna: Just trying not to drool on my phone, thinking about you in a uniform. Any chance I'll get to see you in your dress whites someday?

Marshall: I'm sure that can be arranged. ;)

. . .

Shit, had he just used the winky emoji? Kenna couldn't stop smiling.

Kenna: You sure you still have time to show me around today?

Marshall: Absolutely. Nothing short of world war 3 would keep me from our date today.

Kenna: So it's a date?

Marshall: Yes.

One word. Kenna could practically hear his emphatic response.

Kenna: Cool. So I'll meet you in the parking lot for the Pearl Harbor memorial in an hour?

Marshall: I can still come and pick you up if you want.

Kenna: I know, and I appreciate it. But...as much as we've talked in the last week and as much as I like you, I'm not comfortable with you knowing where I live yet. Sorry.

Marshall: Don't apologize. I'm not comfortable with you knowing where I live yet either.

Kenna wasn't sure if he was kidding or not. It was hard to tell that kind of thing over text. And since he didn't use any funny emojis to help her figure it out, she decided to just move on.

Kenna: You've got a yellow Jeep, right?

Marshall: Yup. I'll text you when I get close. Wouldn't want any other guys with yellow Jeeps horning in on my date.

. . .

Kenna sent an eye-rolling emoji.

Kenna: Not sure you have to worry about that.

Marshall: Their loss is my gain. I need to go. I'll see you in an hour. Drive safe.

Kenna: I will. Later.

Marshall: Later.

Kenna sat back on her couch and couldn't help but smile. One of the things she liked most about Marshall was how much he made her laugh. He simply made her happy, which felt really good.

He'd proven to be a good listener as well. One night after she got home from work, and after an especially hard shift with table after table of assholes, she'd sent him a brief note about how tired she was and wishing him a good night. He'd immediately messaged back and asked if he could call.

They'd ended up talking for an hour. Kenna had gone on and on about the more frustrating parts of her job and the various ways people acted like jerks. He hadn't blown her off or made jokes. He'd listened. Then he'd shared some of his shitty experiences with humans.

It made her feel even closer to him.

But most of the time when they spoke or sent messages, they were light and silly, making her smile much like she was now.

Knowing she needed to get ready to go, Kenna put her phone aside and stood. She'd make herself a grilled cheese sandwich then get changed. She and Marshall hadn't talked about having lunch, and he might not have time anyway. She wanted to see as much of the base as he'd be able to show her. She might be able to sneak onto private beaches, but getting on the Naval base without an escort or a military ID wasn't possible. She didn't want to get arrested, after all.

* * *

An hour later, Kenna climbed out of her Malibu when a bright yellow Jeep pulled up behind her. Marshall had texted just minutes before, like he'd said he would, something else she appreciated...when he said he was going to do something, he did it.

"Hi," she said as she climbed out of her car.

Though she'd expected him to stay in his car while she joined him, Marshall got out to greet her. Her breath caught in her throat when he brushed his lips against her cheek in greeting.

"Hey. You look great."

Kenna hadn't expected the kiss, but it felt natural. He stepped back immediately and wasn't crowding her or making her feel uncomfortable. She'd gone out of her way to try to look nice today. The first time she'd seen him, she was half naked in her shorts and sports bra, and the second, she was in her waitress uniform of khaki shorts and a Duke's T-shirt. Today, she'd put on a pair of jean shorts and a v-neck shirt that showed off her cleavage. Tastefully, of course. Normally she lived in flip-flops when she wasn't at work or going for a run, but because she wasn't sure how much walking they'd be doing, she'd worn sneakers. She'd left her hair down, but had a ponytail holder in her purse in case it got too hot.

All in all, Kenna was very pleased with her efforts, and was happy Marshall had noticed.

"Thanks," she told him, smoothing a lock of hair behind her ear. "You do too." And he did. Marshall had on his camouflage Naval uniform and was just as good-looking as she'd imagined he'd be. His dark hair was a bit mussed and he was clean shaven this morning. She couldn't decide if she liked his face better bare or with a five o'clock shadow. Then she wondered what he'd look like with an actual beard. But a trimmed one, not long and shaggy.

"What are you thinking about so hard?" Marshall asked.

Kenna knew she was blushing. "Um...honestly?"

"Always."

"I was trying to figure out what you'd look like with a beard."

Marshall smirked and reached into his back pocket and pulled out his phone. He tapped the screen a few times before holding it out to her with a grin.

Kenna took it and glanced at the screen. "Holy shit," she said under her breath. She was looking at a picture of Marshall and his teammates. They were dressed in full-on military gear—camouflage, helmets, bulletproof vests, and a ton of accessories strapped to their arms, legs, and chest. Each of them also held a rifle.

But what really caught her attention was that all of them sported full beards and mustaches.

"We'd been on a mission for quite a while," Marshall explained. "There wasn't any time to shave, not that it was high on our priority list. When we finally got back to base, one of our friends snapped the picture."

Kenna brought the phone closer. He looked tired in the photo, but she couldn't deny that Marshall was *hot* in full gear and a beard. She handed the phone back. "I like the beard, but I think I like you clean shaven better."

"Me too," he agreed immediately. "Having a beard honestly reminds me too much of the things I've seen and done while deployed."

"I can see that. I haven't said it before, but thank you for your service. For all you've done."

Marshall nodded and pocketed his phone. "You ready?"

"Yup."

"I have to warn you," Marshall said as they walked around his Jeep. "I don't know how exciting this tour will be."

"I've never been on a military base, so for me, this is cool."

He smiled at her as he opened the passenger door.

Kenna got in and was surprised when Marshall handed her the seat belt. She clicked it on as he shut her door. He walked around and climbed into the driver's side.

"Go ahead and get your ID out. I'll need to show it when we go through the gate."

Kenna dug in her purse and grabbed her driver's license.

"I thought I'd start out by showing you Joint Base Pearl Harbor-Hickam, then we'll head over to Ford Island. I want to show you one of my favorite places over there."

"Awesome," Kenna replied. She hadn't really thought too much about what they were going to do while on the base, she was just excited to see Marshall again and spend time with him.

Going through the gate was uneventful, then Marshall began driving around. He first took her through one of the housing sections, and she was suitably impressed by how clean everything looked.

"Do you live on base?" she asked.

"No."

She waited for more explanation, but when there wasn't any, she asked, "Is it because you're single?"

"Not really. I mean, yes, single sailors don't live here in these larger houses, they're reserved for families, but I like living off base. It somehow makes me feel as if I have a life." He chuckled. "That's not the best explanation, sorry."

"No, it makes sense. I guess it would be like if I lived in the Outrigger hotel connected to Duke's. It would feel too much like I was at work every second of every day."

"Exactly," Marshall said with a small smile. "So...where do you live?"

His question wasn't exactly subtle, but she gave him a pass. "In a small apartment complex not that far from Waikiki. It's on the other side of the Ala Wai Canal, but close enough that I can get to work without having to get on the Interstate. And before you get too excited, it's just a two-level building, and no, I can't see the ocean from my apartment."

"I wasn't going to ask about that," he said.

"It's usually the first thing people from back home want to know. 'You live in Hawaii? Can you see the ocean from your apartment?' As if everyone who lives here has a perfect ocean view." She rolled her eyes. "But I've got a great landlord and my neighbors are pretty cool."

"That's good," Marshall said.

Kenna thought it somewhat odd that he dropped the subject, but he probably remembered her being cautious about telling him where she lived. Which seemed silly now. She suddenly wished she'd let him pick her up, it would've given her more time with him.

They drove past a dog park and an elementary school. He showed her the commissary and the BX, the base exchange... basically like a big-box store that sold everything from snacks to clothes to tools. They drove farther onto the base and Marshall pointed out the building he worked in. He apologized for not being able to take her on a tour of any of the ships that were in port, though Kenna was still fascinated by the sight of them.

"The base isn't as big as I imagined it'd be," she told him.

"Well, the Navy doesn't need a huge post like the Army

does," Marshall explained. "Our playground, so-to-speak, is the ocean."

"Yeah, that makes sense. It's not like you need a huge amount of land to drive tanks around on and stuff."

"Yup. You ready to head over to Ford Island?"

Kenna had no idea how the base was laid out and didn't know what was on the island compared to where they were now, but she nodded anyway.

Marshall smiled, as if he knew she was clueless, but he was a gentleman and didn't comment on it. They drove back through the gates, past the Pearl Harbor Visitor Center and onto a bridge. She had to show her ID again at another checkpoint, but soon they were on their way once more.

"I feel as if I'm getting some super-top-secret tour," Kenna told him.

Marshall chuckled. "It feels that way, but honestly, the base is a lot like any other neighborhood."

Kenna wasn't sure about that, but she didn't comment. Marshall drove through another residential area, smaller than the one on the main part of the base. They passed a hotel for military personnel, another dog park, and then Marshall pulled into a small parking lot for the USS Utah memorial. He parked and met her at the back of his Jeep. He reached for her hand and they walked down the memorial walkway that extended into the harbor. At the end, there was a plaque describing what happened to the ship during the attack on Pearl Harbor in World War Two, and she could see the hulking remnants of the ship in the water.

There was only one other couple there, but they left soon after Marshall and Kenna arrived. It was quiet and serene, and Kenna took the time to reflect on the fifty-four men who'd lost their lives and who were still entombed on the ship under the water. Being there made her really think about Marshall and what he did. He was a SEAL. He wasn't sitting behind a desk, safe here in Hawaii. She had no idea where he was sent or even exactly what he did, but it hit home that he definitely didn't have a safe job.

She stepped closer and leaned into him, resting her head on his arm.

"You okay?" Marshall asked quietly.

It seemed proper to whisper here. In the shadow of the ship where sailors like Marshall had lost their lives.

"I learned about the attack on Pearl Harbor in school," Kenna said. "And the Holocaust. And the Vietnam War, and other major conflicts around the world. But they were always just words on a page. Details to memorize for a test. Standing here, seeing the rusting hull of this ship, it's so real. And now knowing you, and what you do, it just seems more...personal."

"I didn't bring you here to make you sad," Marshall said.

"I know. And I'm not sad...exactly," Kenna said, struggling to explain how she felt. "It's only been a week since I've met you, and I'm not even sure our relationship is really defined yet, but standing here, reading the info on what happened and seeing the names of the men who died, it makes me worry about you all the more."

Marshall put his arm around her shoulder and held her against him. "The circumstances are very different," he told her. "Pearl Harbor was attacked without notice. The men on the ships weren't able to do much to protect themselves. My team and I don't go into any situation without having first researched the hell out of it."

"That doesn't mean something can't go wrong," Kenna protested.

"You're right. It doesn't. But we plan for every contingency we can think of. And, not to be flip about what I do, but you could be killed driving down the street. I don't take my life for granted, and I'm as careful as I can be, but shit happens. Freak accidents, heart attacks, being struck by lightning. There are a hundred different ways you and I could die walking down the street. I'm probably safer with my team on the other side of the world tracking down a terrorist than you are going to work at Duke's."

Kenna snorted. "I'm not so sure about that, but you have a point."

"I know."

Kenna rolled her eyes and turned so she could meet Marshall's gaze. "Sorry for being a downer."

"You aren't a downer. And to address something else you said...it's okay if you're not sure yet, but as far as I'm concerned, we're dating."

Kenna's stomach flipped. "Yeah?"

"Yeah," he said with a smile. "I already can't wait for lunchtime so I can call and hear your voice. I'm constantly checking my phone to see if you've messaged and the guys have been giving me shit about it...but I don't care. I don't even think about sleeping until you text me to let me know that you're home safe and sound after work."

Kenna loved all of that. Freaking *loved* it. "I've never dated a military guy before," she admitted. "And since we're being honest, you being a SEAL scares me. Now I can't stop thinking about the dangerous things you do."

"I can't do anything about that, except to tell you that my team and I don't take risks. Especially now that Mustang is married and Midas has Lexie. When we get sent out, I won't be able to tell you where we're going or when we'll be back. Is that a deal breaker?"

Kenna thought about it for a long moment. Intellectually, she knew that he couldn't tell her about his missions, but emotionally it was a harder concept to swallow.

But then she thought about the last week. How much she'd laughed while talking to Marshall. How he'd made her feel special even though they hadn't seen each other. How nice it was to have someone worried about her well-being and someone who got irritated on her behalf when she had asshole customers to deal with.

He had a good point about the dangers of everyday life. Marshall loved what he did, that was obvious. And she had to guess he was good at it. Not only that, but as he said, his SEAL team was prepared when they were deployed. That didn't mean they couldn't be shot, or blown up by one of those rocket things...but she just had to have faith.

"No," she said, answering his question.

Marshall sighed in relief. "Whew!" He pantomimed wiping sweat from his brow. Then he got serious. "Talk to Elodie and Lexie," he said. "They can tell you how my team and I work since they've seen it firsthand. I'm sure they'd also be happy to discuss their feelings about when we're deployed. One of the most important things for a military spouse is a support system. Having someone to call when you're scared or worried. Someone who can commiserate with how you're feeling and be there for you no matter what. And I can tell you with no hesitation whatsoever that both Elodie and Lexie will be that support for you."

Kenna stared up at him. "You sound like this will be a super long-term thing."

"For me? I hope it is. I'm not getting any younger, and the thought of casual dating gives me hives. I can't see into the future. I don't know where we'll be a month, a year, ten years from now, but I'll tell you this—you aren't a fling for me, Kenna."

"Most guys would have a heart attack talking about a long-term relationship or, God forbid, getting married, a week into a relationship," Kenna said.

"I'm not most men," Marshall said simply. "I know what's important. Family. Friends. Relationships. Not material shit. Not being the most popular or dating as many people as possible. I want what my friends have. I want to come home from a mission knowing the woman I love is waiting for me. Knowing she'll be just as excited to see me as I am her."

"Marshall," Kenna whispered, not sure what to say.

"Sorry. I'm not trying to freak you out. But...yeah. As far as I'm concerned, we're dating. We'll take things one day at a time and see what happens."

"Okay."

"Okay," he echoed. "You ready to move on?"

Kenna looked back at the hunk of rusting metal in the ocean in front of her. She could be afraid to get into a relationship with Marshall. Could push him away because she was scared of him getting hurt, or getting hurt emotionally herself...but that wasn't like her. "Yeah," she said softly.

"Good. Because I've got something else kind of cool to show you. My favorite spot on the island. Although with your response to seeing this memorial, I'm kinda nervous now."

"Don't be. I didn't even know this existed, and I'm honored to have been able to see it," Kenna said.

"All right. You okay? Hungry? Too hot?"

"I'm good. I wasn't sure if we'd be eating or not, so I had a sandwich before I came."

Marshall grinned.

"What?" Kenna asked.

"You're just so...refreshing. You're hungry, you eat. You plan ahead. You don't assume. I can see I'm gonna have to work hard to spoil you."

Kenna shrugged. "I've been on my own a long time. And trust me, you don't want to be around me if I'm hungry. I turn into a raging bitch."

"Now *that* I don't believe," Marshall said, putting a hand on the small of her back and leading her down the walkway toward the parking lot.

"I'm serious," she said.

"Noted," Marshall said. "I'll do my best to make sure I have snacks for you just in case."

Kenna smiled. "I usually have my own snacks," she informed him.

"Right. Then I'll do a better job of planning our dates, letting you know if I'm going to be feeding you or not."

"Now I feel bad," Kenna said. "I'm not going to waste away if I don't eat at a specific time."

"I know," Marshall said as they approached his Jeep. "Here we are."

He opened the door for her again and handed her the seat belt as she got settled. When he was behind the wheel once more, she blurted, "The other reason I'm scared is because you seem so...perfect."

Marshall chuckled as he pulled out of the lot. "I'm not perfect, Kenna. Not even close."

"You've said all the right things, opened my door, and you haven't irritated me once. It makes me nervous."

"I was brought up to treat my girlfriend as if she was the most important person on Earth. My dad made sure I knew how important the little things can be in a relationship. Sure, grand gestures are nice, but it's the everyday things that make the difference. Opening the door for you, handing you the seat belt so you don't have to crane backward to grab it, holding your hand...those are easy. I'm positive I'll annoy you sooner rather than later. It's inevitable. I just hope the small things make up for it."

Kenna had a feeling they would.

"What about you?" he asked.

"What *about* me what?" Kenna asked in confusion.

"From where I'm sitting, you're pretty damn perfect yourself. You jumped into the ocean to rescue me when you thought I was drowning, everyone at Duke's obviously respects and likes you, you've followed your heart even when it was probably scary to quit your job and move to Hawaii. You're beautiful, funny, and somehow you've gotten me to actually enjoy texting."

Kenna laughed. "Point made. I'm not perfect either, Marshall."

"Right. So neither of us is perfect, we're gonna screw up, but we're building a foundation so we can weather the storms that are sure to arrive sooner or later," Marshall said matter-of-factly.

When he put it that way, Kenna couldn't argue his point. And amazingly, her fears that he was somehow pulling the wool over her eyes when it came to who he really was were assuaged. "For the record...I like you opening my door for me," Kenna said.

Marshall shrugged. "Some people don't. They think it's demeaning, as if I think they can't do it themselves."

"Not me. A little kindness goes a long way with me," Kenna said. "I see people at their best and worst at work all the time. So when someone treats me with respect and kindness, I take notice."

Marshall smiled, and Kenna wanted to stop time. The man really was gorgeous. It was hard to believe she was sitting here with him and that he wanted a serious relationship.

They drove around the island and Marshall pointed out the Brig, where Naval prisoners were kept; Kai Beach, the small sandy strip for residents on the island; some of the training centers and the Pearl Harbor Aviation Museum. They went by the Battleship Missouri Memorial, but instead of stopping, he said, "We'll come back another day so you can go onboard...if you want."

"I do," Kenna said immediately. She actually wanted to do some research on her own before they did that though. She felt woefully ignorant when it came to her own country's history and had a feeling knowing the story behind the USS Missouri would make it all the more moving when she *did* board the ship.

Marshall turned down a small road just before the parking area for the battleship, then turned right onto a gravel road. He parked his Jeep off to the side and shut off the engine.

"You been out to the USS Arizona Memorial yet?"

"Yeah, it was one of the first things I did when I moved here," Kenna said. "It was very moving."

"And?"

She wasn't sure what he was asking, but she decided to be honest. "And it was crowded. One of the tourists threw up on the short boat ride out of the memorial. People were talking loudly and being kind of rude."

Marshall nodded as if he wasn't surprised. "Wait there," he said, getting out of the Jeep. He walked around to her door and opened it, holding out his hand. Kenna took it and let him help her out. But instead of letting go, he tightened his hold and started walking toward a tiny path in the trees.

Kenna followed him without question. She supposed maybe it wasn't smart to let a man she'd only known a week lead her into what looked like a thick copse of trees, but she trusted Marshall.

They hadn't walked very long before he turned off the small path and headed through some bushes. Thankful she'd worn her sneakers because of the mud under her feet, Kenna ducked her head and followed Marshall's lead without a word.

Twenty seconds or so later, he stepped out of the undergrowth onto a rocky patch of shoreline. The tide gently lapped at the rocks and he gestured in front of him. "This is my favorite view of the memorial," he said softly.

Looking up, Kenna gasped. Right in front of her was the USS Arizona Memorial. The one she'd taken a boat to when she'd visited it. She was now looking at it from the other side.

She could hear birds chirping and, in the distance, children playing on a playground somewhere.

"Here, sit," Marshall said, nodding to a large flat boulder on the shoreline.

Without taking her eyes from the memorial, Kenna sat. It was more than obvious Marshall had been here before. He sat next to her on the rock and she leaned against him. They didn't talk, just absorbed the view.

After a while, Marshall spoke. "I come here sometimes when I get frustrated with the Navy. When it feels as if what I'm doing doesn't make a difference. I look at that memorial and remember that I'm doing important work. If we can eliminate one enemy who might come over to America to try to kill as many people as he can, then what I do is worth it. If my team and I can take out a terrorist leader who might be planning a sabotage like the one that happened here in nineteen forty-one, it's worth all the angst and hardship.

"I'm only one man, but so were each and every one of the men who died on that ship all those years ago. They had loved ones, doubts, and they were all still serving their country on the brink of war. I respect them, and being here helps ground me."

Kenna gripped his hand harder. "I'm proud of you," she told him softly. "Just like I'm proud of those men under the waves that I never knew. They had families who worried about them, worried what the war would mean for them. While I have a feeling I'll never be all that comfortable when you head off on a mission, that doesn't mean I'm not proud of you for doing it in the first place."

Marshall nodded.

They sat on the rock, listening to the waves splashing at the shore lazily for a while longer.

"You ready to go?" Marshall asked.

She wasn't, but Kenna nodded anyway. He had to get back

to work and couldn't sit out here with her all day. "Thanks for bringing me here."

"Anytime. I mean that. If you need a break, just let me know and I'll bring you out here and you can hang with my homies as long as you want."

Kenna laughed. "Your homies? Who talks like that?"

"Well, no one. But it made you smile," Marshall said.

"It did."

He stood and pulled her up next to him. The ground must've been uneven, because he seemed taller by more inches than usual. He looked down at her with an intense expression on his face.

"What?" Kenna whispered.

"I want to kiss you but I'm trying to decide if it would be weird. If it's too soon."

"It's not too soon," she encouraged.

She saw his lips quirk upward before his head lowered. Kenna went up on her tiptoes to meet him halfway.

The second their lips met, she jolted as if she'd been tased, but she didn't pull away.

God, this man was lethal.

His head tilted and one of his hands came up to rest on the nape of her neck. He didn't grab her, didn't force her head one way or another; his large palm just rested on her skin. Goose bumps broke out on her arms as he slowly and tenderly kissed her. His mouth sipped at hers, and when she thought she was going to go crazy, his tongue licked along the seam of her lips.

She opened to him eagerly. Even then, he didn't get aggressive. He lazily twirled his tongue with hers as they learned what each other liked. Truth be told, Kenna liked *everything* about this man. She pushed her tongue into his mouth, and he let her take control of the kiss.

When it felt like she might pass out from lack of oxygen,

Marshall finally pulled back. But his hand stayed on her nape. He stared down at her as if she was a mythical creature. "I didn't think this place could get any more special," he said. "I was wrong."

Shit. He was killing her. Instead of responding, Kenna put her cheek on his chest and leaned into him. His arms immediately went around her, holding her close. The hug felt amazing.

She felt more than heard him sigh right before he pulled away. "You have no idea how much I hate saying this, but I need to get going."

"I know," she said. "How come when something amazing is happening, time seems to race by? But when shit hits the fan, time crawls?"

Marshall chuckled. "Right? I feel that deeply. Sometimes it feels as if our missions are weeks long when in reality they're only days. And of course when I'm on leave, time flies."

Kenna smiled. "Same with crappy shifts at work. When I have obnoxious customers, they seem to sit at their table all night. And when I have lovely, kind patrons, they eat and run."

They smiled at each other for a moment.

"Seriously, thanks for showing me your special spot," Kenna said.

"You're welcome," Marshall said, then he leaned down, kissed her on the forehead, and grabbed her hand once more, starting back through the bushes toward the path and the Jeep.

Before she was ready, she was once more in the passenger seat and they were headed for the bridge. Wanting to lighten the mood, she asked, "Do you see Elodie and Lexie a lot?"

"A decent amount. Why?" Marshall asked.

"I just wanted them to know that people are still talking

about the mysterious waitress who has connections to *Jurassic Park*. I think Paulo and Kaleen are spreading the rumor every shift they work, but it's been amazing how much nicer people have been acting over the last week."

"I'll make sure they know their plan was, and still is, a success. Although I'm equally sure they'd prefer to hear that from *you* instead of me. I can give you their numbers."

"That would be weird," Kenna protested.

"No, it wouldn't," Marshall countered. "Trust me, they'd love to hear from you."

Kenna wasn't sure about texting people she didn't really know, but then again, she'd really liked both women, and wouldn't mind getting to know them better. Besides, if she really was going to date Marshall, she'd probably be seeing them more often. "Okay, I'd like that."

"Great."

Before she was ready, Marshall was pulling into the parking lot where she'd left her car. He pulled up behind it and, leaving his Jeep running, got out. Sliding out of her own seat, Kenna met him at the back of his Jeep. They walked toward her Malibu and after she'd unlocked it and put her purse inside, she turned to face him. "I had a good time."

"Me too."

"Since you showed me around today, you want to come with me on Sunday to try out a new private beach?" Kenna blurted. She'd been trying to think of how to ask *him* on a date, but had been nervous, which seemed silly now.

"Yes." His answer was short and to the point. "You're working tonight, right?"

"Yeah."

"How's Carly doing?"

Kenna wasn't surprised he'd asked after her friend. "She's okay. She's been on edge since the protection order was delivered to Shawn, but she hasn't seen him."

"Good. Do you think he'll come back to Duke's?" Marshall asked.

"I doubt it," Kenna said honestly. "I mean, he's not allowed within five hundred feet of her, and there would be way too many witnesses to him being there if he showed up. He's more the type who will try to catch her at her apartment or something."

Marshall frowned.

"Don't worry, one of the guys from work has been taking her home every night. And although you probably know this, your friend, Jag, calls her every night and stays on the phone with her until she's inside her apartment."

"He has?" Marshall asked.

"You didn't know?"

"He hasn't said anything."

"Well, he has, and she might not admit it, but I think it's been a relief for her. Anyway, she's okay."

Marshall nodded. "Well, if you do happen to see that asshole, don't hesitate to call the cops and they'll come throw his ass in jail."

"I will."

"Let me know when you get home?" Marshall asked.

Kenna smiled and nodded.

Marshall reached out and ran his hand along the side of her head, smoothing her hair back. "For the record, I'd like to kiss you again, but since I'm in uniform and we're in a public place, it's probably not a good idea."

"Public displays of affection aren't allowed when you're in uniform?" Kenna asked with a frown.

"No, it's not that. But your lips are addicting and I probably wouldn't be able to stop."

Kenna smiled. "Oh."

"Yeah, oh. Can I pick you up on Sunday? Or do you want me to meet you somewhere?"

"If it's not too much trouble, you can pick me up," she told him, feeling somewhat shy. It was a big step forward in their relationship to give him her address, whether he knew it or not. But she should've known he'd realize it.

"I swear you won't regret letting me in," he said, rubbing his thumb against her cheek gently.

"Is eleven o'clock all right?" she asked, not sure what else to say.

"Perfect. You want me to bring lunch?"

Kenna hadn't even thought about food, but it was a good idea, so they could hang out on the beach all day—if they weren't kicked off. "That'd be great."

"Anything you don't like?" Marshall asked.

"Not really. I mean, the beach isn't really the place for something like seafood, but generally I'll eat whatever."

"Okay, I'll come up with something easy to eat that won't spoil in the heat. Kenna?"

"Yeah?"

Marshall shook his head as if he thought better about asking whatever was on his mind.

"What, Marshall?" Kenna asked.

"I was just going to tell you how excited I am about this weekend."

She smiled at him. "Me too," she said quietly. "I don't know what it is about you, but I feel as if I've known you forever."

"Same," he agreed. "Drive safe and don't forget to text me when you get home so I know you got there okay."

Kenna nodded, then stepped toward him. She went up on her tiptoes and kissed him lightly and briefly. "I had a good time today. Thanks."

"I'm just happy we'll have more time this weekend," he said.

"Me too."

Marshall stepped away from her slowly, as if reluctant to leave. Kenna definitely knew the feeling. She stood by her car until he was inside his Jeep once more. Only then did she get into her own vehicle. She followed him out of the parking lot and waved when he turned left and she turned right.

After arriving home and shooting Marshall a text to let him know she got there without any issues, she stood in the middle of her apartment with a silly grin on her face. There was something...soothing...about being with Marshall. She didn't worry about where they were or what they were doing, somehow she just had a feeling he'd take care of all the details. Make sure they were safe.

Had she ever felt this way when she was with a guy before?

She didn't think so.

Looking at her watch, Kenna saw she had a few hours to kill before she had to leave for work. She decided to spend the time surfing the web and finding the perfect beach for them to go to that weekend. It had to be somewhere that had high reviews online, but wasn't too hard to get onto. She didn't want to make Marshall drive all the way up to the North Shore either. Even heading east to the coast could take a while. So she decided to concentrate on beaches on the west side near the Navy base. She hated that he'd have to drive out to Waikiki to pick her up, only to go back where he'd come from, but hopefully she could find a beach that would totally be worth it.

Marshall offering to pick her up was extremely considerate. Especially considering it was so early in their relationship. One of the things she liked best about Marshall was how down-to-earth he was. Being a SEAL probably meant he made more money than the average sailor, but maybe not. She had no idea. Maybe he hadn't talked much about where he lived because he was embarrassed. Hopefully after seeing her not-so-very-exciting apartment, he'd relax a little. Other than his somewhat snobby comment that first night, he seemed to be a lot like her...middle class, with enough money for the important things in life but not a lot of extra.

Smiling, Kenna sat on her couch and fired up her laptop. She remembered seeing a private beach in a previous search that she thought would be perfect. Coral Springs condos looked classy and posh, and the beach was to die for. With Marshall at her side, she thought they just might be able to sneak in. As a couple, they'd blend in more, seem as if they belonged there. Sunday couldn't come soon enough.

CHAPTER SEVEN

Aleck smiled at his phone, then stuffed it back into his pocket.

"Let me guess, that was Kenna," Midas said with a smile.

Aleck shrugged and nodded.

"Things are going well with you guys," Mustang noted. It wasn't a question.

"Yeah. She's great," Aleck said.

"Happy for you, bro," Pid said.

They were taking a short break from the intense meetings they'd been in all morning. An American had been thrown in jail in Iran for some perceived law he'd broken. Talks had been ongoing to secure his release, but had fallen through. Now other alternatives were being discussed; namely, sending special forces to go in and break the man out. But going into Iran without approval from the government was highly risky. The last thing the SEAL team wanted was to be discovered and incarcerated themselves.

"Thanks," Aleck told his friends. "I could use some advice though." He didn't hesitate to ask his team for their opinion. Mustang and Midas had women of their own and could offer perspective, and the others were always up for telling him what they thought.

"Shoot," Pid said.

"What's up?" Midas asked.

The others nodded at him as well, letting him know they'd help however they could.

"So you know how I almost blew it that first night at Duke's?" Aleck asked.

"You mean when you basically told her you didn't approve of her job?" Slate said.

Aleck sighed. "That's not what I said," he grumbled. "And believe me, I've definitely had time to think about it, and Kenna loves what she does and is good at it. If only everyone could have a job they enjoy instead of just tolerate." Aleck was truly happy for Kenna. She was living in a place she loved, working a job that was perfect for her extroverted personality. So what if she wasn't making a shit ton of money? If things worked out like he was beginning to hope they would, she didn't need it. Because he had plenty for them both.

"Go on," Mustang urged.

"Right, well, I think she has the impression that as a sailor, I'm not making all that much money. Normally, she'd be right. But with our hazard pay and rank, not to mention the housing allowance and cost of living bonus, even without my trust, I'd be doing just fine," Aleck said.

"And now you're wondering how, and if, you should tell her that you're loaded," Jag said.

Aleck nodded. "Yeah. And that I live in a fucking penthouse at Coral Springs. I absolutely don't want her to feel weird about me having plenty of money when she doesn't. But the longer I go without telling her about my trust and my parents' wealth, the harder it is to figure out how to spill the beans."

"Just tell her," Slate said.

Aleck wasn't exactly surprised at his friend's suggestion. He was a no-nonsense kind of guy.

"No, man, he can't just blurt that out. He has to finesse it," Mustang said.

"I agree," Midas said with a nod.

"But how?" Pid asked. "It's not something that's likely to come up in casual conversation. He can't say something like, 'Oh, by the way, I live in a penthouse,' and expect that to be that."

"Why not?" Slate asked. "It's true."

"Because!" Pid exclaimed.

"Is she gonna be mad that he's not a broke-ass military guy? Only if she's psycho," Slate said with a shrug.

"She's not psycho," Aleck said with a shake of his head.

"I agree that the longer you go without telling her, the bigger a deal it'll be," Midas said. "But I also think you need to find a good way to tell her that doesn't feel as if you're bragging about it or something."

"You know I never brag about money," Aleck said, somewhat annoyed.

"I *do* know. I wasn't saying you do. But things with Kenna are new," Midas said.

"So? Anyone got any great ideas?" Aleck asked.

No one said a word.

"Shit," he muttered.

His friends all looked apologetic. Aleck was going to have to figure out something on his own. It wasn't that he'd come out and told Kenna that he was barely getting by, and she *had* called him a snob, so she might not be all that surprised. But he didn't like keeping such a big detail about his life a secret, even if it made no difference in how he felt about her.

Aleck had dated a few women who made no bones about the fact that they were thrilled he could afford to buy them gifts and take them out all the time. At first it didn't bother him. But the older he became, the more he wanted a woman who was into *him*, not just interested in what he could give her. And the more he talked to Kenna, spent time with her, the more he was certain she wasn't like that.

So he needed to suck it up and just tell her.

"How's her friend? Carly?" Pid asked.

"Good, as far as I know," Aleck answered.

At the same time Jag said, "Good."

Everyone turned to stare at their teammate.

"You been talking to her?" Mustang asked.

Jag shrugged. "It's not a big deal, but yeah. We text now and then. And she sometimes calls me when she's on her way up to her apartment, you know, as a safety thing."

Everyone smirked.

"Seriously, she's one hundred percent anti-dating right now. So we're friends. I just want to make sure that asshole ex of hers is obeying the protective order and isn't harassing her," Jag said.

"And is he?" Slate asked.

"So far, yeah. But it's only been days, and we all know assholes like that usually don't slink back to their holes so easily."

Aleck nodded. It was true. He worried about Kenna as well, since she'd been up in Shawn's face the other day. He definitely hadn't been happy about that.

"Oh, hey, if you guys aren't busy the week after next, Lexie could use some help moving to the new location of Food For All," Midas said.

"That's finally happening?" Pid asked.

"Yeah. There's not much furniture in the new location, but her boss, Natalie, is letting her take a bunch of extra stuff from the downtown location over there."

"They need a donation to get some things?" Aleck asked. It didn't really matter what the answer to his question was...

he was already planning on making sure Lexie had what she needed to be comfortable and successful at the satellite location of the food pantry where she worked. Located in Barber's Point, it was closer to Midas's house, and would really help out the residents in that area. Traveling to downtown Honolulu was out of the question for the families in Barber's Point who needed help the most.

"It wouldn't go unappreciated," Midas said diplomatically.

Aleck nodded.

"Elodie is super excited to work with her," Mustang told them. "She's been researching all sorts of healthy meals for box lunches. She's also talking about the possibility of making dinners too. She said Lexie is working on finding volunteers who wouldn't mind delivering the meals to the people who can't make it to the center."

"Lexie told me about that," Midas said. "I guess Ashlyn is interested in helping. Maybe even heading up that part of the program."

Slate growled, surprising everyone.

They all looked over at their friend.

"You don't approve?" Midas asked.

Slate shrugged. "Just don't think it's safe for a woman to be driving around to strangers' houses by herself."

"I agree," Pid said.

"Me too," Midas added. "But no one said she'd be by herself, and one thing I've learned after getting to know Ashlyn through Lexie is that she isn't someone you say 'you can't do that' to. It makes her dig in her heels and become more determined than ever to prove you wrong."

Aleck heard the note of warning in his teammate's voice, and wondered if it was aimed at Slate. He'd just opened his mouth to say something sarcastic, because that was what he did, when their conversation was interrupted by a deep voice from behind them.

"Well, well, well, Smart Aleck's gone and got hisself some pats on the back."

Sighing, knowing exactly who was behind him in the hallway, Aleck turned to face the sailor who'd been a pain in his ass ever since the man had arrived on base.

Kylo Braun.

"What the hell are you talking about?" Pid asked the other man.

"I'm just congratulating the big bad SEAL on tackling an unsuspecting civilian and causing a ruckus," Braun said.

Aleck crossed his arms over his chest and glared at the other man. Kylo had taken an immediate disliking to Aleck the first time they'd met. They'd all been on a company run, and a little girl hadn't been paying attention and had dashed out into the street, right in front of an approaching SUV that was driving way too fast.

Braun had yelled, "Watch out!"

Aleck had acted. He'd barely gotten to the child in time, diving for her and snatching her out of the way of the approaching vehicle with inches to spare. He'd gotten a hell of a case of road rash out of it...and a commendation from the base commander.

Aleck suspected Braun was embarrassed *he* hadn't tried to do anything, even though he was closest to the girl. It probably didn't help that he'd most likely gotten a rash of shit from the other guys in his platoon. From that moment on, Braun had taken it upon himself to be a thorn in Aleck's side.

"Thanks," Aleck said, even though he knew that wasn't what Braun wanted to hear. He'd done his best to stay away from the man, especially after reading his service record. He wasn't supposed to have it, but an envelope had appeared at his condo one day and Aleck hadn't been able to resist reading it.

Somehow, Baker Rawlins had gotten wind of Braun's

antagonistic attitude toward Aleck and had taken it upon himself to get a hold of his records. Baker wasn't someone Aleck *ever* wanted to cross. The man was spooky as hell, and could get just about any information he wanted on anyone, as evidenced by the packet on Braun that had appeared on his doorstep.

Apparently, Braun had tried out to be a SEAL but hadn't made it. He'd been cut fairly early in the process, hadn't even made it to BUD/S. He'd failed the psychological assessment, which wasn't exactly a surprise. The man was a bully who hated not being the center of attention.

The fact that the SEAL teams on base definitely got preferential treatment probably didn't sit well with him. Regardless, Braun went out of his way to cause trouble for the teams whenever he could, and for some reason, he'd singled out Aleck for his own special brand of attention.

"Give it up," Mustang told him.

"Give what up?" Braun said not so innocently. "I'm just congratulating a fellow sailor on a job well done."

"You're pissed that once again, Aleck is out there doing good for the community, while you sit around with your thumb up your ass, wishing it was you getting the attention," Jag said in a low, deadly tone.

Jag wasn't usually the first one to jump into a verbal confrontation. Not when they were on a mission and not here at home, on base. But he was the first one to act if one of his teammates was threatened. Aleck wasn't sure why he was suddenly worked up over this asshole, but he had a feeling if something wasn't done, the situation could get out of control.

"I appreciate the kudos," Aleck said, stepping between Jag and Braun. The last thing they needed was a physical altercation, even if the other man was doing his best to provoke one of them into it.

"You're an asshole," Braun hissed, his true feelings finally coming out. "You think you're all badass and better than anyone else just because you're a SEAL."

"No," Aleck retorted. "I'm not better than anyone else because I'm a SEAL, but I'm definitely more observant than the average sailor. I've been trained to be that way. And if that means I'm in a position to help a little girl, or a grown woman who's being harassed, you better believe I'm gonna step in. When's the last time *you* stood up for someone else, Braun? You should try championing other people rather than tearing them down. I think you'd find it makes you a hell of a lot happier."

"Fuck you," Braun said, his eyes narrowed. "I would've saved that girl, but you pushed me out of the way so you could get the glory."

"See? That's where your thinking is fucked up," Mustang said. "Aleck didn't put himself in danger because he wanted a pat on the back. He did it because it was the right thing to do."

"Whatever," Braun said with a roll of his eyes. "You better watch your back. One of these days someone's gonna expose the fact that you're not a superhero, and you'll come crashing down to Earth."

"Was that a threat?" Slate asked, stepping toward him menacingly.

Proving that he wasn't completely stupid, Braun took a step backward. "No," he said, but he didn't sound nearly as cocky as he had a second ago. "Just a fact. You aren't bullet-proof, Smart Aleck, and one of these days your true colors are gonna show through, and I'm gonna be there to see it...and rejoice."

Then, as if knowing he was two seconds away from being laid out on the ground by a bunch of SEALs, Braun turned and walked away as if he hadn't just threatened one of their own.

Aleck's hands curled into fists. "What an asshole," he muttered.

"Please let me go after him and teach him a lesson," Slate said to Mustang.

But their team leader shook his head. "No. The last thing I need is you getting into trouble over him. He's not worth it."

"Oh, it would totally be worth it to smash his face in," Slate said.

Aleck took a deep breath. He didn't like the not-so-veiled threat Braun had lobbed his way, but he wasn't about to stoop to his level and didn't want any of his friends to get in trouble.

"Ignore him," Aleck told Slate and the others. "He's hated me since his cowardice was revealed to the entire company. It's fine."

"Can you imagine if he'd somehow slipped through the cracks and become a SEAL?" Pid asked with a shudder. "What a fucking disaster."

Aleck had to agree. Being on a SEAL team was rewarding, but one of the hardest things he'd ever done. He relied on the five men around him to have his back and had no doubt they would, no matter what the situation. But if Braun was on his team, he wouldn't trust the man as far as he could throw him, which wasn't a good situation when you were balls deep behind enemy territory.

"You need to watch your back," Mustang warned. "I don't trust that guy."

"I will," Aleck said.

"I mean it. We all read the report Baker sent you, and he's unstable. There's no telling what he might do to try to bring you down," Mustang said.

It wasn't Aleck's proudest moment when he'd shared the info Baker had sent with his team. But they shared everything. And Aleck knew without a doubt that none of them would ever admit how they'd gotten Braun's service record. That was the kind of bond SEALs had.

"I'll be careful," Aleck said.

"Good. All right, let's get back inside and see if we can find out more about this Iran situation. I really don't wanna cross the mountains to get into the country to get this guy out. Let's hope negotiations are successful and we don't have to," Mustang said.

"Oh, come on, you know a thirty-mile pleasure hike over a ten-thousand-foot-high peak into hostile territory is just what you want to do next week," Aleck joked.

Mustang just shook his head and headed back inside the conference room so they could continue going over maps and intel.

The rest of the team followed. Aleck grabbed the door and held it open for his friends. Slate was the last one to approach, and he stopped, giving the others time to get far enough ahead so they wouldn't hear him.

"You want me to fuck him up, just say the word," Slate told Aleck.

"I appreciate that," Aleck said, and he did. "But the day I can't handle that pencil-necked douchebag, is the day my Budweiser pin should be taken away."

Slate eyed him for a long moment before nodding once. Then they both headed inside after the rest of the team.

CHAPTER EIGHT

Kenna opened her apartment door and beamed at Marshall over a week later. Their plans the Sunday before had been canceled when Marshall had to participate in a training exercise. But now it was the following Sunday, her day off, and they were going to attempt to sneak onto the private beach at the Coral Springs condo complex she'd been drooling over for quite a while.

"Hi!" she said happily. He looked good. Really good. She enjoyed gawking at him in his uniform, but Kenna thought she liked this laid-back Marshall even more. He had on what looked like a pair of swim trunks with a white T-shirt emblazoned with a large pineapple. It was whimsical and seemed out of character. Which made her like it even more.

"Hi, back," he said before stepping into her personal space and reaching for her. Even though this was only their second in-person date, Kenna was more than comfortable with him initiating a kiss. Probably because of the hours and hours they'd spent talking on the phone and via text.

When he leaned down, she didn't hesitate in the least. She wanted this man.

His lips landed on hers, and Kenna mentally let out a girly squeal.

This kiss was more confident, hungrier, than their first had been. On both their parts.

Kenna eventually forced herself to pull back, when all she really wanted to do was pull him inside her apartment and throw him down on her bed.

They continued to chat every night after she got home from work. What had started as texts to let him know she was home safe, had led to Marshall asking her to call. Every night for the last week, she'd fallen asleep with the memory of his deep voice in her head. She'd even masturbated a time or two while thinking of that rumbly voice saying all sorts of not-so-innocent things.

Marshall licked his lips sensually, and it was all Kenna could do to control herself and not jump him right there. It had been a while since she'd been with a man, and she had a feeling Marshall would be well worth the wait. At least she hoped so. God, if he was bad in bed or had a tiny dick, she might be devastated.

"What are you thinking about so hard?" Marshall asked.

Kenna blushed. There was no way she was going to tell him she was thinking about the size of his cock. "I'm just happy to see you," she hedged.

He smirked as if he knew she was lying through her teeth. But as the gentleman he'd proved himself to be time and time again, he merely smiled at her. "Same," he said, lifting a hand and smoothing a piece of hair behind her ear.

Man, she loved when he did that. She loved this man's hands on her *anywhere*.

"Come on, let me show you around. It's nothing fancy, but it's home." Kenna gestured behind her and Marshall came in and shut the door. She walked him through the galley kitchen, definitely not pointing out the peeling Formica countertops or the appliances that had probably been there for twenty years.

"I love that I can watch TV while I'm in the kitchen," she said, playing up the positive aspects of her apartment. "I never miss anything when I'm doing dishes or grabbing my popcorn from the microwave."

Then she led him into the small living area. "Here's where I spend a lot of my time. I know the beanbag is a little ridiculous for someone my age, but seriously, it's the most comfortable thing ever."

Marshall raised an eyebrow.

"What? You don't believe me? Go on. Sit in it."

"It's okay. I believe you," Marshall said.

"Nope, now that I've seen your skeptical face, you have to."

"My skeptical face?" he asked with a laugh.

"Yup. Admit it, you looked at it and thought it was ridiculous," Kenna teased.

"I'm gonna plead the fifth on that one," Marshall said as he walked toward the ginormous beanbag Kenna had splurged on.

He lowered himself into it and wiggled around until he was comfortable.

"It's called a Lovesac. I know, I know, the name is horrible, but I did a ton of research and it had amazing reviews. And believe it or not, this isn't even the biggest one they had. I got the second to largest one, and I probably could've gone a bit smaller. There have been plenty of nights that I've fallen asleep in that thing, it's that comfortable. I do have to turn it around and plump it up every now and then, but otherwise it's perfect."

"There's one thing wrong with it," Marshall said.

Kenna frowned. "What?"

He held out his hand and without thought, Kenna grabbed it.

He immediately yanked her forward, and Kenna let out a yelp as she landed half on top of him in the oversized beanbag.

"You weren't in here with me," he said, finishing his thought.

Kenna laughed. "Jeez, Marshall, I thought there was really something wrong!" she accused.

"As far as I'm concerned, I stand by my statement."

Kenna was plastered against Marshall's side, the beanbag seeming to smoosh them together even tighter than they'd be if they were in a bed. Her hand rested on his chest and she could feel the thumping of his heart under her fingers. She stared at him as he gazed into her eyes.

"You look amazing," Marshall said quietly.

"Thanks." Kenna didn't think she was wearing anything special. She had on a brightly colored cover-up dress that went down to her knees. It was black with huge purple and yellow hibiscus flowers. It was gaudy, but when she'd seen it in one of the iconic ABC Stores in Waikiki, she couldn't resist.

"I haven't seen you in a dress yet," Marshall told her.

"It's not really a dress," Kenna admitted. "Just something to wear over my bathing suit."

"Please tell me you're wearing a bikini," Marshall said with a twinkle in his eye.

Kenna rolled her eyes. "You're such a guy."

"Yup, I sure am," he agreed.

"I don't own a bikini. I'm fairly confident with how I look, but I'm just more comfortable in a one-piece."

"You have nothing to worry about," Marshall reassured her. "Remember, I've seen you in nothing but a sports bra and shorts when you jumped on top of me."

"Don't remind me," Kenna groaned, wrinkling her nose. "And I didn't jump on you."

Marshall's hand came up and he brushed the back of his fingers against her cheek before moving his hand to the nape of her neck.

Goose bumps broke out on her arms, and of course he noticed.

"You like when I hold you like this?" he asked.

Kenna nodded. "It's been a while since anyone's really touched me. If you grabbed me and hauled me around, I'd hate it. But you touch with me with the perfect mix of assertiveness and gentleness."

"You don't like anything I do, all you have to do is say so. Or push me away or something," Marshall told her. "And I love touching you. I feel as if it's my reward for getting through the week without seeing you. Don't get me wrong, I've enjoyed talking to you and getting to know you. But I've missed this...being with you in person."

"This is only our second date." Kenna felt obligated to point out, even though she felt exactly the same way he was describing.

"So?" he said. "I know you, Kenna Madigan. And I more than like what I've learned about you. Being with you is icing on the cake."

"Shit, you're being too nice. You need to stop," Kenna begged.

"Nope. No can do," Marshall said with a smile. "And, by the way, you're right."

"About what?"

"This is the most amazing beanbag I've ever sat in, and now I want to order one for myself."

"They're super expensive," Kenna told him. "How about you borrow mine whenever the mood hits?"

"Every night?" he asked.

Kenna couldn't tell if he was kidding or not, and decided he had to be. His nickname was short for smart aleck, after all. "Sure. You can just move on in and take up residence in my beanbag," she joked.

He didn't respond, but his thumb swept back and forth over the sensitive skin of her neck as he stared at her.

"I do have to warn you, it's tough to get out of," she said.

Marshall licked his lips, and suddenly Kenna had no desire to go anywhere. She took the initiative and leaned toward him, feeling his hand tighten subtly on the back of her neck as she moved.

How long they made out in her beanbag, Kenna had no idea. All she knew was that his hand had moved under her cover-up to her bare thigh. Her own hand had snaked under his T-shirt. He was nothing but rock-hard muscles, and she felt extremely powerful when he inhaled sharply as her hand brushed against his nipple.

He pulled back and took a deep breath in through his nose before saying, "Holy shit, woman."

Kenna smiled. She could still taste him on her lips, and she really, really wanted more. But she was aware that this was technically only their second date. She wasn't ashamed of her sexuality; she was more afraid she'd fall head over heels for him, then find out something about him that she couldn't live with...thus breaking her heart.

"This beanbag is lethal," he quipped.

"Right?" she replied.

"Come on, we need to get up before I cross a line I swore I wouldn't cross today."

Kenna tilted her head as she stared at him. "Oh?"

"Yeah. I want you, Kenna. I don't think that's any surprise," he said, nodding down his body toward his erect cock. She hadn't missed it but was trying to do the polite thing by not staring.

"But I also want to spend more time with you before rushing our physical relationship."

Aaaaand, there he went again, being considerate and irresistible. "Tell me something negative about you," she blurted.

Marshall smiled as if he could read her mind. "I drink straight from the carton. Milk, orange juice, soda...you name it," he said without hesitation. "You?"

Kenna smiled. That was gross, but she could probably live with it. It wasn't as if they weren't swapping spit already. "I hate doing dishes and usually let them pile up until I literally can't do anything in the sink, so I have to give in and do them."

"I have a dishwasher," he told her.

"La-dee-da," she singsonged.

Marshall laughed. "You ready to go?" he asked.

Kenna nodded.

"Okay, I'll push to help you get out."

Kenna was used to getting out of the beanbag, so it wasn't an issue for her. Of course she copped a feel while she did it, just because she could.

Marshall smirked, but didn't call her on her boldness. He held up a hand.

Kenna grabbed it and, between the two of them, got him out of the super-squishy seat. He stood and shook his head. "I probably need to admit another annoying thing about me," he said.

"Yeah?"

"Yeah. I can fall asleep anywhere, at any time. Usually within like five minutes. In that thing?" he said with a shake of his head. "It would probably be under two."

Kenna liked the thought of him sleeping while she puttered around her apartment. It seemed cozy. "I'm sure you've learned to fall asleep anywhere because of your job.

Assuming when you need sleep, you grab it where you can. I can handle that. But the real question is...do you snore?"

"No," he said with a completely straight face, but Kenna saw something in his eyes that made her think he was lying.

"I wouldn't think snoring would be safe in your profession."

"It's not," Marshall said. "Which is why when I start, one of my teammates kicks me until I roll over and stop."

Kenna laughed. "Noted. Kick the man when he snores." The second she said it, she thought about what that would mean. That they were together in the same bed. And of course, that made some pretty carnal thoughts run through her head. Again.

"Right. On that note, we *really* need to go. That all you need for today?" he asked, nodding toward a large bag on the floor.

"Yeah, I packed an extra towel, just in case, and I've got plenty of snacks and cash. I have no idea if the beach will have a bar or food truck parked nearby or anything, but I don't want to risk leaving to get lunch or something to drink in case we can't get back in."

"You gonna tell me where we're going yet?" Marshall asked as he lifted her bag over his shoulder and put his other hand on the small of her back to lead her to the door.

"Nope," Kenna said with a grin. "It's a secret. But trust me, it's swanky and posh, and the beach looks amazing from what I've seen online."

"Do you have a plan for getting us on the beach?" Marshall asked.

"Yup. I'm a professional at this."

"You ever been kicked off a property before?"

"Of course," Kenna told him. "Probably fifty percent of the time. But the ones where I've been able to stay under the radar have been so worth it."

"Right, then let's get this show on the road. Because I'm super curious about this beach adorned with golden sand and mermaids and perfect snorkeling."

Kenna burst out laughing as she locked her door behind her. "I'm not sure about all that," she said.

"From the way you talk about these private beaches, I just thought they had to be lined with diamonds or something," Marshall joked.

"Do you like the beach?" Kenna asked as they headed down the hall toward the stairwell. The elevator in the building had been broken for months. She didn't mind, it let her get in a bit more exercise to counter the calories from the food she ate while on shift at Duke's.

"Hate it," Marshall said.

Kenna looked up at him in shock, hoping he was kidding. "Seriously?"

"Yup. I mean, who likes sand in their shorts?" he asked.

Shaking her head, Kenna said, "Well, I'm sure that would suck. But we aren't going to be rolling around in the sand today. I can imagine Hell Week probably didn't give you a great feeling about the beach, huh?"

"Cold water, covered in sand twenty-four seven, and feeling as if you were literally going to freeze to death? No," Marshall said. "But I have a feeling if anyone can change my mind about spending time on the beach, it's you. Hell, you could probably change my mind about just about *anything* I don't like."

That was a really nice thing to say. Kenna was falling for this guy. Hard. "Trust me, I've seen pictures of this beach. It's perfect. There's even a grassy area we can sit on if you truly don't want to be on the sand itself. The waves there aren't terribly intense, but from what I've seen online, because of some rocks, the east side of the beach has waves that are good for bodyboarding, while the west side is calmer. There's a huge pool if we want a change of pace, and they have free umbrellas and chairs too. It's gonna be awesome."

Marshall smiled down at her. "I can't wait to spend the day together," he said. "Doesn't matter what we do, as long as I get to hang out with you."

Kenna felt herself leaning toward him. "I feel the same."

She smiled the rest of the way down the stairs and out into the parking lot. She was still smiling when he opened the door to the Jeep and handed her the seat belt.

"Where to?" he asked as he started the engine after he'd gotten into the driver's side.

"Get on the interstate and head toward the Naval base."

"You got it," Marshall said as he backed out.

Kenna knew she still had a goofy smile on her face, but she was so looking forward to today. She hoped she and Marshall could sneak in without being caught. There was a backup public beach nearby if needed, but she hoped it wouldn't be. The thought of doing something a little illicit with Marshall made adrenaline rush through her veins.

Shit, she was so screwed. If she was this excited about spending a day with the man, how would she feel when they eventually slept together?

Because there was no doubt in her mind that was where they were headed. And she couldn't wait.

CHAPTER NINE

Aleck's stomach dropped to his feet when Kenna directed him to turn into the Coral Springs condo complex the private beach was connected to.

His condo complex.

"Here it is," she whispered as if a security guard might hear her all the way out in the parking lot. "I've been drooling over this place ever since I saw it online. They've got a beautiful beach, the pool has a slide, which is awesome, and they even have hammocks strung up around a grassy barbeque area. It's perfect."

"No place is perfect," Aleck mumbled. He knew he should just straight up tell her that he lived here, and he opened his mouth to do just that. To make a joke about how he knew all about the amenities because he paid a shitload each month in home owner association fees. But she spoke again before he could.

"I bet the people here don't appreciate what they have. They probably sit up in their overpriced condos and complain that it's too sunny. Or the water is too blue or something." She rolled her eyes. "I don't get rich people. As pretty as this place is, there's no connection to the locals out here. Most of my neighbors are native to Hawaii, and they're generous and funny and have welcomed me with open arms. I love walking around my neighborhood and playing with the kids and being a part of a community. I bet everyone living here is from the mainland and they probably don't even *know* their neighbors. It's kind of sad, really."

Well, shit. That wasn't exactly the opening he wanted to confess that he lived here. Aleck wanted Kenna to like him, not think of him as pathetic. And it wouldn't help to admit that he owned a penthouse.

His opportunity to not only tell Kenna that he lived here, but that he was one of the rich people she didn't seem to think much of, was cut short again when she opened her door excitedly and hopped out.

Not sure how this was gonna go, Aleck slowly got out as well. He reached into the backseat and grabbed both their bags and met Kenna at the front of the Jeep.

"Okay, this is what I'm thinking," Kenna said as she reached for her bag.

Aleck gave it to her, only because he knew it wasn't very heavy.

"There's only a few entrances and the beach has a fence around it to keep it private, so we're going to have to go in the main door and right through the lobby. That's tricky, because if they have security, they might ask for our IDs or something. But if we're in the middle of a conversation, maybe they'll feel as if it's rude to interrupt us. If there's a security desk, you can give the person that chin lift thing you do so well. Whatever you do, stay casual. Don't look guilty. Try to blend in." She chuckled. "Although, everyone is probably wearing overpriced name-brand clothing and you've got...a pineapple on."

"Hey, I love this shirt," Aleck told her.

She smiled up at him and patted his chest. "I do too. But I'm thinking the people around here wouldn't be caught dead in it. Come on, we've got this."

It was obvious Kenna was amped up and totally excited about the possibility of getting onto the private beach. Aleck wasn't all that happy about how she constantly seemed to put down the residents, though. Yes, most people who lived here probably had very comfortable bank accounts, but that didn't mean they were assholes. He might not hang out with many of his neighbors, but he'd met a lot of them, and they seemed like perfectly nice people.

Not wanting to be a downer when Kenna was so excited, he took her hand in his and they headed for the entrance. If they really were trying to slip onto the property without being noticed, Aleck knew they'd fail. The security here was top-notch and no one got past the front desk without being recognized or without showing ID and letting them know who they were visiting.

But he went along with Kenna's plan. The idea of sneaking in clearly thrilled her. The time to admit he lived here had definitely passed, and an uneasy feeling churned in his gut. He should've said something immediately, when he'd found out what beach she wanted to visit.

He'd already put his foot in his mouth about her job and didn't want to say or do anything else that would give her a reason to decide they weren't compatible—and it was abundantly obvious she thought she had nothing in common with rich people.

Now he'd have to find a way to tell her another time.

Funny thing, remember the other day when we went to the beach at that condo complex? Well, I live there.

Shit, that wouldn't work. He'd have to come up with something much better, and if she couldn't forgive him for not fessing up sooner, well...at least he could give her this adventure.

"Marshall, pay attention," Kenna scolded. "We've only got one shot at this and I really want to check out this beach."

"What happens if we get caught?" he asked.

Kenna scrunched her nose adorably. "I've got another beach in mind as a fallback. But it's not as nice as this one."

"I don't care where we go or what we do," Aleck told her. "I'm just thrilled to get to spend time with *you*."

She looked up at him and smiled. "Wow, I think that's the nicest thing anyone's ever said to me."

"It's true. Fancy private beach, hanging out in that amazing beanbag of yours, or sitting in a dive restaurant eating peanut butter and jelly. I just like being with you. You make me feel...happy."

Aleck regretted the words the second they left his lips because they were so sappy.

But he changed his mind when Kenna stopped walking and leaned into him. Aleck put his arm around her waist to hold her close.

"You make me happy too. I could be in the worst mood, but then I get a text from you and it's like whatever upset me is completely forgotten. I don't recognize myself lately."

Aleck couldn't have stopped himself from leaning down and kissing her if his life depended on it. Cognizant of where they were, he kept the kiss light, but it was still intense.

Kenna reached up and put her hand on his cheek, but she didn't say anything.

A loud honking made both of them jerk in surprise, and Aleck chuckled as he hustled them out of the middle of the road. He waved at the man behind the wheel of the large SUV in apology and saw the man laughing as he continued on.

Kenna took a deep breath. "Okay, this is it. Act natural."

Aleck didn't know if she was telling him or herself, but he nodded anyway.

As they neared the front doors to the complex, she started babbling about what they needed to buy at the grocery store later.

Aleck knew she'd picked a topic that would make it seem as if they lived here, and he couldn't help but hope for a time when they'd be shopping together for real, or leaving each other notes about what they needed at the store. It was somewhat surprising, as he'd never considered living with a woman before, but with Kenna, he couldn't seem to *stop* thinking about it.

The automatic doors opened and they walked into the lobby of the condo complex. Just as Kenna had ordered, he gave the security guard a chin lift as they approached the desk. Of course, he knew Robert fairly well. He'd come home from a mission very early in the morning a few months ago and they'd gotten to talking. Robert had a brother in the Army, and he wanted to make sure Aleck knew he appreciated his service.

Kenna had a death grip on his hand and she started talking even faster. Aleck wanted to end this farce right now. He didn't like seeing her all worked up, but now definitely wasn't the time. She'd be embarrassed if he told her he lived here after she'd tried so hard to look like they belonged.

They passed Robert, who looked back down at the papers on the desk in front of him. They headed toward the doors at the back of the large hotel-lobby-like space, which led out to a grassy area where Aleck and his team had barbequed often.

The second the doors shut behind them, Kenna turned to him with a huge smile on her face. "We did it!" she half-whispered, half-screeched. Then she hugged him once more.

Now it was *Aleck* who was too embarrassed to tell her

they'd made it past Robert because the man knew him—because he was a resident.

"That was awesome!" Kenna said, a smile lighting up her face.

Aleck wanted to bottle her energy and enthusiasm and pull it out when he needed it the most...probably right after he told her they didn't actually "sneak" anywhere.

"Come on. I want to see this beach. And I'm telling you right now, it had better live up to my expectations." She chuckled. "Man, my heart is beating out of my chest and my adrenaline is making me shaky," she said as they headed toward the beach.

Aleck moved closer and put his arm around her shoulders as they walked. "You liked that." It wasn't a question.

"I like winning," she said with a grin. "I don't really like the stress that comes with actually breaking the law."

Aleck couldn't help but laugh. "I'm not sure sneaking onto a private beach constitutes breaking the law."

Kenna shrugged. "I'm a goody two-shoes," she said without any artifice. "I don't like breaking the rules. Never have."

"Well, we're here now. And as far as anyone else is concerned, we belong here. So no feeling guilty, okay?"

"Absolutely!" Kenna said happily.

Then she pulled away from him and ran ahead to where the grassy area met the sand. She stood there as he caught up to her.

"It's beautiful," she breathed.

And it was. While Aleck wasn't a beach person, he could certainly understand the appeal. And his complex always went out of their way to try to make sure the beach itself was as inviting as possible. There were umbrellas and chairs spread out across the sand, with a satisfying distance between each. Someone raked the sand every night to keep it smooth and to get the leaves, sticks, and other debris out of it. There was a shed where people could check out boogie boards, stand-up paddle boards, snorkel gear, and even blow-up floats. A small stand served canned drinks—alcoholic and not—as well as snacks. Even the restrooms were fastidiously cleaned and serviced every hour to make sure they were up to the standards of the complex.

"Where do you want to sit?" Aleck asked.

"Oh, um...somewhere away from the service hut. I don't want someone wondering who we are and asking for our IDs after the fact. Maybe over there on the other end?"

Once again, guilt ate at Aleck. He hated that Kenna was still worried about getting caught. He wanted to reassure her that no one was going to kick them out, but she'd probably ask *how* he was so sure.

On second thought, maybe that was a good way to bring up the topic. Then he could admit everything.

But he warred with his conscience too long. Kenna grabbed his hand once more and was leading him to the farthest umbrella from where condo employees manned the equipment shack and snack stand.

Kenna fussed with the umbrella and the chairs until she was completely satisfied with their arrangement. "Look! They even provide towels," she said with a pleased smile. "And they're *nice* too. Fluffy and thick." She spread a blue and white striped towel with the condo's name on it on her chair, then reached for the hem of her cover-up without hesitation.

Aleck almost swallowed his tongue when he saw Kenna in her black and red swimsuit. It was modest compared to a lot of suits women wore these days. Cut high on her thighs and dipped low between her breasts, showing off a bit of cleavage.

She turned to grab something out of her bag, and Aleck's breath whooshed out.

He'd checked out her ass as she'd climbed out of the water

when they'd first met, but this was so much better. Her suit basically had no back to it. There was a tie behind her neck, and her ass was covered, but otherwise he could see her entire back.

Moving without thought, Aleck stepped toward her. His hands reached out and caressed her smooth skin.

Kenna jerked in surprise, then relaxed as his hands ran up either side of her spine.

"Marshall?" she asked.

"You are so damn beautiful," Aleck said softly as he stroked her. He dug his thumbs into the muscles at the top of her spine and she arched against him.

"That feels so good," she moaned.

Aleck's cock twitched. Fuck, he wanted to hear her say that when they were both naked in his bed and he was—

"While you're back there, will you put some of this on my back?" she asked, grinning and holding up a tube of sunscreen.

So much for his daydream. But Aleck was determined to get to her as much as she was getting to him. Although, she certainly *seemed* affected, if their time in her beanbag was any indication. He decided to play a bit.

"Of course," he told her, taking the sunscreen. Her head was turned, watching him as he stripped his T-shirt over his head and dropped it on the chair next to him.

Kenna's eyes widened as she stared.

Internally, Aleck grinned. He knew he was in shape. He and his teammates worked hard to keep their bodies in tip-top condition.

"Holy shit," she whispered, turning slowly. "I felt your abs earlier, but damn, Marshall. What is that, like a twenty-seven pack? I didn't know the stomach even had that many muscles."

He laughed. "Just a normal six-pack," he told her, tightening his muscles to show off for her.

Her hand reached out and smoothed over his stomach, much as his hands had done to her back. "Damn!" she exclaimed again.

"Turn around," he ordered, "so I can put this on."

It took her a moment to drop her hand from his skin, but then she took a deep breath and turned so her back was to him once more.

Aleck squeezed a healthy amount of the coconut-smelling lotion on his hands and got to work. He smoothed them up her spine again, loving how she arched into his touch. He took his time, making sure he reached every inch of exposed skin, rubbing the lotion in thoroughly. Even after she was appropriately covered, he couldn't take his hands from her.

His fingers slipped just below the elastic, caressing the top of her ass crack.

"Marshall..." she complained weakly.

"Yes?" he asked, continuing to tease. He made sure not to be indecent, even though he wanted nothing more than to reach around and slip his fingers under the front of her suit.

Her ass pushed back against him, and Aleck's cock twitched under his suit.

Kenna looked at him over her shoulder. "I want you."

Aleck nearly choked. But he did his best to hang on to his control. "I want you too," he said, as one finger dipped even lower under her suit. He let himself enjoy the feel of her silky skin for another second, before moving his hand to safer territory. He put his hands on her shoulders and leaned down and kissed her temple. "You're good to go sunscreen wise," he told her.

Kenna chuckled and took a deep breath.

Aleck knew he'd remember this moment for the rest of

his life. The ocean breeze, the smell of coconut, and Kenna in his arms.

"Right, turn around and I'll do you."

Aleck raised an eyebrow at her. "I thought you didn't want to get kicked off the beach?"

She laughed and rolled her eyes. "Turn around," she repeated.

As Aleck turned, he realized he was having a great time, despite the guilt he still felt. Bantering with Kenna was fun. She was sensual, wasn't too self-conscious, and she obviously loved this little escapade.

Having her hands on him was torturous, but he did his best to control himself. What he *really* wanted to do was pick up Kenna, throw her over his shoulder, and head up to his bed. But for the moment, until he could figure out how to tell her about his trust fund, he would make do with her touch.

Kenna took her sweet time spreading the sunscreen on his back, but Aleck didn't mind in the least. Eventually, after slathering the rest of their bodies with more lotion, they both lay down on the lounge chairs.

Aleck heard Kenna chuckle under her breath. He turned his head to look at her. "What's funny?" he asked.

She nodded to his lap. "That doesn't look comfortable," she quipped.

Aleck shrugged. "What did you expect with you touching me like that?" he asked, having a feeling he'd be half-hard all day. "Besides," he nodded to her chest, "you aren't much better."

He never would've brought attention to a woman's hard nipples in the past. But everything with Kenna was different.

She simply laughed. "Touché," she said.

They fell silent for a few minutes, then Kenna said, "I like this," she said.

"The beach?" Aleck asked.

"Yes, but *this*. You and me. Being comfortable with each other. Being turned on and not embarrassed about it. I like how open and honest we are."

Of course, her words made his erection deflate as if it'd been pricked with a pin.

Fuck. He *wasn't* being honest, and the longer it went on, the worse he felt.

"I love spending time with you," he managed to say after a moment. Then, needing the connection with her and afraid his deception was going to end up pushing her away, Aleck reached for her hand. She twined her fingers with his without hesitation.

* * *

Kenna laughed as she rode another wave all the way to the shore. She and Marshall had been at the beach for hours and at one point, he'd suggested getting two of the boogey boards. She hadn't wanted to, in case the employees found out they didn't live at the condos, but he'd finally convinced her.

He'd come back from the equipment shed with not only the boogey boards, but a couple of sodas and soft pretzels.

At first, Marshall had sat under the umbrella while she'd gone out to play in the ocean, but he'd eventually joined her, grumbling about sand in his suit. They'd had a water fight, a swim race—which Kenna had handily lost—then they'd grabbed the boogey boards and started body surfing.

As she'd suspected, Marshall was a natural at everything. Of course, being a SEAL, he was more than comfortable in the water, but it went beyond that. He looked completely at home in the ocean. He wasn't constantly spitting out the salty water. Didn't look as if the sun bothered him at all. And even when he was sent tumbling when a wave caught him by surprise, he looked like some sort of merman as he rose out of the water laughing, rivulets of water glinting as they dripped down his body.

And seeing him in nothing but a suit wasn't exactly a hardship. Kenna had a feeling she'd remember the moment he'd stripped off his T-shirt for the rest of her life. Intellectually, she'd already known he was in great shape, but seeing all his muscles up close and personal was almost a religious experience. She'd commented on his abs, but what had really caught her attention were the v-muscles near his hips that pointed straight toward his groin.

And his cock.

Lord love a duck. Kenna wasn't a virgin, she had seen her share of dicks, but she had a feeling Marshall was going to ruin her for all other men. He was long, and from what she could tell from his shape through his suit, thick. And she absolutely loved that he wasn't shy about his body at all.

Her thoughts about trying to be good had gone out the window as he stood in front of her in his suit and nothing else. She wanted this man. Wanted to get down and dirty with him, feel him deep inside her. Wanted to take his cock in her mouth and make him lose his mind.

Pretty much she wanted to do all the carnal things with him that had been flitting through her head ever since seeing his chest and feeling his erection.

But she couldn't deny she was enjoying the foreplay. His fingers on her back were heavenly, and she felt herself drip with excitement when those fingers snuck under her suit and played with her ass. It was just as fun to caress him, as well.

Yeah, they were totally engaging in foreplay. It was exciting, making anticipation flow through her veins.

It was nice to know they had physical chemistry to go along with their intellectual connection. It might be awful of her to say, but as much as she wanted to be with a man she could *talk* to, she wanted someone who would be compatible with her in bed as well.

And she had no doubt Marshall would rock her world when they finally did give in to their lust.

"Incoming!" Marshall yelled from behind her. Kenna had been so lost in her head, she'd forgotten where they were. She turned and let out a girly screech as she saw Marshall barreling toward her on his boogey board. She tried to stand, but a wave knocked her feet out from under her. She was laughing and doing her best to get out of Marshall's way when he ran into her.

For a split second, his board ran right over her, but Marshall, being the water expert he was, had thrown himself to the side so he didn't crush her.

Kenna felt arms go around her and pull her from under the water. Then she saw Marshall's concerned expression. "Shit, Kenna. Are you all right? I thought you'd move."

She couldn't help it. She laughed again. She was so incredibly happy, she couldn't hold it back.

Marshall stared at her as if she'd finally lost it and looked like he was two seconds away from hauling her out of the water and calling an ambulance. He moved them closer to shore.

Kenna did her best to control herself, then threw herself into his arms. Marshall stumbled and went to his knees in the surf. She put a hand on his chest and pushed, until he was sitting. She then straddled him, wrapping her arms around his neck. "I'm fine," she said. "I wasn't paying attention. Serves me right."

"I almost ran you over," Marshall murmured, running his hands up and down her back as he held her to him.

Kenna scooted closer, until she could feel his cock against her folds. It was an intimate position, even if neither of them was turned on. She loved being close to him like this. "You didn't," she reassured him.

Marshall met her gaze and nodded, finally understanding that she was fine. He reached up and ran his hand over her hair, gripping a fistful. He pulled on it lightly, until her chin tipped up. Then he leaned forward and kissed the underside of her chin. He relaxed his grip a bit but didn't let go of her hair.

Kenna tilted her head back down and wiggled on his lap. Yeah, okay, now she was turned on, and she could feel Marshall's cock throbbing against her pussy. The waves lapped around them and the sun was beating on their heads. Kenna knew there were other people on the beach, enjoying the beautiful day, but she only had eyes for one man.

She gazed at him and licked her lips, tasting nothing but salt. She knew she'd never forget today and being with Marshall.

"Don't look at me that way," he said.

"What way?" Kenna asked.

"As if you want to strip me bare and have your wicked way with me right here on the beach."

"Can't help it," Kenna admitted.

"Woman, do you know how awful that would be?"

She blinked in surprise. "What?"

"Sex on the beach. It's a great fruity drink, but the actual physical action is the worst idea ever. I can't think of anything worse than sand on my cock when I want to fuck you."

His words made her shiver in excitement. "You ever done it?"

"Are you listening to me, woman?" he asked in mock exasperation. "No. Fuck no."

"We'd have to be careful," she mused. "But I have a feeling you could figure out a way to make it work."

Marshall was already shaking his head. "Nope. Not happening. I'll have sex on a boat, in a cabin at the beach, on a grassy piece of land *near* the beach, but on the actual sand? No way."

Kenna giggled.

"Hey guys, are these yours?" a man asked from nearby.

Kenna turned to see a guy holding their boogey boards.

"Yeah, thanks, man. Can you just throw them up there on the sand? We'll get them in a second."

"No problem," the man said with a smile. "If I had a pretty girl on my lap, I wouldn't want to deal with the boards either."

Kenna smiled at him, then looked back at Marshall. He was watching her with an intense look in his eyes she couldn't interpret. One of his hands went to the small of her back, pressing her even tighter against him.

"I'm not perfect," he said.

Kenna frowned. It wasn't what she'd expected him to say. "We've had this conversation. I know you aren't."

"No, I mean it. I've done things in my life that would scare the shit out of any rational human being. When I'm in a bad mood, I can be an asshole to my friends and to strangers on the street. I'm a cynic, and the first thing I think when I see someone panhandling on the side of the road is that they're a scammer and just trying to get money for drugs. I'm suspicious of people's motives in general, and I don't really know my neighbors."

"Marshall—" Kenna started, but he kept talking.

"I want to be the man you think I am, but I'm human. I say the wrong thing all the time, and I'm scared to death that you're gonna realize I'm not the man you've built up in your head and you'll break up with me. All I'm asking is that if I do something you don't like, or you hear something about me that pisses you off or you don't understand...talk to me about it. If my answer isn't good enough, then you can leave."

"I'm not leaving." Kenna had no idea where this was coming from, but she desperately wanted to soothe him.

"I think I need you, Kenna," he said. "I need you to bring me out of my shell. To force me to see the good in the world rather than the bad. It's been so long since I've met someone I feel as if I can just be myself with. Be Marshall, rather than the smart aleck. The SEAL."

Kenna leaned forward and rested her forehead on his. "You've got me," she told him earnestly.

"Promise me," he said, moving his hand to the nape of her neck. "Promise me if you hear shit about me that bothers you, you'll talk to me about it."

For the first time, Kenna got nervous. "What shit?"

He shook his head. "Promise me," he repeated, squeezing her neck. Not hard, but enough to get her attention.

"I promise," she whispered.

At her words, every muscle in Marshall's body seemed to loosen. He ran his thumb over her nape as if in apology for how hard he'd been gripping her. "Good. Thank you for today, Kenna. I can't remember a date I've enjoyed as much as this one."

"Thank you for humoring me and coming with me. I knew this beach would be awesome."

"Anytime you want to try to crash a private beach, count me in. Although I'm not sure we'll always be as successful as we were today."

"Right? It seemed almost too easy. But I'm not looking a gift horse in the mouth," she said.

Marshall chuckled. "That is the weirdest saying. I mean, why would you want to look into a horse's mouth anyway?"

"I don't know. But now I want to look up the origins of that saying," Kenna said with a grin.

"Well, we've got our phones in our bags..." he said, letting his voice trail off.

"That's one of the things I like so much about you...you don't think I'm weird for some of the things I think about. And so far, you've been down for the crazy things I want to do."

Marshall smiled. Then he kissed her, licking the salt from her lips before he put his hands on her biceps. "Ready for a break from the water?"

Kenna nodded.

"Me too. And now since I've been sitting here, I've got sand in my shorts."

Kenna couldn't help but giggle at him. She scooted backward off him and stood, holding out her hand. "Come on, you big baby. I can't believe you're a SEAL, whining about the sand as much as you do."

"Hey, I learned that being a sugar cookie in BUD/S wasn't my idea of a good time. There was chafing. Lots and *lots* of chafing," he said as he put his hand in hers.

He stood and didn't even stumble as a wave crashed against his legs. He truly was completely comfortable in the water, and Kenna thought it was sexy as hell. A vision of them making love in the ocean flicked across her mind before she pushed it away. Today wasn't about sex, it was about getting to know each other better. But she was fairly sure sex wasn't too far in their future.

Marshall grabbed their boogey boards and they walked back to their lounge chairs. He insisted on going to get her a fresh, cool water and another snack without her even having to ask.

As she watched him go, Kenna thought about what he'd said in the water. She had no idea what he thought she might find out about him. She knew he was a SEAL. Knew he'd killed people. Knew he wasn't always a happy-go-lucky person. But it had to be something big, since he was so worried. She couldn't imagine anything making a difference in how she felt about him, but if that time ever came, she'd keep her promise to discuss it before making any snap decisions about their relationship.

Pushing the odd conversation out of her mind, she got settled on her chair and sighed in contentment. This beach was perfect. Everyone had been polite and friendly and she hadn't seen even one piece of trash. She hadn't worried about someone stealing their stuff while they were in the water either, which was a relief. Having money couldn't be all bad if it meant having a place like this to hang out in your off time.

Closing her eyes, Kenna relaxed. The day would end soon enough, but for now, she was going to enjoy every second she had left to spend with Marshall.

* * *

They'd stayed longer at the beach than she'd planned. Marshall had stopped at a Wendy's on the way back to her apartment so she could get a hamburger and fries for dinner. He'd offered to take her somewhere nicer for dinner, but she loved fast food. She couldn't eat it as much as she wanted, but she was a sucker for fries. It meant she needed to go for a longer run in the morning, but it was a price she was willing to pay.

Besides, she wasn't dressed appropriately to go to Helena's or any other sit-down restaurant. She was still in her suit, her hair was an absolute mess with the salt and wind, and she didn't feel like talking to anyone other than Marshall.

Yes, she was an extrovert, but she had her limits with people. And today had been so amazing, with just her and Marshall, that she didn't feel like bringing anyone else into her circle at the moment.

Kenna desperately wanted to ask him to come up. They could eat their meal—he'd gotten a burger too—then maybe she could suggest they jump in the shower to clean up. Not that they'd fit together in her tiny shower, but a girl could fantasize.

Shaking her head, Kenna knew she wouldn't do any of that. The day had been perfect and she didn't want to mess it up. Not that spending more time with Marshall would mess it up, but it didn't feel like the right time to get physical.

"What are you thinking about over there?" Marshall asked.

Maybe it was because she felt so mellow and had such a great day, but Kenna found herself being completely honest. "Whether or not to ask you to come up. And maybe to suggest we conserve water by showering together. But then I realized that we wouldn't fit in my shower together anyway, and I decided that it doesn't feel like the right time for anything more, physically, right now."

Marshall reached for her hand and she gladly wrapped her fingers around his.

"I think we both know where this relationship is heading. At least I know where I *want* it to go. But I agree, today's not the time."

Kenna sighed in relief.

They didn't speak for the rest of the trip to her apartment, but it was a comfortable silence.

Once they arrived, he pulled into a parking space, turned off the engine, and turned to her. "What's your schedule like this week?"

"I work Monday, Tuesday, Thursday, Friday, and Saturday," she said. "I've got some errands I need to do, but tomorrow I'm gonna go for a long run first."

"Don't jump on any unsuspecting scuba divers," Marshall teased.

Kenna chuckled. "I didn't jump on you, and I think I've learned my lesson on that one," she said. "What about you?"

"PT and meetings. There's a chance we might have to ship out, but we're waiting to see how things go. Hopefully everyone can get their heads out of their asses and we won't have to go anywhere."

Kenna's belly clenched, but she merely nodded. "I hope so too."

"Did you know that Lexie works at Food For All downtown?" he asked.

Grateful for the subject change—Kenna wasn't ready to think too much about Marshall and his friends heading into a dangerous situation yet—she nodded. "She said something about that the last time she texted me. Talked about one of her favorite people who frequently visited. I think his name was Theo?"

"Yeah, that's him. Anyway, she's going to be in charge of a second location of Food For All out in Barber's Point and will be moving this week. The guys and I will be helping with some of the big stuff, but if you have the time, and you want to, I'm sure she wouldn't mind help with organizing the new space. Elodie's going to be volunteering there as well. Making healthy and somewhat gourmet box lunches for people."

"I'd love to help," she said honestly.

"Awesome," he said with a smile.

Kenna eyed him for a second, then said, "It's important to you that I like Lexie and Elodie, isn't it?"

"Yes," he said without hesitation. "First off, they're awesome, and I know you'd click with them once you really get to know them. But second, they're around the guys and me a lot. And like we talked about before, I think they'll be a great help and resource when I get deployed."

Kenna smiled.

"What?" he asked.

"I just love that you're talking long term."

Marshall leaned over and once more put his hand behind her neck. It was obviously his go-to way to get her attention. And she loved it.

"I was already pretty sure I wanted something serious with you, but today clinched it. You're everything I've ever wanted in a woman, Kenna. You're funny, outgoing, kind, friendly, fun to be around, and I can't deny that I'm physically attracted to you. And before you say it, I know you aren't perfect, and we've already been over how *I'm* not. But your good qualities shine through so strong, I can't imagine ever getting pissed over something silly, like you not wanting to do the dishes. Lexie and Elodie are not only my friends' women, they're my friends too. I desperately want you guys to all get along."

"We will," Kenna said. "I have no doubt. I already like them. And the fact that they went out of their way to stand up for me at Duke's and make up that story so those bitches would be nicer...that said a lot about who they are as people."

"Good. You'll be okay with them by yourself? I can't get off work to help out during the day. We were planning on moving the big stuff early in the week."

"Marshall, I'm a professional waitress. I can talk to anyone about anything. I'll be fine." She thought it was cute that he was worried.

"Okay. Good. For the record?"

When he didn't continue, Kenna said, "Yes?"

"If you'd have invited me up to eat and shower with you, I would've said yes. At this point, I can't deny you anything."

Kenna smiled. She loved knowing she had that kind of power over him...the same power he had over her. Leaning forward, Kenna kissed him. He quickly took over, holding her close with the grip on her neck and devouring her mouth.

They were both panting when they finally pulled apart for some air.

"Damn," Kenna breathed.

"Yeah," Marshall agreed. "Come on, I'll walk you up."

"You think that's a good idea?" Kenna teased. She could feel her nipples pressing against her suit and she was damp between the legs.

"I just need to make sure you get inside safely. I'd be a shitty boyfriend if I left you in the parking lot."

Kenna shook her head. "No, you'd be normal."

"I don't like to be normal," Marshall said. Then he kissed her hard and fast and turned to get out of the Jeep.

Kenna knew she was smiling like a crazy person, but she couldn't stop. Marshall grabbed her bag, and her hand, and they walked into the complex.

They were at her door in less than a minute. Marshall handed her the beach bag with her fast food he'd put inside. He pulled her against him in a long, heartfelt hug. Then he stepped back as she unlocked her door.

"Have a good night," he said.

Kenna might've been offended that he didn't look like he was going to give her a goodbye kiss, but she had a feeling if he did, they'd definitely end up inside. "You too. Let me know when you get home?"

He nodded. "You have next Sunday off, right?"

"Yes."

"I'd like to take you to my place and cook for you...if that's all right."

Kenna tingled. "Can you cook?"

Marshall chuckled. "I'm not a chef like Elodie, but I've been taking pointers from her, and I can grill a mean steak."

"Sounds good. You want to go to the Aloha Stadium swap meet with me in the morning?" she asked.

"Yes," he said immediately.

Kenna smiled. "You ever been?"

"Nope."

"You're in for a treat. They have everything from clothes to souvenirs, ethnic food to antiques. I love talking to the artists. They usually have amazingly interesting stories."

Marshall smiled. "I like seeing you get all worked up and excited about doing stuff," he said. "We can work out the logistics later."

"Sounds good."

"Be safe this week."

"I will," Kenna reassured him.

For a second they both stood stock still, staring at each other, before Marshall took a deep breath and backed away.

Kenna watched him walk backward down the hall.

"Go inside," he ordered.

It was reassuring that he felt the same pull toward her that she did toward him. Kenna gave him a little wave, then pushed her door open and went inside her apartment.

She closed the door and leaned against it with another smile on her face. It was safe to say that she was head over heels for Marshall Smart. She had no idea what he was so worried about her finding out, but she had a feeling whatever it was, it wouldn't matter.

Feeling happier than she'd been in a very long time, Kenna dug her dinner out of her beach bag and headed to the couch to eat. Food first, then shower, then she'd text Lexie and find out the details about helping her with the new location of Food For All.

It would be a busy week, and Kenna was already excited about seeing Marshall next Sunday. Yes, she'd talk to him as the week progressed, but seeing where he lived, him cooking for her...it seemed like a perfect time to move their physical relationship forward.

Saying it like that almost seemed too tame. In reality,

Kenna wanted to fuck Marshall more than she'd wanted anything in a long while. And she had a feeling next weekend would be their time.

She was still smiling as she took a big bite of her burger. It was lukewarm, but nothing could dim her excitement from the day.

CHAPTER TEN

The week was moving quickly. Between working out, doing errands, talking to Marshall, and working, time had flown by.

It was already Wednesday morning, and Kenna was headed to the Barber's Point area to meet up with Lexie, Elodie, and another woman named Ashlyn, who worked with Lexie, to organize the satellite location of Food For All. She'd even convinced Carly to come with her. She hadn't lied to Marshall, she could have a conversation with anyone about anything, but she was glad Carly had said yes to coming all the same.

Kenna was also worried about her friend. Carly hadn't been going anywhere since the confrontation with Shawn at Duke's, preferring to stay in her apartment as much as possible until it was time to go to work. It wasn't as if Kenna blamed her; if Shawn was *her* ex, she'd be extremely careful as well, but it wasn't exactly healthy for Carly to lock herself away.

One more reason to hate Shawn.

But today she'd convinced Carly to come with her, and

was looking forward to spending time with her friend outside of work.

As they drove toward the western side of the island, Kenna said as nonchalantly as she could, "So...how are things with Jag? You guys still talking?"

"They're fine. And yes."

Kenna could tell Carly didn't want to talk about the handsome SEAL, but she wasn't ready to drop it. "Marshall said he's worried about you."

Carly sighed and looked over at Kenna. "Look, I know you're deliriously happy with Marshall, but don't go getting ideas that I'm gonna end up with his friend. I'm done with guys. Seriously. Maybe not forever, but for the foreseeable future. Okay?"

"Okay, okay," Kenna said. "I want you to be happy. And just because Shawn wasn't the man for you doesn't mean someone else isn't. Not to mention, they're not all abusive assholes either."

"I know. And I really do like Jag. He's nice and he makes me feel safe. But I'm still not ready. I feel like I need to get my feet under me again. Learn to be happy on my own for a while. It also wouldn't be fair to him to be a rebound."

"I get it," Kenna said. And she did. She had a feeling if Carly let Jag in, she wouldn't regret the decision, but *she* had to be the one to decide when she was ready to move on. "Thanks for coming with me today," she said, changing the subject.

Carly smiled. "Thanks for asking me. I know I need to get out more, but I just imagine Shawn jumping out and hurting me the second I leave my apartment."

"I understand. But no one is gonna hurt you today. This should be fun."

"Who's gonna be there again? The two women from Duke's the other night, I know, but who else?"

"Yeah, Elodie and Lexie. Lexie works for Food For All and they're expanding into this new location. She's apparently in charge of getting it all set up. Another woman who works with her, Ashlyn, will also be there from what I understand."

"Cool. So the guys aren't coming?" Carly asked a little too nonchalantly.

Kenna suppressed a grin. She had a feeling if Jag had just a little bit of patience, he'd totally wear Carly down. "No, they're working. I think they helped move some of the bigger pieces of furniture yesterday."

Carly nodded.

They talked about work gossip and their schedules the rest of the way to Barber's Point. Kenna pulled into a parking spot a block from the Food For All building, and she and Carly climbed out of her trusty Chevy and headed down the sidewalk.

The windows of the building were covered with tan paper, indicating to the general public that they weren't open yet, but Lexie had told Kenna to just come on in when she arrived.

Kenna pushed open the door and walked into a large, bright and welcoming space. She smiled. If she happened to be down on her luck and felt bad about having to ask for help with feeding herself or her family, she'd feel much better about it after walking in here. It wasn't depressing. It was almost uplifting. The walls were bright white and the lighting was vivid as well, but without the harsh glare of fluorescent bulbs. And once the paper was off the front windows, she knew the sunlight would help even more.

"Hi!"

"Yay! Kenna and Carly are here!"

"Good to see you again!"

The immediate welcome from the three women made Kenna smile even wider. It reminded her of the old television show *Cheers*, where everyone always greeted Norm when he walked into the bar.

Kenna waved at everyone. "Hi! You guys remember Carly, right?"

"How could we forget the best waitress ever?" Elodie said with a grin.

"And this is Ashlyn. She works with me at Food For All," Lexie said.

"It's nice to meet you," Kenna said politely.

"Same. I've heard a lot about you from Lexie," Ashlyn said.

"You can put your purses down over there," Lexie said, pointing to a table along one of the walls where their own bags were sitting. "Then we'll get to work."

"What are we doing today?" Kenna asked as she headed for the table.

"The taskmaster has quite the list," Ashlyn quipped.

"Shut it," Lexie said, throwing a balled-up piece of paper at her friend.

Everyone laughed.

Kenna had a feeling today was going to be a ton of fun. She needed this. Needed to connect with women outside of work.

Hearing the door open once more, Kenna turned to see a man entering the space. He was tall, fairly skinny, and had long, disheveled hair. His lips were moving as if he was talking to himself, but no words were audible. He stared at the floor as he stopped near the door. He carried a large bag, which was full of empty tin cans, and his clothes were tattered and worn.

Kenna waited for Lexie or Ashlyn to tell the man that they weren't open yet, but instead, Lexie greeted the man by name as she approached.

"Hi, Theo. Did you sleep okay last night?"

He nodded but didn't pick his head up or answer verbally.

"Good. You think you can be happy here instead of being downtown?"

At that, Theo looked up for the first time. He stared at Lexie as if she hung the moon. "I like my bed. And my place. It's quiet. And there's a park nearby. With trees."

"You like trees, don't you?" Lexie asked gently.

Theo looked back down at his feet and nodded once more.

"Good. We're just getting started in here. You can stay if you want."

"Stay," Theo mumbled under his breath.

Ashlyn startled Kenna when she spoke quietly from right next to her. Kenna hadn't even heard her approach. "Theo helped save her life. Lexie would do anything for him. He's protective of her in his own way. When she knew she'd be working down here, she couldn't bear to leave him downtown. She asked if he wanted to come over here and he agreed. She arranged for a one-room studio apartment for him, and he seems to be doing really well so far."

Kenna didn't know the details of Lexie's story, and was extremely curious as to what happened and how this previously homeless man had saved her new friend's life, but now wasn't the time or place to ask about it.

Theo shuffled over to a small table in the corner and sat on a chair, making sure his bag was between his feet, as if he thought one of the women might try to take it from him. Kenna didn't take offense. If she'd been homeless, she supposed she'd be paranoid about someone stealing her stuff too.

Lexie walked over to a cooler and pulled out a bottle of water. She brought it over to Theo and left it on the table without a word. Then she turned to the women and said, "Okay, so Elodie wants to set up the back room so we can get the boxed lunch program underway quickly. It'll involve moving some of the shelves the guys brought in yesterday. We also need to sweep this place, clean the bathroom, unstack the tables and chairs, and generally make everything look as inviting and welcoming as possible."

Ashlyn groaned and bent over with a hand on her back as if she were a hundred years old.

Everyone laughed.

"And while I love the brightness of the room, it's a little... stark. I thought before we unpacked or cleaned, we could paint the walls. I wanted to do a colorful mural like the ones in Kakaako."

"What's that?" Carly asked.

"It's a neighborhood between Waikiki and downtown Honolulu. It used to be an industrial ghost town with mostly auto body shops and old warehouses. But a bunch of local artists used the old buildings as their canvases and as a result, it revived the area. There are a bunch of breweries and other businesses there now, and there's even a monthly food truck gathering."

"How come I didn't know about this?" Kenna asked no one in particular.

"Because you have no reason to really drive through there?" Elodie suggested.

"I do now," Kenna said. "I'm gonna look it up and Carly and I will go through on our way back to Waikiki."

"Awesome," Ashlyn said with a smile.

"So...who's gonna draw this mural, Lexie? Because I don't have a lick of artistic ability, and I don't think you do either," Elodie said.

"Count me out," Ashlyn chimed in.

"I don't suppose either of you is an artist?" Lexie asked Kenna and Carly.

"Sorry, I'm not," Kenna said.

"I can't even draw a straight line," Carly agreed.

"Well, shoot. There goes my grand idea," Lexie said with a sigh.

"I can draw."

All five women turned to look at Theo. He was still sitting at the table, looking down at the top of it, drawing imaginary circles with his finger in the light dust covering the surface.

Lexie walked over to him and crouched next to his chair. "You can draw, Theo?"

He nodded.

Lexie turned and gestured to Elodie. "Will you bring me a piece of paper and a pen?"

Elodie rushed over to the table with their purses on it and grabbed a piece of paper out of a folder, bringing it over to Theo and Lexie.

Kenna watched with interest as Lexie turned back to her unconventional friend and put the supplies on the table in front of him. "Can you draw me something?"

"Yes."

"Maybe the ocean, with a pretty beach, some buildings off to the left and a mountain."

"Like Diamond Head?" Theo asked, looking up at her.

"Yes, exactly! And maybe a bright rainbow in there somewhere too. Everyone likes rainbows. They're happy."

Theo nodded and bent over the paper.

Lexie stood and backed away from the table, giving Theo room to do his thing.

"Do you really think he can draw?" Carly whispered as Lexie came back over to where the women were standing.

"I sure as hell hope so. Otherwise the walls are gonna be super boring in here," Lexie said. "We don't have the money to hire an artist right now."

"We could ask Aleck," Elodie suggested.

Kenna blinked in surprise at the seemingly out-of-the-blue statement.

"We could," Lexie agreed. "But he's already donated so much, I hate to ask for anything else."

"He can afford it," Elodie said nonchalantly.

"I know, but I don't want to take advantage. Especially if I need to hit him up for help with something else later."

Elodie and Ashlyn nodded in agreement, but Kenna just looked at Carly in confusion.

Elodie caught the look and asked, "What's wrong?"

Kenna shrugged. "I guess I'm just confused about why you've singled out Marshall to donate money."

"He's loaded," Lexie said casually, already unstacking chairs. "You'd never know it by looking at him or talking to him. He's one of the most down-to-earth millionaires I've ever met. I swear I'm not taking advantage of him though. That's why I wouldn't ask him to pay for an artist to come in and paint a mural on the wall. He's been more than generous as it is."

Kenna was still stuck on the first part of what she'd said, struggling to wrap her mind around the fact that Marshall was a *millionaire*.

"You didn't know? I'm sorry if we let the cat out of the bag," Elodie said gently. "He doesn't go around bragging about the fact his parents made a ton of money in real estate and set up a trust fund for him."

"And he's even paying them back for his penthouse at Coral Springs too. He told us they bought it as a vacation place, but when he was stationed here, they insisted he move in. They switched it over to his name and everything," Lexie explained.

Kenna froze completely at hearing where Marshall lived.

God, she was an idiot.

No wonder it had been so easy to get onto the private

beach. Marshall freaking *lived* there. And he hadn't said a word.

Humiliation swept over her like an ocean tide.

And just like that, the best date she'd had in her entire life was tainted.

Carly obviously saw how upset she was, though she didn't know why. She put her hand on Kenna's arm in support.

Kenna knew she should say something, but she was still processing the fact that in all the conversations they'd had, Marshall hadn't said one word about being rich. It stung. Bad.

She was saved from the awkward silence by Theo saying, "Done."

Everyone's attention turned to him as he put the pen down on the table. Lexie walked back over and picked up the piece of paper. Her shock was easy to see on her face.

"Can you draw this again? But on the wall? Really big?" she asked him.

Theo nodded.

Kenna turned to the women with a huge smile on her face. "Looks like we found our artist," she said.

Elodie and Ashlyn cheered and rushed over to see what Theo had drawn. Carly took the chance to ask Kenna quietly, "You okay?"

"No," she replied honestly. "But I'm not going to think about that right now. We've got stuff to do and I want to get to know everyone here. I can't do that and think about how Marshall lied to me."

Carly frowned. "Okay, but I'm here if you want to talk."

"Thanks," Kenna said. "That means a lot."

Carly nodded and pulled Kenna toward Theo and his drawing. She went willingly, wanting to put what she'd just learned about Marshall out of her mind. It was too hurtful to dwell on right now.

The rest of the morning and early afternoon went by

quickly. Elodie ordered lunch for all of them and they pigged out on burgers, French fries, and malasadas for dessert. Theo turned out to be amazingly talented. He might have a mental disability and questionable hygiene, but it certainly didn't affect his artistic talent. He finished drawing the beach scene on the wall and they all got a good start on painting it in by the time Kenna and Carly had to leave.

Since Carly had to work that night, she needed to get home so she could change and drive to Duke's for her shift. They hadn't gotten a ton of work done on organizing the space, but Kenna was thrilled with how well everyone got along. Elodie and Lexie were just as fun as they had been the night they came to Duke's.

Kenna heard abbreviated stories of both their dramas, and was suitably horrified. She wasn't all that surprised to hear how Marshall and his SEAL team banded together to rescue the women. She also couldn't help but be interested in hearing about the missions they were on when they'd met Elodie and Lexie in the first place. It was hard to visualize Marshall in full-on SEAL mode, but she had a feeling it would be impressive.

Hearing about Marshall and his friends was also a little painful. It reminded her of his deception. It didn't help when Lexie went on and on about the ocean view from his penthouse condo at Coral Springs.

But every time he was brought up, Kenna refused to dwell. She'd have plenty of time tonight to think back over everything they'd talked about and to pick it apart.

Ashlyn was just as nice as the other two women, and when Lexie started to tease her about Slate, Kenna was surprised. The man struck her as impatient and not all that interested in a relationship. Then again, she didn't know him very well. Ashlyn, however, was outgoing and bubbly, and Kenna had a hard time picturing her with Slate.

Of course, talk had then turned to Carly, her ex, and Jag. Carly had opened up and talked about Shawn and how good things had seemed at first, until his personality had completely changed. Lexie and Elodie told Ashlyn all about what happened at Duke's, and how Kenna had shoved him, trying to get him to let go of Carly, before Midas and Marshall had tackled him.

By the time Kenna and Carly left, all five women were fast friends. They'd gotten Carly's phone number, and Ashlyn had shared hers. Kenna felt good about having a new group of friends. While she enjoyed the women she met at work, it was nice not to talk shop all the time.

After promising to get in touch soon so they could figure out another time to hang out, Kenna walked with Carly toward her car.

Neither spoke until they were on their way back toward Waikiki.

"You want to talk about it?" Carly asked.

Kenna didn't need to ask her what she meant. She knew. Sighing, Kenna shook her head. "I had no idea. I feel like an idiot."

"I'm sorry," Carly said.

"The thing is, I told him more than once that I hated being lied to. And here he was, keeping such a big secret from me."

"*Did* he lie to you though?" Carly asked.

"Of course he did. I didn't know he was a millionaire!" Kenna exclaimed.

"But did he come right out and say that he *wasn't*?" Carly pushed.

"Why are you on his side?" Kenna asked. "You're supposed to be my friend. Be supporting *me*."

"I am," she said calmly. "But trust me, I know how a liar operates. Shawn was really good at it. And it seems to me

144

that not telling you he has a truckload of money is way different than flat-out lying about it."

"I feel like an idiot. I was so excited about sneaking into Coral Springs—and he *lives* there! He was probably laughing his ass off at me."

"I doubt that. If I had to guess, I bet he was panicking."

"About what?" Kenna scoffed skeptically.

"Did you tell him what beach you wanted to try to sneak onto before he picked you up?"

"No. I wanted it to be a surprise."

"Right. So when you directed him to pull into his own parking lot, I bet he was shocked."

Kenna sighed. She could see that. But she wasn't ready to let him off the hook yet. "He had plenty of time after that to tell me," she insisted. "We spent all day there. He could've told me at some point."

"Look, I'm not saying you don't have a right to feel embarrassed or even let down, but, Kenna, you're kind of a bons."

Kenna frowned and looked over at Carly. Thank goodness the traffic was light. She could handle both driving and this intense conversation as a result. "A what? What the hell is a bons?"

"A snob spelled backward. You're a reverse snob. Instead of looking down on people who don't have money, you judge them harshly for being wealthy."

Kenna snorted. Her friend's observation was kind of ironic, since she'd called Marshall a snob that first night on her break at Duke's. "No, I don't," she said.

"You do," Carly said gently. "I've noticed it before. Anytime someone comes in who looks like they have a lot of money, you kind of look down your nose at them. You're much more comfortable with people who you think are middle to lower class than you are with the rich tourists or locals who come into the restaurant all the time."

Kenna wanted to protest. To say that wasn't true. But she knew it kind of was. "I just...people look down at *me* because I'm not interested in being in the corporate world and making six figures a year. I'm happy being a waitress."

"Fuck them then," Carly said.

Kenna couldn't help but laugh. Her friend didn't swear that often, so it was somewhat surprising to hear her do so now.

"I mean it. You're an adult and can do what you want. And if you're happy, who cares what others think. But seriously, girl, you've got a boyfriend who's loaded. Why are you mad about that? Most women would be jumping for joy. If things work out between you two, you can live in a penthouse with a kick-ass ocean view and *still* be a waitress. You just maybe won't have to work as much or worry about pesky things like rent and grocery money."

Kenna sighed. She knew Carly was right, but she couldn't get over the fact that Marshall had spent the entire day with her, at his own damn private beach, and hadn't said a word. "I know," she said after a moment.

"I've never seen you as bubbly and happy as you've been the last couple of weeks," Carly said. "And it's because of *him*. Not because of his money, but because of his texts. Because of your late-night conversations. A man like that doesn't come along very often. Trust me, I know."

"Carly—" Kenna began, but her friend interrupted before she could continue.

"I'm not bringing up Shawn to turn this conversation to me. I'm just saying...I don't want to see you end what's so far been an amazing relationship before it even truly begins. Not over something as silly as him having money."

Kenna didn't think it was silly, but she still understood Carly's point.

"Talk to him," she urged. "Hear him out. You're a really excellent judge of character, you'll know if he's blowing smoke up your ass when he explains why he didn't tell you. But you have to give him a chance. Don't blow this."

Kenna couldn't help but snort-laugh. "You sound invested in our relationship," she quipped.

"I kind of am. I mean, Jag is becoming a good friend. And it would be awkward for me to talk about him or even to see him if you break up with Aleck."

Kenna grinned. "So you're admitting you like Jag?"

"Of course I like him," Carly said.

"*Like*-like him," Kenna clarified.

"No," Carly said stubbornly.

But the fact that she was talking about seeing Jag in the future was a big deal. They both knew it, even if Carly wouldn't admit to being interested.

As the conversation waned, Kenna sobered as she thought about what she had to do later that night.

She remembered what Marshall had said. That if she ever heard something about him she didn't like, that he wanted her to talk to him about it. She'd promised. She hoped like hell *this* was what he was talking about. If he had some other deep dark secret, she wasn't sure she could deal.

Kenna had forgotten to drive though Kakaako on the way home to look at the murals, but figured she could do it another day. She pulled up outside Carly's apartment to drop her off and her friend turned to her once more.

"Thank you for inviting me today. I had a good time."

"Anytime."

"I haven't made a ton of friends here, and hiding from Shawn in my apartment has been lonely. I'm going to try to make an effort to start living my life again, thanks to you."

Kenna smiled. "Just be careful, okay?"

"I will. I have no desire to run into that asshole again. All I'm saying is that I really liked hanging out with the women today, and I hope I'll get to see them again."

"I'm sure you will. They all got our numbers, and I have a feeling it won't be long before we get roped into some scheme with them soon."

"I hope so," Carly said with a smile. "See you tomorrow at work."

"See ya," Kenna said. She idled at the curb until Carly was safely inside the lobby of her apartment, then pulled away and headed for her own place.

She wasn't looking forward to what she needed to do, but she had a few hours to think about what she wanted to say to Marshall. She wasn't happy he'd lied by omission, and she didn't want to be a bons, as Carly had called her, but the embarrassment Marshall had made her feel lingered just below the surface, and she hated that.

If she and Marshall were going to be able to continue with their relationship, she had to find a way to get over that feeling. But she wasn't sure how. And that worried her.

So, she'd try to sort out her feelings that afternoon and would call Marshall later. They'd talk, and then she'd make the decision of whether or not she wanted to keep seeing him.

Just the thought of not talking to him, not getting to hang out at the swap meet as they'd made plans to do, was painful...which said a lot about her feelings already. She didn't want to break up with him. But she also didn't want to feel as if she was the butt of one of his jokes.

A pit formed in her belly when she thought about their call. This time tomorrow, she and Marshall would either be completely all right, or they'd be done.

She wanted to throw up.

CHAPTER ELEVEN

Aleck frowned at the text he'd just received from Kenna.

Kenna: We need to talk.

The joke was that if a woman ever said that to a man, it didn't mean anything good. But it was one hundred percent true. And Aleck had a feeling he knew what she wanted to talk about.

He mentally kicked himself. He should've told her that he lived at Coral Springs on Sunday. He'd been enjoying the day too much to bring it up, to possibly ruin the mood—and her perception of him.

He hadn't thought much about her hanging out with Elodie and Lexie, but he probably should've warned the two women that he hadn't told Kenna about his money, and maybe asked them if they could please not say anything until he had a chance to tell her himself.

But he hadn't. Kenna had spent the afternoon with Elodie

and Lexie—and now she had a "need" to talk. It was likely they'd spilled the beans. He'd asked Kenna to promise she'd talk to him if she heard anything she didn't like, and it looked like she was at least keeping that promise.

He quickly sent a text back.

Aleck: Of course. Anytime. I'm home and not busy.

He'd prefer to get this over with. To apologize and grovel if he had to.

Kenna: Okay.

She didn't say when she'd call, but Aleck didn't press. He paced back and forth with his phone in his hand, trying to think of the best way to explain his reasoning behind not telling her he lived at Coral Springs. To tell her that he had a healthy seven figures in his bank account. It was almost amusing that Kenna was pissed that he had money. Most women would be thrilled. But not his Kenna.

His Kenna.

Shit. *Was* she still his?

"Come on, call," he muttered. He wanted this done. He hated that she was upset.

Aleck stopped pacing and chuckled. Not because something was funny, but because he didn't even know if she *was* upset. He was working himself into a frenzy. For all he knew, Kenna wanted to talk about something else.

No. He knew deep down, his money was causing problems for her.

Maybe he'd subconsciously hoped Elodie and Lexie *would* let something slip, so he didn't have to figure out a way to bring it up.

Either way, he hated the feeling of dread that had settled deep within him.

Kenna made him wait for another half an hour before his phone finally rang.

"Kenna," he said as he answered the phone.

"Hi."

Her voice was flat and didn't have the welcoming tone it usually did when she called.

"You said to talk to you if I ever heard something I didn't like about you," Kenna said, not beating around the bush. "You live in Coral Springs."

It wasn't a question.

"Yes," Aleck said without prevarication.

"You're rich," Kenna added.

"Technically, my parents are rich. But yes, I have access to a very comfortable trust fund and have a healthy amount of money in my bank account."

Kenna didn't say anything for a long moment, and Aleck was afraid to say anything else that would exacerbate the situation.

"Why didn't you tell me? Say something when we pulled into the Coral Springs parking lot on Sunday? You had plenty of time to let me know that you lived there and it wouldn't be an issue getting onto the private beach."

The hurt in her voice killed him. Aleck hated having this conversation over the phone, but he wasn't about to ask her to wait until the weekend. "I should've."

"Yeah," she agreed.

"I don't really have a good excuse," Aleck told her. "But my bank account isn't something I go around talking about to people I just met. I only use the money my parents put aside for me very rarely. Yes, I live in a penthouse at Coral Springs. My parents bought the place a few years ago as a vacation home. When I got stationed here, they gave it to me. I tried to protest, but it was pointless. I'm paying them back for it... out of my Navy salary, not the trust fund."

Aleck took a deep breath and kept going. Kenna hadn't hung up on him or interrupted, he wanted to think those were both good signs, but the truth was he had no idea. She could be waiting until he was all the way done explaining before telling him she never wanted to see him again. The thought made him talk faster.

"You accused me of being a snob that first night we met, and while that stung, you weren't exactly wrong. My parents did their best to make me work for what I wanted, but holidays were always awesome. I usually got exactly what I wanted. Birthdays too. And yes, I got a car when I turned sixteen. I've never really wanted for anything. So yeah, it was hard for me to understand why you were satisfied with a waitress's salary. But the more I came to know you, the more I got it.

"Life isn't about money. It's about relationships. Connections with people. And you've got the unique ability to connect with just about everyone you meet. It's a beautiful thing, Kenna. And Sunday, when I picked you up, you were utterly adorable. So excited about crashing the private beach. I had no idea you'd picked my condo's beach to sneak onto until we pulled into the lot. There was no good way to just blurt out that I lived there. I mean, I could've, and should've, but the truth is...I was nervous. You made your opinion of rich people more than clear, and the kind of people you assumed lived in my complex. The very last thing I wanted was for you to paint *me* with the same brush, or break things off because of where I lived."

He sighed. "For what it's worth, I felt guilty all day, and

since Sunday, I've felt even more like shit for deceiving you. I was going to tell you this weekend. And I know that's a convenient thing for me to say now...but I hope you remember that I invited you to my place for dinner. I'd hoped even if you were pissed at me, I could woo you with a delicious meal."

Aleck stopped and took a deep breath. When Kenna still didn't say anything, he tentatively said, "Kenna?"

He heard her sigh. "You embarrassed me," she said quietly. "I can't help but think that you were laughing at me internally the whole time."

"Never," Aleck said emphatically. Then he decided to tell her something he'd never told anyone else—not even his teammates. Something that had played a huge part in keeping the details of his finances close to the vest. "When I was twenty-five...I met this woman at a bar. She seemed different, not like the other Frog Hogs."

"Frog Hogs?" Kenna asked.

"Yeah. The generic term is 'tag chaser,' women who go after any man in the military. But a Frog Hog is someone who only wants to date the best of the best...a Navy SEAL."

"Conceited," Kenna muttered.

But Aleck caught the humor in her tone, and he much preferred that than the humiliation he'd heard earlier. "We prefer the word 'confident,'" Aleck said. He took another deep breath and continued his story. "Anyway, she was tall, blonde, had a master's degree, and she was pretty, so I felt proud that she'd singled me out. I knew about Frog Hogs, of course, but she seemed so different that I ignored the warning signs. We dated for a few months, and I thought things were going pretty great. My team *hated* her though. They didn't come out and say it, but I could tell.

"We were all out together one night, and she went to the restroom. She was gone a really long time, and I got worried, so I went to check on her. She was drunk, and laughing and talking to a girlfriend really loud in the bathroom. I could hear every word through the door."

Aleck paused. He hated remembering how he'd felt when he'd stood in the dim hallway in that bar.

"What'd she say?" Kenna asked quietly.

Deciding to treat the conversation like a bandage and just rip it off to get it over with, Aleck continued. "She was talking about me, and how she was sure I was on the verge of asking her to marry me. Basically said she'd encourage me to go to Vegas and get it done quickly, then it would only be a matter of time before I was killed on some mission. And as my wife, she'd get not only my life insurance from the Navy, but my trust fund too. She and her friend actually *laughed* over that, agreeing that I was a sure thing. That she wouldn't have to—in her words—put up with me for long because of my dangerous job."

"Holy shit, what a cunt!" Kenna exclaimed.

Aleck couldn't help but chuckle, more because of Kenna saying "cunt" than anything else.

"I hope you dumped her right then and there," she continued.

"I did," Aleck said. "I turned around and left the bar. Didn't even tell my friends why I was leaving. I had brought the bitch to the bar, so she had to get a ride home with her friend. She called me several times but I never spoke to her again. I texted her that we were done...and that's it. It was juvenile, and I should've been the bigger person and broken up in person rather than ghosting her, but I just couldn't."

"No, you should not have. She didn't give a shit about you, so why would you give her the decency of breaking up in person? Fucking bitch."

As much as Aleck was enjoying her support, he still wanted to make sure she understood why he was telling her the story. "She got under my skin—in the worst way. I didn't date for over a year after that because I couldn't trust anyone, and when I finally started, I was much more careful when it came to telling anyone about my wealth. Hell, I might've even been able to handle the bitch wanting to be with me because of my money; at least that wouldn't be very surprising. But the fact that she wanted to marry me because my job is dangerous, and she was counting on me getting killed in action so she could get her hands on my money sooner...that was nearly impossible to wrap my head around."

Kenna took a deep breath and let it out slowly. "I understand. I'd probably be just as wary as you are if I was in your shoes."

Aleck couldn't believe she was letting him off the hook so easily. "I should've said something," Aleck told her. "It was cowardly of me."

"I didn't really give you a chance," Kenna offered. "And I *was* pretty judgmental about rich people. I'm sorry for that."

"Still. I could've said something before we got out of the Jeep. Or when you told me your plan on getting past Robert at the security desk. Or even after we were sitting on the beach."

"Are you seriously trying to talk me *into* staying pissed at you?" Kenna asked with a small laugh.

Was he? It hadn't been his plan, but now that she'd pointed it out, Aleck realized that was exactly what he was doing. Unintentionally, but still. "Shit," he muttered.

Kenna giggled, and the sound seeped into his pores and settled into his heart.

"You hurt me," Kenna said honestly. "I was mortified when Elodie and Lexie let it spill that you lived at Coral Springs. I bitched about you to Carly on our way home from Food For All today, and you know what she said?"

"What?"

"That I was a bons. A reverse snob. She pointed out that most women would be over-the-moon excited if their boyfriends had money. I thought about that a lot this afternoon before I called. I've had so many people look down on me because of my job and tell me I could do so much better, that it's made me wary of anyone who makes a ton of money. I don't like you because of what you do, Marshall. Or because of how much is in your bank account. I like you because of who you are. But I've said it before and I'll say it again—I don't like secrets. Is there anything else I need to know? Any other big reveals you need to make? Now's the time if you do."

"No. Although I have to point out again that there's a lot I'll never be able to tell you about my job," Aleck said a little warily.

"I understand that, and it's okay. I'm more concerned about things like you having a fatal disease or that you're married with children or something."

"No, absolutely not. Kenna?"

"Yeah?"

"I really am sorry. I hate that I made you feel bad."

"Me too. But now that I know, we're moving on. I had fun with the girls today."

"Yeah?"

"Uh-huh. Did you know Lexie's friend Theo is a damn good artist?"

"He is?"

"Yeah."

For the next few minutes, Kenna talked about her day and about the mural Theo had painted on the wall of the annex of Food For All. Then they talked about Carly and if she'd seen Shawn—she hadn't—and how the rest of the day had gone.

"I know you work the next three nights, but I was

wondering if maybe we could hang out Friday for a while?" Aleck asked. "Maybe go to lunch?"

"Don't you have to work?" Kenna asked.

"If you had time, I was going to ask my commander if I could take a few hours off. I just...I want to see you. Apologize in person. Make sure we're okay."

"We're good," Kenna told him. "And you don't have to apologize again."

"Yeah, I think I do," Aleck said.

"I'd love to have lunch with you on Friday," Kenna told him.

Aleck let out the breath he'd been holding. "And we're still on for Sunday? For the swap meet and dinner?"

"Yeah."

"Good."

"So...is the view from your balcony as good as Elodie and Lexie said it was?" Kenna asked.

"Yes," Aleck said simply.

"I can't wait to see it," Kenna said.

Aleck fully relaxed for the first time since he'd read her text earlier. Instinctively, he knew not telling Kenna about his money could be an issue, but he hadn't realized how terrified he'd be that she'd tell him she didn't want to see him anymore.

Kenna was different. Special. And he wanted to see where their relationship could go. And making her feel humiliated wasn't exactly the best way to bring them closer. But he felt ten pounds lighter now that she knew.

They continued their conversation after that, about everything under the sun. Their jobs, friends, families, hometowns, she even told him a little about her accounting job back in Pennsylvania. He told her some funny stories about SEAL training and admitted that it was the hardest thing he'd ever done in his life, but it was the thing he was most proud of as well.

When Kenna yawned, he glanced at his watch and saw they'd been talking for an hour and a half. It wasn't exactly late, but Kenna had been busy all day, not to mention probably extremely worked up over what she'd learned about him. This was her one night off all week, and he wanted her to get some sleep.

"I'm gonna let you go," he said gently. "You're tired."

"I shouldn't be. On a work night, I probably walk about twenty-five thousand steps. I haven't come close to that today."

"Still," Aleck said. "Get some sleep."

"Okay. Marshall?"

"Yeah?"

"Thanks for being honest with me."

"Thank *you* for coming to me with what you heard. Communication is the key to a good relationship, and while I obviously failed at that, I promise to be better."

"I'll talk to you tomorrow?" she asked.

"Of course. I'll call during my lunch as usual," he told her.

"Okay."

"Sleep well, babe."

"I will. Bye."

"Bye."

Aleck hung up the phone and collapsed back against the cushions of his couch. He stared into space as he did his best to process everything. He knew he could've lost Kenna. He hadn't meant to embarrass her, and he'd do anything in his power never to do so again.

It was crazy how fast a woman could change his life. He lived to talk to her and to hear how her day was going. Even though they'd only hung out in person a couple of times, he craved more. It sucked that their schedules were so different, but that wasn't going to deter him. He had a feeling Kenna could be the best thing that ever happened to him, and he made a pledge to do everything in his power to show her how much she meant to him.

With that thought, he shot off a text to Elodie, asking for dinner menu suggestions. He wanted Sunday to be perfect, to prove to Kenna that he was a man she could rely on, trust, and be happy with.

CHAPTER TWELVE

Kenna was in a great mood when Saturday rolled around. Lunch with Marshall on Friday had been awkward at first, but he'd taken her in his arms and apologized once more, asking for her forgiveness. She'd reassured him that she'd already forgiven him and they were good.

He'd taken her to Chiba-ken, a sushi restaurant she'd been dying to try, but hadn't had a chance to yet. Apparently, he didn't even like sushi, and when she'd asked him why on earth he'd picked this restaurant for lunch, he'd simply said, "because you wanted to eat here." Her heart just about melted right then and there.

He'd ended up getting the asparagus wrapped with pork. She'd gotten the sushi platter, and proceeded to stuff her face with the three different kinds of sushi that were included.

It was clear to her that Marshall Smart was one of the good ones, as Carly promised. Kenna had been afraid he was *too* perfect, and she now knew that wasn't true. He'd messed up by not coming out and admitting he lived at Coral Springs. But he was sorry, and Kenna had apologized again too. If she hadn't been so judgmental, he might've fessed up sooner.

She was also still pissed off at the woman he'd dated who'd been hoping he'd die so she could get her hands on his money.

Kenna knew money was important. She wasn't an idiot. But who he was as a person far outweighed the importance of his bank account, in her opinion. She could take care of herself. Had *been* taking care of herself. She didn't need a man, or his money, to make her happy. She just wanted and needed someone who enjoyed being with her, treated her and others with respect, and who she could *talk* to.

And Marshall fit the bill on all accounts.

Work on Thursday and Friday had been fairly normal. Saturday nights at Duke's were usually a bit crazier. More tourists, more alcohol, and—most of the time—more tips.

Halfway through her shift, a family came in...and Kenna just knew they were going to be trouble. She got a vibe from them that made her feel as if all was not right in their world. The man was large, more round than tall, and he wore a scowl on his face. How anyone could be grumpy in a place like Duke's, in Hawaii for goodness sake, was beyond Kenna.

The woman was thin and fairly short. Her shoulders were hunched as she followed behind her husband when Vera led them to their table in Kenna's section. They had a child, a little boy, who looked to be around four or five. His eyes were wide as he took in everything around him, but he didn't say a word as they were seated.

"Thanks, Vera," Kenna told the hostess after she handed them their menus. "I've got it from here."

"Enjoy your meal," Vera said cheerfully.

"If we didn't have to wait for an hour to be seated, I might've had a better shot at doing that," the man muttered.

Kenna mentally sighed, but did her best to stay upbeat and positive as she went over the specials for the night and taking their drink orders.

The man didn't ask his wife or son what they wanted to drink, he just ordered for them. But since neither protested, Kenna assumed it was probably what they always ordered. She wasn't thrilled that the man ordered a bourbon, neat, but she wasn't the alcohol police. She just hoped he wouldn't get drunk. She had a feeling the more alcohol he had, the worse his mood would get.

As she headed for the kitchen, Kenna said a silent prayer that she was misinterpreting the situation and everything would be just fine.

But an hour later, she knew her concerns had been spot on. The man had ordered four drinks so far and proceeded to down each almost as soon as Kenna had put them on the table. He was loud and obnoxious, complaining about how long it took for the food to be delivered and the temperature of their meals. He didn't like how noisy the restaurant was, or the music out by the Outrigger Hotel's pool. He constantly glared at his wife, though Kenna had only heard her say one thing the entire time she'd been serving the family. And that was to apologize profusely when she admitted that she'd dropped her fork and needed a new one.

Of course, her husband called her a clumsy bitch, which made Kenna want to scream. Their son seemed unnaturally quiet, and she hoped he was just uncertain about his surroundings. Or shy. She'd done her best to engage both the wife and the little boy, but the man's complaints made it hard to have any kind of conversation.

Kenna had just returned to their table with the man's credit card when the shit *really* hit the fan.

He'd tipped a measly ten percent, but Kenna was honestly pleased he'd left her a tip at all. It seemed the more obnoxious a customer, the less they always gave. She still needed to package up the leftover hula pie they hadn't been able to finish, and had just turned to head back to the kitchen for a box when the little boy stood and wandered off toward the beach, as his father bitched about something or other. Since Duke's was an open-air restaurant, there weren't any walls between the tables and the beach. Just a couple of stairways with maybe four or so steps each.

The boy had been looking wistfully toward the beach and ocean throughout the meal, and Kenna smiled to herself when she saw him give into his longing to get a closer look.

But his father obviously wasn't happy with his son wandering off. He sprang out of his seat and took the few steps required to reach him, grabbed a handful of his shirt, and jerked him backward.

Kenna could only stare in horrified shock as the man smacked his son across the face, then swatted his butt, hard. "You do *not* leave our sides!" he shouted, pointing a finger into the boy's face. "Hear me?"

"Yes, sir."

"Sit your ass back down. Now."

Kenna already had her phone out. There was no universe she lived in where she would *not* report abuse. Didn't matter if it was an adult to a child, a man to a woman, or even a woman to a man. She quickly explained to the police what had happened and implored them to hurry as the family was getting ready to leave.

She managed to stall them by lingering in the kitchen for much longer than she would normally when a customer was waiting for something. But she needed to give the cops time to get there. Luckily, just like the other day, they arrived quickly, and Kenna met them at the front of the restaurant. She explained what had happened and pointed out the man.

The second the man saw the police officers headed his way, he completely lost his cool. He stood up and started swearing loudly. Kenna watched from a distance as the officers tried to have a calm and rational conversation with him, but when he drew back his fist to hit one of them, all bets were off. They had the man on the ground with his hands cuffed behind him before he could follow through with his physical threat. One officer hauled him up and out of the restaurant, while the other stayed behind to talk to his wife and son.

On his way past her, the man glared and hissed, "You'll be sorry, bitch. You're *nothing*! Lower than the dirt on my fucking shoes. You shouldn't have fucked with me. I'll—"

"Come on," the officer said harshly, cutting off whatever threat he was going to spew next. "I think you're in trouble enough, let's not add threatening your waitress to that list, shall we?"

Then he hauled him down the small hallway toward the exit...and hopefully right to his cop car sitting at the curb on Ala Moana Boulevard.

Kenna was a bit shaken at the hatred in the man's tone, but did her best to shake it off. She looked back at the table where his family were still sitting. The little boy had a large red mark on his face from his dad's abuse, and was quietly playing with a toy police shield the officer had obviously given him.

Kenna couldn't hear what was being said, but she prayed the woman would press charges. If anyone dared to hit her child like the man had done to his son, Kenna would've lost her mind. She hurried back into the kitchen to grab a fresh piece of pie and a side order of French fries. She'd noticed the little boy seemed to love them, while he'd only nibbled on his hamburger. She supposed that giving him more of the greasy fried potatoes maybe wasn't the healthiest thing, but she wanted to comfort him in some way. And since she knew he enjoyed the fries, that was the first thing she'd thought of.

As Kenna suspected, when she approached the table, the

woman was shaking her head and telling the officer she didn't want to press charges.

Mentally sighing, Kenna knelt by the boy's chair.

"Hey, I brought you some French fries to take home. The cook said he made too many and was about to throw them away. I figured you might want them instead."

His eyes lit up, but before he accepted, Kenna saw him look over at his mother. She nodded at him, and only then did he reach for the container.

Kenna put the piece of pie on the table. "And I brought you a full slice of hula pie instead of the half-eaten one from your dinner."

"Thank you," the woman said distractedly. Kenna could tell her mind was on other things. Probably how mad her husband was going to be when he was released and able to return to their hotel room.

"Can I call you a taxi?" Kenna asked.

"No, thank you," the woman said.

"We're gonna need your statement," the officer told Kenna.

She nodded.

"You shouldn't've called the police," the woman said quietly.

"And your son shouldn't *ever* be hit in the face. Especially not by his father," Kenna returned.

The woman looked away without meeting her gaze.

Kenna sighed again. She hadn't exactly saved the boy or the woman from being abused further. In fact, there was a chance she'd made things worse, and she fervently hoped that wasn't the case...while adding a silent prayer that maybe, just maybe, the woman would eventually realize her son's well-being was more important than staying with her bully of a husband.

The paperwork with the police didn't take too long and

luckily the other servers dealt with her tables while she completed her statement. By the time she got back to work, Kenna was exhausted. It was more emotional than physical. She never hesitated to stand up for what she felt was right, but that didn't always mean it was easy.

By the time she headed home from her shift, Kenna was dead on her feet. Usually after situations like this, she didn't want to talk to anyone. She just wanted to be alone. She'd normally rewind the incident over and over in her mind, finally falling into a fitful sleep in the wee hours of the morning.

But tonight, all she could think about was getting home and talking to Marshall.

She was able to resist calling him until she'd showered and put on the oversized T-shirt she liked to sleep in. She crawled into her bed, pulled the covers up, and reached for her phone.

Marshall answered after only one ring.

"Good evening, beautiful."

"Hi."

"What's wrong?"

It was pretty wonderful how easily this man could read her. She'd only said one word, and that was enough to convey her state of mind. "Work sucked," she said.

"Talk to me," Marshall implored.

So she did. She told him everything. How she'd suspected the man was going to be trouble from the second she saw him. How cowed his wife and son seemed to be. How Kenna had worried as the man downed one drink after another. And then her horror when the guy had struck his son. She even told him about the man's threats as he was hauled out of the restaurant. By the time she was done rehashing everything, Kenna felt drained.

"I'm so sorry, babe. That sounds awful. But I'm proud of you for calling the police on his ass."

Kenna smiled and turned onto her side. This is what she needed. Marshall's voice in her ear, saying he was proud of her. "Thanks."

"Although I'm not thrilled with his threats. You need to be extra careful. It was bad enough with that Shawn asshole being pissed at you, I can't stand the thought of someone *else* wanting to get back at you."

Kenna hadn't even really thought about that. "I hate to even tell you this, because you might get upset, but honestly, people threaten the servers all the time. Well, maybe not *all* the time, but they generally aren't happy when we refuse to serve them alcohol when they're obviously drunk as hell already, or if there's anything wrong with their meal. We've even had people accuse us of stealing their credit card numbers to use later. Most customers are great. Happy to be in Hawaii and enjoying the food and ambiance, but there are always those assholes who want to throw their weight around."

"Not making me feel better by telling me tonight's incident wasn't unusual. Just please be careful. I can't have found you now, only to lose you."

Kenna smiled. "You aren't going to lose me. I'm right here."

Marshall chuckled in her ear. "You know what I mean."

"I do. But I don't remember signing a contract that said I'd live to be a hundred years old. All I can do is live my life the best I can here and now. I can be kind, and helpful, and stand up for others, no matter what's thrown in my face."

Marshall didn't answer immediately, and Kenna frowned. "Are you still there?"

"I'm here," he said quietly. "I think that's one of the reasons I'm so drawn to you. You're the antithesis of the people we're sent to battle against when we're deployed.

You're the light to the dark that sometimes threaten to over-take my damn soul."

Wow. Kenna both liked and hated that. "I've just learned that a little bit of kindness goes a long way. Maybe I made that woman and boy's situation worse tonight. But then again, maybe they'll remember the kind waitress they had and realize there are people out there who are more than willing to help."

"I hope so too," Marshall said.

Kenna's voice lowered. "And maybe when you start feeling that darkness creep in, you'll think about me and how much I respect and admire you, and you'll beat that shit back."

"What time can I come over tomorrow?" Marshall asked.

Kenna blinked at his change of topic. "Um...whenever you want? The stalls at the swap meet don't open until eight, I think. But they're open until eleven, so we have plenty of time."

"Is six too early?"

Kenna nearly choked. "In the morning?"

"Yeah. It's taking everything I have not to get up and drive over there right now. I've missed you this week. Lunch yesterday was amazing, and I really liked seeing you on a weekday. And after the night you've had, and with what you just said...I really want to be with you."

Kenna was tempted to tell him to come on over, but it was late. She was exhausted and she knew Marshall had to be too. She'd talked to him before her shift started and knew he'd spent all day in training. He and his team had been dropped off in the middle of the ocean and left to make their way back to shore on their own. He'd nonchalantly mentioned it was a four-mile swim, which seemed insane to her, but for her SEAL, it was apparently just another day. "Six is fine. Although don't expect me to be fully awake."

"You drink coffee?" he asked.

"Um...who doesn't?"

"You like it sweet or black?"

"The sweeter the better," Kenna said.

"No wonder you and Lexie get along," Marshall said. "I'll bring coffee. And malasadas."

Kenna's mouth watered. "Deal. Thanks for letting me vent."

"Anytime. I mean that," he told her. "And maybe in the future, you'll do so while I'm holding you."

God. The image that sprang into her head made Kenna's heart pound. She wanted that. Badly. "I'd like that."

"Me too. Sleep well, babe. You did the right thing tonight."

"Thanks."

"See you soon."

"Bye."

"Bye."

Kenna clicked off her phone and realized she was smiling like a loon. She set an alarm for five fifty-one the next morning—she was going to get every minute of sleep she could—and put her phone on the table next to her bed.

Usually after an intense situation like the one that happened tonight, it was difficult for her to fall asleep, and she frequently had at least one nightmare. But with Marshall's words of praise rattling around in her brain, she was adrift in a dreamless sleep within minutes.

CHAPTER THIRTEEN

Aleck took a deep breath before knocking on Kenna's door the next morning. It was five fifty-eight and he couldn't wait one more minute to see her. He knew how close he'd come to losing her, and it still haunted him.

He heard the locks click open, then Kenna's face appeared in the crack of the door.

"Marshall?"

"Yeah, it's me." He'd have a conversation with her later about opening the door before knowing who was on the other side.

The door opened all the way—and it was all Aleck could do not to burst out laughing. Kenna's hair was sticking up on one side and matted on the other. She was squinting as if the light in the hallway bothered her, wearing an oversized T-shirt that swamped her frame.

"Come in," she said, then turned and headed back into her apartment.

Aleck pushed the door open all the way and closed it behind him. There was a light on over the stove, and that was it. The apartment was dark, but he could make out Kenna climbing into the large beanbag in her living area.

"Not a morning person?" he asked softly.

"No," she said.

"How long have you been awake?"

"About four minutes. I set my alarm, got up, brushed my teeth, and then you were here," she told him as she grabbed a blanket and curled up into the squishiness of the beanbag.

Aleck placed the coffee he'd bought for her on the kitchen counter, along with the bag of malasadas. They could wait. Without hesitation, he kicked off his shoes and headed straight for Kenna. Her eyes were already closed, but when he eased himself onto the beanbag next to her, they popped open.

"What are you doing?" she asked sleepily.

"Napping with you," Aleck informed her. He held his breath to see if she would kick him out. But to his relief, she nodded, closed her eyes and, once he was settled, snuggled into him. They were squished together just as they'd been the other day, and nothing felt better than having Kenna curled up in his arms.

He wasn't tired in the least, but he wasn't going to pass up the opportunity to hold her. Aleck stroked her hair slowly and felt her sigh. She shifted a little, burrowing closer.

"Did you sleep okay last night?" he asked.

"Mm-hm. I fell asleep immediately, which is amazing after everything that happened. But I'm just so tired still."

"Then sleep," he said.

"I should get up," she protested halfheartedly.

"Why? The swap meet doesn't close until eleven. We have plenty of time. That's what you said."

"But you're here, and I want to spend time with you," she said.

Aleck fucking loved hearing that. "You are. Sleeping in my arms," he said quietly.

"Is this weird?" she asked.

"No."

"Okay. Wake me up in an hour. I'll get up and shower and eat the food you brought—which smells amazing by the way —and then we'll go."

Aleck nuzzled her temple but didn't answer. He wasn't going to wake her up at seven. There was no need. He'd let her sleep as long as she wanted to.

"Marshall?"

"Yeah, babe?"

"I needed this."

"This?" he asked.

"You. Hugging me."

Closing his eyes in gratitude that Kenna was as forgiving as she was. And that she'd done what he'd asked and talked to him when she'd heard about his lie by omission, he took a moment to compose himself before he responded. "I should've come over last night," he whispered.

He felt Kenna shrug. "You're here now."

Yes, he was. And he wouldn't take her for granted. "I am," he agreed. "Sleep," he told her.

"Bossy," she muttered.

Aleck saw the smile on her face though. He leaned over and kissed her temple and soon she was fast asleep once more.

Aleck was a man who didn't necessarily like to sit still. He liked to be doing something at all times. But at the moment, he couldn't think of anything he wanted or needed to do more than he needed to lie there with Kenna. There was something immensely satisfying about her trusting him enough to hold her while she slept. She was extremely vulnerable like this, but Aleck would never hurt a hair on her head. The day she'd jumped into the ocean to save him was the best day of his life, he just hadn't known it at the time.

At seven forty-six, Kenna stirred in his arms. Aleck had dozed lightly a time or two, but mostly he'd stayed awake, just enjoying the intimacy of being with her.

She mumbled something under her breath, then her eyes opened and she looked up at him sleepily. "What time is it?"

"Almost eight," he told her softly.

Her eyes widened. "Eight? Shit! I meant to get up an hour ago."

Aleck held her tight when her body tensed as if she was going to leap up. Not that there would've been much leaping out of the beanbag.

"Easy, babe. It's fine. We've got three hours to browse the market."

"But the good stuff'll be gone," she sighed, settling back against him.

Her T-shirt had risen up while she slept, and Aleck could feel her bare legs against his own. But he wasn't feeling horny, exactly, just wildly content.

"You okay about last night?" he asked gently.

Kenna sighed, and Aleck felt her warm breath against his neck above his shirt. Goose bumps broke out on his nape. It was a surprising reaction, but he merely smiled.

"I keep thinking about what might be happening *today*. His wife said she wasn't pressing charges, so the cops probably had to let him go."

"If he was drunk, they could've decided to keep him until he sobered up," Aleck suggested.

"Maybe. But I can't imagine he'd be any happier whenever he was finally released to go back home. I hope he doesn't take out his anger on his wife or son."

"Do you see that kind of thing a lot?" Aleck asked.

"Not really. I mean, in public, people are usually on their best behavior. And it's Hawaii and most are on vacation."

"Which in itself can bring out a lot of stress sometimes," Aleck noted.

"True. I'm thankful though that Alani and the rest of management is supportive of us making a judgement call and calling the cops if we think it's necessary," Kenna said.

"Me too," Aleck said.

Kenna lifted her head and met Aleck's gaze. "Thank you for talking to me last night. I needed that."

"Of course. As long as I'm around, I'll always pick up when you call, no matter what time it is or when you need to talk. And this is probably way too soon, but fuck it. Before too long, I'd like to be there in *person* to discuss your night."

Aleck mentally kicked himself when she didn't immediately answer. He held his breath as he waited for her response.

"I think I want that too," she said quietly.

Aleck smiled. He brought his hand up and ran it over her hair before sliding it under the messy locks, gripping the back of her neck.

"I love when you do that," she said, her eyelids drooping.

"Do what?" he asked as he leaned forward and kissed her forehead.

"Hold me by the nape," she told him.

Making a mental note to do so as often as possible, he kissed her nose. Then her cheek. Then he brushed his lips against hers lightly. Teasing her. Enjoying the intimacy of the moment.

When she squirmed against him and grumbled under her breath in frustration because he refused to deepen the kiss, Aleck smiled. "Something wrong?" he asked.

"Kiss me already," she ordered.

"With pleasure," Aleck said. He tightened his hold on her

so she couldn't pull away—not that he thought she'd do so—and dropped his head once more. This time there was no more teasing. His tongue immediately sought entry to her mouth, which she granted.

She tasted slightly of mint from when she'd brushed her teeth earlier, and he savored each tiny moan as their tongues dueled erotically. Her hands eased under his shirt beneath the blanket, and his nipples immediately hardened. He only had one hand free because he wasn't about to let go of her nape, especially now that he knew how much she liked it when he held her possessively, but he eased it down her body, making sure she was all right with his touch before moving further.

When she arched against him, he ran his hand up her bare thigh, then her side.

She squirmed against him and mumbled, "Ticklish," before taking his lips once more.

Some men might have taken advantage of her ticklishness, but he didn't want to make her laugh right that moment. He wanted her to moan even more.

So he moved his hand from her side to her belly. He was tempted to ease it down, under the elastic of her panties, but instead shifted it upward. Not willing to tease her, or himself, Aleck boldly palmed her breast, and they both moaned. Kenna pulled her head back and arched harder into him.

"Yes," she whispered.

He gave her another squeeze, then flicked her hard nipple with his fingernail. To his surprise, she reciprocated, doing the same to his own nipple.

"Fuck," he muttered.

He saw the satisfied smile on Kenna's face and freaking loved that she wasn't just lying docile against him. She was just as into this as he was.

He removed his hand to throw the blanket back, ignoring her pout. Then he ventured back under her shirt, the pout fading as he began to tease her nipple once more. Her own hand had stilled, as if her brain had short-circuited. He was all right with that. He wanted to please her more than he wanted or needed to be taken care of. She would come first. Always.

"That feels amazing," Kenna whispered.

Shifting so he was hovering above her now, Aleck still didn't remove his hand from her nape. His thumb brushed back and forth over the sensitive skin there, as he did his best to arouse her with his other hand.

Her nails dug into his chest, and it turned him on even more. His cock was as hard as it had ever been, but he didn't spare a moment to do anything about it. This was all for her. His woman had a hard night, and he wanted to help make it better.

He lowered his head and suckled her nipple, biting and nipping through the wet cotton of her shirt.

"Oh my God, yes," Kenna said.

Then she delighted the shit out of him by reaching for the hem of her shirt and pulling it to her chin, exposing herself fully.

For a second, Aleck was struck dumb. She was so fucking beautiful. Her round tits sat high and firm on her chest, her pink nipples beckoning. Her hand went to the back of his head and she gripped his hair, pulling him down to her chest.

Aleck didn't need to be told twice. He immediately took one of her nipples into his mouth and sucked. Hard.

She cried out in pleasure and pushed his head closer.

How long he spent worshiping her tits, Aleck didn't know. He was lost in the pleasure of her reactions.

It wasn't until he felt her hips rhythmically thrusting against him that he realized she was on the verge of an orgasm. He felt ten feet tall that he could get her to the edge just by playing with her breasts...before movement between them, down low, caught his attention. He glanced down her body, realizing that she'd snaked a hand into her panties. She was frantically rubbing her clit.

"Don't stop!" she pleaded.

There was no way Aleck was going to miss her going over the edge in his arms for the first time. Even if it was by her own hand. He pinched her nipple. Hard. He was no longer tender and loving as he worked her, squeezed her tit and rolling her nipple roughly in his fingers.

"That's it," he murmured. "Get yourself off. Show me what you look like when you come."

She whimpered, her eyes closed as she concentrated on reaching orgasm.

Aleck continued to stimulate her breasts as she got closer and closer to the edge.

"Open your eyes," he ordered as he hovered over her. "Look at me when you come." Her beautiful brown eyes popped open and he could see her pupils were dilated with lust. "That's it, babe. Come for me. Come hard."

He stared into her eyes as he pinched her nipple once more, and that was all it took. Every muscle in her body tensed and her thighs shook as she flew over the edge. She curled into him and cried out as she gave into the pleasure coursing through her.

Her hand stopped moving under her panties—but Aleck wanted more.

Knowing he was pushing his luck, yet unable to stop, he eased his hand down, gripping her sex possessively. She'd slipped her own hand away, and he ruthlessly began rubbing her clit through the wet cotton.

She jerked in his hold and said, "Too sensitive!"

But Aleck shook his head. "One more," he rasped.

"Oh shit..." Kenna breathed as her eyes closed once more and within seconds, began shaking again.

It was all Aleck could do not to pull her underwear down and bury his head between her thighs. He could smell her arousal all around them and it was like an aphrodisiac. He wanted to taste her. Lick her until she came again and again.

But he was more than aware that this interlude could make her feel embarrassed. He'd done that once, and had no desire to repeat it. Ever.

So he stilled his hand, cupping her pussy as she jerked against him a few more times, then went still. He'd kept his hand on her nape the whole time, and when she didn't open her eyes, he tightened his hold. "Kenna?" he said softly.

"Shhhh," she mumbled. "I'm basking."

Aleck smiled. Fuck, she was amazing. "Bask away. I'll just be here enjoying the view," he said, taking in her gorgeous breasts, still heaving as she caught her breath.

Instead of trying to cover herself, Kenna chuckled. "You're such a guy," she mock-complained.

"That I am," he agreed.

Her eyelids opened and she gazed up at him with a look he couldn't interpret. He still had one hand on her soaking-wet folds, the other at her nape.

"Good morning," she said with a huge smile.

Aleck couldn't help but laugh. "Morning," he echoed, knowing he had to let go of her eventually. Reluctantly, he moved his hand from between her legs and reached for her shirt. He pulled it down, covering her tits, then rested his hand on her belly as he lay beside her.

They lay together quietly, and for the first time in his life, even though his cock was throbbing, he didn't feel the need to get off. This was for Kenna. And he was so damn thankful she'd let him share it with her, he wasn't sure what to say or do.

"That was...amazing."

"I didn't hurt you?" Aleck asked, recalling how rough he'd been with her breasts.

"Not at all. It felt wonderful. The way you took control and held me so tightly...it was obviously hot."

Aleck sighed in relief. "Thank you for sharing that with me," he told her.

Kenna's head tilted as she looked at him. "You're so different from most guys I've been with," she said.

"Yeah?"

"Uh-huh. Most would be pressing me for sex right about now. Or wanting me to reciprocate. You're still hard."

It wasn't as if he could hide his erection. His cock was pressed up against her bare thigh, and even though he had on shorts, it was pretty damn obvious.

He shrugged. "You needed that. You've been stressed, and some of that stress is my fault. It was a privilege to do that for you."

"Still..." Her hand moved toward his cock, but Aleck shook his head.

"No, Kenna. I can wait. Sex between us will never be tit for tat, so to speak. And for the record, if there's anything I ever do that you really don't like or want to do, tell me no and I'll stop."

"I was really sensitive, and you forced me to orgasm a second time," she pointed out, not taking her gaze from his.

"But you didn't say no," Aleck said. "And that second orgasm was even more intense than the first. You loved it."

She took a deep breath and nodded. "I did."

"Right. I'm not a very gentle guy," Aleck told her. "But I'll never hurt you. I might push you, but if you say no, I'll stop. No questions asked. Okay?"

Kenna nodded.

After a few moments, Aleck asked, "Feel better? Less stressed?"

"Yes, absolutely," she replied.

"Good. Hungry?"

She chuckled. "Yes again."

"How about you go shower and get ready, and I'll warm up the coffee I brought for you and throw the malasadas into the microwave?"

She nodded but didn't move to get up. Not that Aleck had taken his hand from her neck either.

Then she took a deep breath. "So...dinner tonight...is that only a dinner invitation, or is it...more?"

Aleck's heart jumped into his throat. "You have an open invitation to spend the night with me whenever you want," he said. "I'd love for you to stay, but I don't want to rush you into anything."

Kenna laughed. "I just masturbated in front of you, and you got me off a second time. I don't think you're rushing me into anything," she said with a laugh.

Aleck loved how comfortable she was with her sexuality.

"Then I want you to stay the night," he said, excitement rising within him. "As much as I fucking love this beanbag, I'm looking forward to laying you out on my bed and not being quite so cramped when I make love to you."

"Oh yeah," she said on an exhale.

"And seeing you masturbate for me again," he added.

"Only if you reciprocate," she retorted.

His cock jerked in response to her words. "You want to watch me get myself off, Kenna?"

She nodded.

"Fuck. We need to get out of this beanbag. I think it's an aphrodisiac," he muttered.

Kenna laughed. "I've never felt like this when I've been in it before. It's all you," she said. "Us."

"Us," Aleck echoed. Then he took a deep breath. "On that note, I'm getting out."

"I'll give you a push," Kenna said.

"Hands off the ass," he warned.

She giggled.

Aleck leaned down and kissed her, loving the feel of her smile under his lips, then did his best to maneuver himself out of the beanbag without kneeing Kenna. She took advantage and let her hands stray as she attempted to "help" him out of the big bag.

After Aleck got to his feet, he reached down and pulled Kenna up as well. Then he wrapped his arms around her and just held her for a long moment.

"Not that I'm complaining, but what is this for?" she asked.

Without loosening his grip, and keeping his nose in her hair, he said, "It's the hug I wanted to give you last night, but couldn't."

Kenna pulled back and Aleck allowed it. She looked up at him. "You're a sappy fool under that badass Navy SEAL exterior, aren't you?"

Without feeling self-conscious about her words in the least, Aleck said, "Only with you."

She smiled. "Suck-up."

"Nope. Just being honest. Go shower and change. Your breakfast will be waiting when you get out."

"I could get used to this," she quipped. "Being waited on hand and foot."

"Me too," Aleck said seriously. "Me too."

They stared at each other for a long moment before Aleck dropped his arms and stepped back. Kenna looked like she wanted to say something else, but she simply smiled at him, then turned and headed for her bedroom.

As he heated up her coffee and pastries, Aleck couldn't help but feel proud. She looked a hundred times more relaxed now than she had when he'd arrived. Granted, she'd been half asleep, but still. She even *sounded* more relaxed. It had been extremely difficult last night not to drive over here to comfort her. But his Kenna was tough. She'd proven it time and time again. She didn't *need* him to comfort her, but he sure felt good that she'd *let* him.

* * *

Kenna turned to look at Marshall. He was driving them to his condo after spending the morning at the swap meet at Aloha Stadium. He'd been a good sport. It was obvious shopping wasn't his favorite thing to do. He'd bought only one thing—a ring she'd looked at and had decided against buying.

But he hadn't haggled over the price at all. Had simply asked the woman who ran the stand how much and didn't hesitate to hand over the twenty bucks she'd quoted. Kenna had tried to protest, but when he'd grabbed her right hand and slipped it down her middle finger, she'd practically melted into a pile of goo right there at his feet.

The ring obviously didn't have any monetary value, but emotionally, it was priceless. Kenna knew she'd remember this day every time she saw it on her finger. It was a daisy, and probably made in China, but Kenna treasured it.

Their morning had been a wonderful surprise. She hadn't meant to sleep so long, but when she'd woken up in Marshall's arms, she'd felt amazingly good. She hadn't meant to touch herself while in his arms, but she couldn't help it. Marshall's mouth on her breasts had felt incredible, and it had been so long since she'd let down her guard with a man that before she'd even realized it, she was touching herself.

It turned out to be one of the hottest moments she'd ever shared with a man. Looking into Marshall's eyes when she'd come had been...earth-shattering. Even through her pleasure, she could see his own reflecting back in his eyes. He enjoyed seeing her come, and hadn't been concerned about getting himself off afterward, which was quite a change from most men she'd been with.

When he'd brought her to orgasm again, his touch was so different from her own. She always backed off touching herself when she felt her orgasm approaching, but he'd been forceful, dominant, refusing to let up and making her pleasure seem to go on and on. It felt...incredible.

Kenna didn't even feel guilty about basically asking him if she could spend the night at his place. She wanted this man. *All* of this man. Yes, things were moving fast between them, but she didn't care. Being with Marshall—in every way—felt right.

"What are you smiling about over there?" Marshall asked.

"This morning," Kenna said without hesitation.

She loved seeing the satisfied smirk on her man's face at her words.

"About how good breakfast was?" he teased.

"That too," she told him.

Glancing at his lap, Kenna saw he was half hard. She loved having that effect on him.

"Shit, you're gonna be the death of me, woman," Marshall groaned.

"For the record, I like sex," Kenna explained. "And this morning was..." She struggled to find the right word. Then decided to just say what she felt. "The best I've ever had...and we didn't even *have* sex."

"Shit, you *would* decide to have this conversation now, when I'm driving," Marshall grumbled, shifting in his seat and adjusting his cock in his shorts.

Kenna merely grinned. "Sorry," she said, knowing she didn't sound sorry at all. "Look, here's the thing. Women are judged because of sex all the time. If we like it, we're easy. If we have too many partners, we're whores. We're supposed to be virginal and chaste until we get married, while a guy can fuck as many people as he wants and society doesn't think twice about it, as if it's expected. It's never made sense to me. I'm thirty years old, I like orgasming, and even though I haven't had a boyfriend in a while, that doesn't mean that I haven't been taking care of myself.

"But what you did today...it made me realize that I'm still a little clueless about my own body. You making me come a second time when I thought I was done...it was enlightening. And hot. And now I want to know what *else* I don't know about myself when it comes to sex."

She could see Marshall's jaw flexing, and she scrunched her nose in contrition. "Sorry, too honest?"

"No," he said in a low, rumbly tone that made Kenna shiver. She hadn't heard him sound like that before.

No—she *had*.

That morning...when he'd said "one more."

"You're right. Society is way harder on women than men when it comes to sex. I like how open you are about your sexuality. How you aren't afraid to go after what you want. And I can't fucking wait to get you in my bed and learn everything you like and don't like when it comes to being intimate with each other."

Kenna smiled. "But you're going to feed me first, right?" she teased.

"Fuck, you really *are* gonna be the death of me," Marshall complained.

"But you love it."

He turned and met her gaze then, and Kenna inhaled sharply at the intensity she saw in his eyes. "I do," he agreed, then looked back at the road in front of them.

Kenna was turned way the hell on. She totally wanted to jump this man as soon as they were inside his condo, but she also loved foreplay. And they were engaged in the longest and most intense foreplay she'd ever experienced.

She was still smiling when they pulled into the Coral Springs parking lot. For a second, she was embarrassed all over again about everything she'd said while trying to "sneak" onto the beach. But she pushed it away. That was over and done.

"I'm sorry," Marshall said after he turned off the engine.

Kenna shook her head. "You've already apologized. And we're past that now. I want to see this amazing penthouse. And the view. I've heard a lot about it."

"You're too good to be true," Marshall said. He picked up her hand, kissed the palm, then turned to get out of the Jeep.

Kenna swore she could feel tingles all the way to her toes with just that short kiss. Oooh boy, sex with this man was going to ruin her, she just knew it.

He met her at her side of the Jeep and grabbed the bag she'd packed. He left the things she'd bought at the swap meet in the car to take back to her apartment later.

Marshall took her hand in his as they walked toward the entrance. He stopped at the security desk and greeted the man who was sitting there. "Hey, Robert."

"Good evening, Mr. Smart."

"I want to introduce you to my girlfriend, Kenna Madigan," Marshall said.

Kenna reached out and shook the security officer's hand. "It's nice to meet you."

"Same. I hope you had a good time last weekend when you were here," he said politely.

Kenna smiled and nodded. It was now obvious that they never would've made it past this man if Marshall hadn't lived there.

"I'd like to add her to my approved visitor list," Marshall told him.

"Of course. If I can just see your ID, Ms. Madigan," Robert said.

Kenna had no idea Marshall was planning on adding her to anything. She looked up at him, and he smiled and nodded. Reaching into her purse, Kenna took out her driver's license and handed it to the security officer. He filled out a piece of paper with her information, then stood.

"I'll need to take your picture for our records," Robert said.

"Oh, um, okay," Kenna said, taken aback at the level of security in the place.

"It's so the other security employees know what you look like," Robert said, obviously noticing her unease. "I'll input your picture into our system and that's it. No one else has access to our files. The next time you come, you won't even have to stop. We'll know you're allowed to access the property."

"If you're not comfortable, we can do this another time," Marshall said.

"No, it's fine," Kenna said. "I was just surprised." She posed for Robert and he took the picture without fanfare.

He handed her a piece of paper and said, "These are the rules and regulations for Coral Springs. Even though you're a guest, you're expected to comply with them. Read it at your leisure, sign, and return it back here to the desk when you're done," Robert told her.

Kenna nodded and folded the paper, putting it, and her ID, into her purse.

"Ready?" Marshall asked.

"Ready," Kenna said with a smile.

"Have a good afternoon and evening, Robert," Marshall told the security officer.

"You too."

As they got into an elevator, Kenna turned to Marshall. "I

wouldn't have gotten two steps past that desk if you weren't with me, would I?"

"No," he said with a small smile. "Robert and the other security officers are very good at what they do."

"What did your teammates think about having their pictures taken and having to sign the rules?" she asked.

Marshall shrugged. "They aren't on my approved visitor list."

She frowned in confusion. "But they're your best friends."

"Yup. And when they come over to visit, I add them to a daily visitor log. They're allowed to come in for the day, but not to come and go as they please."

Kenna stared at him in disbelief. "Seriously?"

"Yes. You're the only person I've ever added to my list."

Kenna swallowed hard. "You're *so* getting lucky tonight, sailor," she told him.

Marshall burst out laughing and tugged her into him. "Yeah?"

"Oh yeah."

He bent his head to kiss her right when the elevator dinged to let them know they'd arrived on his floor. "Later," he muttered, more to himself than to her.

Kenna couldn't get the smile off her face. She loved surprising this man. She didn't think it happened very often.

He kept his arm around her shoulders as they walked down the hall toward his condo. He placed his palm on a bio-reader next to his door, and she shook her head in disbelief. "Really?" she asked.

"Yup," he said. "It's easier than having a key, especially when I go on missions. I don't have to worry about losing or misplacing it."

"You take your keys on a mission?" she asked, her brows shooting up in surprise.

He laughed. "No way. They stay back at the office."

"Whew. I was just imagining some terrorist in the wilds of a desert somewhere finding a Jeep key in the sand and wondering how the hell it got there."

Marshall grinned. "Exactly. Give me your hand."

She did without hesitation. Kenna had a feeling she'd do whatever this man said without thinking about it.

He pushed a series of buttons on the bio-reader, then pressed her palm to the screen. "There, now you can get in whenever you come over."

Blinking in surprise, Kenna stared at him. "Did you basically just give me a key to your place?"

Marshall shrugged. "Are you gonna come over and rob me?"

"No."

"Then, yes." Marshall turned to open his door, and Kenna did her best to get her reactions under control.

This man was nothing at all like she thought he'd be when she first hung out with him on the beach at Duke's. He was so much...more.

Marshall led the way into his condo, and Kenna closed the door behind her. Her eyes widened as she took in her surroundings.

The place was so incredible, she didn't know where to look first. From the kitchen—which had beautiful white cabinets, concrete countertops, and a refrigerator that was double the size of hers—to the bamboo floors, to the extremely comfortable—and expensive—looking couches and the huge TV...it was all overwhelming.

But she could also see Marshall's touches here and there. This was no showroom. She saw a pair of boots lying on the floor near a hallway. There were a few dirty dishes in the sink and crumbs on the countertop. A bookcase against the wall had books haphazardly placed on the shelves. A half-filled glass of water sat on a table next to one of the couches. Accent pillows were tossed casually on the furniture.

Then there were the pictures. Kenna wanted to examine all of them, as they were strewn everywhere throughout the living area. He'd even enlarged and framed the picture of himself and his team that he'd shown her on the base, which hung on a wall near the television.

The place was fancy, yes. And expensive. But it looked lived in. Comfortable. Which made Kenna feel much more relaxed.

While she was looking around, Marshall had walked over to a wall to her left. He pulled the curtains back—and Kenna could only stare in disbelief at the view he'd exposed. She walked as if in a trance toward the balcony. She knew Marshall was grinning like a boy with his hand in a cookie jar, but she ignored him. He opened the door for her, and she walked outside.

There was a breeze blowing in from the ocean and it made her hair ripple as she gripped the railing. There were a few lounge chairs on the balcony, along with a table and six chairs. The space was huge, but Kenna turned her attention back to the ocean in front of her.

She felt Marshall come up behind her. He put his hands on the railing on either side of hers and leaned in close.

Kenna took a minute or so to study the view. She could see the beach where they'd spent the day, the umbrellas looking tiny from this vantage point. There were sailboats out on the water, and she could even see a large cargo ship in the distance. It was absolutely beautiful, and Kenna could suddenly understand the appeal of an ocean view. If she had a view like this at her place, she'd spend all her time on her balcony enjoying it.

"It's amazing," she said in awe.

"This is the main reason why I stopped fighting my parents

about this place. It's pretentious and over the top, and way too fucking expensive. But this is my favorite place to hang out with my friends, or after a hard mission. You should see it when a storm moves in. It's like you're in the middle of it."

"I bet."

"You want to see the rest of the condo?" he asked.

Kenna shook her head. "Nope. I'm staying right here. I think I'm moving in and I'll sleep and eat and do everything out on the balcony."

She felt more than heard him chuckle against her back. "It might be hard to waitress from here."

"Don't care."

"And you haven't seen my bedroom yet," he added suggestively.

Kenna smiled, then turned in his arms. "True. Tell me you have a king-size bed."

"I have a king-size bed."

"And that the master bathroom is to die for."

"It is," he agreed. "Rain shower, huge claw-foot tub, double sinks, heated tiles on the floor, and the toilet is in a separate little room with a door."

Kenna burst out laughing at that. "And that's a plus?" she asked.

"Of course. I like my privacy when I'm doing my business," he said with a straight face.

"Hmmm. I think maybe I would like to see your room then. But if it doesn't compare to this balcony, I'm coming right back out here."

"I think you'll be pleased," Marshall said mysteriously. "Come on." He took her hand in his and led her back into the living area of the apartment.

Kenna let him tow her down a small hallway toward a door at the end. She caught a glimpse of a guest bathroom on her way that was bigger than her master bathroom back at her apartment.

Marshall didn't hesitate to throw open the door at the end of the hall, gesturing for her to enter.

Kenna was about to make a joke, something about a spider and a fly, but her words stuck in her throat when she walked into the room.

The entire wall next to the bed was windows. Floor to ceiling. It was almost like being out on the balcony, but without the breeze. "Holy crap," she whispered.

"Told you you'd like it," Marshall said smugly.

Kenna looked up at him. "It's incredible! But doesn't the light bother you when you're trying to sleep?"

In response, Marshall walked over to a panel on the wall next to the windows and pushed a button. The windows went from clear to black within seconds.

"*What*? How is that possible?"

Marshall shrugged. "No clue. They've got some sort of mechanism in the glass." He pushed another button and the windows changed once more to a light gray, letting in some light, but still muted. He then pushed one last button, and the glass cleared again, letting in the afternoon sunlight.

"Wow," she said after a long pause.

"You're speechless," Marshall joked. "I'm impressed."

"No, *I'm* impressed," Kenna told him.

"Wait until you see the bathroom."

She followed him to another door and had to admit that it was pretty damn spectacular. Again, it was fancy as hell, but his toiletries were spread over the counter, along with a hand towel sitting next to one of the sinks, instead of hanging on the rack nearby. Another towel barely clinging to a rack on the wall made the space seem less hoity-toity.

She couldn't help but imagine her and Marshall inside the

huge shower stall. There was a small bench inside that she knew they could put to good use.

"I see your mind working," Marshall said.

Kenna grinned. "Yup," she said without embarrassment.

"So, you like?"

"I like," Kenna told him. "And if I had the money, I'd totally want to live here."

Marshall nodded, then grabbed her hand and started pulling her out of the room.

"Where's the fire?" Kenna asked on a laugh.

"Just think it's a good idea we get out of my bedroom," Marshall said.

Kenna laughed harder. Being with him was...easy. Fun. She genuinely enjoyed the man's company. "So, what are we going to do to pass the time until dinner?" she asked. She wasn't trying to make an innuendo, but when Marshall turned and raised a brow at her, she laughed again. "I mean, other than the obvious."

"You want a tour of the property?" he asked tentatively.

"Yes." Kenna wanted to know everything about this man. And that included seeing where he lived.

An hour and a half later, after seeing the pools, the workout room, the sauna, the spa, the restaurant, the lounges, and being introduced to just about every single person they passed, they were back up in his condo, sitting on the balcony. She was in a lounge chair, with Marshall in another. They were close enough that Kenna could reach out and touch him. It felt intimate and cozy. And she still couldn't get over how perfect his view was.

Kenna was nursing a glass of wine while Marshall had a glass of tea.

"I'm impressed that you know so many people here," she said.

Marshall shrugged. "I don't *know*-know them," he said. "I

don't know anything about their lives or their work, but we're all friendly when we see each other."

"I really *was* rude when I said that rich people stayed inside their apartments and didn't talk to each other," Kenna blurted, feeling the need to apologize again, having met a few of the residents.

"No, you're right. I'd guess you know everything there is to know about your own neighbors. The relationships are more superficial here. But if someone needed something, I'd happily help them out."

"I know you would," Kenna told him, reaching for his hand. He took it without hesitation and squeezed reassuringly.

They talked about nothing important for a while, but then the conversation turned to Carly and her ex. Marshall wanted to know how she was *really* doing.

"I think she's okay. She struggles with feeling safe still, I think. She's hardly going anywhere, basically to work and back."

"But she hasn't seen Shawn since he came to the restaurant?" Marshall asked.

"Not that I know of, but she could be keeping it to herself if she has," Kenna said honestly. "I just don't understand men like him."

"What do you mean?"

"I mean, if you made it clear that we were over, that you didn't want to see me anymore, I wouldn't get all weird and psycho and insist that you weren't allowed to break up with me. And I know that some women get that way too, but from what the statistics show, I don't think it's as prevalent as guys. Can you explain it to me?"

"No."

Marshall's answer was short and to the point.

Kenna sighed. "I also don't understand why some

men get off on scaring and raping women. I mean, I get that it's a power thing, but where does that *come* from? Why do they think it's okay to violate someone like that? Why does it give them pleasure? And I'm not talking about the serial killers who most likely have messed-up brains. I'm talking about the men who have friends, and secure jobs, and good families...the ones who you'd never guess could act that way. Who seem to harass and overpower women just because they can. I don't get it."

Marshall's thumb brushed back and forth over the back of her hand, making Kenna feel calmer. "I don't know," he said. "I can't imagine what goes through someone's head when they decide to do something like that. And I'm like you, if a woman says she wants to break up, I might not be happy about it, but I'd respect it. Why would I want to be with someone who doesn't want to be with *me*?"

"Exactly!" Kenna exclaimed. "The whole, 'if I can't have you, no one can,' makes no sense to me. People aren't possessions. And the angst and hatred that would have to be present in that relationship would be unbearable. I have such a hard time understanding why Shawn is acting the way he is toward Carly. Why isn't he moving on? Finding a woman who *does* want to be with him?"

"I wish I had an answer for you. All I can do is reassure you that there are more of us in the world who respect women and would never act like that asshat."

"I know," Kenna said with a sigh. "I just hate that Carly is dealing with it. I just want him to *go*. To move on."

"Me too," Marshall said.

They were quiet for a long while, each lost in their own thoughts. It was one more reason Kenna liked being around Marshall. They didn't have to talk constantly. They could simply exist in the same place at the same time.

"Want to go to the store with me?" Marshall said after a while.

Kenna looked over at him. "For what?"

"Stuff to make dinner."

She laughed. "You planned to make me dinner and you don't have the ingredients?" she asked.

Marshall shrugged. "I had planned on shopping this morning before picking you up, but those plans changed last night when I asked if I could barge in at dawn, wanting to make sure you were all right."

She loved that. "Sure."

"Great. Let's go."

Kenna chuckled. "You don't just sit and enjoy the world going by very often, do you?"

"No. Now get up, lazy bones. I'm trying to prevent you from actually making a nest in the corner of my balcony and not ever leaving."

Kenna laughed and let Marshall help her up.

"What are you making me?" she asked as they headed back inside and toward the front door.

"Well, I told you that I grill a mean steak, but I was thinking about going in a different direction, if it's okay."

"Depends on what you want to change it to," Kenna told him honestly.

"You like seafood, right?" he asked.

"Of course. We had sushi, remember."

"I remember, but sushi is different from seafood in general. Anyway, I thought maybe about doing sriracha-glazed seared scallops. With a side of roasted garlic broccoli, meatless taco cups, and a skillet brownie sundae for dessert."

Kenna knew her mouth was hanging open, but she couldn't help it. "Seriously?"

"Yup."

"I was expecting hamburgers or spaghetti or something."

"I wanted to spoil you for our first dinner date," Marshall said simply.

"Well, consider me spoiled, even though we haven't been shopping yet," Kenna told him. "I do have one question."

"Shoot."

"What's a taco cup?"

Marshall grinned. "You take those little nacho chips that are in the shape of a bowl, and fill it with pico, sour cream, cheese, black beans, and a jalapeno slice if you want. Then you shove the entire thing in your mouth and enjoy."

Kenna could picture Marshall doing just that. "Sounds delicious."

"It is. Come on, I'm getting hungry just thinking about it. The only problem is that the dinner I have planned takes some prep work."

"I'd love to cook with you," Kenna told him.

At the door, Marshall leaned down and kissed her. It was a swift kiss, a mere brushing of their lips together.

Kenna pouted. "That's all I get?"

"For now, yes. If I take your mouth the way I want, we'll end up in my bed, and I won't let you up for hours. And if I do that, I can't feed you. So shopping, then cooking, then eating. *Then* I'll take you long and hard and every way you can imagine."

Kenna grinned. "Can we leave the windows clear?" she asked.

Marshall shook his head and opened the door. "I think I'm insulted that the windows are what you're thinking about."

"Oh, I'm thinking about you, have no doubt. I can't wait to see what you've been keeping to yourself in your pants," she told him.

"You want my cock, Kenna?" he growled.

"Yes," she answered simply.

"Then you'll get it. Later."

She mock pouted, and Marshall laughed. She would never get sick of hearing that sound.

He closed the door behind them and once more took her hand in his. Smiling, Kenna had a feeling she could get used to being with this man on a much more substantial basis. Doing everyday things like shopping and cooking...and ending each night in his arms.

CHAPTER FOURTEEN

Dinner was amazing. Aleck couldn't remember a time when he'd been as content as he was now. Kenna had helped him cook, and they'd both had a hard time keeping their hands off each other in the process.

He'd purposely brush up against her ass, and she'd retaliate by "accidentally" touching his cock as she passed him in the large kitchen. She was carefree, fun, sexy...and instead of his mind turning to some of the horrifying things he'd done and seen as a SEAL, as it often did in the evenings when he was alone, he was fixed in the here and now with Kenna.

He hadn't planned on adding Kenna to his approved visitor list so soon, but while introducing her to Robert, it just seemed like the right thing to do. Some people would think he was crazy to give a woman he'd just met access to his condo, but he trusted her instinctually. He had no doubt Kenna would never betray him. They had clicked in a way he'd never experienced before, on a level that surpassed even his best relationships.

He had no idea what the future held for them, but for now, he could admit that he was head over heels for this woman and wanted to be around her as much as possible. Spending the day with her had been wonderful so far. And watching her haggle over the price of a trinket at the swap meet was enlightening. She was stubborn and liked to win.

He was too—no wonder they got along so well—though he didn't like to haggle over prices. Maybe it was because he didn't have to worry about money, but he'd almost rather pay too much for something than try to save a buck or two. And paying extra helped the vendor as well.

Kenna had said she wanted to eat out on his balcony, which wasn't a surprise. They'd just finished their meal and were watching the sun slowly set, enjoying the evening breeze, when Aleck heard his phone ring from the other room.

"Shit," he muttered.

"What? How do you know who's calling?" Kenna asked.

"I don't. But I'm not expecting anyone to call."

"That doesn't mean it's something bad," she reasoned as Aleck got up and headed inside to get his phone.

But Aleck suspected otherwise. His teammates all knew he was spending the day with Kenna, so they wouldn't interrupt him. It could be either one of his parents, but he didn't think so. He had a bad feeling the call was about work.

Gritting his teeth, he answered. "Hello?"

"This is Commander Huttner. You're being called in for a mission."

Generally, Aleck liked his commander. Dylan Huttner was fair and genuinely cared for the SEALs he managed. But his timing was complete shit. "Can you give me any details?" Aleck asked.

"Just that the situation we've been looking at for the last two weeks has gone to shit and we need to move, and move fast," Huttner said.

Which meant Aleck and his team were headed to Iran.

Fuck. "Understood. What time do I need to report?" he asked.

"Immediately."

Aleck was too well trained to react in surprise, but if they were being called in without any prior warning, the situation had to be extremely urgent. "Yes, sir."

"See you soon. You'll get details when you get here."

Huttner hung up without another word and Aleck put his phone down. Damn. His and Kenna's plans for the night had just changed...for the worse. And he had to figure out how to not only let her down, but tell her he was headed out on a mission for which he couldn't give her any details.

"Everything okay?" she asked tentatively from the doorway to his balcony.

Taking a deep breath, Aleck turned toward her. "No," he said. "I have to go."

"Go?" she asked.

Shit, he was fucking this up. He couldn't just leave. He needed to reassure her. Explain. Something. He strode across the room and pulled Kenna close. He put his hands on either side of her neck and held her gently as he said, "The team's been called in. We're heading out on a mission."

"Now?" Kenna asked in disbelief as she grabbed hold of his wrists.

"Unfortunately, yeah."

"Well...shit. What can I do to help you?"

That so wasn't the reaction Aleck had expected. "You aren't upset?"

"Of course I'm upset," Kenna said. "But being pissed, or sad, or hysterical isn't going to help you or change the situation. I'm disappointed that I don't get to jump your bones tonight, but you're going to come home safe and sound, then we'll have something to *really* celebrate." Her voice wobbled a bit at the end, but she took a deep breath and got herself under control.

"Fuck, you're amazing."

"I'm not," she countered. "I'm scared to death on your behalf, but this is what you do. What you love."

The first thing that sprang to his mind was that he loved *her*, but he kept that to himself. Because that was crazy...wasn't it?

"So...what do you need me to do to help you?" she repeated.

Taking another deep breath, Aleck forced himself to start getting into SEAL mode. "Can you put the dishes away while I pack?"

"Of course."

"Just throw everything in the dishwasher. Once they wash, they'll be fine in there until I get back. And please take the leftovers with you."

"Okay, no problem."

"I can run you back to your place before heading to the base," Aleck said.

"No way. That's completely out of your way. I can take a taxi or an Uber."

Aleck frowned. "It's late."

"Not *that* late," Kenna said.

"Would you consider staying here for the night and heading to your apartment in the morning?" Aleck asked tentatively. He dropped his hands to her waist and held her in a loose embrace.

She was quiet for a moment before asking, "You wouldn't mind me being here without you?"

"No, of course not. In fact, come over whenever you want. Maybe on days you don't have to work the next day. You're on my list of approved visitors so it won't be an issue. You can get in because I programmed your palm print into the reader.

And," he added as he thought of something, "if you want to invite Lexie and Elodie over and have a girls' night, feel free. They'll probably be down because Midas and Mustang are gone too."

"Wow, um, okay. Maybe."

He smiled at her.

"But I'm sure I'll be fine going home tonight."

"Stay," he cajoled. "I might not be able to join you in my bed, but I love the thought of *you* being there."

"Well, shit. How can I say no to that?" she teased.

"You can't."

"Okay. I'll stay."

"Good. I'll get the bags with the stuff you picked up this morning at the swap meet from the car, and give them to Robert or whoever is on duty to store for you until tomorrow. I'll also arrange for a taxi for you."

"You don't have to do that."

"Yes, I do." They stared at each other for a moment before Aleck pulled her closer. "Come 'ere," he said gently.

Kenna snuggled into his embrace. They both sighed.

Aleck hated that this was how their night was ending. Not because he wouldn't get the chance to go to bed with her, but because he could tell she was now stressed and sad.

"I'll be back before you know it."

"I know. Marshall?"

"Yeah?"

"I know your job is dangerous, and your team is one of the best, but..." Her voice trailed off.

She didn't need to continue. Aleck was pretty sure he knew what she was going to say. "We're good at what we do. We're coming back," he told her. He really shouldn't promise anything of the sort, but there was no way he could just stand there and *not* reassure her.

Kenna nodded against him. He felt her take a deep breath

before she pulled back. Tears shone in her eyes, but she blinked them away. "Right. So...you need to get packed so you can go kick some ass."

Fuck, this woman killed him. "I'm gonna miss you. I think we've talked and texted every day since you jumped on my head."

"I didn't jump on your head," she protested automatically, as she always did. "And yeah, I think we have. I'll miss you too. But you need to go and do your thing."

Aleck nodded.

Kenna gave him a little push. "Go. I'll clean up our dinner stuff."

Reluctantly, knowing he really did need to get moving, Aleck headed for his bedroom. By the time he'd packed, Kenna had filled the dishwasher and put away the leftovers. She was standing on his balcony looking out at the ocean when he returned to the living area with his duffle bag and wearing his camouflage uniform.

She obviously heard him and turned. She gave him a wobbly smile and walked toward him. "I don't know how much this place costs, but that balcony makes it worth every penny."

Aleck knew she wasn't fishing to find out how much the condo was worth. She was making small talk to try to make his leaving easier. He met her halfway across the room and cradled her nape in his hand, his other arm sliding around her back. It felt natural now to hold her like this. "I'm coming back," he said gruffly. "There's no way I'm fucking dying before I taste your pussy. Before I get inside you."

She choked out a laugh. "Okay. Good. Because I haven't gotten to suck you off either," she returned.

Aleck lowered his mouth and kissed her long, hard, and deep. He was only torturing them both, but he couldn't seem to stop. He'd always assumed that deployments were harder on the ones left behind. Mustang and Midas always talked about how difficult they were for their women. But he hadn't realized how tough it would be for him to *leave* her behind.

When he finally pulled back, they were both breathing hard. Kenna's fingers were digging into his chest and as he stared into her eyes, a tear finally broke free and fell down her cheek. She immediately used her shoulder to wipe it away.

"I'm fine," she said almost defiantly.

"I know you are," Aleck said gently, then kissed her forehead. "Stay here," he said. "You don't need to walk me down."

She shook her head. "No, I want to—"

"It's hard enough for me to leave you," Aleck interrupted. "I'd like my last sight of you for a while to be here. In my space."

Kenna took a deep breath. "Okay," she said, giving in immediately.

He stared at her for a long moment before swallowing hard and backing away. He needed to just leave already. Staying here looking at her longingly wouldn't make his departure any easier. "Like a bandage," he muttered.

"Get it over with fast," Kenna agreed, on the same wavelength as him, as usual.

Aleck backed away, not taking his gaze from hers until he almost tripped over his duffle bag.

Kenna giggled, and Aleck knew the sound would stay with him the entire time he was gone. He smiled and winked at her, picked up his bag, then backed toward the door. He opened it and gave Kenna a chin lift, then turned, exited his condo, and shut the door behind him.

Taking a deep breath, he forced himself to walk down the hall toward the elevator. This sucked.

* * *

This sucks, Kenna thought to herself as she stood in the middle of Marshall's empty condo. She wanted to run after him and tell him not to go. But he had to. It was what he did. Who he was. She'd so wanted to ask where he was going and if it would be dangerous, but of course it would be. He was a SEAL, for God's sake.

Sighing, she headed into the bedroom and got ready for bed. It was early, and she'd planned on doing something much more exciting tonight, but perhaps it was for the best. She and Marshall had been moving really fast. Maybe some time away from each other would be a good thing.

She headed over to the panel on the wall to black out the windows, then hesitated. Why should she? The windows faced the ocean, and the sun rose on the other side of the island, so she wouldn't be blinded by it in the morning. In fact...

She pushed a button that opened one of the windows a couple of inches, letting in the breeze. The opening was a portion of the window near the ceiling, so no one could accidentally fall out. She couldn't quite hear the ocean, but the fresh air felt great.

She backed away from the wall of windows and fell onto Marshall's bed. Immediately she was surrounded by his scent. She had no idea how to describe it, but knew she'd never forget it. She pulled one of his pillows into her arms and buried her face against the softness, inhaling deeply.

Then she cried.

Cried because she was disappointed that Marshall wasn't fucking her brains out right this second.

Cried because she was scared to death for him.

Cried because she already missed him and he wasn't even off the island yet.

It had been a long time since she'd bawled that hard, but

by the time she got herself under control, she felt a little better.

Marshall *would* be back; she refused to believe otherwise. In the meantime, she had friends and her job to keep her busy.

She fell asleep in Marshall's big bed and dreamed about him all night.

Kenna woke up feeling slightly sad, but not quite as scared as she'd been the night before. She took a shower in Marshall's amazing bathroom and decided that even though it might feel weird, she was totally going to hang out here whenever she could while Marshall was gone. The heated tiles under her bare feet and the warm towel from the heated rack were decadent luxuries, and she had a feeling her own shower would feel totally inadequate now.

But more importantly, being in his space, surrounded by his things, made her feel as if he was still with her.

She rummaged in the fridge for some breakfast and ate out on the balcony, enjoying the view once more. It was around eleven o'clock before Kenna decided she had to get going. She had to work in a few hours and needed to stop at the store on her way home for her weekly groceries.

She packed her things and found a reusable grocery bag she could use to carry the leftovers from last night. Putting the containers in the bag made her relive yesterday all over again, how great it had been...before he'd left, of course. Kenna loved cooking with Marshall. And the fact that he'd wanted to go out of his way to make something special for her put a smile on her face.

She made sure the windows were all closed, the bed was made, her towel was hung up, and the balcony doors were closed and locked, then she picked up her bags and made her way to the door. She looked back before leaving and sighed. She'd been a bitch about the people who lived at Coral

Springs, and had judged them unfairly. It was clear it wasn't cheap to live here, but she had to admit, Marshall's condo had totally spoiled her. She was officially a fan.

Taking a deep breath, she closed the door and heard it latch behind her. Just to test it out, she put her hand on the reader next to the door. It immediately opened. Kenna smiled and pulled the door shut once more.

She was still smiling as she headed down the elevator and into the lobby. She walked toward Robert, who was sitting at the security desk once more. She assumed he hadn't been there all night.

"Good morning," she said cheerily.

"Ms. Madigan, good morning," he returned as he reached for an electronic device on top of the desk and pushed some buttons.

Kenna had no idea what it was, but supposed it didn't really matter. "I guess you work days?" she asked.

"Right now, yes. I heard Mr. Smart headed out last night for a while," Robert said.

Kenna wrinkled her nose and nodded.

"On behalf of myself and the entire staff here at Coral Springs, we appreciate his service to our country, and if there's anything you need, anything at all, just say the word and we'll do our best to accommodate you."

Kenna blinked in surprise. "Um...thanks. I'm not staying here while Marshall's gone. But I might come by a time or two. If that's okay."

"Of course," Robert told her with a smile.

"Cool. Um, can I get you to call me a taxi?"

"Already done. Mr. Smart requested one for you last night. He wasn't sure when you'd be ready to go, but I've already called one for you."

"Oh, wow, thanks," Kenna said, realizing just how valuable Robert and the other staff members could be. She didn't mind waiting around or being inconvenienced every now and then, but she could certainly get used to being spoiled by the staff at Coral Springs. Her irritation over learning Marshall had money now caused a flicker of guilt, since she was reaping the benefits.

"Also, Alfonso will be right out with your other things."

"Oh, that's right. I forgot," Kenna said, figuring maybe that's what Robert had been doing on the electronic pad, sending a message to his coworker to bring the stuff she'd gotten at the swap meet yesterday from wherever they'd been stored.

"Understandable. You had other things on your mind," Robert said.

Kenna bit her lip, then blurted, "I feel like I should apologize to you."

Robert looked confused.

"I just...before I knew Marshall actually lived here, and in the penthouse no less, I judged the residents pretty harshly. In my mind, they were stuck-up snobs who sat around in their expensive condos and counted their money."

Robert chuckled.

Kenna continued. "But now that I've spent a little bit of time here, and met some of the residents and employees, I realize how unfair I was. So...I'm sorry."

"You have nothing to apologize for," Robert told her. "When I first contemplated applying to work here, I thought the same thing. But in the last year or so that I've been here, I've found the residents are just like everyone else. Some are rude and demanding, some are generous and friendly to everyone they meet. Money doesn't seem to make much of a difference, at least in my experience."

"Mine too," Kenna agreed. "And I shouldn't judge people based on someone's bank account. I work at Duke's in Waikiki, and I've seen the good and bad in countless people, just like you have. And some of the nicest customers I've had were wealthy enough to leave me huge tips. So I should've known better."

"*That's* why you look so familiar," Robert said with a smile. "I go to Duke's all the time. I must've seen you there before. Their hula pie is my weakness."

"It's everyone's weakness," Kenna agreed, feeling better now that she'd apologized.

"Here's Alfonso with your things. Go ahead and leave your other bags, he'll get them."

"Good morning, ma'am," Alfonso said as he stopped next to her.

"Morning. You don't have to carry all my crap. I've got it."

"How about if I grab the bigger bag and you carry the smaller one?" Alfonso offered.

Here was another person who was being extremely nice. Kenna knew it was his job, and he probably got paid very well to be helpful and accommodating, but still. "Sounds good," she said, giving in.

"There's your taxi now," Robert said. "And it's already been paid for, so if the driver tries to get you to pay a second time, don't. Also, if that happens, let me know the next time you're here and we'll mark them off our list of taxi services to use."

"Wow, you'd do that?" she asked.

"Absolutely," Robert said, his voice stern. "Anyway, be safe, Ms. Madigan. Until we meet again."

"Thanks. And I don't know when I'll be back...do I need to call first?" she asked, not completely sure of the rules. Which reminded her she still needed to read the paper Robert had given her yesterday and sign it. It had slipped her mind until right this moment.

"No. You can come and go as you please."

"Oh, and if I want to bring some friends with me sometime, that's okay, right? It's a couple women Marshall knows, of course. I'm not planning on having a wild and crazy party," she said quickly, not wanting either man to think she was taking advantage of Marshall being gone.

"It's no problem. Are you talking about Ms. Winters and Ms. Greene?"

"Um...I don't know their last names. Elodie and Lexie."

"That's them. Mr. Smart said something about that last night. It's no problem. They just need to stop by the desk and check in before they head upstairs," Robert told her.

"Okay. Thanks." She had another thought. "And if two other friends come too...is that all right?"

"Of course. Again, they'll just need to stop here and check in before they'll be allowed onto the property."

"Great. Thanks!" Kenna wasn't sure if a girls' night would actually happen or not, but if it did, she figured Carly and Ashlyn might want to come too. She had a feeling if it was just her, Elodie, and Lexie, they might get too sad about the guys being gone, so adding in the other two would be a good balance, help them focus on something other than how worried they were for their men.

"See you later, Robert. Have a good day."

"You too, Ms. Madigan."

Kenna smiled at him and headed out of the lobby, with Alfonso holding the door for her. He opened the door to the backseat of the taxi and, once Kenna was seated, closed it and headed for the trunk to store her bags.

The ride to her apartment was uneventful, and Kenna was pleased when the taxi driver helped carry her things up to her place. As soon as her door closed behind her, Kenna's gaze went to the large beanbag in her living room, and she sighed. She had a hunch she'd see and hear things that reminded her of Marshall all the time while he was gone.

Taking a deep breath, she carried her overnight bag into

her room to unpack. With that done, she put the leftovers in her fridge and put away the things she'd picked up at the swap meet. Finally, she sat down to make a list for the grocery store.

It felt weird to be going about her own business while Marshall was somewhere doing his best to keep the world safe. But life went on, no matter what was happening in her personal life. Or anyone's, for that matter. Determined to not wallow in fear or worry—she knew Marshall would hate that —Kenna concentrated on her list once more.

* * *

Work that night seemed to go by much more slowly than in the past. Probably because Kenna didn't have any texts from Marshall to look forward to, and she knew when she got home, she wouldn't be talking to him either.

When Alani asked why Kenna seemed so down, she realized that she wasn't doing a very good job of hiding her worry for Marshall. Carly surprised her when she brought up the deployment, and Kenna could only assume she'd heard about it from Jag. She wanted to tease her about being "just" friends with Marshall's teammate, but she wasn't in a teasing mood.

The two women talked about where the men might be for a while, but because neither kept up with international news, they had no idea where the hot spots were at the moment. And, ultimately, it didn't matter where they were, just that they came home safe and sound.

By the end of the night, after dealing with a customer who got so drunk he puked all over himself, the table, and the chair he was sitting in, being stiffed a tip by another table, and having to deal with what seemed like more than the normal amount of screaming and misbehaving children, Kenna was more than ready to head home.

Paulo walked her and Carly to the parking garage they always used, and after giving them both a hug, Kenna headed for her car. She unlocked her Malibu and got in, locking the doors behind her and putting her purse on the passenger seat. She put the key in the ignition and started to turn the car on—when something on her windshield caught her attention.

A piece of paper was stuck under her wiper blade.

Looking around carefully, Kenna didn't see anyone lurking, so she got out and grabbed the note. She sat back in her car and locked the doors again, being extra cautious. She unfolded the note—and stared in confusion, then anger, then a little bit of fear at the words written there.

You should've minded your own business.

That's all it said. It wasn't signed, and there was no clue as to who had left it on her car. But Kenna had a feeling she knew. The man from Saturday night...the one she'd called the cops on. Men like him wouldn't take kindly to anyone putting a nose in their business, but especially not a woman.

Had he followed her to the parking garage from work the other night? She'd hoped the police would keep him at the station until he sobered up, at least, but maybe that didn't happen since his wife didn't press charges. Maybe he came back to Duke's and watched her leave...

She'd guessed he and his family were tourists, but plenty of locals frequented Duke's. If they lived here, he had plenty of time to come up with some way to get back at her.

Shit. Time to go. She was freaking herself out and needed to get the hell out of the dark parking garage. She didn't want to be like one of those "too stupid to live" heroines in a cheesy horror movie who did all the wrong things and put herself smack dab in the middle of the bad guy's path.

Kenna knew she should probably take the note to the police, but she just wanted to get home where she felt safe.

No, what she *really* wanted was to talk to Marshall, but that wasn't possible. And she'd touched the note, so now her fingerprints would be all over it. She had no idea if the parking garage she used had cameras, but while she thought the note sounded threatening, technically it wasn't...at least that's what she assumed whoever left it—and the police —might say.

Hating that she felt so vulnerable and off-kilter, and knowing it was largely exacerbated because Marshall was gone, Kenna took a deep breath. She'd never relied on a man for anything before, but despite that, in the short time she'd known Marshall, he'd become her rock.

As she'd thought last night, this deployment was probably good for her, proving that she needed to continue to be the strong and independent woman she'd always been. But Kenna still missed Marshall.

She drove home with one eye on the road and another on the cars in her rearview. Of course, since she wasn't a super-spy, she had no idea what to look for or how to know if someone was following her. Unless they were sitting on her bumper, she wouldn't know if one of the sets of headlights belonged to the man who'd left the note on her car.

When she arrived home without incident, and once she was in her apartment safe and sound, Kenna let out a wobbly, relieved breath. She was being ridiculous. She'd taken self-defense courses; if that asshole decided to confront her in person—instead of being a coward and leaving her notes like they were in grade school—she'd kick his ass, then run like hell.

Deciding to sleep in her beanbag tonight didn't mean she

SUSAN STOKER

was a scaredy-cat. Nope. It was just comfortable. And if she concentrated really hard, she could still smell Marshall from when he snuggled with her while she napped.

Kenna slept like shit that night. She had nightmares of a man with no face breaking into her apartment and shooting her. Then Marshall showed up while she was trying to staunch the flow of blood, and he apologized for not being able to help her, as both his arms had been blown off on his mission.

Needless to say, Kenna was more than happy to get up the next morning.

"Today's a new day," she said out loud, scolding herself. "Get your shit together, Kenna. One step in front of the other and one day at a time. Marshall will be back soon, and if that guy from the other night does decide to get stupid, you'll deal with it."

Feeling better after the small pep talk, Kenna headed into her room. She needed to get out and go for a long run. Some people would say that was stupid after getting the note last night, but she hadn't worked out for a while and needed the release of endorphins running provided.

Right before she headed out the door, Kenna turned back around and grabbed the pepper spray her parents had badgered her to buy for her safety. She might be confident and independent, but she wasn't stupid.

"Be safe, wherever you are," she whispered, hoping somehow, someway, Marshall would know she was thinking and worrying about him. Then she took a deep breath...and got on with her life.

CHAPTER FIFTEEN

"Are you sure we're allowed to be in here?" Carly asked Kenna as they entered the lobby of the Coral Springs condo complex.

She chuckled. "I'm sure." But Kenna couldn't blame Carly for being uneasy. She'd felt the same way when she'd come back the first time by herself. Robert had been working, and he'd recognized and welcomed her, making her feel much better about being there.

She'd stayed at Marshall's condo several times in the last month. It made her feel closer to him. She hadn't expected him to be gone so long. For some reason, she thought the SEAL team would dash into whatever country they were deployed to, take out their target or rescue whoever they were there to rescue or find the information they were going to find, whatever their mission was, and be back within a week.

When she'd finally given in and sent Elodie a text to ask if it was normal for them to be gone so long, she hadn't been comforted when the other woman replied they'd never been gone this long before. At least, not since she and Mustang had gotten together.

So Kenna decided the girls' night Marshall had suggested was long overdue. She should've done this a couple weeks ago, but was reluctant since the condo didn't belong to her. But she'd finally gotten over that, and had asked Elodie and Lexie if they wanted to spend a night at Marshall's place with her. And when she'd asked Lexie if she thought Ashlyn might want to come, Lexie had said she'd be thrilled.

It seemed a little junior high-ish to arrange a sleepover, but Kenna was almost giddy with excitement about it nonetheless. She'd gone a little overboard in buying drinks and snacks, but didn't feel a bit embarrassed. She wanted everyone to be comfortable and happy.

Kenna had just met Carly outside and was escorting her in.

"Good afternoon, ladies," Robert said with a smile.

"Hi, Robert. This is my friend, Carly Stewart. She's gonna be spending the night with me in Marshall's condo."

"Got a fun night planned?" Robert asked with a twinkle in his eye. Kenna estimated him to be in his late forties to mid-fifties. He was always smiling, so friendly and helpful. The more she got to know him, the more she liked him.

"Yup."

"Well, if you need anything, you've got my number," he told Kenna. "If you want to use some equipment on the beach, or reserve one of the barbeque grills on the plaza, just let me know."

"I will. But I think we're gonna stay in tonight," Kenna said.

"We've got a whole room of DVDs, if you prefer. No one really rents them out anymore, now that there are so many subscription services on TV, but if you get bored and want a specific movie, I'm sure we probably have it and it can be brought up."

"Thanks," Kenna told him.

They got Carly signed in and headed up to Marshall's penthouse. When Kenna put her palm on the panel next to the door, Carly couldn't keep quiet anymore.

"Wow! This place is super fancy!" Carly exclaimed with wide eyes as the door automatically unlocked.

Kenna grinned. "Believe it or not, you get used to it."

"So, you're no longer a bons?" Carly asked.

Kenna burst out laughing. "Apparently not. I've found there are definitely perks to having money." She gestured for Carly to enter the condo first, knowing exactly what her reaction was going to be when she walked in.

And she wasn't disappointed. Carly gasped and made a beeline for the balcony.

Laughing, Kenna followed and they both went outside.

"Holy shit, girl," Carly said. "This is...I don't know what this is. It's amazing. Stupendous. Awesome. Incredible. And every other superlative adjective you can think of."

"Right?" Kenna asked. "I told Marshall I was moving out here the first time I saw it. That I was going to put a mattress in the corner and live here."

Carly turned to her friend. "I'm happy for you."

"Because my boyfriend has money?" Kenna asked.

"No. Well, yes, that doesn't hurt. But more because you're so happy. Content in a way I didn't really notice before you met Marshall. And before you get all weird on me, I'm not saying that you need a rich guy to be satisfied. You guys just fit. You're perfect together."

"Thanks. I miss him so much, but I'm also damn proud of him at the same time. And yes, I feel settled."

They smiled at each other for a moment before Kenna

headed back inside. "Come on, help me get everything organized before the others get here."

An hour later, Kenna headed back down to the lobby to meet Elodie, Lexie, and Ashlyn. After getting them checked in with Robert, they all headed back up to the penthouse.

The second they entered, Elodie sighed and said, "I'll never get over how much I love the view from up here."

"Me either," Lexie chimed in.

"Wow!" Ashlyn exclaimed as she walked toward the balcony as if in a trance.

"And another one bites the dust," Kenna quipped.

Everyone laughed.

"I thought you, Elodie, and Lexie could stay in the guest room together. Marshall's got a king-size bed in there, so you'll have plenty of room. Carly, do you want to stay with me in the master?" Kenna asked.

"Um, not only no, but *hell* no," her friend retorted.

"What? Why not?"

"Because that's where you and Aleck do the nasty," Carly explained, wrinkling her nose.

Kenna nearly choked, while everyone else burst out laughing. "For your information, Marshall and I haven't 'done the nasty,' as you called it. Not that there would be anything nasty about making love with that man."

"Holy shit, you haven't?" Carly asked. "I just assumed you had."

"Yeah, well, we were planning on it the day he left. I decided I was enjoying the anticipation and foreplay too much to jump his bones the second we got back from the swap meet. So we went to the store, made dinner, and were working our way up to what I know would've been the most amazing night of my life...but then his phone rang."

"Shit," Lexie mumbled.

"Yup," Kenna agreed with a sigh.

"Well, that sucks, but I'm still not sleeping in his bed with you," Carly said.

"And I'm not either," Ashlyn piped in. "I mean, I like you and all, but now that Carly's brought it up, I don't want to think of a naked Aleck lying in the same bed I'm in."

Kenna wanted to tell the other woman not to think of a naked Aleck *any* time, but decided that might be a bit too cantankerous. "Fine, you guys can each take one of the couches out here. Marshall has a ton of sheets and blankets, so it should be comfortable enough." She didn't bring up the fact that it was likely Marshall had probably sat on *all* the furniture in his condo butt-ass naked at some point. He was a guy, after all, and in her experience, guys were much less self-conscious about walking around without any clothes on. Especially if they lived alone.

"That'll work," Carly said with a smile.

"We can leave the balcony doors open and get some fresh air too," Ashlyn said in excitement.

Yep, Kenna should have done this sooner. She liked seeing her friends so happy.

After Lexie and Elodie had put their bags in the guest room, and Carly and Ashlyn had stashed theirs against the wall out of the way, they all headed into the kitchen to grab drinks.

For the next few hours, they sat on the balcony, eating snacks and drinking the wine Kenna had bought. When they went inside to make dinner, Lexie ended up kicking Elodie out of the kitchen because she kept trying to make their simple meal of baked chicken and a salad too fancy. Luckily, she just laughed about it—but she didn't stop trying to take over from her spot at the table in the dining room either.

Dinner was filled with more laughter, and by the time they all wandered back out to the balcony, Kenna was tipsy, feeling relaxed and mellow.

It was after they'd oohed and ahhed over the sunset—which was even more brilliant and beautiful because of the number of clouds in the sky—when the elephant in the room was finally brought up.

"I miss Scott," Elodie said somewhat sadly.

"Me too. Well, not Mustang, but I miss Midas," Lexie agreed.

"Do you think they're okay?" Kenna whispered. She figured it was a given that she missed Marshall and there was no need to actually say it.

"Yes," Elodie said firmly. "They're so damn good at what they do. I've seen them in action firsthand."

"But didn't Mustang say that you saved his life? That if you weren't there, that pirate guy would've shot him?" Lexie asked.

"I did, but if I wasn't there, they probably would've cleared the engine room faster and would've found that guy, and he wouldn't have been able to sneak up on him," Elodie argued.

Kenna hadn't known Elodie had actually saved Mustang's life, and it was definitely a story she wanted to hear. Later.

"If something happened, wouldn't the Navy call you?" Ashlyn asked.

"Probably not me, as Midas and I aren't married, but they'd definitely call Elodie," Lexie explained.

"And I've gotten no calls," Elodie pointed out.

"Which means they're probably fine," Carly said.

"I hate that word, probably," Kenna muttered.

"Yeah," Elodie agreed.

"We have to think positive," Ashlyn announced. "The guys are good, they're doing their thing, and they'll be back to annoy us before we know it."

"So...Slate annoys you?" Kenna asked, preferring to tease Ashlyn and Carly about their non-relationships with Slate and Jag than think about any of the guys being hurt or killed.

"Duh. Yes," Ashlyn said.

Everyone chuckled.

"What are you all laughing about? He *is* annoying. And impatient. And bossy. Did you know he called me before he left and scolded me about driving food out to people who need and request it?" she asked. "He flat-out ordered me *not* to do it."

"What'd you say?" Lexie asked with a smile.

"I told him he wasn't the boss of me, stuck my tongue out at the phone—not that he could see it—and hung up," Ashlyn said.

Everyone laughed harder.

"And what'd he do?" Lexie asked.

Ashlyn couldn't hide her smile. "He called me right back and gave me a fifteen-minute lecture about the dangers of going to strangers' houses. It wasn't until I promised to add Lexie to my circle on the tracker app on my phone, and always carry mace, that he shut up."

"He likes you," Elodie said with a firm nod.

"Yup," Lexie agreed.

"I like him too...sometimes," Ashlyn said.

"No, he *likes* you," Elodie clarified.

"Whatever. I'm too busy to date anyone. I'm not sure I'd even want to date a military guy. Look at you three, all mopey and worried," Ashlyn said.

"And you aren't? Worried, I mean?" Kenna asked.

Ashlyn looked down at her wine glass and muttered, "Scared to fucking death."

Kenna reached over and squeezed her forearm in support. No one really needed to say anything, they knew exactly how she felt. Even though she and Slate weren't dating, they seemed to have a connection.

"What about you, Carly?" Elodie asked.

"What about me?" Carly returned.

"What's up with you and Jag? Scott tells me that you two text all the time."

"We're friends," Carly said firmly. "*Just* friends."

"Hmmm," Elodie mused.

"You should've seen him that night at Duke's, when Carly's ex showed up and was all pissed off," Lexie told Ashlyn. "I swear that asshole wasn't there two seconds before Jag had shuttled Carly away and out of his sight."

"He was being helpful," Carly insisted.

"You can protest all you want, but it's obvious you guys are more than friends," Kenna said.

Carly sighed. "I'm the worst judge of men. The *worst*. I thought Shawn was amazing when we met, and look how that turned out."

"So, what, you think if you don't actually date Jag that he won't turn out to be a jerk?" Lexie asked.

"Something like that," Carly said a little defensively.

"He won't," Elodie and Lexie said at the same time.

Everyone laughed at how they were on the same page.

"It's just that I hate having to constantly look behind me. To see if Shawn is following me," Carly said.

"Is he?" Kenna asked with concern.

"Not that I can tell. But I did see his son on the beach at Duke's the other day."

"Wait, wait, wait! Shawn has a *son*?" Kenna asked.

"I never mentioned that?" Carly asked.

"No, you certainly have not. How old is he?"

"Twenty-two."

"Wow, so almost your age," Kenna said.

"Yeah. And I think that's why he definitely did *not* like me dating his dad. I guess Shawn was married briefly when he was twenty or so. They had a son, his wife dumped him and left him with Luke, and Shawn raised him. I was impressed with that when I first met him. Until I realized they don't have the healthiest relationship."

"In what way?" Elodie asked.

"It's just...odd. Like they're best friends, rather than father and son, yet *really* close. Which I don't have a problem with, but Luke still lives with Shawn. And they do everything together. I can't really explain it, but it's just...weird."

"Should you report Luke?" Lexie asked.

Carly shrugged. "I don't have a protective order against *him*. And he didn't even look my way. He was just sitting by the pool."

"Which is odd in and of itself," Kenna said.

Carly shrugged. "Anyway, that's why I've given up men. I don't want to live the rest of my life thinking that one of my exes, or their children, are waiting for the right moment to leap out at me with a machete or something, since I'm clearly the worst judge of character. I'm done with dating."

"You aren't the worst judge of men," Ashlyn said. "I could give you a run for your money. I moved to Hawaii because of a guy I met in a bar. I thought he was awesome. I uprooted my entire life by coming here. Then I found out he was looney tunes. Trust me, you don't own the market on hooking up with crazy men."

Ashlyn and Carly shared wry, commiserating smiles.

Kenna took a deep breath and held up her wine glass. "A toast!" she said, probably a bit too loudly, but she didn't give a shit at the moment.

"A toast!" everyone else said immediately, holding up their glasses.

"To good friends. To our men—and yes, they're *all* our men, no matter what you two will admit to or not," she added, giving both Ashlyn and Carly the stink eye before continuing. "And may the bad guys hurry up and die or give up or whatever so our SEALs can come home."

"I'll toast to that!"

"Amen!"

"Hear, hear!"

"Drink up, bitches!"

Kenna almost spit out her drink at Ashlyn's words. She swallowed, then laughed along with everyone else.

After polishing off another three bottles of wine, and long after the sun had set, they all decided it was time for sleep. They wandered inside and headed off to their respective beds for the night.

Other than Marshall not being home, Kenna was happy as she prepared for bed. She had a group of friends she'd really bonded with, a job she enjoyed, and nothing had come out of the note that was left on her car. It had been over a month, and she hadn't heard hide nor hair of the asshole who'd smacked his son at Duke's. Like most bullies, he'd gotten his jollies over trying to scare her, then had slunk off into the night.

Yeah, things were definitely going well...except for missing her boyfriend.

Kenna lay in Marshall's bed, cuddling his pillow—which still held the slight scent of him—and stared out at the stars she could see through the windows. She had no idea what time it was where Marshall and the rest of his team were, or what they were doing, but she prayed they truly were all right. This being with a SEAL stuff wasn't for the faint of heart.

The women in the condo certainly made the deployment easier, and once more, Kenna kicked herself for not getting them all together before now. Next time, she'd be sure to suggest a sleepover sooner.

Next time...

Would there be a next time?

Yeah, Kenna was pretty sure there would be. Unless something drastic happened, she had a feeling she and Marshall would be together for the long haul.

"Please don't let anything drastic happen," she whispered, then closed her eyes. The room was spinning and she already had a headache, but Kenna wouldn't change anything about the night.

CHAPTER SIXTEEN

"Fuck," Aleck muttered as he and the rest of his teammates stumbled toward the plane in Germany that would take them back home. It had been six weeks since they'd left for Iran. Six long, hard, frustrating, and grueling weeks.

They'd been dropped miles away from where intel on the American they were sent in to rescue claimed he was located. They'd done a HALO parachute drop, high altitude, low opening, into the Iranian mountains. From there, they'd hiked through the wilderness for days, doing their best to stay off anyone's radar, which meant moving a lot slower than they might have otherwise. They'd finally located their target and had extracted him without any issues—but at the last minute, they'd been spotted.

They'd had to flee with the civilian they'd rescued back into the mountains. It had been another couple of weeks before they were able to make their way across the border to Iraq. Which didn't mean they were clear to head home. They'd had to lie low for a while, then there were video meetings with their superiors and intel they'd needed to pass on about Iran.

The entire team had been on guard for six weeks, their adrenaline on overload. By the time they'd finally been able to start preparations to head back to the States, everyone was more than ready to go home.

But they'd done what they'd set out to do, rescued a fellow American. Not that the man was very grateful. He'd bitched and moaned the entire time they were on the run, trying to get out of Iran so they wouldn't *all* be tossed into a prison cell with the key thrown away. The man had slowed their escape considerably—not that they hadn't expected that part—and hadn't muttered even one thank you before he was taken away by medical personnel to be checked out.

Aleck and the rest of the team didn't do what they did for thanks. They did it for their country, because it was the right thing to do...but a tiny bit of appreciation, or at the very least respect, would've been nice.

Now, they were simply too exhausted to be overly bitter that the man hadn't been grateful for their efforts.

They'd been flown to Germany, where they were switching planes before heading to Hawaii. No one had wanted to stay overnight, even though it would mean a comfortable bed and a shower. They just wanted to get home.

Aleck couldn't fucking wait to see Kenna. He'd worried about her more than he probably should've, considering the focus required for his job. He'd been gone much longer than he'd expected. Was she okay? Had she decided she couldn't handle dating a SEAL?

Feeling so unsure about a relationship wasn't something he'd really dealt with before, and Aleck didn't like it.

He collapsed into a seat and Mustang grabbed the one next to him. The plane wasn't crowded, which Aleck appreciated. Hell, the other military men and women headed home probably did too, considering his team had come straight from the field after not partaking in a proper shower for the last six weeks.

"You okay?" Mustang asked as he got settled and after the plane had taken off.

"Exhausted, dirty, impatient to get home and see Kenna, but yeah, otherwise good," Aleck said honestly, no hint of the smart aleck in evidence.

"Same," Mustang said with a nod. "Except I want to see my wife instead of your Kenna."

Your Kenna. Damn, that sounded good.

"Though, you don't look all that happy for a man who will get to see his girlfriend soon," Mustang observed.

"Can I ask you something?" Aleck asked.

"Of course. You can always ask me whatever you want."

"Things were pretty intense between me and Kenna when I left Hawaii. We went from one to a thousand really quickly. I mean, I was thrilled about it, and I think she was too. But we hadn't slept together yet—damn Huttner and his bad timing." Aleck paused to snort and shake his head. "But anyway, I haven't talked to her in six weeks. The first week was the hardest, because I'd gotten used to texting and calling her every day. Hearing her laugh and listening to her talk about work somehow made *my* day better." He paused for another moment.

But he didn't have to even ask Mustang what he was worried about. He knew.

"And now you're worried that because you've been gone so long, things won't be the same when you get home," Mustang finished.

"Exactly," Aleck said with a relieved sigh that his team leader had pinpointed exactly what was bothering him.

"You want me to be honest, or do you need me to tell you what you want to hear?" Mustang asked.

"Honest. Always."

"Right, so there's a chance that both of you got caught up in the heat of the moment. That your hormones took over. You might get back and things won't be the same. She'll seem distant. You both got used to not talking, and it might be hard to pick up where you left off. Hell, she could've met someone else in the last six weeks, for all you know. Someone who isn't in the military and won't leave without being able to say where they're going or how long they'll be gone."

"Damn," Aleck breathed.

"You told me to be honest," Mustang reminded him.

"I know. And I appreciate it. But that sucks."

Mustang chuckled. "It does. But I wasn't done. I was going to add that you might find you're even closer because of the time you spent apart. They do say that absence makes the heart grow fonder."

"Who the hell is 'they' anyway?" Aleck muttered.

Mustang laughed again. "Who the hell knows. Do you trust Kenna?"

That was easy. "Yes."

"And how do you feel about her, now that you've been gone?" Mustang asked.

"I miss her. She has a way of making me see the positive aspects of life. And she's made me really think about some of my beliefs. I grew up without having to worry about money in the least, and while I try really hard not to let that affect me now, it obviously still does. She calls me on my bullshit, in a nice way. I also like that we never run out of things to talk about."

"Well, you did only know her a few weeks before we left," Mustang said with a snort.

"You know what I mean," Aleck told his friend.

"I do. Because I feel the same about Elodie. I don't really have any great advice other than to see where things between you stand when you get home. Are things awkward? Is she thrilled to know you're back? Does she make excuses as to why she can't see you? Does she seem reticent? All the worrying in the world isn't going to help. You're just going to have to assess the situation when you see her again."

"Shit. I was hoping you had some awesome advice that would magically make me feel better," Aleck grumbled.

"Wish I did, man," Mustang said. "Here's the thing. I like Kenna. And the chemistry between the two of you is obviously electric. I have good vibes about her. I have a hunch the second you see each other, you'll know if her feelings have changed about you...and yours about her."

"I hope so. And for the record...thanks for taking out that tango before he could put a bullet in my brain. I don't think Kenna would've been too happy about that," Aleck said.

"Fuck you. You know you don't have to thank me for that," Mustang said. It had been right after they'd liberated their target and were slipping away from the prison where he'd been stashed. They'd been spotted, and Mustang had taken out a guard before he could get off a round—straight into Aleck's skull—and alert the rest of security.

Aleck knew he didn't have to thank his team leader, but now that he had a pretty damn good reason to get back to Hawaii in one piece, he felt the need. "You sound like Tex," Aleck said with a grin.

Mustang burst out laughing. "God forbid. That old bastard never can take thanks, can he?"

"Nope."

"Then you're welcome," Mustang said, still grinning.

"You know who else reminds me so much of Tex?" Aleck asked.

"Who?"

"Baker."

"Shit yeah, he does," Mustang agreed.

"You heard from him lately? After going to New York on Elodie's behalf, has he said anything else about that?"

"Nope. As far as I know, the mob is content to stay in their corner of New York and Elodie's still in the clear. Baker is hanging out at his place on the North Shore, surfing as much as he can as he tries to outrun his demons."

"Do we know what happened with him to make him such a hermit?" Aleck asked. "Is there anything we can do to help?"

"I don't know for sure, but I think it had to do with his SEAL team. Something happened, the team broke up, and he retired not too much longer afterward. And I think he likes being alone. But I also truly believe that helping others is what's keeping him sane."

"Midas said he thinks there's a woman he's interested in," Aleck said.

Mustang whipped his head around to stare at Aleck. "Really?"

"Yeah. He doesn't know her name or anything, but when he brought Lexie up to the North Shore to meet him, a woman pulled up in a VW van, and Midas said it was like a switch was flicked. He totally ignored him and Lexie and headed for her."

"Interesting," Mustang mused. "I hope it works out for him. I've never met anyone who needs someone in his corner as much as Baker does. He knows everyone, has some pretty scary contacts, yet he doesn't seem to let anyone get too close. This may sound sappy as fuck, but now that I've got Elodie, I know firsthand how a good woman can be life-changing."

Aleck couldn't keep the amused grin off his face.

"Fuck you," Mustang said with no heat. "Just wait. When things get even more serious with you and Kenna, you'll understand."

Aleck's smile dimmed. "I already do," he said softly.

"It'll get worse. Wait until after you've been inside her," Mustang said, without sounding lecherous. "There's something about being with the woman you love that completely changes you. And in my case, having Elodie in danger seemed to flip *my* switch. I know it's cliché to feel like she was a damsel in distress who I rescued, but...there it is. She's mine. Body and soul."

"Well, I can do without having to rescue Kenna. Hell, she'd probably just rescue herself. She's pretty self-sufficient," Aleck joked. "But I'm totally down with being inside her."

Mustang nodded, then sighed and rested his head on the seat back.

"Thanks, Mustang," Aleck said. "I'm just so impatient to get home and see her, and it occurred to me that she might not feel the same."

"You'll find out soon enough. I've found that sleeping makes the time go by faster," he said as he closed his eyes.

"Wow, you aren't being subtle at all," Aleck told his friend.

Mustang grinned again, but didn't open his eyes.

Deciding to follow his lead, Aleck did his best to get comfortable on the not-so-comfortable seat. He closed his eyes, and even though he hadn't slept more than four hours in a row throughout the last six weeks, he couldn't seem to make himself do so now. He was too keyed up. Too anxious. He prayed Kenna would be glad to hear he was back.

* * *

After way too many hours traveling, Aleck was finally in Honolulu. He and the rest of his team had debriefings they needed to take care of, but for the rest of the day, they were off duty. Tomorrow afternoon, they'd go to the base for just a few hours, and the next few days after, they'd be working eight-hour days until every single minute of their mission had been accounted for. *Then* they'd finally get a few days of R&R to decompress before starting their usual routines all over again.

As he walked through the parking lot to his car, Aleck had only one person on his mind. Kenna. He hadn't called her yet —he was scared to. Him, a deadly Navy SEAL, was fucking terrified to call his girlfriend to let her know he was back safe and sound.

If she said she was too busy to see him, or that she hadn't handled his deployment well and wasn't interested in a relationship any longer, it would destroy him.

Looking at his watch, Aleck saw that it was three in the afternoon. She might be heading to work, anyway. He also wanted to look his best when he saw her. And right now, he was anything but. His beard was even longer than it had been in the picture he'd shown her, and he felt as if he had sand and dirt ground into every pore. He needed a long, hot shower, a shave, and something to eat that wasn't a damn MRE.

His bright Jeep wasn't hard to spot in the small parking lot reserved for military personal and civilians with access to the base, and simply seeing it made Aleck smile. He and the rest of the team had retrieved their keys and phones out of storage, and he clicked the fob to unlock the doors as he approached his Jeep.

Something caught his eye on the windshield. After stowing his duffle bag in the backseat, he reached for the piece of paper that had been stuck under his wiper. Annoyed that someone had come through the parking lot and left advertisements on the cars, Aleck unfolded the paper.

But this was no advertisement.

The paper was faded from the sun and had obviously been rained on several times, telling Aleck that it had been placed on his Jeep at least a few weeks ago. He read the smeared words—and every muscle in his body tensed.

You're not as awesome as you think you are.

The first person who came to mind when he read the words was Kylo fucking Braun.

The man had gone too far this time.

Refolding the note, Aleck climbed behind the wheel. He put the note in his glove compartment and took a second to inhale a deep breath.

He assumed Braun had found out that he and his team had been deployed, and he certainly knew what kind of car Aleck drove, so he had taken the opportunity to place the note when he knew he wouldn't be caught in the act. The man was a coward, and not worth a second of Aleck's energy, but it still pissed him off to no end.

Since he and Mustang had talked about Baker on the plane, the man was fresh in Aleck's mind. Maybe he'd give him a call and see what, if any, dirt he could dig up on Braun. Get him transferred.

Aleck didn't feel bad in the least that he was seriously considering fucking with the man's career. He'd brought it on himself with his constant harassment, and just from being a jealous asshole. Braun wanted to play games? Aleck was all in. The other man would find out the hard way that you don't mess with a SEAL.

Satisfied with his decision to get rid of the thorn in his side once and for all, and knowing Baker would definitely be able to discretely do what needed to be done to get Braun transferred out of Hawaii, Aleck reached to put his key in the ignition—and had another thought.

Midas and Mustang had immediately called Lexie and Elodie after retrieving their phones. He wouldn't be surprised if Jag had texted Carly as well.

Shit.

He had no idea if Kenna had done as he'd suggested, getting together with the other women, but if she had, she'd probably be getting a text from one of them, letting her know that the team was home.

And if she heard from someone other than *him* that he was back, like she'd learned about his condo, Aleck knew he'd be in deep shit. It might embarrass her again, make her feel bad that he hadn't called her right away like his teammates had.

He was reaching for his phone before he'd even finished his thoughts. He didn't even consider sending a text. He clicked on her name and held his breath as he brought the cell up to his ear.

It rang twice before she answered. "Marshall?"

"Hey, babe."

"Oh my God!" she screeched. "Are you back?"

He chuckled. "I'm back," he confirmed.

Then Kenna shocked the hell out of him by bursting into tears.

Shit!

"Kenna? It's okay. I'm all right. We all are. Nothing's wrong, we're all good."

"I'm just so h-happy that you're home," she hiccupped.

"Breathe, babe. You're worrying me," Aleck told her. He heard her take a deep breath, then another. "Better?"

Instead of answering him, she asked, "When can I see you?"

"The sooner the better," he said honestly.

"Are you at your condo?" Kenna asked.

"Not yet. I'm still on base. I wanted to call and let you

know I was back before you got a text from one of the other girls."

"I appreciate it. Are you going home or do you have to go into work?" she asked.

"Home. We have a meeting tomorrow afternoon, but we're free until then."

"Can...would you mind if I came over?"

Aleck felt his heart rate kick up a notch. "You're not working?"

"I am, but I can call in. Alani will understand."

Aleck blinked in surprise. "Seriously?"

"Yes. Are you really that surprised?" she asked.

"Kind of," he said honestly. "You love your job, and you've said more than once that you hate people who call in, that the business and managers rely on the servers to be there when they're scheduled."

"Marshall, I've spent the last six weeks worrying about you and missing you like crazy. If you think I'm gonna be worth a shit at work, knowing you're finally here but I can't see you, you're wrong. If you don't want me to come over, just tell me. I'll be disappointed, but I'll try to understand."

Fuck, he loved this woman. Flat out. No ifs, ands, or buts about it. How could he not love her when she would drop everything, including the job she enjoyed, to see him?

"Not want to see you? Damn, Kenna, I've spent every minute I've been gone missing you," he blurted. "So yes, I want you to come over. I look pretty gnarly right now, and I need to get cleaned up and try to scrape this hair off my face, but I want to see you more than I want to breathe."

He heard her sniffing and figured she was crying again.

"Don't cry," he ordered.

"Then don't say such nice things," she retorted.

Aleck realized he was smiling like a crazy man, and anyone watching him would probably think he'd seriously lost it. "Please come over," he said gently. "I can't wait to hold you."

"Same," she said. "Do you need me to stop at the store on my way? Anything you've been craving while you've been gone?"

"Yes, but no," Aleck said. "That would take too long. I just want to see you."

"Okay. And for the record, you've got stuff to eat at your place. You said it was okay for me to stay over there sometimes, so I have been. There's not a ton of stuff in your fridge, but there's enough to get you by until you can get to the grocery store."

Knowing she'd been puttering around his condo, sleeping in his bed, had Aleck's heart flipping—and his dick going hard. "Drive safely," he ordered. "Do not get in a wreck driving like a bat out of hell to get to my place."

"I will. And I never drive crazy," she retorted.

"Kenna?"

"Yeah?"

"It's so good to hear your voice. I've missed our phone calls and texts."

"Same," she said softly.

"I'll see you soon."

"Soon," she echoed. "Bye."

"Bye."

Aleck felt like a ton of bricks had been lifted from his shoulders. He started the engine and backed out of the parking space, the note he'd found already forgotten in his glove compartment as he accelerated out of the lot. He needed to at least shower before Kenna arrived. She might be anxious to see him, but she wouldn't be very impressed with how he smelled if she got there before he had a chance to clean up.

CHAPTER SEVENTEEN

Kenna couldn't believe Marshall was actually home. She'd dreamed about this day for so long, and it was finally here. After she hung up with Marshall, she immediately called Alani and explained the situation. Her manager was very understanding, and because Kenna rarely called in when she was supposed to work, she was more than happy to give her the night off. Considering her shift was starting soon, it was even more generous of Alani to be so cool about the request.

She took the time to change out of her Duke's uniform, putting on a pair of shorts and a T-shirt, not even bothering to do anything with her hair, which she'd put up in a ponytail for work.

While she was changing, her phone began to ding with texts from the girls.

Elodie: They're back!!!!

Elodie: If you don't hear from me for a while, don't be alarmed, I'm just hibernating in bed with my husband!

. . .

Lexie: Did you hear? The guys are home!

    Lexie: Midas told me Aleck talked about you all the time.

    Lexie: Get it, girl!

Carly: I got a text from Jag. He said they're finally back. I'm so relieved!

Ashlyn: Holy crap! I can't believe Slate messaged to tell me he's home. I'm way more excited than I should be about this. He's kind of a jerk, but it was super nice of him to let me know!

Not wanting to take a second longer than necessary to get to Marshall, Kenna shot a quick text back to each of her friends before heading out of her apartment. Even though Marshall said he didn't need anything from the store, she still made a quick stop on her way to Coral Springs. She wanted to make his return special in some way.

She gathered up some of the things she knew he loved to eat. The Maui onion potato chips he was addicted to, a bag of Kona coffee because she thought she'd finished up the last bag he had, some fresh mangos, some POG juice—passion, orange and guava juices—and a bag of the Hawaiian popcorn he liked so much, the kind with mocha crunch and furikake. Kenna thought it was gross, but if Marshall liked it, he was getting it.

She also wanted to stop and get some malasadas from Leonard's Bakery, but that would take too long. So she cheated and picked up some generic malasadas and dough-nuts from the grocery store. They wouldn't be as good, but they'd do in a pinch. She'd make it up to Marshall later by getting the good stuff.

Everything within her was urging her to get to Marshall's condo as fast as possible. Intellectually she knew he wasn't going to disappear before she could get there, but emotionally, she wasn't as certain.

Kenna did her best not to be impatient as she checked out, but it seemed to take forever before she was finally on her way. The closer she got to Marshall's condo, the more nervous she became. It was silly. He'd sounded excited to see her and more than welcoming, but she couldn't help but wonder if things between them would be any different.

For her part, she felt the same toward him. She'd missed him terribly and had resorted to going back and rereading his old texts and messages that he'd sent before he was deployed, just to feel closer to him.

Butterflies were swirling in her belly by the time she finally arrived and parked.

Robert had obviously seen her pull into the lot—the man didn't miss anything—and by the time she had opened her car door, Alfonso was walking quickly toward the vehicle.

"Hi," she said as he approached.

"Good afternoon, Ms. Madigan. Let me take those for you," he said, reaching for the bags in her hands.

"Thanks," she said as she handed them over gratefully.

Alfonso smiled at her as they walked toward the entrance. "Mr. Smart is back."

It was kind of cute how excited Alfonso sounded as he said that. "I know," she said with a smile. "It's why I'm here. I was supposed to work tonight, but how could I concentrate on anything knowing Marshall had returned?" Kenna knew she was babbling, but she was excited and nervous at the same time.

"If you need anything, don't hesitate to contact us," Alfonso said as he held open the door to the lobby.

"I stopped and got some of Marshall's favorite foods, although I didn't want to wait on Leonard's malasadas," she continued. "So I got some generic ones. His sweet tooth should be assuaged either way."

Alfonso smiled at her.

As they approached the security desk, Robert stood. He had a huge smile on his face too. "Hello, Ms. Madigan. I'm guessing you're happy Mr. Smart is back."

"Oh yeah," Kenna said with feeling.

Robert chuckled. "I'm sure Alfonso has said this already, but if you need anything, please let me know."

"I will. Thanks. I've kept Marshall's pantry and fridge stocked since I've been hanging out here, so we should be good."

"Very well," Robert said. "Have a good night."

"I plan to," Kenna muttered. Then she turned to Alfonso. "I've got those," she said, nodding at the bags in his hands.

"Are you sure? I can carry them up for you," he offered.

"I'm sure. The day I can't carry a few grocery bags is the day I...well, I guess have you bring them up for me," she ended lamely.

Both Robert and Alfonso laughed.

"Here you go," Alfonso said, handing over the groceries.

Kenna thanked him, took a deep breath, and headed for the elevators. She supposed she should've texted Marshall to let him know she was there, but it was too late now...and her hands were full.

She did her best not to throw up from nerves as the elevator rose to the top floor. She walked much quicker than usual down the hall toward his door. Before she could put down the bags in one hand to knock, the door opened.

She almost didn't recognize Marshall. His face was

covered with a fairly substantial beard and his hair had gotten longer.

"Get in here," he growled, wrapping an arm around her waist and pulling her against him before stepping back.

The second she got close, Kenna recognized his smell, the one that had finally dissipated from his pillows. She'd been so upset the night she realized she couldn't smell him on his sheets anymore.

Kenna dropped the bags, not caring if she smooshed the chips, and clung to Marshall. She heard him shut the door behind them, then he had one hand around her back as the other snaked under her ponytail, where he gripped her nape.

Sighing in contentment, Kenna buried her nose in the side of his neck and held on to him as tightly as she could. His beard tickled her face, but it was much softer than she would've expected. His hold on her was just as tight and desperate. Being with him, seeing with her own two eyes that he was safe and unharmed, holding him...it was all too much.

Once more, to her chagrin, Kenna burst into tears.

Marshall didn't let go. He held her even tighter and did his best to comfort her.

"I'm okay," he said, knowing exactly why she was overwhelmed with emotion. "I'm here. It's so good to see you, hold you. You smell just like I remembered. I never thought coconut could be so comforting. Damn, I missed you."

How long they stood in his foyer holding onto each other, Kenna had no idea. All she knew was that she could finally relax. She hadn't realized how tense she'd been for the last month and a half, until right this second.

Eventually, she took a deep breath and pulled back a fraction. He didn't let go of her.

"Hi," she said. "It's so good to see you."

"Same," he replied. "You look so damn good...so beautiful. I can't even begin to tell you."

Kenna smiled. She hadn't done anything special to her hair or even put on makeup, other than what she was already wearing to go to work. She loved how generous Marshall was with his compliments.

She reached up to touch his face, then hesitated. "Can I?"

He took her hand in his and pressed it to his cheek. "You can touch me anytime you want."

Smiling, Kenna ran her hand over his face.

"What do you think? Should I keep it?" Marshall asked.

Kenna shrugged. "It's different. I'm definitely not used to seeing you like this. But I don't have enough information to decide if you should keep it or shave it off."

He looked confused. "Information?"

Kenna did her best to keep a straight face. "Yeah, I mean, I guess I've have to see how it feels when you kiss me."

"Yeah?" Marshall growled.

Kenna didn't even have time to respond before his head lowered and his lips were on hers.

It was like coming home.

She'd needed this. Neither was hesitant, they kissed as if they hadn't seen each other in years, rather than six weeks. By the time Marshall pulled back, they were both breathing as if they'd just run a mile.

"So?" he asked with a crooked grin.

Kenna reached up once more and ran her fingers through his beard. It was that long. "Are you gonna be upset if I tell you I like kissing you better when you're clean-shaven?" she asked.

"Nope. In fact, I've got the scissors and razors in my bathroom right now, all ready to go. Want to help me?"

Kenna eyed him for a moment. "So if you were already planning on shaving, why'd you ask me what I thought? What if I'd said I wanted you to keep it?"

Marshall shrugged nonchalantly. "Then I would've kept it."

"Just like that?" Kenna asked skeptically.

"Just like that," he agreed. "I had a lot of time to think about us while I was deployed."

Kenna scowled at him. "You're supposed to be thinking about where the bad guys are, and not stepping on one of those explosive bomb things. And how to get home safely," she scolded.

Marshall chuckled. "I was. But if I thought about that stuff nonstop, I'd go crazy. So when things got to be too much, I thought about us. You."

Fuck. This man. "And?" she asked.

"And I realized how much you mean to me. Things have been fast with us, but they've felt...right. I wondered what you were doing. How you were. If you've had a lot of annoying customers, if you were coming over to my condo. If you were eating all right. You name it, I thought it. I know I'm a lucky bastard, and if you can handle my job, me leaving for unknown amounts of time here and there, then I can do no less than bend over backward to make your life easier and full. So...that means if you want me to keep the beard, I will. If you want me to shave, I will. It makes no difference to me."

"Marshall," Kenna whispered, extremely touched.

"Don't cry," Marshall ordered. "I didn't say any of that to upset you."

"Major fail," Kenna said with a sniff, wiping the tears from under her eyes.

Marshall squeezed her neck, where his hand still held her possessively, and said, "Look at me, babe."

Kenna took a deep breath and looked up at the man she'd fallen head over heels for. She should've known she was in love when she'd missed him so terribly. She'd never felt so much for a man. Ever. She'd gone a week once without talking to one of her boyfriends, and it hadn't fazed her in the least.

"You're the most capable woman I've ever met. I have no doubt you can do whatever you set your mind to. The fact that you're with me is something I've been pinching myself over for the last six weeks. You've got me in the palm of your hand. All you have to do is say the word and I'll give you anything you want."

"You. I want *you*," Kenna replied without a second thought.

"Thank fuck," Marshall breathed.

Kenna was surprised to see the relief in his eyes. How could he not know that?

"Come on. Help me scrape this crap off my face, then we'll see about getting something to eat."

Kenna nodded, and he gave her nape one more affectionate squeeze, then bent and picked up the bags she'd been carrying. After he'd oohed and ahhed over the things she'd bought for him, they put everything away and headed for the master bathroom.

Kenna had left some of her things in his bathroom, since she'd been going back and forth from here to her apartment. Nodding toward the counter, where she'd put her toothbrush, toothpaste, and lotion to the side of one sink, he smiled. "I love seeing your shit in here." Then, looking around the room, he added, "I think the best way to do this is if I sit on the side of the tub. It'll be easier for you to reach me."

"But hair will get all over the floor," Kenna said.

"Yeah, so?"

"So it'll have to be swept up. Then vacuumed to make sure we got it all."

"And?" Marshall asked. "We'll make a mess, then we'll clean it up. Not a big deal."

"Okay," Kenna agreed, liking his laid-back attitude. "But

why don't we at least put a trash can under you to catch as much as we can."

He nodded, and Kenna grabbed the small plastic trash can from under the sink and put it on the floor between his legs as he sat on the edge of the bathtub.

Marshall then held up a pair of very sharp-looking scissors, handing them to her handle first, and said, "Madam, if you would do the honors."

"Um, I have no idea what I'm doing," Kenna said tentatively as she took the scissors from him.

"You can't screw it up...well, unless you stab me with those. Just hack away at the hair. Get as close as you can to my face. The shorter it is, the easier it is to shave off the rest."

"Okay, but if I stab you and you bleed out on the bathroom floor, don't blame me," she joked as she stood in front of him.

Marshall reached up and took her wrist in a loose grip. "I trust you," he said solemnly.

Kenna swallowed hard and nodded. It wasn't as if she was actually cutting his hair in some kind of style. She couldn't mess this up...unless she cut his face. Mentally grimacing at that image, she took a deep breath, then got to work.

She started with the easy stuff, the hair hanging down from his chin, snipping it off and letting it fall into the bin. Carefully, she cut off more and more of his beard, until she got to a point where she had to put the scissors right next to his skin to get as much hair off as possible.

"Relax, Kenna, you're doing fine," Marshall told her.

She nodded, still tense.

It didn't help when she felt his hands grip her hips. She looked down. "What?" she asked, thinking she'd done something wrong.

"Keep going," he urged.

Kenna snipped some more hair—and luckily had paused to inspect her work when his hands snaked under her T-shirt and caressed her bare skin.

She squirmed and reminded him, "Ticklish."

His touch immediately firmed, but she still froze as his hands roamed.

"You done?" he asked, knowing full well she wasn't.

"No."

"Well, don't take all night," he teased. "I'm thinking we have other things to do."

And just like that, the mood in the room changed, electrified.

Kenna's nipples hardened under her shirt, and since they were at Marshall's eye level, he definitely noticed. His hands slipped upward, pushed under her bra, and cupped both her breasts.

Kenna closed her eyes and moaned as she put her hands on his shoulders to steady herself, careful not to poke him with the scissors.

"You are so damn responsive," he muttered as he kneaded her flesh.

"It's just you," she said honestly. Kenna couldn't remember reacting like this to any other man's touch. All Marshall had to do was *breathe* and she was putty in his hands.

After a moment, Kenna said his name in almost a whine.

It was his turn to take a deep breath, then he stood, startling Kenna. He removed his hands and reached for the scissors. Then he pulled her over to the counter.

Kenna watched quietly as he made quick work of removing the last bits of hair he could with the scissors. Then he grabbed a can of shaving cream and slathered it on his face, his movements quick and economical. He picked up a razor and asked, "You want to do the honors again?"

Kenna's eyes widened in horror. "No," she said emphatically.

Marshall chuckled, then got to work shaving off the rest of the facial hair he'd grown in the last six weeks.

The thought of wielding a razor anywhere near his face made Kenna shudder, but she watched in fascination as he quickly did what he'd likely done thousands of times in his life. She snuggled up behind him, wrapping her arms around his waist as she watched him in the mirror.

When he took a break to rinse the razor, she grinned and slid her hands under *his* T-shirt.

His gaze immediately met hers in the mirror. Even with his face half covered in shaving cream—which should've looked ridiculous—Kenna was turned on. He was a beautiful man.

Her fingers roamed upward until she reached his nipples, which she began to play with. Pinching and flicking. They immediately hardened, and Kenna couldn't help but press closer to his back.

"You want me to finish this?" he asked.

She grinned. "Yes."

"Then you're going to have to move your hands."

Move her hands? She could do that.

Slowly, she ran her palms down his flat belly and left them resting just above his waistline. He made a few more swipes with the razor before she made her next move.

Marshall wore a pair of gray sweatpants, which should be illegal. Well-endowed men wearing sweatpants were a turn-on for most straight women, but the sight of *her* man, in *his* sweatpants, made Kenna want to throw them all away so no one else could see what was hers.

The thought wasn't even startling. Marshall *was* hers—just as she was his.

She quickly slipped her hands under the elastic waistband and got her first feel of his cock.

It was half erect already, but as soon as she touched him, he hardened, lengthening in her hand as she tightened her grip around him.

"Fuck," Marshall groaned when she caressed him.

He tolerated her touch for another moment before leaning forward and aggressively shaving the rest of his beard off. He was much rougher than Kenna would've dreamed of being, and she'd opened her mouth to tell him to be careful just as he threw the razor into the sink. He reached over, grabbed a towel and swiped it over his face, removing the remnants of shaving cream before throwing the towel onto the counter.

He pulled Kenna's hands out of his pants before turning. She had a split second to admire his clean-shaven face—much happier, now that he looked more like the Marshall she remembered—before his lips landed on hers.

Then all she could think of was trying to get even closer to her man.

She tilted her head and hitched a leg up as they kissed. Marshall spun them both, lifting her in the process, and Kenna found herself sitting on the counter. He didn't stop kissing her as he shoved her legs wider and stepped between them. With a hand on her ass, he pulled her to the edge of the counter, so his cock was pressed right where she wanted it most.

Their kiss was messy and uncoordinated, and the hottest thing she'd ever experienced. His hands went to the hem of her shirt and he took his mouth off hers just long enough to say, "Arms up."

Kenna didn't even think about protesting. She was one hundred percent in for whatever he had planned...as long as it ended up with them both naked. Her ponytail holder came out as he whipped her shirt over her head, but Kenna barely noticed. Her hands went to the back of his head as he leaned over to suck on the mounds of her breasts plumped over the top of her bra.

His hands were busy at her waist, unbuttoning and unzipping her shorts. He glanced up at her and ordered, "Lift your hips so I can get these off."

"Yes," she said, licking her lips. She knew she was wet, she could feel how damp her panties had gotten. She reached for his sweats after kicking off her shorts, but he brushed her hands away and palmed her ass once more. He didn't hesitate to crouch and put his mouth right over her soaking-wet panties.

"Holy shit!" Kenna exclaimed as she bucked in his grip.

"I need you. Need to taste you. I was cheated out of getting to feel you come on my tongue six weeks ago, and I'm done fucking waiting," he said, more to himself than her, before roughly pulling the gusset of her panties aside and lowered his head once more.

Kenna had been with men who'd gone down on her, but no one had shown nearly as much enthusiasm as Marshall.

It was all she could do to remain on the counter as he ate her out as if he were starving for her taste. His tongue licked the length of her slit, then he flicked her clit, making her jerk in his grip.

"Easy," he murmured. "Reach down and hold your underwear out of my way," he said.

"Bossy," Kenna complained, but she didn't hesitate to move one of her hands down between her legs. "You know this would be easier if you took my underwear off," she informed him.

"Can't wait," he said, before he was once more licking and sucking at her soaking-wet folds.

Now that he had both hands free, he held her firmly

against his face and drove Kenna out of her mind. He sucked, nipped, licked, and it wasn't long until she felt herself on the verge of coming.

"I'm close!" she said, panting.

Marshall moaned and increased his ministrations between her legs. As if he knew exactly what she needed to get off, he closed his lips around her clit, used his tongue as a vibrator, and sucked at the same time.

Kenna began to shake and before she knew it, flew right over the edge. Marshall didn't stop stimulating her clit. He actually sucked harder, making her orgasm go on and on. It wasn't until she pulled on his hair and said, "Enough, please! Shit, Marshall," that he licked her one last time and looked up at her.

He had a very satisfied expression on his face, but Kenna couldn't find it in her to tease him about it. Then he shocked her by leaning down again and gently licking her folds, collecting her juices with his tongue.

"If I'd have known what I'd missed out on by just an hour or so, I might not've survived that deployment," Marshall mumbled.

That was...

Kenna didn't know what that was.

Without warning, Marshall stood and lifted her off the counter with his hands on her ass. Kenna shrieked and grabbed at him, holding on as he walked them into his bedroom. He dropped her on the bed without finesse. But Kenna wasn't offended. She was too busy watching avidly as he stripped off his T-shirt, letting it fall to the floor without a second thought.

"Panties and bra off," he said, reaching for his sweatpants.

Kenna didn't take her eyes off the bulge between his legs as she lifted her hips and removed her underwear, then arched her back and unhooked her bra, throwing it to the side.

Her eyes widened when his cock bobbed free of his underwear as Marshall shoved them down his legs, along with his sweats. He was huge. And thick. And her mouth began to water.

She needed him inside her. Now.

He was obviously on the same page, since he reached over and opened a drawer next to the bed. She already knew there was a new box of condoms in there, because she'd seen them one night. He ripped open the box and was soon smoothing a condom down his magnificent cock.

She wanted to touch it. Touch *him*. But she was much too eager to feel him between her legs at the moment to try. She'd have time to explore later. Much later.

One of his knees hit the mattress, and Kenna grinned.

"You ready for this?" he asked, holding the base of his cock and caressing his balls at the same time.

"Yes," she rasped. And she was. She'd dreamed about this for weeks. About being with him.

Marshall reached out and grabbed one of her ankles and pulled her toward him.

Kenna laughed as she fell onto her back, but her humor faded as Marshall shoved her legs apart with his knees while inching forward. She thought he was going to take her quickly, right then and there, but he surprised her by leaning forward and putting his hands on either side of her shoulders. He stared down at her, and she could feel his cock throbbing against her belly.

"You're mine," he almost growled. His voice was deeper than normal, and Kenna shivered at the lusty sound.

"And you're mine," she answered.

He smiled then, and Kenna almost melted. Damn, he was so freaking good-looking.

"I'm going to fuck you. It's gonna be hard and fast. You good with that?"

"Oh yeah," she breathed.

"Then, after you come on my cock, I'm gonna make long, slow love to you until you come again."

"That doesn't sound like much fun for you," Kenna quipped. "When do you get to orgasm?"

"Oh, I'm gonna come, babe," he said with a smirk. "After you. I want to watch you, feel your muscles ripple along my dick, know that *I'm* the man who's inside you, the one who gets to see those fabulous tits shake as I take you, the one who's making you cream all over his cock."

Kenna chuckled and rolled her eyes. "So far you're all talk and no action," she complained, squirming against him, wanting to feel him inside her.

He moved then, straightening on his knees and pulling her closer. He reached down and used his thumb to rub her clit, and Kenna jerked.

"You ready to take me?" he asked.

"Yes."

"I don't think so, not yet. I don't want to hurt you."

His words seemed more for himself than for her, and Kenna had a feeling this man was about to change her life forever. She wouldn't be the same after tonight. She knew it.

With more restraint than she thought he had, with way more than *she* had, he played with her clit, ramping her arousal back up. He used the head of his cock to rub her wetness around her pussy lips, and when he was finally satisfied that she was slick enough to take him without pain, he eased himself inside her body.

Once he'd entered her, he didn't stop until he was all the way in. He didn't give her time to adjust to his size, simply pushed slow and steady until she could feel his balls against her ass.

Kenna moaned and widened her legs, trying to get closer. She was wet enough that he hadn't hurt her at all. She felt full, *very* full, but there was no pain. "Ummmm," she said.

"Good?" he asked.

"Very," she reassured him.

That was all he needed. Marshall pulled back, then slammed inside her, forcing a grunt from Kenna's mouth.

He did it again. And again. He fucked her hard and fast, just as he'd promised. Kenna had no idea what other women liked when their men were inside them, but she loved being taken like this. She didn't have to think about what she needed to do to achieve orgasm. All she had to do was take what Marshall gave her.

And he was giving her all he had. Every time he slammed home, a jolt of ecstasy went through her entire body. It wasn't easy for her to come without stimulation to her clit, but because of all the foreplay before he'd entered her, she was on the verge of coming once more.

The orgasm itself snuck up on her. One minute she was enjoying the feel of Marshall inside her, loving the look of concentration and intensity on his face, and the next she was coming. Her legs shook and her belly tightened.

Kenna arched as Marshall continued to fuck her through the tremors that shook her body.

"So damn beautiful," Marshall gasped.

When she'd stopped shaking, he pushed all the way inside her and reached down between them once more.

"Marshall, no," Kenna panted.

"No?" he asked, stilling above her.

Shit. Kenna remembered that he'd told her once if she ever said that word, everything would stop. She didn't want to stop what they were doing, but she was extremely sensitive right now. "I need a small break," she told him. "But feel free to keep going," she said with a smile, running her hands up and down his thighs.

He grinned. "All right. But I'm only human. And I've been dreaming about this for six weeks. There's only so long I can fuck you before I'll come."

"So come then," she said reasonably.

Kenna almost laughed at the pout that crossed her man's face. "But I wanted to feel you come against my cock again. I missed it the first time because I was too busy fucking you."

She *did* laugh at that. "Right, sorry." She loved that they were teasing each other. Loved that sex with Marshall was fun. Yes, it was intense, and she was almost overwhelmed by how good he felt inside her, but laughing brought a whole new dimension to sex that was rare, in her experience. "Just go easy. I haven't had this many orgasms so close together...ever."

"Ever?" he asked.

"Shit, I've created a monster, haven't I?" she quipped.

"Fuck yeah, you have. One that's addicted to his woman's pussy," Marshall said crudely.

"Make love to me," she whispered. "But go easy on my poor clit," she added.

Marshall nodded and slowly pulled out of her body, then pushed back in. It felt...nice Almost soothing. Not overwhelming like when he was fucking her hard. One of his hands went to her chest as he lazily pumped in and out of her, and he squeezed her nipple.

Arching her back, Kenna groaned and felt her Kegel muscles tighten around Marshall's cock.

"You like that," he said. He wasn't asking. It was pretty damn obvious when she'd nearly strangled his dick.

The next few minutes were spent with Marshall playing with her nipples as he learned where and how she liked to be touched. It wasn't long before Kenna was ready to come again.

"Touch yourself," he said. "That way I won't hurt you."

As Marshall pinched her nipples and played with her breasts, Kenna massaged her clit. She used her pinky to caress his cock every time he pulled out of her body, wanting to make him feel as good as she did at that moment.

"You need to come," Marshall warned. "But tell me right before."

Nodding, Kenna flicked her fingers over her extremely sensitive bud a little faster. "I'm close…"

Marshall pushed back inside her body and held still as he pinched one of her nipples harder than he had before. The extra stimulation was enough for Kenna to once more reach her peak. The orgasm wasn't as intense as the others she'd had earlier, but she could feel herself trembling, and her inner muscles spasmed around Marshall's cock, still buried deep within her body.

"There is literally no better feeling in the world than you coming on my cock," Marshall panted. Then, without thrusting, she felt him shudder above her as he finally let himself come.

They were both sweating, and Kenna felt as if she'd just worked a marathon twenty-four-hour shift, but she couldn't remember ever being more satisfied after sex than she was right this moment.

"I think you killed me," she said when Marshall fell forward and to the side, pulling her with him. He slipped out of her body as they moved, and they both sighed at the feeling.

He kissed her temple and said, "But what a way to go."

"True," Kenna agreed.

They lay together for a moment before Marshall sighed again. "I need to take care of this condom."

Kenna nodded and watched as he slid out of the bed and headed for the bathroom. His ass was a thing of beauty. Round, tight, and drool worthy. But it was nothing compared to the view when he returned.

She wasn't nearly done with ogling him when he pulled the sheet back and gestured for her to get under it. They hadn't even bothered pulling the covers down, and Kenna laughed. They'd both been too eager to finally be together to worry about something as mundane as getting *under* the covers.

It was still very early, but Kenna didn't care. She snuggled into Marshall and ran her fingers over his now clean-shaven face. He had a bit of razor burn, which didn't surprise her. He hadn't been gentle those last few strokes.

"You know," she said as nonchalantly as she could. She was an adult. She could talk about birth control without blushing. Maybe. "I'm on the pill."

He stared at her without blinking.

"I mean...in case you didn't want to use a condom. I'm also clean, don't have any diseases or anything. I know the pill isn't one hundred percent foolproof though, so if you want to keep using them, that's okay too. I'm not ready for a child. No way."

"I get tested twice a year by the Navy. And I've passed every test with flying colors," Marshall said.

"That's good," Kenna said softly.

"You're saying I can be inside you without a condom?" he asked.

"Well, yeah. We didn't really have a chance to have this conversation earlier. But thank you for not being an ass about the condom..."

Marshall didn't say anything for a long, painful moment, and she started to feel self-conscious. Had it been too early to bring that up? Should she have waited?

Then he moved swiftly. Pushing Kenna to her back and crouching over her. She could feel the tip of his now weeping cock brush against her wet folds. Without a word, he pushed inside her once more. He wasn't as hard as he'd been the first time, but he still filled her easily.

"Marshall?" she questioned as she gripped his biceps.

He didn't thrust, just pushed inside her and held still.

"I'm sorry, I couldn't help it. I needed to get inside you bare right now. You're so hot. And fucking wet as hell. If you could feel what I do, you'd understand."

Kenna laughed, and he groaned.

"Fuck, even that feels damn amazing," he semi-complained.

"Don't mind me, I'll just be lying here," she teased.

"I'm gonna come pretty fast. I'm sorry."

She got serious, realizing how close to the edge Marshall was. "Does it really feel that much different?" she asked.

"I've never been inside anyone without a condom before. This is so damn amazing. You have no idea."

Weirdly enough, it was a very intimate thing to watch Marshall's reaction to fucking her without a condom. This big bad SEAL wasn't very intimidating at the moment. "Move, Marshall. I bet it'll feel even better." She felt like a madam teaching a virgin how to make love. The thought made her smile.

Marshall's gaze met hers as he slowly began to thrust inside her. His pupils were dilated so much, she almost couldn't see his beautiful brown eyes.

"I'm sorry, babe! I can't hold back."

"Then don't," she said.

A few more thrusts, and she felt Marshall's dick twitch inside her as he came for the second time. She was impressed he'd been able to not only get hard as fast as he had, but that he was able to come again so soon.

He shuddered, then fell sideways once more. But this time, he kept his hand on her ass, keeping them connected. Kenna ended up lying on his broad chest, his cock long and thick enough to not immediately slip out of her body.

"Oh my God, I don't have to get up," Marshall said with a smile of wonder on his face.

"Perks of no condom. Although the drawbacks are... messy," she warned.

"I'll wash our sheets every day," he said, his voice slurring.

He was so damn cute, and Kenna had never been happier.

She rested her head in the crook of his neck and felt his arms tighten around her. One snaked up to her nape and rested there. The familiarity already something she craved.

"Kenna?"

"Yeah?"

"I love you."

She stilled. Was he half asleep? Had he meant to say that?

She felt his hold on her nape tighten. "Did you hear me?"

Guess that answered her two questions. "Yes," she said softly.

"Good. You don't have to say it back, because I know I probably freaked you out, but I couldn't keep it inside anymore. The day you jumped on my head was the best day of my life."

"I didn't jump on your head," she protested automatically.

"I just wanted to make sure you know this isn't a fling for me. Not a short-term thing. I want you in my life for the long haul. And...I've never told a woman I loved her before."

"You haven't?"

"No. The connection we have is special, and I know it. I'd be an idiot if I didn't hold on to you with both hands. I love you. I say that with no strings, but now you know where I stand."

Kenna knew this was crazy. They hadn't known each other

all that long, but deep down in her heart, she knew he was right. Their connection *was* special. "I think I love you too," she whispered.

He chuckled. "I'll take that."

"I just—"

"Shhh, you don't have to explain yourself. I'm fucking thrilled to get even that from you. Just know that I'm going to do whatever I can to change that 'I think' to an 'I know.'"

Kenna smiled. "I don't think it'll be difficult," she admitted.

They were both silent for a few minutes before Marshall asked, "It's still early, but do you want to sleep?"

Kenna wasn't all that tired, but she nodded anyway.

"Good. I'm exhausted," Marshall admitted. "And I have a feeling I'm gonna want more of you when we wake up."

Kenna chuckled. "I've created a sex fiend."

"Only with you," he reassured her. Then he turned his head and kissed her temple once more. "Thank you for being here. For wanting to see me as soon as I got home. For sweet-talking Robert—and yes, he babbled on about you nonstop when I got back. And for just being you."

"Thank *you* for coming back to me in one piece," Kenna countered.

It didn't take long for Marshall to fall asleep. Kenna supposed if she'd traveled from wherever he had, probably from halfway around the world, she'd be exhausted too. Not to mention the two orgasms on top of it.

He finally slipped out of her body, groaning in his sleep. Grinning, Kenna shifted so she was no longer lying on top of him, but snuggled up against his side. She stared out the window as the sun slowly set and couldn't remember a time when she'd been this content.

CHAPTER EIGHTEEN

Aleck woke up in the evening, alert and as ready to go as if he'd slept for twelve hours straight. It took him a moment to figure out where he was and that Kenna was lying next to him. He hadn't been able to resist easing down her body and tasting her once more. That had led to her climbing on top of him and giving him the show of a lifetime as she rode him hard, fucking him until they both came once more.

Then they'd slept again.

He'd woken up a few hours later to the feel of Kenna's mouth on his cock, and it was all he could do not to explode immediately.

It was safe to say he and Kenna were more than compatible in bed, and Aleck knew he was a lucky son-of-a-bitch. He also knew their sex life might eventually taper off a bit...but not anytime soon. He couldn't get enough of the woman.

By the time they woke a third time, the sun was just peeking over the horizon. They'd been in bed for at least twelve hours, and Aleck felt amazing.

He was enjoying holding Kenna while she slept when he heard a knock at his door.

"What the fuck?" he muttered, immediately easing out of Kenna's hold. Having someone at his door this early couldn't be a good thing.

"What's wrong?" Kenna asked sleepily as she came up on an elbow.

The vision in his bed almost made Aleck crawl right back under the covers. One tit was exposed, her hair in disarray, and the sight of the few light hickies he'd accidentally given her last night made his cock twitch.

When another knock sounded on the front door, he swore under his breath. "Stay here. I'll go get rid of whoever's here and we can take a shower."

"Together?" she asked with a smile.

"Oh yeah," he told her.

The sultry look on her face reassured him that he'd given her the answer she wanted to hear.

He pulled on his sweats, which were still lying in the middle of the floor, and didn't bother with a shirt. Whoever was at his door would have to deal with his naked chest. That's what they got for daring to knock so early in the morning.

When Aleck pulled up the video monitor on the panel next to the door, he was surprised to see Robert standing there. He opened the door, praying nothing was terribly wrong. He wanted to spend the morning spoiling Kenna.

"Robert," he said with a nod.

"I'm very sorry for disturbing you this early, Mr. Smart. And I'll get out of your hair in a moment. My shift starts in a bit, but yesterday when Ms. Madigan arrived, she mentioned to Alfonso that she was disappointed she hadn't been able to stop at Leonard's and get some malasadas to welcome you home. So I stopped on my way into work to pick some up for you both."

Aleck was speechless. He reached for the box that Robert

held out. "Wow, um, thanks."

"You're more than welcome. It's the least I can do to thank you for your service." Robert gave him a nod of respect, then turned and headed back down the hall.

Aleck watched him go for a beat, then smiled as he shut his door. As the smell of the pastries wafted up to his nose, Aleck's stomach growled. He couldn't remember the last time he'd had a good meal, and while the sweets in the box probably weren't all that good for him, he could more than afford to splurge after the stuff he'd eaten, or not eaten, over the last six weeks.

And Aleck had a hunch that Robert hadn't actually gone out of his way to get the malasadas for *him*. There were plenty of times he'd come home from a long deployment in the past and hadn't gotten the royal treatment from Robert. It was all because of Kenna. She was just the kind of woman people wanted to be near. Wanted to make smile. And Aleck knew with certainty that the iconic Hawaiian pastries would do just that.

Not bothering to get a plate or cutlery, he carried the box into the bedroom.

"Who was it?" Kenna called out from the bathroom.

Aleck couldn't help but close his eyes in contentment. Was this how Mustang and Midas felt? It had to be. The morning was so...normal. Her asking who was at the door while in the bathroom brushing her teeth. It was everything Aleck hadn't known he wanted.

Grinning, he opened the box and stood just inside the bathroom door. "The malasada fairy," he told her.

Kenna had just wiped her mouth after rinsing, and she turned to him with a look of confusion on her face—but as soon as she saw the box of treats, she grinned. Huge. "Oh my God, I'm starving! We didn't exactly have dinner last night!" she exclaimed, reaching for one of the gooey doughnut-like pastries. She took a huge bite, and her eyes rolled to the back of her head in ecstasy as she chewed.

"Robert brought them by."

As soon as Kenna swallowed, she asked, "*Our* Robert? From downstairs?"

"The one and the same. I guess you mentioned to Alfonso you weren't able to get some yesterday, and he must've mentioned it to Robert. So he stopped by on his way to work to pick them up."

"Seriously?" she asked.

"Yup."

"Wow. We'll have to figure out how to thank him. That was...that was definitely going above and beyond. I know, I'll get him a gift certificate to Duke's. He said he's been there lots of times."

Aleck merely grinned at how the word "we" fell so easily from her lips. He liked being a part of a couple with Kenna. No, he *loved* it. "Want to go sit on the balcony and stuff our faces before we shower?"

"Yes," she said immediately. She'd put on a bathrobe Aleck knew for a fact hadn't been in his condo when he'd been deployed. The fact that she'd brought over more of her things made him even happier.

Aleck couldn't remember a better morning. Normally after a mission, he had a hard time getting it out of his mind. He'd go over what he'd done and what he could've done better. But this morning, all he could do was appreciate the beautiful sunrise and the equally exquisite woman by his side.

They ate a few sweet pastries on the balcony, showered—which turned into another long round of lovemaking—then he made omelets for both of them. After a proper breakfast, they sat on his couch, Kenna resting against him, and got caught up on what had happened in Oahu while he'd been gone. Aleck was feeling happy and mellow. Yes, the sex played a large part in why he felt that way, but it was more Kenna's comforting presence. She didn't ask questions about his mission, and while she'd missed him, she'd clearly gotten by just fine on her own, as he knew she would.

And now he truly understood how much he appreciated her independence. Previously, when he'd thought of the woman he might end up with, he assumed it would be someone who *needed* him...or at least his money. And as conceited as it was, he'd also thought he wanted someone who would worship the ground he walked on. Which was ridiculous, now that he thought about it. If Kenna had been like that, she would've had a much harder time with his deployment.

After hearing about the sleepover Kenna and the other women had at his condo, and about some of the more memorable customers—for both good and bad reasons—that she'd served recently at Duke's, and how well she'd gotten to know Robert and the other security employees, Aleck was deeply satisfied, and grateful, that he'd found someone like her.

The clock was inching toward the time when he needed to leave for the base for the initial AAR—after-action review. The team and their superior officers needed to go over what had happened in Iran, and why and how things could be done better in the future, both by the team and those who planned the missions. Kenna also needed to get home to get ready for her shift at Duke's.

"You get off at your regular time tonight, right?" Aleck asked.

"Barring anything crazy happening, yes. Why?"

"If it's all right, I'd like to come to your place tonight."

Kenna was snuggled up against his side, and Aleck had his arm over her shoulders. She tilted her head so she could see his face. "But you said you have to work all day for the rest of the week. It's a long drive from my apartment to the base."

"It's not that far. I mean, people commute from all over the island to the Naval base," he said.

"Still..." Kenna protested.

Aleck felt his stomach clench. Did she not *want* him to stay at her place?

"Here's the thing," he said softly. "Now that I've spent the night holding you in my arms, I don't really want to sleep by myself if I don't have to. I know there will be plenty of times when we have no choice, but driving an extra ten or so miles is nothing when it means I get to see you after your shift and hold you as I sleep."

Kenna just stared at him, and Aleck couldn't read her expression.

"If you'd rather I didn't, say the word," he said.

Her eyes widened and she immediately shook her head. "No! It's not that. I mean, yes, I'd freaking *love* it if you stayed the night. But wouldn't it make more sense for me to come here? I don't have to get up early tomorrow and you do."

Relief swept through Aleck. "You're a seriously independent woman."

She looked confused at the topic change. "Yeah," she agreed.

"You've been on your own a long time. You're perfectly able to take care of yourself. It's more than obvious...but I have to admit that I still don't like the idea of you driving out here after dark."

Kenna frowned slightly.

He went on. "If you come here after you get off work, it'll be late. I'll be in my meeting by the time you leave to go to Duke's, so I can't drive you there. It's probably not a good idea for me to pick you up, because then your car will be in the garage in Waikiki all night. I could come to your place and pick you up after you get home, and bring you back here, but if I'm going to drive out there, I might as well stay. I just...I've thought about you for six weeks, and being with you relaxes me in a way I can't fully explain. You calm the demons in my head."

"Marshall," Kenna whispered.

"But if you're not ready for regular sleepovers, that's okay," Aleck tried to reassure her. "I'll do what I can to see you as much as possible some other way. I don't want to go back to the way we were before I left though. Seeing you once a week just isn't going to be enough." He finally took a breath, realizing how fast he'd been talking, as if that would help convince her.

"You done?" Kenna asked with a small smile.

"I'm done," he confirmed a little sheepishly.

"I would love it if you came over tonight. My place is nothing like this one, but anytime you want to come over, you're welcome to. There aren't any kick-ass security guards like Robert, and there's no beach to lie on, but I do have a pretty amazing beanbag," she said.

"I love you," Aleck blurted. He refused to feel bad for saying the words so early in their relationship.

"I love you too," she returned a little shyly.

"You *think* you love me or you *know* you love me?" he prodded.

She smiled confidently. "I know I do. I've known it for a while. But last night I was feeling off-kilter, I think. I was blown away that you could actually love me back."

Aleck leaned down and kissed her gently. As much as he wanted to push her back on the couch and show her physically how much he cared about her, they didn't have time. So he kept his kiss light. "If you text me a bit before you're done working, I can head out there and meet you at your apartment."

"I'll make a copy of my key this afternoon before I go to

work," Kenna said. "So you can come and go as you want. I also don't have a nifty biometric lock. You're going to have to deal with a regular ol' key."

Aleck closed his eyes and let the warm feeling from her words flow through him for a moment.

"Marshall?"

"I'm good," he said without opening his eyes. "I'm just memorizing this moment."

He felt her shift next to him and then straddle his thighs. He opened his eyes and found himself face-to-face with Kenna. She used one hand to grip his nape, the other on his cheek. He felt surrounded by her, and immediately wrapped her in his arms, holding her close. If this was how *she* felt with his hand on her nape, it was no wonder she liked it. It was an intimate hold, and he loved how it felt.

"I *am* independent," she said. "I've been on my own a long time. I pay my own rent, buy my own groceries, make my own decisions about where to work, who my friends are, and what to do in my spare time. But that doesn't mean that I don't want you in my life as much as possible. Sometimes it's lonely being independent. I didn't realize how much until I met you. I've been driving in the dark for years, and no one has ever said a word about it. I like that you're worried about me. I like that you want to make things as easy as possible for me. But I feel that way about you too. You work damn hard, and I never want to add to the stress in your life."

"You don't," Aleck told her without thinking twice about it.

"Well, things are still new with us," she said with a smile, running her thumb over his clean-shaven cheek. It felt a little odd after having a beard for so long, but he wasn't sorry he'd shaved it off. He liked being able to feel her touch against his skin.

"You are not an added stress in my life," he insisted. "And

I have a feeling you never will be. I don't care if we've been together a month or forty years. I know how damn lucky I am to have you, and I'm going to do whatever it takes to not fuck it up...and to spoil you as well. Driving an extra twenty to thirty minutes to go to work is completely worth it if it means I get to say goodnight in person and wake up next to you in the morning."

"You're too good to me," Kenna whispered.

"No such thing," Aleck said.

Her fingers flexed on his neck, and he leaned forward and kissed her forehead gently.

After a moment, she said, "Feel free to bring some stuff over so you don't have to worry about bringing a bag all the time."

"I will," he said with satisfaction. He couldn't think of anything better than seeing his clothes and toiletries mixed in with hers at her apartment.

Actually, yes, he could—having *all* her things here, in his condo.

But if she lived here, that meant she'd have to make the drive in the dark after work all the time. He frowned as he thought about the logistics of moving their relationship forward.

"What are you frowning about?" she asked.

"Logistics," he answered honestly.

"Of what?"

"Us. And we can talk about that stuff later. For now, I'm excited that I'll get to see you tonight," he said. But he was already thinking about the future. Maybe he could sell his place here and find a condo down in Waikiki. There were plenty of luxury condos closer to her work.

"Me too," she agreed.

Sighing, Aleck knew he needed to go if he was going to be on time for the AAR.

"You need to go," Kenna said, as if she could read his mind. She caressed his cheek once more, then climbed off his lap. She held out her hand as if to help him up.

It made Aleck grin. He took her hand and stood. Then he hugged her. "Thank you."

"For what?" she asked into his neck as they embraced.

"For being so amazing. For loving me. For letting me love you. For being so supportive of what I do."

She didn't answer, but tightened her hold on him. "You're welcome," she said softly. He felt her take a deep breath, then she pulled back. "I'll head out with you."

"Sounds good."

Within a few minutes, they were holding hands as they headed down the hall toward the elevator. They exited in the lobby, and Aleck was somewhat amused when Kenna dropped his hand and went around the security desk to give Robert a hug. "Thank you *so* much for the treat this morning. It was such a great surprise! You totally didn't have to do that, but we're both so appreciative."

"It was my pleasure, Ms. Madigan," Robert said with a grin.

"Do you think you'll ever call me Kenna?" she teased.

"Probably not. Company rules, you know," Robert told her.

Kenna just shook her head. "Well, I don't care what you call me, I'm just glad to call you a friend."

Robert looked taken aback for a moment, but then he smiled so big, Aleck thought he was going to dance a jig of happiness right there in the lobby.

"Drive safe, both of you," he said as Kenna took Aleck's hand once more and they headed for the front doors.

"We will!" Kenna called back.

Aleck gave the man a chin lift.

When they arrived at Kenna's Malibu, Aleck took her face in his hands, studying her silently.

"What? Why are you looking so intense all of a sudden?" she asked as she held onto his wrists.

"I want to take you back inside, tear off your clothes, and bury my face in your pussy again," Aleck blurted.

Kenna blushed, and her grip on his wrists tightened. "Yeah, well, we have to be adults and do adulty things," she said.

"Fucking you until we both explode is an adult thing," he quipped.

"True," she said. "But I meant things like work, shop, take care of responsibilities...those kinds of adult activities."

"All kidding aside, last night was the most amazing night of my life," Aleck said seriously.

"Well, you were basically a virgin," she said with a straight face.

"Everything seemed like it was the first time...because it was with you." Aleck didn't know where this sappiness was coming from, but he didn't give a shit. He was well aware Kenna was talking about the fact that he hadn't ever made love to a woman without a condom before, but everything they'd done had seemed...bigger...more intense.

"Okay, where's my big bad SEAL?" she asked.

"Right here, babe," Aleck said. "I'll fucking kill anyone who dares to hurt one hair on your head. Or I'll get my friend Baker to track them down and make them wish they'd never touched you."

"Wow, all right then. There he is," Kenna said. She leaned forward and kissed his chin lightly. Then his cheek. Then his lips. "I like your sappy side as much as I respect and admire your SEAL side," she reassured him. "And while I suppose I should protest the killing thing, it's kinda hot."

"You aren't helping me control my urge to throw you over my shoulder and haul you back up to our bed," he told her.

She laughed, then put her hands on his chest and gave him a push. It wasn't a small shove either. Aleck dropped his hands from her face and took a step back so he didn't fall on his ass.

"How's that?" she asked with a grin.

"It sucks," Aleck said. "But...thank you. I was on the verge of saying to hell with the Navy and damn the consequences."

"I'm sure they wouldn't have fired you," Kenna said breezily. "Your team would've just come looking for you and made fun of your hairy ass for the rest of your life if they caught us in the act."

"My ass isn't hairy," Aleck complained.

Kenna's lips twitched.

"It isn't!" he insisted.

Kenna burst out laughing. "Okay, okay, it's not. But you should've seen your face!"

Aleck realized he'd smiled and laughed more in the last day than he had in ages. His cheeks almost hurt.

"Go on, get to work," she said when she'd controlled herself. "I'll talk to you later and see you tonight."

"Yes, you will," he confirmed.

He snagged her behind her neck and pulled her close for one more long, deep kiss. They were both breathing hard when he stepped away. "Drive safe," he said.

"You too."

"Love you, babe."

"Love you too."

Aleck followed Kenna's Malibu out of the parking lot, honking once when she turned right and he turned left. It wasn't until he was almost to the front gate at the base that Aleck realized he was still smiling. Life was good. Very good.

CHAPTER NINETEEN

The next week was one of the best of Kenna's life. She'd spent every night with Marshall, either at her place or his. And she wasn't ashamed to admit that she much preferred his condo than her small apartment. His bed was bigger, for one, and Marshall was a man who liked to have his space, both while sleeping and when making love to her. Not to mention, his shower and bathroom were much more conducive to hanky-panky. And she loved his heated floors and having a warm towel when she finally got out of the shower.

And then there was Robert. And Marshall's balcony. And his amazing kitchen.

Shit. She loved every single thing about Coral Springs. It was hard to believe she'd been so upset when she'd learned that Marshall lived there. She'd more than gotten used to the small luxuries at his place.

And Marshall himself was all she'd ever dreamed a boyfriend could be. He was definitely doing what he could to spoil her...and it was working. The only thing that worried Kenna about their relationship was wondering when he'd have to leave again. Now that she was seeing him every day, it would be that much harder when he had to go on a mission. Because she'd both worry about him and miss him all the more.

But...she'd manage. Because that was what military girlfriends and spouses did.

It was Friday, and she'd spent the previous evening at Marshall's condo. He'd had the last few days off work and they'd spent them together. His team, and Elodie and Lexie, had come over for a barbeque down at the condo plaza, and Kenna couldn't remember ever laughing so much. Elodie had bossed the guys around as they'd attempted to grill burgers, and it was obviously a familiar routine. After they ate, everyone went upstairs to Marshall's condo and Kenna had fun getting tipsy with Elodie and Lexie.

The second the door closed behind their friends, Marshall had ravished her. They hadn't even made it back to his room; he'd taken her right there on the dining room table, fucking her with a primal ferocity Kenna had never experienced.

She was a little sore this morning, but wouldn't have traded last night's erotic experience for anything in the world.

Now she was heading to work, and Marshall, Jag, and Pid were coming to Duke's later that evening. Marshall promised they'd stay out of her way, hang out at the bar for a drink or two, then he'd follow her back to her place. Saturday night, after her shift, they'd go back to his condo. The plan was to spend Sunday up at the North Shore. Marshall had a friend who lived up there that he wanted to introduce her to.

Kenna had heard all about the mysterious Baker, and was almost as excited about finally getting to meet him as she was when she'd thought she and Marshall were sneaking onto the Coral Springs private beach.

So she was in a great mood—how could she not be, after the last week with Marshall—and smiled cheerfully at everyone on her way through the shops at the Outrigger, heading to Duke's.

Things were crazy from the second she walked into the kitchen. The restaurant was crowded and there was almost a hyper vibe from the customers. Everyone seemed happy to be out with friends or family, eating good food and toasting the start of the weekend.

It wasn't until an hour into her shift when Kenna had a chance to take a short breather. She was in the kitchen trying to relax for ten minutes or so when Carly entered.

The good mood Kenna had been in all evening faded when she saw her friend.

"You look like hell," she blurted.

"Gee, thanks," Carly said with a slight chuckle. The laugh turned into a dry, hacking cough almost immediately.

"Go home," Kenna ordered.

Carly shook her head. "I don't have a fever. Promise. I'm good."

"Yeah, but that cough sounds horrible and you have a killer headache."

Carly winced. "How can you tell?"

"Because you're squinting. And instead of turning your head, you turn your whole body. Besides that, you're pale. Go home," she repeated.

"I'd feel horrible if I did. It's Friday night. And there was that marathon today. We're packed," Carly protested.

"Charlotte and I can cover your tables until Alani calls someone. You know Justin will probably be happy to come in, especially on a Friday when he knows the tips will be good. Besides, it's supposed to storm like hell later. Like, crazy high winds and apocalyptic rain. The last thing you need is to be out in that when you feel like crap. You're allowed to take a day off," Kenna finished gently.

Carly sighed and looked at the floor. "But Jag's coming," she said in a soft voice.

Kenna wanted to do a fist pump and yell, "I knew it!" Instead, she kept her triumph at her friend's obvious interest in the SEAL to herself. "Yeah, but how do you think *he'll* feel if he sees you looking so miserable? He won't like it," Kenna continued, answering her own question before Carly could.

She sighed. "I know you're right. But I haven't seen him since they got back, and I was looking forward to tonight."

Kenna had a feeling if her friend didn't feel so crappy, she never would've admitted that out loud. "But you've talked to him, right?" she asked.

"Yeah, we've been texting. And he called me the other night," Carly admitted.

"You can text him and let him know that you're sick and heading home. He'll understand."

Carly's shoulders slumped, but she nodded. "I really do feel like shit," she said.

"Talk to Alani. Text Jag. Go home. The last thing you want is for this to get worse. Trust me. I had a fever once for ten days and thought I wanted to die. I couldn't stand up without being dizzy. Being cold one second and hot the next sucked too. You definitely don't want to get a fever on top of whatever you already have."

"All right, I'm going. Will you..." Carly's voice faded.

But Kenna knew what she was going to ask. "I'll talk to Jag. Tell him that you hated to go without seeing him."

"Thanks. But don't make me sound as if I'm on death's door. The man would probably show up on my doorstep with a bowl of chicken noodle soup and a truckload of medicine."

"And that would be a bad thing?" Kenna asked, not being sarcastic in the least.

"Yes," Carly mumbled. "I can't fall for someone right now. I just can't."

Kenna wanted to protest. Convince her friend that Jag was a good guy and nothing like her ex. But she had a feeling she could talk herself blue in the face and Carly would still dig in her heels. She was stubborn like that. She honestly couldn't blame her, not after the hell Shawn had put her through.

Carly turned to go find Alani before abruptly turning back to Kenna. "Oh, I wanted to mention...I think I saw Luke earlier."

"Who?" Kenna asked, confused.

"Luke. Shawn's son. He was out on the beach in front of the restaurant again."

"What was he doing?"

"Nothing. He was just standing there. He wasn't watching Duke's at all. He was staring out at the water. I got distracted by a table and when I looked back, he was gone. I don't think it means anything, and you know my protection order is for Shawn, not his son, but I've been on the lookout for my ex, so it kind of surprised me to see Luke here again."

"So you think that means Shawn is here too?" Kenna asked. "Or that he's spying on you for his dad?"

"I don't know. But I wanted to mention it just in case you see Shawn. He's not supposed to be anywhere near Duke's, so if you see him, call the police."

Kenna was glad Carly was being so diligent, and relieved that she was more than all right with getting the authorities involved if Shawn broke the protection order. Kenna had been half afraid that, after all this time, Carly would just want to forget about the entire drama. "Okay, I will. Be extra careful going home."

"I will. Especially after the notes he's been sending me."

"Notes?" Kenna asked, unease suddenly churning in her gut.

"Yeah. The asshole thinks he's so sneaky. As if I wouldn't know he's the one leaving them."

"I didn't know you were getting notes from him. Have you told the police?" Kenna asked.

"What good will that do? I mean, I've been keeping them, just in case, but I have a feeling turning them in will just egg him on even more. I've been trying not to give him any attention whatsoever, in the hopes he'll realize he's not getting the reaction out of me that he wants—namely, me going back to him, which is never going to happen."

"That's not good," Kenna said. "That he's sending notes, that is. I think you should talk to the cops."

Carly sighed. "If I get another one, I will."

"Thank you. I just worry. I don't want anything to happen to you," Kenna said.

"I appreciate that more than you know. Trust me, I've been the most alert and aware woman on the island the last couple of months. I don't trust Shawn in the least. Just because he hasn't done anything beyond leaving cryptic notes on my car, that doesn't mean he isn't planning something. He's patient. And sneaky. And scary as hell. Is it bad that I kind of *want* him to just make his move already? I know that protective order had to have pissed him off, and I have a feeling he's just waiting for the perfect time to be a colossal asshole again."

"Well, if he is, he's gonna go to jail," Kenna said. Then she hugged her friend tightly. "I'm proud of you, and I love you very much. I don't know what I'd do if something happened to you. Go home and sleep. And text me tomorrow to let me know if you feel any better."

"I will. And I love you too. Thanks for being such a great friend. When I first started here, I wasn't sure if I was going to like it, but you made me feel right at home."

Kenna smiled at her before Carly headed off to find their manager.

She *hated* that months later, Carly was still living on pins and needles, waiting for her ex to do something. She'd naively thought Shawn would have gotten the message by now that he and Carly were done.

Then, as Kenna stood there pondering her friend's situation, something else struck her.

If Shawn was sending *Carly* notes...maybe the one she'd received hadn't been from the angry Duke's customer, after all. Maybe it was from Shawn.

Shit! She hadn't even suspected him. But it made sense. If Shawn was pissed that he couldn't get to Carly, it was possible he'd strike out at those who were close to her. Not to mention, Kenna had pissed him off by getting in his face the last time he was at Duke's.

Making a mental note to be extra observant for her friend —and for herself—and to talk to Marshall about the situation as soon as possible and get his take on things, Kenna took a deep breath and got back to work.

An hour later, Vera told her that Marshall and his friends had arrived. She didn't have a lot of time, but there was no way she wasn't going to greet them. As if Marshall could sense her, he turned just as she approached.

Kenna walked straight into his arms, sighing in contentment. She loved how excited she always felt to see him, and how he seemed to feel the same. Pulling back, Kenna smiled at Marshall, then turned to his friends.

"Hey. It's good to see you guys." Kenna gave Jag a small smile. "Carly's sad she missed you."

He shrugged. "I would've been pissed if she'd stayed just to see me when she felt like shit. I'll see her another time."

"For the record," Kenna continued, not able to keep her

mouth shut, "she's gonna come around. She's just a little skittish right now."

She swore she saw Jag's shoulders relax a fraction at her words. "I can't blame her. Her ex really did a number on her."

Kenna nodded.

"As much as I want to stand here and chat, you probably need to get back to work," Marshall said. He kissed her briefly, then said, "You're still cool if we hang out at the bar?"

"Of course," Kenna told him. "I'll stop by when I can."

"We'll be fine," Marshall said. "Just do your thing."

Kenna watched the three men head off for the bar area and couldn't keep the smile off her face.

"Shit, woman, those are three fine-looking men," Vera said. "If I wasn't into girls, I might give you a run for your money."

Kenna laughed at the hostess. "For the record...only one is my boyfriend."

"Damn, I was hoping you were into some kinky shit," Vera said quietly with a wink before heading back to her spot at the podium near the front of the restaurant.

Shaking her head at her coworker's antics, Kenna got back to work.

* * *

An hour later, Aleck couldn't keep his eyes from Kenna as she moved around the restaurant. He'd spent almost every minute since his arrival thinking about what he wanted to do to her later that night, when they got back to her place.

"Glad to see things with you guys are working out so well," Jag said from next to him.

Aleck forced his attention from Kenna to his friend. They were sitting at a table near the bar, shooting the shit, enjoying some downtime.

"She's amazing," Aleck said. "What's up with you and Carly?" he couldn't help but ask.

Jag shrugged. "Complicated."

Pid snorted. "I think that's the understatement of the century," he muttered.

"I'm pissed because her ex has terrified her so much, she's practically a recluse. The asshole even left a note on my car when I came to see if Carly was at work the other day. He's escalating...and Carly still thinks if she ignores him, he'll just go away."

"Wait, what? A note?" Aleck asked, putting his glass down on the table a little too hard.

"Yeah. It just said, *She's mine*. It wasn't signed, but I know it was from him. Who else could it have been from?" Jag asked.

Aleck's mind spun with the implications of Jag's revelation. He couldn't help but think about the note that had been left on *his* car. He'd assumed it had been from Kylo Braun. But what if it wasn't? What if Shawn had left that one too?

He opened his mouth to tell Jag and Pid that he'd received a note as well, but just then, a strong gust of wind surged in from the beach, knocking over a mostly empty glass on a nearby table, and making the woman sitting there squeal in surprise.

The storm had moved in with a vengeance—and a shiver rolled through Aleck as the hair on the back of his neck stood up. He felt exactly as he did right before the shit hit the fan during a mission.

His gaze swept the restaurant, searching for Kenna. He needed eyes on her. To see for himself that she was all right. It wasn't a feeling he could explain, but he knew without a doubt that danger was near. Way *too* fucking near.

* * *

The predicted storm had moved in and the staff at Duke's was kept busy unfolding the plastic barriers around the perimeter of the restaurant. They closed them at night, but they were almost always kept unzipped while Duke's was open. They'd waited a little too long, however, and currently the wind was whipping through the bar and restaurant, sending napkins flying and glasses crashing. Luckily, the dinner rush had come and gone, and the patrons sitting nearest the beach moved toward the interior of the dining area as the staff did their best to zip the barriers as quickly as possible.

Kenna had just zipped up the last plastic window when she heard a commotion behind her. The first thing she did was look toward the bar, where the guys were still sitting. Marshall was staring at her with an intense look on his face that she couldn't interpret.

She had no time to wonder about it before a woman's screech registered.

She turned toward the sound—and froze in shock at the scene that greeted her.

Striding quickly through the restaurant, straight for her, was Shawn. Carly's ex.

And he did *not* look happy.

He was wearing a vest that looked a lot like the one she'd seen in Marshall's picture from when he was deployed. It had just as many pockets—but what caught her attention was the large box strapped to the front.

There was a red light in the center that blinked on and off.

Even as he approached, Shawn reached into one of his pockets and pulled out a pistol. He stopped four feet from Kenna, pointed the gun straight at her face and growled, "Where's Carly?"

For a split second, as cliché as it sounded, Kenna's life flashed before her eyes.

As she looked down the barrel of that gun, she realized how much she wanted to live. She suddenly longed to call her parents; it had been too long since she'd talked to them. She wanted to spend another night with Marshall. A lifetime of nights. She wanted to travel. Get married. Have children.

"Where's Carly?" Shawn barked again, stepping closer. Before she could even think of moving, he grabbed her upper arm, shoved the pistol against her temple, and began dragging her toward the bar.

Exactly where she wanted to go. Toward Marshall and his friends, who could hopefully take this asshole out just as they'd done before.

Kenna heard people screaming around her, almost falling over each other trying to get to the beach and away from the crazy man with a gun.

"She got off early," Kenna told Shawn without hesitation, and she'd never been so glad in her entire life that her friend wasn't there.

The string of curse words that came out of Shawn's mouth at her answer was surprising. Not that Kenna was offended by cursing. She'd been known to spew the occasional bad word herself. But she hadn't even *heard* some of the words Shawn was muttering.

She jerked on her arm, trying to get away from him, but Shawn's fingers dug into her flesh, forcing her to continue toward the bar.

As she figured, Marshall, Jag, and Pid hadn't run in the opposite direction at the first sound of trouble. All three were standing near their chairs, taking in the scene with narrowed eyes. Paulo and Kaleen were frozen behind the bar.

Shawn turned the weapon in their general direction and

without warning, shot off a round, shattering a bottle of booze on a high shelf behind the bar.

It was Kenna's turn to screech. For a split second, she'd thought he'd been aiming for Marshall.

Jag and Pid cleared the bar in one jump, landing behind it and grabbing the two bartenders, hauling them down behind the dubious safety of the wood.

But Marshall, the crazy man, simply straightened from where he'd hunched slightly, and glared at Shawn. She wanted to tell him not to do anything stupid, that he needed to live, but she didn't get the chance.

"Of course the big bad SEAL doesn't flinch," Shawn sneered.

"I'm not scared of bullies," Marshall said in a deep, hard, chilling tone of voice that Kenna had never heard before. She'd gotten to know Marshall as a man. He was funny, sarcastic, and had never spoken to her in anything other than a respectful, or sexy, or loving tone. This was an entirely different facet of him. A different man.

This was the no-nonsense, deadly Navy SEAL.

"Put down the weapon before this gets even worse," he ordered.

"Don't think so. See this?" Shawn asked, gesturing toward the box with the blinking red light. "It's a bomb. A *big* fucking bomb. With enough ANFO to blow up not only this restaurant, but the entire fucking building. I can take it all down just like *that*."

Kenna didn't know exactly what ANFO was, but she'd watched enough episodes of *Mythbusters* to know the situation wasn't good.

"And even better, it's got a mercury tilt switch as a detonator."

Kenna wasn't sure what that meant either, but at the look on Marshall's face, knew it was bad. Very bad.

"That's right, asshole. If you or your friends try to tackle me again, we all go boom. If you shoot me and I fall over, we go boom. If I even bend over at the waist too far, *we fucking all go boom*. So...now that I have your attention, and we know who the fuck is in charge here," he glared at Jag and Pid, who'd stood from behind the bar, "Get. The. Fuck. Out."

The two SEALs looked extremely pissed, but they did as Shawn ordered.

It was now only Shawn, Kenna, Marshall, Paulo, and Kaleen left in the restaurant, as far as she could tell. At least, if her coworkers had fled, they'd done so without standing. She hoped they did—and that they'd hit the silent alarm to summon police on their way out. Everyone else had fled onto the dark beach, into the storm, or through the front entrance of Duke's.

Shawn kept his tight grip on Kenna's biceps as he walked toward Marshall.

Kenna could see a muscle in her man's jaw ticking, his hands fisted tight, but otherwise, he stood stock still.

Shawn stopped just out of Marshall's reach and raised the pistol once more.

Kenna's heart flew to her throat and she almost stopped breathing.

Instead of killing Marshall right then and there, it seemed Shawn was in a chatty mood. "Just as I thought...you're not as tough as you think you are," Shawn smirked.

Kenna saw something flash through Marshall's eyes at the words—she could've sworn it was respect. But that had to be a trick of the light.

Or Marshall was just fucking with Shawn until he could find a way to take him out.

"Good job. I had no idea you'd left that note on my Jeep. How'd you get into the military parking lot? It's strictly monitored."

Kenna's mind whirled. *Note?* He'd gotten a note too?!

"The military sticker on my car. I've done some work on base," Shawn told him. "Who'd you *think* the note was from?"

Kenna felt as if she was in the twilight zone. If Shawn wasn't holding a gun on Marshall, and if he didn't have a freaking *bomb* strapped to his body, she might've thought the two men were old buddies catching up after some time apart.

"There's a guy on base who's been a pain in my ass for a while," Marshall answered, seemingly unfazed by the fact he was looking down the barrel of a gun. "He said almost those exact words to me not too long ago. Figured he was still messing with me."

Shawn laughed. It wasn't a happy sound. It was one of deep satisfaction.

"What about your note?" he asked, shaking Kenna. "Did it make you wanna shit your pants?"

"No," she said with more bravado than she really felt.

"Fucking liar. *All* bitches lie," Shawn seethed, shaking her even harder, his grip painful.

Kenna knew she was going to have some pretty damn vivid bruises in the next week or so...if she lived that long. Her arm throbbed where Shawn held it, and once more she tried to wrench herself out of his grip, but he simply laughed.

Kenna had already been terrified enough by this point, but the crazy look on Shawn's face made her blood run cold. She could hear sirens now, and she prayed the police would hurry. But at the same time, she worried about what they'd do. If they didn't know about the bomb, they might try to take Shawn out. And if he fell, that bomb would go off.

Shit!

Shawn began walking backward without warning, the gun at her temple once more, and Kenna almost tripped as she was yanked along with him.

"I was just gonna take what belonged to me and go,"

Shawn informed them. "But that fucking bitch ruined every-thing, like usual. I know she was here earlier. I've been watching and waiting for all three of you to be in the same place."

"What were you going to do?" Marshall asked, stepping forward, following slowly as Shawn headed for the exit that led out onto the beach. The wind had really picked up, howling outside the flimsy plastic windows Kenna had zipped into place. Rain was falling in heavy sheets. In fact, she couldn't even see the shoreline, and the ocean wasn't that far from the restaurant.

"Take what belongs to me after killing you and this meddling whore," Shawn said without hesitation.

Kenna quaked. God, this was a nightmare.

"And now?" Marshall asked.

"I still want Carly," Shawn said. "I want what's mine." He shook Kenna yet again, making her stumble. "But I'll make do with *this* bitch until I can get her back."

"Not happening," Marshall said in that deadly tone.

Shawn laughed. "Sorry, SEAL boy. It is. It's all planned out, and you can't do a goddamn thing about it. Once we're gone, you'll just have to suffer thinking about what I'm doing to your fuck hole. Wonder if she's scared, if she's in pain. And I'll tell you right now—she will be. She'll regret sticking her goddamn nose into my business—just like you will."

Then Shawn swung the pistol toward Marshall.

Kenna acted on instinct the second his arm moved. She slammed her free hand against the underside of his arm as hard as she could, shoving it up just as he pulled the trigger.

Marshall was already leaping to the side, crashing into a chair that was in his way.

Shawn punched Kenna in the face with the pistol, making her cry out as pain bloomed in her temple. She felt blood oozing down the side of her face, but she didn't fall.

Throughout it all, he never let go of her arm. The sirens wailed, much closer now, and Shawn didn't wait for Marshall to get back up. He walked backward again, much faster this time, obviously trying to get out of there before the police showed up—which Kenna hoped would be any second.

"Time to go," Shawn growled.

Kenna had no idea if he was talking to her or Marshall, but ultimately it didn't matter. She didn't know where they were going. It wasn't like they could just take a stroll down the beach and blend in with the nonexistent crowd. It felt and sounded like a damn hurricane was going on and everyone had sought shelter. But Shawn obviously had a getaway plan.

Kenna just prayed that somehow, someway, she'd be able to escape before his plan succeeded.

CHAPTER TWENTY

Aleck was *pissed*—so angry he was having a hard time thinking straight. His options were also severely limited. Shawn was fucking insane, but he wasn't stupid. He'd made it extremely difficult for anyone to do anything to stop him.

As far as he could tell, the bomb was legit. He wasn't a bomb expert, and for a second he wished the former SEAL Mustang had mentioned meeting in California—when he'd flown out for their friend Phantom's Admiral Mast—was there. Dude was his name. He had a reputation for being one of the best explosive experts the SEALs had ever had. He'd know if the bomb was real or not, and how to take this asshole down without turning the beach into one giant crater. But he wasn't here. And Aleck had to figure out how to end this situation without setting the damn thing off.

He guessed Shawn hadn't activated the bomb until he'd arrived at the restaurant. Mercury switches could be tricky, and *tilt* mercury switches even more so. One jerky movement could make it blow, and Aleck wasn't going to do anything to put Kenna in more danger than she was already in.

But the thought of this asshole torturing her made his

adrenaline skyrocket. Aleck would sacrifice himself before letting Shawn get away with Kenna.

He hadn't missed the way the man's gaze had constantly flicked toward the ocean, not that he could've seen much through the rain and wind. The most obvious escape route was the water. Cops would be converging on Waikiki by now, and there was no way he'd be able to escape by vehicle or on foot. Not after threatening to take down an entire damn building.

As pissed as Aleck was, he was proud of Kenna. She hadn't panicked. Hadn't done anything rash. Was staying reasonably calm under the circumstance, probably waiting to see how he would get her out of this.

The bitch of it was—Aleck had no idea. Shawn had the upper hand.

The second Aleck stepped onto the beach after leaving the shelter of the restaurant, he was soaked to the bone. If the situation hadn't been so precarious, he might've been awed by the power of the storm currently raging around them. The normally calm and serene Waikiki Beach was anything but. The ocean surged and frothed angrily. While the waves weren't quite North Shore worthy, they were as high as anything Aleck had ever seen on this side of the island.

It was the one thing working in his favor. The storm might hinder any quick escape Shawn had planned.

Jag and Pid hadn't gone far when they'd exited the bar. He knew they were at his back as he stalked his target. But Aleck had no idea what they could do to help mitigate the situation. There was no place for them to hide on the beach; Shawn would see every move they made. His mind raced as he attempted to come up with some sort of plan, but at the moment, all he could do was wait for Shawn to hopefully screw up—and not start shooting again.

Shawn and Kenna were about thirty feet in front of him. Aleck was scared to get any closer. Scared Shawn would hurt Kenna.

"Let her go!" Aleck yelled, making himself heard over the howling wind.

"Fuck you!" Shawn shouted back, dragging Kenna as he shot off another round.

Aleck felt the bullet graze his leg, but he didn't even stumble. He wasn't going to die here. No fucking way. Not after all he'd seen and done in his lifetime. He'd faced down some of the worst terrorists the world had ever seen. Men and women who held no respect for human life. He'd been beaten and tortured, hiked for miles and miles through every type of terrain, had gone a week without eating...had even been shot before.

No, this asshole wasn't taking him down—not when this was the most important mission of his life. Keeping the woman he loved safe. He hadn't found Kenna, only to lose her now.

He couldn't. He wouldn't survive it.

Shawn was backing into the water—and dread swamped Aleck. The crazy asshole knew how little it would take to set off the bomb. Why was he risking going into the rolling waves and possibly losing his balance?

Nothing the man was doing made sense.

"Easy," he muttered, more to himself than to the insane man in front of him.

"You want me? Come at me, asshole!" Shawn yelled. "You won't take me alive, and if I'm dead, so is this bitch!"

Aleck heard more people now. The police had finally arrived. When they didn't immediately begin shouting at Shawn, or threatening to shoot him, he knew they'd been briefed on the situation. Probably by either Jag or Pid, who were still somewhere behind him.

"Stand back now, sir," the closest officer said. "We've got this."

But Aleck didn't retreat; instead, he took a step closer to the water. Adrenaline coursed through his veins, fighting with the anger and frustration, urging him to act. To rush toward the woman he loved and snatch her away from danger. But he couldn't do *anything*, not without possibly hurting or killing her.

He wasn't in a position to help Kenna.

He'd never felt more helpless in his life.

Sheets of rain were still coming down from the sky with a vengeance, as if Mother Nature herself was pissed off on his behalf.

Shawn looked behind him at the ocean again, and Aleck realized he was searching for a boat. That was his escape plan. Either his partner was late or he'd capsized in the storm. Aleck couldn't help but hope it was the latter. It was a blood-thirsty thought, but anyone who was in cahoots with Shawn, who'd planned to help him kidnap an innocent woman, deserved to die.

Pain and regret filled Aleck as he watched Kenna struggle in Shawn's grasp. What use was all his SEAL training if he couldn't employ those skills when he desperately needed them most—to save the woman who meant more to him than anyone else on the planet?

Kenna wasn't as calm as she seemed on the outside. In her head, she was screaming bloody murder. But letting Shawn see how petrified she was wouldn't help her *or* the situation.

She kept her eyes on Marshall, mourning everything they'd never have a chance to do...

Shaking her head, Kenna banished any defeatist thoughts.

She wasn't dead yet. Neither was Marshall. If anyone could get her out of this, it was him.

But even from a distance, through pounding rain, she could see the fear and frustration on his face.

Marshall and his teammates couldn't risk charging them. The bomb would definitely go off, killing them all in the process.

Shawn backed them right into the surf, and Kenna frowned in confusion. "What are you doing?"

"Shut up," Shawn said.

But she ignored him. "Are you going to swim away? That's insane! You'd be killed. This storm is unlike anything I've ever seen and—"

"I said, shut the fuck up!" he snarled. "I've got a plan. We're getting out of here, gonna have some fun together. When Carly's delivered to me, you're dead. And I'll make sure that bitch knows she's the reason. My word is law. She'll regret even *trying* to break up with me..."

He continued to mumble under his breath—and Kenna realized the man had completely lost it. She'd had a feeling he wasn't exactly stable to begin with, but now, unable to get his hands on Carly and with his plans falling apart...he'd gone over the edge.

And a crazy man, a bomb, and a gun was never a good combination.

Marshall yelled, "Let her go!" and Kenna jerked in fright when Shawn fired the pistol.

"Stop it!" she screamed, anger overtaking her fear. "You're gonna kill him!"

"That's the idea." Shawn laughed. "Asshole thinks he's a badass. Who's in charge now?"

The waves were crashing against their calves, and every time one of them hit, Shawn staggered a bit. Not enough to be obvious...but enough that it gave her an idea.

The sand was already sucking her feet down, and the farther into the ocean they went, the harder it was to stay upright. It was only a matter of time before Shawn lost his balance and fell, taking her down with him, and setting off the damn explosives strapped to his chest.

Eying the distance between the restaurant, Marshall, and where she was standing in the surf, she knew this was the best chance she had to mitigate damage to property and other people, while also getting away. Any farther, and she wouldn't be able to run through the churning water fast enough to get any distance between her and the bomb.

And just like that, all the noise around her disappeared.

Kenna had no idea if her plan would work. He might shoot her in the back the second she moved. But she refused to just stand there docilely and *let* Shawn kill her—or haul her into the boat he was obviously waiting for.

The arrival of a swarm of police forced Shawn's attention away from Marshall.

The hand on her arm loosened a fraction.

Kenna met Marshall's gaze one last time. She could practically see the tension vibrating off his body. He was about to do something. She could feel it.

But Shawn still had his gun. He'd kill the man she loved before he could even get close. She knew that as well as she knew her own name.

Mouthing *I love you* to Marshall, she took a deep breath.

He shook his head, fear swamping his features—

And at that moment, a wave crashed against their legs.

Shawn shifted to keep his balance.

And Kenna moved.

Jerking her wet arm out of his grasp, she took off, lurching through the waves doing their best to knock her off her feet, their momentum actually helping to push her toward the shore.

Another wave crashed against her as she stepped out of the water. Kenna stumbled forward, gaining her balance and running as fast as she could in the sand, away from the gun. Away from the bomb. Hoping and praying the police would deal with Shawn.

For an excruciating moment, she heard nothing.

Then several shots rang out.

Kenna ran faster.

A heartbeat later, a massive explosion erupted and a shockwave hit her so hard, Kenna was thrown forward. She landed hard, her chin bouncing off the sand.

A wave of heat seared her back. She heard the sound of windows shattering even over the howling wind and crashing waves.

Kenna lay still, not daring to even breathe. She was in pain—but she was alive.

"Kenna!"

She'd never heard a sound so beautiful in her entire life.

Swallowing a moan, she rolled onto her back and looked up at the man she loved with all her heart.

"Kenna, talk to me! Are you all right? Shit, your chin is bleeding!"

She smiled. Rain was falling into her eyes, making her blink rapidly. Her arm hurt. Her head hurt where Shawn had hit her. Her chin throbbed. But she was still breathing. As was Marshall.

So she felt fucking fantastic.

Reaching up, she wrapped her hand around the back of Marshall's neck and pulled him toward her. "Told you I didn't need a man," she said weakly, her voice a little wobbly. Then she kissed him as if her life depended on it.

CHAPTER TWENTY-ONE

Aleck growled at the nurse as she finished stitching his leg. All he wanted was to take Kenna home. He'd insisted on waiting to have his leg looked at until she'd been taken care of. The sand had helped cushion her fall somewhat, and somehow she'd escaped any wounds on her back from the bomb, but she'd managed to break open the skin on her chin. The wound had to be cleaned, since there had been sand packed inside it, then stitched. He'd held her hand throughout the procedure, refusing to let go.

He'd almost lost her.

He'd seen the moment she'd made the decision to do something, and he'd never been so scared in his life.

But she'd timed her escape perfectly. Shawn had stumbled when a wave crashed into them. He'd struggled to maintain his balance for a few precious seconds—long enough for Kenna to reach the beach.

The last decision Shawn made in his miserable life was to aim his pistol at Kenna as she fled.

The officers hadn't hesitated, shooting several rounds at Shawn.

Aleck had enough time to yell "down!" before all hell broke loose.

It turned out Shawn hadn't been lying about the amount of ANFO he'd used. Luckily, he'd fallen backward into the angry sea, another wave crashing over his body just as the fuse had been triggered. Anything less and the explosion most likely would've taken out Duke's, as well as a huge chunk of the Outrigger resort. But the water helped to essentially muffle the blast.

Still, there was a huge crater in the sand, and parts of Shawn's body were strewn over the beach. But the hostage situation had ended with no other deaths.

Aleck had run toward Kenna's motionless body with his heart in his throat. She'd rolled over and smiled at him, the feel of her hand on the back of his neck bringing tears to his eyes. But it wasn't until she'd kissed him hard and deep that he'd truly comprehended she was all right.

And now that she'd been stitched up, it was his turn. Aleck hated hospitals. He would've preferred to let Pid or Jag close up the gash from Shawn's bullet grazing his leg, but Kenna wasn't having it. And because he would do anything for the woman he loved, he caved.

"Don't be a baby," she said, smiling at him.

"The biggest, baddest men usually are," the nurse said with a chuckle.

Aleck barely heard them. He couldn't stop staring at Kenna. Her hair was in complete disarray and still filled with sand. She'd been given a set of scrubs to change into that swamped her frame. She looked tired and dark circles shadowed her eyes...but she was alive and in one piece. Aleck couldn't ask for anything more.

The nurse finished stitching his leg and said she'd be back in a moment, leaving Aleck and Kenna alone in the small examination room.

Before he could move, before he could pull Kenna into his arms and simply hold her, the curtain was thrown back and his team filed in.

Mustang, Midas, Slate, Jag, Pid—even Baker fucking Rawlins—were all suddenly there.

Aleck swallowed hard at the emotion that balled in his throat at seeing his team.

He had no idea how they'd talked their way into being allowed back there, but at the moment, he didn't care. He sat up on the table and swung his legs over the edge, ignoring the twinge of pain. Kenna snuggled into his side and the second he touched her, Aleck felt as if he could finally relax.

"Damn good to see you alive and not in a million pieces," Pid said.

"That was fucked up," Jag muttered, running a hand through his hair.

"The storm tapered off about five minutes after that bomb exploded," Mustang said. "As if Mother Nature said 'fuck you' to that asshole and was satisfied he was in hell where he belonged after he blew up."

"Heard they'll probably be picking body parts off the beach for days," Midas said.

"Gross," Kenna muttered, before taking a breath and standing up straight. "But he deserved it."

"Too bad his death was painless," Baker said.

Kenna glanced at him, as if just realizing there was someone she didn't know in the room.

"Baker," he said, holding out his hand. Kenna shook it, but he didn't let go. "I've seen the security tapes. That was a ballsy move," he said.

If she was surprised that Baker had somehow already seen security video from either Duke's or the Outrigger, she didn't let on. "It was a no-win situation," she replied. "It was either do something myself, or let Marshall do something that might get him hurt or killed, or wait for whoever was coming to pick us up, then suffer even more at Shawn's hands."

"There was literally nothing I could do that wouldn't end in that fucker blowing Kenna up," Marshall said, his voice haunted. "I've never felt more helpless in my life."

"Sometimes the best thing you can do is wait for the right opening," Mustang said.

"Which I did," Kenna interjected.

"Mind giving her hand back?" Aleck couldn't help asking as he stared at Baker, who still had Kenna's hand in his.

Baker's lips twitched, but he nodded and took a step back.

"So, you're the infamous Baker," Kenna said.

"That's me," he said.

Kenna opened her mouth to say something else, but there was a commotion outside the curtain.

Everyone turned as Elodie and Lexie rushed into the room, followed by the nurse who'd just stitched up Aleck's leg.

The nurse sighed. "You all have two minutes to say what you have to say, then you're out of here. And I'm only allowing that much because I heard about what happened tonight, and I know how harrowing it must have been. Your friends aren't being held overnight, so you can fawn over them soon. Somewhere else. *Not* in my emergency room."

Aleck nodded at the woman gratefully, even as Elodie and Lexie went straight to Kenna and pulled her into a three-way embrace.

Baker moved closer. "I'm gonna figure out who was helping him," he said in a low tone. "No one fucks with the SEALs."

"First on the list is his son, Luke," Jag muttered.

"Already on my radar," Baker said.

Aleck glanced at the older man. "I want in," he said simply.

Baker shrugged noncommittally.

Aleck frowned. He knew Baker had a code. He didn't mind stepping outside the bounds of the law, and he liked working alone.

"She's mine. My responsibility," Aleck argued quietly, glad that Kenna was busy with her friends instead of paying attention to him and Baker. He was well aware that the rest of his team was listening. They all had a stake in this, especially Jag. He hadn't said much, but the fact that Shawn was Carly's ex was likely eating at him.

Baker didn't seem fazed by Aleck's declaration. He merely shrugged again. "She's all of ours," he said. Then he nodded at Aleck and the rest of the team before heading out of the room without another word.

"Darn it, I wanted to talk to Baker," Elodie protested. "He always slips away before I can have an actual conversation with him."

"Well, it'll have to wait for another day," Mustang told her.

"Shoot," Elodie pouted.

Kenna sidled back over to Aleck. He stood slowly, testing his leg, pleased that the pain killers they'd given him were doing their thing. He barely felt a twinge. But he was well aware that for the next few days, both him and Kenna would be hurting. He planned to hole up with her in his condo, neither coming out for a week. They'd take care of each other...and bask in the fact that they were still alive.

"At least we don't have to worry about that asshole coming after Carly again," Elodie said as she leaned against Mustang.

Aleck met Jag's gaze and knew he was thinking the same thing. Yes, Shawn was out of the picture, but his accomplice wasn't.

Carly might not know it, but she was about to have a Navy SEAL glued to her hip. Jag would make sure she was safe until whoever had been out in that ocean was discovered —and any threat to Carly ended once and for all.

"I can't believe someone was crazy enough to be out on the ocean in that storm," Kenna mumbled. "I mean, assuming that's how Shawn was going to get off the beach like the cops think. It was probably Luke. Shawn's son."

"We'll figure out who it was and make sure he's not a threat to Carly in the future," Jag said, determination easy to hear in his tone.

"Can we talk about the note you got...and didn't tell me about?" Aleck asked Kenna.

She turned to him. "I honestly thought it was that stupid guy from Duke's. The one who was abusing his wife and kid, who I'd called the cops on," she said. "It said something about minding my business. I got it right after that incident, the day after you were deployed. I honestly forgot about it with everything else going on, especially since I didn't get any others. Besides, you didn't tell me *you* got a note either."

Aleck took a deep breath. He had no right to be upset with her when he'd also gotten a note and dismissed it. He was sorrier than he could say that he hadn't taken it more seriously. "You're right. I should've said something. Jag got one too," he told her.

Kenna looked at his friend with wide eyes. "You did?"

"Yes. I figured it was from Shawn, but like everyone else, I never expected he'd do something as extreme as he did," Jag said.

"The second I learned about Jag getting a note, I put it together, but it was too late," Aleck said. "Shawn was already at the restaurant."

"Carly got a note. More than one, actually." Kenna shivered. "I'm just so glad she wasn't there."

"Anyone *else* get any fucking notes?" Mustang asked, looking at Elodie and Lexie.

"Don't look at me," Elodie said immediately, shaking her head.

"Nope, not me," Lexie added with a shrug.

"Well, in the future, if anyone *does* receive any threatening notes, no matter who you think they're from, can we all agree to say something about it?" Mustang asked.

Everyone immediately nodded.

The realization that he wasn't the only one who'd dismissed the note should've made Aleck feel better, but it didn't. Because his mistake had almost meant Kenna's death. He never would've forgiven himself if she'd been hurt worse than the cut under her chin.

"Okay, time's up," the nurse said as she stuck her head back into the room. "Everyone out."

The guys each approached and gave Kenna heartfelt hugs. Aleck was almost brought to tears again, seeing how much they all worried and cared about her. Some men might've been jealous, but not him. He *wanted* his friends to like his woman, as much as he liked theirs.

Elodie and Lexie took a bit longer saying goodbye, with Elodie promising to make several meals so Kenna didn't have to worry about cooking.

"Bring them to my place," Aleck told her.

She smiled. "Of course."

Kenna gave him some side-eye, but she didn't complain or protest.

Lexie promised to come by and see her soon, and to bring Ashlyn as well.

Slate told Aleck he'd wait and drive them both home. "We'll get both of your cars to Coral Springs," he reassured them before heading out.

After their friends had all left, the room almost felt too quiet.

"I'll bring by your discharge papers," the nurse told them. "Sit. Get off that leg. Relax," she ordered, then left.

Aleck ignored her. He was fine. His leg was fine. All he needed was to hold Kenna. He gathered her against his chest and sighed deeply. It had been a hell of a night, and there were a few times he hadn't been sure he'd get a chance to hold her again.

"That sucked," she muttered against his neck.

"Yeah."

"Is that what it's like when you're on a mission?" she asked.

Aleck couldn't help but chuckle. "Not even fucking close," he told her.

Kenna looked up at him. "Really?"

"Really. I've never felt as helpless on a mission as I did tonight. I had no plan. I was frozen in fear for you. I knew if I made the wrong decision, it could result in your death. I didn't have my team at my side—well, not all of them, and Jag and Pid didn't have a plan either. That's a shitty feeling for a SEAL. And above everything else, I knew I wouldn't be able to survive if something happened to you. I'd never recover. So yeah, it sucked."

"Marshall," she whispered.

"I'm proud of you," he told her, moving one hand to her nape in the familiar hold they both loved so much. "From the first time you jumped on my head, I've known you're a woman of action. You'd never sit back and do nothing when someone was in danger, including if that someone was you."

"I didn't jump on your head," she grumbled without heat.

"I love you," Aleck said. "So much it almost scares me. You've somehow changed my whole outlook on life. The sun seems brighter, the water is crisper, the air is cleaner. I wake up thinking about you, and I go to sleep with you on my mind as well. You're literally the best thing to ever happen to me, and I have no idea what I'd do without you in my life."

"I'm not going anywhere," she told him. "You're stuck with me."

"Forever?"

"Yup."

"Good. So we're getting married?"

Kenna snort-laughed. "Um..."

"You said forever."

Kenna leaned up and kissed his lips. It was a short kiss, and Aleck so badly wanted to deepen it. But there would be time to reaffirm that they were both alive later. He had plans to make love to her for days. Long and slow, hard and fast. Staying inside her long after they were both satisfied. He needed their connection. Needed to feel her heartbeat against his chest as he held her.

"Yes," she said simply. "But not tonight. And not tomorrow. And I want a luau. With the whole roasted-pig-in-the-ground thing. It should be a big party, not all dressy. I want everyone to be comfortable and happy. Um...if that's all right," she said a little sheepishly.

Aleck chuckled. "As long as we end the day with my ring on your finger, and yours on mine, you can have any kind of wedding you want."

"And our parents should be here," she added.

"Of course. I can't wait to introduce you to mine," he said, knowing his mom and dad would fall head over heels in love with Kenna, just as he had.

"Same," she agreed. "I love you, Marshall. So much. I was so scared about you doing something that would get you killed."

"It's over," Aleck told her, ignoring the niggling voice in the back of his head that reminded him of the loose end in the situation.

"You two ready to go?" the nurse said as she came back into the room, making Kenna flinch against him as the woman startled her.

Aleck tightened his hold for a second, then slowly let go. She turned and nodded at the woman. "We're ready."

Twenty minutes later, they were sitting in the backseat of Slate's black Chevy Trailblazer. Kenna pretty much kept the conversation going all the way back to his condo, being careful not to mention anything about Shawn, Duke's, or what had happened.

Slate pulled up as close to the front doors as he could and walked around to hold the door as Kenna and Aleck climbed out. It was nearly three in the morning now, and no one was around, which Aleck was glad for. He wanted to get Kenna upstairs and in bed before she crashed.

Slate surprised the hell out of him when he yanked Aleck into his arms for a quick but heartfelt hug. "I'm glad you didn't get dead."

Then he nodded at them both before jogging back around to the driver's side of the car.

"I love your friends," Kenna said softly.

Aleck did too. "Come on, let's get you inside."

"And *you*. Your leg has to hurt."

It was beginning to throb a bit, but Aleck wasn't going to admit that to Kenna. He was more concerned about getting her settled.

They nodded at the nighttime security guard but didn't stop to chat.

Without discussion, as soon as they entered the condo and the door shut behind them, Kenna and Aleck headed for the master bedroom. They changed, brushed their teeth, and climbed into bed.

Kenna carefully snuggled into Aleck's side, and for the

first time since he'd seen Shawn holding her captive at Duke's, he relaxed.

Neither spoke. There were no words that needed to be said. They were both alive, and for the moment, that was enough.

Kenna nodded off almost immediately, but it took Aleck a bit longer. He lay in the dark holding the most precious and important thing in his life, reflecting on how differently the night could've gone. He finally fell asleep to the vision of Kenna, covered in sand, lying in the pouring rain and smiling up at him. She might not need a man, but he sure as hell needed *her*.

EPILOGUE

"No. Absolutely not," Kenna said emphatically. She and Marshall were mostly healed from that horrible night two weeks ago. They'd spent the first week holed up in his condo. Robert had heard what happened and had taken it upon himself to make sure they had everything they needed. Elodie had sent over the most mouthwatering meals, and Lexie and Ashlyn texted nonstop.

Marshall's teammates had also been sweet in their own ways. Making sure their vehicles were retrieved from the parking garage in Waikiki and keeping Aleck appraised about what was happening at work.

The only dim spot was Carly. Kenna had spoken to her only briefly, and Carly had sobbed, apologizing profusely, devastated over what had happened. No matter how many times Kenna swore it wasn't her fault, Carly wouldn't accept it.

Then Kaleen texted Kenna to tell her Carly had quit Duke's.

Now her friend wasn't answering her calls or texts.

Kenna was all set to drive to Carly's apartment to *make*

her talk, when Aleck told her that Jag was in constant contact with her, and assured her that Carly just needed some time to process what had happened. Kenna wasn't happy, but she trusted Jag, and now that she knew he was keeping an eye on Carly, she'd decided to leave her alone...for now.

She and Carly were definitely going to have a long talk, but if she truly needed some time to process everything, Kenna would give it to her.

Marshall had gone back to work, and she'd done a couple of lunch shifts at Duke's. Kenna was itching to get back to normal sooner than later. Shawn had disrupted their lives long enough.

She and Marshall had just finished dinner and were sitting on his balcony, enjoying the evening, when he'd dropped a bombshell on her.

"It's for the best," Marshall soothed.

Kenna shook her head. "No, seriously. Not happening," she informed him. "I can't believe you'd even *think* about selling this place."

"It makes more sense for us to live in Waikiki," Marshall said, keeping his voice calm. "I've been looking online and there are some incredible condos down there. With ocean views, since I know how much you love this balcony."

"It's not just the balcony," Kenna insisted. "It's the beach where we had our first real date. It's Robert—I can't imagine not seeing him every day. It's the master bathroom where you went down on me that first time...It's the *memories*, Marshall. I love this condo. I don't want to live anywhere else."

"Come 'ere," Marshall said as he held out his hand.

Kenna wasn't sure she wanted to cuddle right now, but she stood and took his hand anyway. He pulled her down beside him on the chaise and wrapped an arm around her back, holding her securely. They lay there for several minutes before he spoke.

"I just thought getting a condo in Waikiki would make your life easier. You've spent every night here for the last two weeks, and it's a pain for you to have to drive so far to work."

Kenna came up on an elbow so she could meet Marshall's gaze. "I know I pitched a fit when I first discovered you lived here, but I've come to love everything about Coral Springs. The memories we have here are irreplaceable. And yes, I understand that we probably won't live here for the rest of our lives, and memories live on forever, but there's no need to move right now."

"I don't like you driving so late at night," he argued.

Kenna knew this was what a relationship was about. Give and take. She wanted to protest that she was perfectly capable of driving at night by herself. But after everything that had happened, she also understood his obsessive need to keep her safe.

"What if I picked you up after your shift?" Marshall suggested. "I'm not going to be able to sleep until you get home anyway. Maybe we can look into a ride-share or a taxi or something for you to get to Duke's in the afternoon, since I'll still be at work. Would you be okay with that?"

"If it means us staying here at Coral Springs, yes," she told him. "This is closer to the base for you, so if there's an emergency, you can get there faster."

Marshall leaned down and kissed her thoroughly. By the time he lifted his head, Kenna was way-the-hell turned on. His gaze flicked to her chest, then back to her face. She could feel her nipples rubbing against the T-shirt she was wearing. She hadn't bothered with putting on a bra when she'd changed after getting home from the lunch shift earlier that afternoon.

Without a word, Marshall stood, grabbed her hand, and headed inside so fast, she stumbled after him. But she wasn't afraid of falling, Marshall would never let her hit the ground.

He didn't stop until he'd reached the side of their bed. Didn't speak as he stripped her shirt off her body and pushed her leggings and underwear over her hips. Then he picked her up and threw her onto the mattress as if she weighed nothing more than a feather.

Laughing, Kenna came up on her elbows to watch Marshall take off his own clothes. Within seconds, he was looming over her. They didn't speak as he settled between her legs, shoving them farther apart before he went down on her.

Kenna gasped, excitement filling her. She and Marshall had made love since that awful night two weeks ago, but Marshall had been extremely careful. And while she loved when he treated her gently, she'd missed this part of him. The bossy, impatient, dominant side that took what he wanted without hesitation or permission.

Kenna's libido went crazy when he got like this. She moaned as he ate ravenously, as if he couldn't get enough. He licked, sucked, and finger-fucked her, his mouth closing around her clit. It didn't take her long to orgasm, and she was still shaking when he rose to his knees, stroking his cock a few times and spreading his own precome down the length. Before long, he'd notched the mushroomed head of his cock to her opening.

"Yes," she encouraged as he hesitated a fraction of a second.

Then he was inside her once again. She was so wet, so turned on, she took him easily, as if she'd been made just for this man—and she felt like she was.

He fucked her hard and fast, groaning every time he bottomed out inside her. One of his hands moved between them and he flicked her clit with a firm touch. He knew exactly how and where to touch her to make her fly.

And fly she did. Her inner muscles gripped him tightly as she came. Marshall moaned as he fucked her through her orgasm, pushing inside her so deep, Kenna felt a pinch of pain. Then he came. And came. And came. So much, she wasn't sure he would ever stop.

When he finally opened his eyes and looked at her, she melted at his loving expression.

He fell to his side, holding her ass so she wouldn't lose his cock, then rolled to his back. This was one of Kenna's favorite positions. Straddling his waist, his dick deep inside her, and using his chest as a pillow. His hand stayed on her butt, making it clear he was happy right where he was.

He spoke for the first time since bringing her into the room. "I love you, Kenna. I'd live on the moon if you wanted to. I just want you to be safe. And happy."

"I am," she reassured him. "I can't imagine us being anywhere else."

"All right."

"All right?" she asked. "We'll stay here? No more talk about selling and moving to Waikiki?"

Marshall nodded.

"Yay!" Kenna said with a huge smile.

Marshall grinned and shook his head in exasperation.

"You know it's early, right?" she asked. "Are we going to sleep now?"

His easy grin turned a bit wicked. "A nap, yes. Then you're gonna suck my cock and I'm gonna eat you out. Then I want to take you from behind, before fucking you face-to-face again."

"Do I have any say in this?" she teased.

"No."

But she knew otherwise. He'd never do anything she wasn't one hundred percent all right with. "Okay. But I want to try reverse cowgirl. You know, on top but facing your feet."

"Done," he said without hesitation.

As if she even thought he'd disagree.

She squirmed a bit on top of him and his hand tightened on her ass cheek.

"Stay still," he told her. "I want to fall asleep inside you."

Damn, she liked his bossy side.

She clenched around his cock, and felt him twitch.

"No," he said, slapping her ass gently. "It's too soon, and I took you hard. You need to recover."

Yup, she definitely liked this side of him. "Then stop turning me on," she complained.

He smiled then, and she sighed in contentment when his free hand came up to her neck. "I love you," he whispered. "So damn much."

"I love you too," she returned.

They were quiet for a long while, basking in contentment and love.

Marshall's hand on her neck eventually relaxed as he fell asleep. Kenna wasn't sure he'd really meant it when he'd suggested a nap. He must've been a bit stressed, telling her about moving.

She wasn't tired in the least but loved lying on top of her man as he dozed. He'd wake up soon enough and do exactly as he promised. He was a man of his word, and it was one of a million things she loved about him. She'd stopped looking for his faults. He had them, there was no doubt, but she also knew they'd seem inconsequential compared to all his positive qualities.

Kenna stared out the window at the fluffy clouds and blue sky. The sun would set in thirty minutes or so...and she couldn't help but think about how different the weather was two weeks ago. On *that* night. If there hadn't been a storm raging, she didn't want to think about how different the outcome might've been. While the rain and wind had been scary, it had also saved her life. And Marshall's.

"Kenna. You aren't napping," Marshall muttered as his hand tightened once more on her nape.

"Sorry," she whispered, not sorry in the least.

"You're gonna need your sleep," he warned.

"Okay, okay, I'm closing my eyes," she told him.

He turned his head, kissed her temple, and almost immediately started snoring once more.

Kenna may have thought that she didn't need a man, but she was wrong.

She needed *this* man.

She fell asleep with a smile on her face, knowing whatever might come in the future, she would *always* need Marshall, right by her side.

* * *

A month later, Pid and the rest of the team were tense as they flew in a helicopter toward the American Embassy in Algeria. The country was in the midst of an intense power struggle...the people versus the president, who'd been in power for over twenty years. An unprecedented ten percent of the population had taken to the streets in protest of his continued rule. At first, the protests had been peaceful. Over time, they'd turned more and more violent, and the United States had made the decision to evacuate their representatives until things were more stable.

The saddest part was the number of foreigners who'd made their way to the country to take advantage of the unstable infrastructure. Homes and business were broken into or burned down, and looting was rampant.

"Test, test, test," Mustang said into his microphone, making sure their radios were working properly.

"Got ya."

"Loud and clear."

"Ten-four."

The rest of the team chimed in, letting their team leader know they could hear him without any issues.

"We're going to touch down in five. The families are desperate to escape, so we're gonna have to do our best to keep order. Reassure them that everyone will be evacuated, but there will be several trips and a few different choppers coming and going," Mustang said.

Pid nodded along with the rest of his team. He knew the plan, they'd gone over it several times, along with contingency scenarios. They were SEALs; having a backup plan for their backup plan was what they did. They'd all studied the maps of the area around the embassy and they knew where to meet up if they got separated.

Four minutes and forty-three seconds later, the chopper touched down on the landing pad on the roof of the embassy.

Pid and his teammates quickly exited the helo and made their way to the group of men, women, and children huddled near the stairwell.

Mustang took the lead and spoke to the group, explaining how many people would be going in this first trip. Pid and Midas checked IDs to make sure they were only taking American citizens. That was one of the hardest parts of the job; many times they'd had to turn away friends and loved ones of the Americans they were rescuing because there simply was no room for everyone, not to mention they didn't have the proper paperwork to get them out of the country.

Ten people would be leaving on the first chopper. Pid checked the IDs of the middle-aged ambassador and his wife as they waited to board. She had two little boys huddled against her sides, and they all looked terrified. Pid did his best to smile reassuringly at the children, but he'd never been that great with kids, and they merely stared at him and hugged their mother tighter.

Pid turned toward the next person in line when he felt a tug on his belt. Looking down, he saw one of the little boys—the older one, he guessed—standing next to him.

Pid kneeled so he was eye-to-eye with the boy. "It's going to be all right," he said.

"Monica," the boy said in a shaky, scared voice.

Pid frowned. "What?"

"Monica's not here."

"Who's Monica?" Pid asked.

"Our nanny. Daddy said there wasn't time to go back to the house but I don't want to go without her. She's waiting for us and probably scared!"

Pid patted the boy awkwardly on the shoulder. "We'll find her."

"Promise?"

He hesitated just a second before nodding. "Promise."

The boy gave him a plaintive look just as his mom grabbed his hand, fast-walking him toward the chopper as if afraid someone would change their minds and they wouldn't be able to leave.

Pid stood and turned to Slate. "You hear that?"

Slate nodded. "We're not supposed to be running all over the city looking for stragglers. We have orders," he reminded Pid.

"I know, but it sounds as if she thought they were coming back for her."

"We don't even know if she's American," Slate said reasonably.

Pid nodded, even as he frowned. He didn't know why the boy had struck a chord in him. Maybe because even though the kid was scared, he'd loved his nanny enough to brave talking to Pid. "Once we get this chopper loaded, it'll be a while before the next one arrives. I know from studying the maps that the ambassador's house isn't far from here..."

Slate stared at him for a beat, then nodded. "I'll talk to Mustang and go with you."

Pid mentally sighed in relief and he gave Slate a chin lift. They'd dash to the house, talk to the nanny. If she was American, they'd bring her back here for extraction. If not, they'd inform her that the family was safe and she should lay low. They could be there and back within twenty minutes. Thirty, tops.

* * *

Monica Collins paced anxiously back and forth. Where were they? The family should have been back by now.

Desmond Laws, the US ambassador to Algeria, and his wife had left with their two little boys two hours ago on an errand, and hadn't returned. It was her morning off, so she'd stayed behind. It wasn't exactly smart to go *anywhere* with the protests going on, but Desmond had told her not to worry and left anyway. And now they weren't back, and the protestors were creeping closer and closer to the house.

She was scared to stay, but even more scared to leave. Growing up, her dad's mantra was, *Stay put. Protect what's yours.* But Monica didn't think the house was the safest place to be right now.

The crowds had gotten more and more unruly as the protests continued. She'd watched on the news as people broke windows of businesses and homes, looted stores, even burned cars and buildings. The house the US government had provided for the Laws' was in a neighborhood that was usually very safe. But nothing was as it had been when Monica had first arrived in the country.

A sound at the back door startled her—and she turned to see a man standing on the other side of the glass. He wore green camouflage pants and shirt, his sleeves rolled up. He had material over his mouth and nose, and black paint smeared on his face above the covering. He also had a rifle slung around his chest, and she caught a glimpse of a black tattoo on his forearm.

They stared at each other for a moment before the man smiled. She knew he was smiling because she could see wrinkles form around his eyes. But something in their depths said he was trying to put her at ease...

More like he was excited about whatever he was planning to do next.

Military men weren't her favorite people in the world. After her childhood, that was to be expected.

"It's okay!" he shouted so he could be heard through the glass. "I'm a Navy SEAL and I'm here to rescue you. Open the door."

When she didn't move, the man frowned. "My friend is circling around to the front. We're here to help you. Come on, open the door so I don't have to break it."

Instead of moving toward the glass sliding door, Monica spun and ran for the stairs.

Instinct and the years of conditioning as a child told her to hide. To get away from the military man.

Flashbacks of her dad in his camo uniform ran through her brain, making her even more desperate to get away.

Just as she reached the top of the stairs, the sound of gunfire echoed throughout the house, along with the sound of glass breaking.

A deep voice called out, "I'm a SEAL! You can trust me!"

Nope. Monica was the queen of hiding, and with the way her skin crawled at hearing the man's voice, and remembering the look of interest in his eyes when their gazes met, she had a feeling her life depended on getting to her hiding spot and not making a sound. Navy SEAL or not, she didn't trust him.

She didn't trust *anyone*.

She'd been shown time and time again that most people were extremely untrustworthy and unpredictable. She only let her guard down fully with children. They were untainted by life. They were honest to a fault. They said what they were thinking, instead of hiding their disdain and disgust.

Just after she slipped into her hiding spot, she heard the familiar creaking of the floorboards on the landing.

She held her breath, not daring to move a muscle. She hadn't heard the man coming up the stairs. He'd gone into stealth mode.

He was a hunter now—and she was his prey.

Closing her eyes, Monica did her best to slow her heartbeat. If he found her hiding spot, it wouldn't go well for her. She knew that down to the tips of her toes.

As the SEAL entered the room, Monica prayed harder than she ever had before.

Don't let him find me. Don't let him find me.

Monica looks like she's in big trouble...or is she? Pick up *Finding Monica* today!

Want to talk to other Susan Stoker fans? Join my reader group, Susan Stoker's Stalkers, on Facebook!

Also by Susan Stoker

SEAL Team Hawaii Series

Finding Elodie
Finding Lexie
Finding Kenna
Finding Monica (May 2022)
Finding Carly (TBA)
Finding Ashlyn (TBA)
Finding Jodelle (TBA)

Eagle Point Search & Rescue

Searching for Lilly (Mar 2022)
Searching for Bristol (Jun 2022)
Searching for Elsie (Nov 2022)
Searching for Caryn (TBA)
Searching for Finley (TBA)
Searching for Heather (TBA)
Searching for Khloe (TBA)

SEAL of Protection Series

Protecting Caroline
Protecting Alabama
Protecting Fiona
Marrying Caroline (novella)
Protecting Summer
Protecting Cheyenne
Protecting Jessyka
Protecting Julie (novella)
Protecting Melody
Protecting the Future
Protecting Kiera (novella)
Protecting Alabama's Kids (novella)

Protecting Dakota

SEAL of Protection: Legacy Series
Securing Caite
Securing Brenae (novella)
Securing Sidney
Securing Piper
Securing Zoey
Securing Avery
Securing Kalee
Securing Jane

Delta Force Heroes Series
Rescuing Rayne
Rescuing Aimee (novella)
Rescuing Emily
Rescuing Harley
Marrying Emily (novella)
Rescuing Kassie
Rescuing Bryn
Rescuing Casey
Rescuing Sadie (novella)
Rescuing Wendy
Rescuing Mary
Rescuing Macie (novella)
Rescuing Annie (Feb 2022)

Delta Team Two Series
Shielding Gillian
Shielding Kinley
Shielding Aspen
Shielding Jayme (novella)
Shielding Riley
Shielding Devyn

Shielding Ember
Shielding Sierra (Jan 2022)

Badge of Honor: Texas Heroes Series

Justice for Mackenzie
Justice for Mickie
Justice for Corrie
Justice for Laine (novella)
Shelter for Elizabeth
Justice for Boone
Shelter for Adeline
Shelter for Sophie
Justice for Erin
Justice for Milena
Shelter for Blythe
Justice for Hope
Shelter for Quinn
Shelter for Koren
Shelter for Penelope

Ace Security Series

Claiming Grace
Claiming Alexis
Claiming Bailey
Claiming Felicity
Claiming Sarah

Mountain Mercenaries Series

Defending Allye
Defending Chloe
Defending Morgan
Defending Harlow
Defending Everly
Defending Zara

Defending Raven

Silverstone Series
Trusting Skylar
Trusting Taylor
Trusting Molly
Trusting Cassidy (Nov 2021)

Stand Alone
Falling for the Delta
The Guardian Mist
Nature's Rift
A Princess for Cale
A Moment in Time- A Collection of Short Stories
Another Moment in Time- A Collection of Short Stories
Lambert's Lady

Special Operations Fan Fiction
http://www.AcesPress.com

Beyond Reality Series
Outback Hearts
Flaming Hearts
Frozen Hearts

Writing as Annie George:
Stepbrother Virgin (erotic novella)

ABOUT THE AUTHOR

New York Times, *USA Today* and *Wall Street Journal* Bestselling Author Susan Stoker has a heart as big as the state of Tennessee where she lives, but this all American girl has also spent the last fourteen years living in Missouri, California, Colorado, Indiana, and Texas. She's married to a retired Army man who now gets to follow *her* around the country.

She debuted her first series in 2014 and quickly followed that up with the SEAL of Protection Series, which solidified her love of writing and creating stories readers can get lost in.

If you enjoyed this book, or any book, please consider leaving a review. It's appreciated by authors more than you'll know.

www.stokeraces.com
www.AcesPress.com
susan@stokeraces.com

facebook.com/authorsusanstoker
twitter.com/Susan_Stoker
instagram.com/authorsusanstoker
goodreads.com/SusanStoker
bookbub.com/authors/susan-stoker
amazon.com/author/susanstoker

CPSIA information can be obtained
at www.ICGtesting.com
Printed in the USA
FSHW021045290921
85081FS